NYMPHS

SARI LUHTANEN AND MIIKKO OIKKONEN

headline

Original title: NYMFIT – MONTPELLIERIN LEGENDA

Copyright © 2013 Sari Luhtanen, Fisher King Ltd & Gummerus Publishers

Published by agreement with Gummerus Publishers, Helsinki, Finland,
through Stilton Literary Agency, Finland

English translation copyright © 2015 Kristian London

The right of Sari Luhtanen and Miikko Oikkonen to be identified as the
Authors of the Work has been asserted by them in accordance with
the Copyright, Designs and Patents Act 1988.

First published in Great Britain in 2015 by
HEADLINE PUBLISHING GROUP

First published in paperback in Great Britain in 2016 by
HEADLINE PUBLISHING GROUP

1

Cataloguing in Publication Data is available from the British Library

ISBN 978 1 4722 1328 0

Typeset in Fournier MT by Avon DataSet Ltd, Bidford-on-Avon, Warwickshire

Printed and bound in Great Britain by Clays Ltd, St Ives plc

MIX
Paper from
responsible sources
FSC® C104740

Headline's policy is to use papers that are natural, renewable and recyclable products and
made from wood grown in well-managed forests and other controlled sources. The
logging and manufacturing processes are expected to conform to the environmental
regulations of the country of origin.

HEADLINE PUBLISHING GROUP
An Hachette UK Company
Carmelite House
50 Victoria Embankment
London EC4Y 0DZ

www.headline.co.uk
www.hachette.co.uk

CHARACTER LIST

Nymphs
Didi Tiensuu (Desirée Volanté/Tasson)
Kati (Ekaterina, Katya)
Nadia (Ninette) **Rapaccini**
Rose, Kati's sister
Frida, nymph captured by Erik
Ana-Claudia, Frida's lover
Albena, servant to Erik Mann
Nicoletta, servant to Erik Mann
Aurelia, an ancient nymph

Oakhearts
Dr Elina Tiensuu, Didi's foster mother
Samuel Koski, childhood friend of Didi's
Pentti Koski, Samuel's father
Pauliina Koski, Samuel's mother
Matias van der Haas
Matilda van der Haas, his daughter
Salma van der Haas, his mother
Janos, Kati's lover of old
Laertes, Aurelia's lover of old

Satyrs
Professor Erik Mann
Jesper Janssen, Nadia's lover
Mitchell Brannegan
Lucas
Gabriel Korda, Head of the Conclave

Police
Detective Harju
Detective Heikki Hannula

Humans
Laura Maasalo, Didi's best friend
Lasse, Laura's boyfriend
Johannes Metso, Didi's first boyfriend
Janne Malasmaa, Didi's lover
Valtteri Vaara, Didi's boss
Baron Savichny, imprisoner of Nadia and Jesper
Roland Gyllen, business partner of Erik Mann

When the moon goes dark above the pale hills, a nymph will be born in the forest eaves, her hair is as red as the rose . . . Bearer of the Knot of Astarte, this nymph will be raised in the cities of man, and she will not fear to wage war on behalf of the freedom of all nymphs everywhere.

Prologue

The last rays of the setting sun penetrated the whitewashed hall, creating an amber glow. Before long, the southern night would turn pitch black, and even the plants surrounding the villa seemed to be anticipating the evening cool with relief. Didi stood there, looking at herself. She couldn't understand how she could be in two places at once. Then the dream revealed itself in all of its familiarity. She was gazing at a marble statue of herself standing in the middle of a grand hall. She stepped in to examine it more closely, and marveled at the die-cast precision. The artist had captured every single strand of hair. And that wasn't all. The artist clearly knew her intimately, because the statue wasn't wearing a stitch of clothing. Didi reached out to touch the surface of the statue. The marble was both cool and warm. But it was the smoothness that aroused the sensation in the pit of Didi's stomach that she both craved and feared. It was desire. Didi was at a complete loss as how to react to it. The statue, on the other hand, smiled knowingly. It stood there on its bed of moss, hands at its sides, hiding nothing, utterly unashamed of its nakedness.

Suddenly Didi sensed that she was no longer alone in the magnificent hall. She turned around and saw a dark, broad-shouldered man in a starched white shirt and black trousers. The evening heat didn't appear to faze him in the least. Meanwhile, beads of sweat gathered on Didi's forehead and between her breasts. The man stared as one of the pearls of perspiration rolled lower, lower . . . Didi wanted to brush it away, but she was unable to move. A wine glass had appeared in the man's hand, and he held it out to Didi.

'Taste,' he said. 'It's an old vintage, but that statue is older. I commissioned it centuries ago. I hadn't seen you in the flesh yet. You are perfection, Desirée Volanté.'

Didi raised the glass to her lips. The wine was cold; she tasted apricot, a hint of resin.

The man's gaze continued to linger on her and the sensation in the pit of her stomach intensified. A red glimmer appeared in the man's eyes; a moment later they were burning like embers. They scorched her skin, she could feel them somewhere inside her, deeper than anything she had ever felt before. Pain, and yet not pain . . . Didi wanted to scream, but she couldn't make a sound.

Didi snapped awake, her heart still hammering. Her belly was on fire, and her limbs were possessed by an agonizing tension.

It was only the dream again, Didi told herself, trying to breathe more steadily. She had had it so many times she ought to be used to it by now. And yet each time she had it, it was more vivid, somehow closer. *A clear case of pent-up sexual energy*, Laura had teased, and Didi had accused her friend of putting too much stock in what she read in *Cosmo*.

What Laura didn't know was that, in the dream, Didi was also terrified she would die. She never wanted to have that dream again.

Didi rolled onto her side and slipped her hand lower, down past her belly. If Laura was right, she ought to take appropriate measures. Maybe that would keep the restless dream from tormenting her again.

CHAPTER 1

The sight facing Didi in the bathroom mirror was becoming far too frequent. She had dressed for school and was giving herself the final once-over before she headed out the door, but at the last minute she had to stop and take a peek under the collar of her aquamarine hoodie.

'Fuck!'

She heaved her bag onto the bed and grabbed the tube of concealer from beside the mirror. She squeezed out a little too much, and the mess frazzled her nerves even more. She calmed herself and tried to spread the makeup as evenly as possible over the bruise that was starting to stick out above her collar. Then she assessed her handiwork. No one would probably notice.

Didi raced down the stairs, into the kitchen and over to the fridge, flying past her mom. She'd down a quick gulp of juice and then head out before they had time to start fighting.

'You're going to be late,' Elina nagged, just like Didi knew she would.

Didi filled her glass with one slosh. 'I couldn't sleep.'

'It's probably the moon. It kept me up, too. I was reading a detective novel until it was almost time to get up.'

'Sounds like it was the book, not the moon.'

'You're going to have to run,' Elina said, putting the juice carton back in the fridge.

Elina picked up her gargantuan coffee mug with both hands. She examined Didi as she drank her juice and before Didi could turn away, Elina had swept Didi's long red hair away from her throat. Didi shoved her mother's hand away in irritation.

'They're not hickeys,' Didi said.

'I never said they were.' Elina clearly had no interest in starting her morning off bickering either, but she couldn't hide her concern any more than Didi could hide the marks on her skin.

Didi didn't have to say what she was thinking; her eyes said it all. She slammed the glass down on the counter and rushed out.

But she did tell Laura what she was thinking.

'Why does Mom have to treat me like a little kid?' They were in the gym locker room, and Didi handed her best friend the extra pair of clean panties she was loaning her.

A couple of other girls walked past, already clothed, and Didi and Laura waited a second so they could talk privately. Earlier, Didi had spilled the entire contents of her bag onto the bench to find the panties Laura needed, and now she was cramming everything back in.

'That's just how moms are, I guess,' Laura said, wrapping the towel more tightly around her. Water was still dripping from her brown hair onto her shoulders. 'Besides, you have less to complain about than I do. I'd be so goddamn grateful if I didn't have to deal with periods.'

'It's not as great as you think it is, believe me.'

Didi shut the red metal door to her locker and sat down next to Laura. Laura was shorter than she was and more delicately built, but in Didi's mind she was still somehow more feminine. Didi lowered her bag to the floor.

'It's not some disease, is it?' Laura said. 'God, you're so lucky, you can jump around in your shorts as much as you want without having to worry.'

'As usual, Mom has a diagnosis. Like she does for all of my problems,' Didi said. 'At least it has a fancy name: *Primary amenorrhea*. Your period just never starts; it's some hormonal thing. There's still nothing to worry about if you're only sixteen.'

'I guess.' Laura collected her clothes and headed for the bathroom. 'I think it's a gift. Think about it. No migraines, no insatiable craving for chocolate, no bloating.'

'I wouldn't mind being a woman, though,' Didi said.

'Yeah, but you get to be a woman without this,' Laura said, pointing at the cheerful red pimple sticking out in the middle of her chin. 'See ya!'

Didi waved her fingertips at Laura, signaling that she was leaving and Laura should take her time getting ready. Didi yanked the zipper on her bag shut and headed out to the bike rack. *Easy for Laura to say*, she thought, kicking at the gravel with the tips of her tennis shoes. Laura was fun, popular, she got to live her life without someone breathing down her neck all the time, she got to date . . . Didi wasn't so sure about Laura's boyfriend, but Laura refused to listen to any criticism about him.

Didi unlocked her bike, tossed her bag over her shoulder, and started pedaling. At least Mom wouldn't be home from work yet. She'd have a moment's peace before the badgering began.

This pleasurable thought inspired Didi to pick up her pace, and before long, she was turning onto her street. She had almost reached their white wooden house with the mansard roof when something buzzed out of nowhere and flew into her hair. Didi was startled and tried to rake the creature out, but whatever it was seemed to be getting more and more entangled in her tresses. Didi started to panic. She lost control of her bike, and immediately her front tire hit the curb.

'Goddammit . . .'

Didi barely had time to swear before her knee was scraping nastily against the asphalt; the pain made tears spring to her eyes.

The bike crashed over on its side. Didi lay there on the ground, wondering for a moment whether she was dead or alive, and then she could tell she was alive from the pain. She heard someone honking behind her. The stupid idiot was probably getting a good laugh.

Didi half-crawled over to the edge of the sidewalk and pulled herself up. Luckily her bike had toppled to the side of the street. She examined her wound and tried to straighten her leg. Then she heard footsteps. Didi got even more worked up. *Now the jerk is going to come over and tell me to be more careful. What a dick,* she thought.

'Did you fall?' asked a young man's voice.

Didi squinted into the sunlight. She gradually made out a tall young man in khaki cargo shorts and a gray T-shirt that had seen better days. He had brown hair and a nose that was a little too big for his face.

'Impressive deduction,' Didi said, immediately wishing she had bitten her tongue. *The guy is hot,* Laura would have pointed out. *Come on, at least try a little.*

He knelt down next to Didi.

'Can I take a look?' he asked, pulling a handkerchief out of his pocket and pressing it against Didi's wound. 'It's clean.'

Didi didn't even have time to be thrown off by the sudden contact, because she was staring so intently into the boy's eyes. 'Ouch,' she said, a second too late.

'It doesn't look too bad. What exactly happened back there?'

'Some bug flew out of the bushes and attacked me,' Didi said. A nervous giggle struggled to get out, but she managed to stifle it.

'Show me who did it and I'll kill the bastard,' the boy said.

This time Didi dared to laugh. She was on the verge of saying something, but of course right at that moment, her mom appeared on the porch. Elina wasn't even supposed to be home yet!

'Didi!' Elina's voice was angry from the get-go. 'Didi, get in here right this instant!'

The boy stood up and tried to wave at Elina, but Didi's mother refused to look in his direction. He looked at Didi inquisitively.

'That's my mom,' Didi explained.

'You didn't manage to get too far on your escape, did you? My name's Johannes.'

'Didi. I guess I'd better get going. My mom's a doctor. She ought to be able to patch up a scratched knee.'

Johannes picked up Didi's bike and carried it along, following Didi as she limped into the yard. Elina had already gone back inside, but she was monitoring the young people from the window. She gestured sternly at Didi.

'I really have to go,' Didi said. She limped up the porch stairs a little theatrically. But the bee that had flown into her hair and the pain were long forgotten.

Once she got inside, Didi scurried into the bathroom without any trouble at all. She pulled the door shut and twisted the lock. She could hear Elina waiting on the other side of the door, though, and she totally lost it.

'Stop spying on me like I'm some fucking twelve year old,' she shouted, while she searched the cabinets, looking for Band-Aids and antiseptic.

'You're the one who's acting like a twelve year old,' Elina retorted.

'Can't I even go to the bathroom in peace? Or is that also too much to ask these days?'

'Didi, knock it off,' Elina said, listening to the sounds Didi was making. 'I was just worried.'

Didi sat down on the toilet lid. Mom had always been protective when it came to her, but lately she had practically turned into a stalker. 'Worried about what – that I'm going to go off with some guy, get shit-faced, and next thing you know I'll be pregnant?'

'You know why.'

'I'm serious.' Didi tried to pull the backing off the Band-Aid.

'I never met that guy before and I wasn't trying to get anything past you. Not all men want to get into your pants right away. Some are just nice guys.'

'Didi, teenage boys are only nice for one reason.'

Why did Mom always have to blurt out the wrong thing? On some level, Didi knew that Elina was trying to comfort her, even make up to her, but instead all she heard was bitching and nagging. Didi didn't say anything so Mom would have time to calm down. A moment later, there was a tentative knock at the door.

'Let me in so I can have a look.'

Didi had no intention of giving in. She knew Mom had agonized over every tiny bump and scratch of hers since she was a little girl, so Elina may as well agonize a little longer.

'I'm putting disinfectant on it. Stop bugging me.'

Didi poured antiseptic over the scratch. But when she thought about Johannes' smiling eyes, she couldn't even feel the sting.

CHAPTER 2

D idi was standing in the middle of her room, gazing at her reflection. She was perplexed by what she saw. Earlier that day, when she had carried the pastel floral bra and panties over to the cashier, she was certain that the salesperson, a disapproving old sourpuss, assumed that they were meant for someone else's enjoyment. That had flustered Didi, but Didi had known what she wanted, and she had put on an air of self-confidence. Now she wondered how she had ever been capable of such a performance. There was a stranger looking back at her from the mirror, a stranger who looked like a woman. But Didi didn't feel like a real woman at all.

Still, Didi had wanted something special for tonight. Her gaze focused on the inviting red bow between her breasts. The first time she and Johannes met they had gone to a movie, and then for coffee, and then they had started to see each other without any pretenses. And each time, things had gone a little further. Tonight they were going to Laura's party, and there was no reason why it shouldn't be just a totally normal date. But ever since they had made plans over the phone, Didi had felt a growing desire within her. Was there something in Johannes' voice this time that had responded to Didi's cravings?

These days it's not like your virginity is some major achievement that you have to guard with your life, Didi thought. Laura had encouraged her to take the final step plenty of times. But was it a little over the top to prepare for it by buying a new bra and panties?

Didi bent in closer to the reflective surface of the mirror and scanned her skin for the teeny-tiny bruises with a practiced eye. They had appeared for as long as she could remember. When she found one, she deftly covered it up with concealer and highlighter. Her highlighter was about to run out, too – it was almost time to get a new one.

Didi glanced over at the bed, where the floral spring dress she had bought on the same shopping trip was laid out. Now she slipped into it. The lightweight fabric put her in a party mood. Didi spun around in front of the mirror once, but her sense of satisfaction proved momentary. Back in the store, Laura had called the dress frumpy, even though it was cut beautifully at the breasts and caressed Didi's hips as it skimmed down. Laura had carried a couple of her own suggestions into the dressing room. They were a lot sexier and more revealing, and Didi had liked them for a second, but then she realized that they would make her too self-conscious, too embarrassed at the party. This dress was cute, the cotton felt so wonderful against her skin. Maybe if she put her hair up, or knotted it in a cute bun, or . . .

Didi was overcome with frustration down to the hairs on her neck. She had envisioned herself gliding into the party, carefree and beautiful. The other guests' gazes would be drawn to her, but the gaze of only one guest would be important, and both of them knew it . . . That's how it always happened in the books and the movies. But probably not in real life. Didi tugged the zipper down and let the dress fall to the floor in a heap. After a moment's thought, she went over to her closet and pulled out a blouse and skirt, but thirty seconds later they ended up on the floor too. As did her black miniskirt. She reached for her cell phone.

'Laura—' Didi didn't have time to say anything except her friend's name.

'Flirty white skirt, pink top and your new patent heels. Ponytail, nude makeup, maybe a little extra lip gloss. Done and out the door,' Laura said.

'Am I really that hopeless?'

'Yes,' Laura replied. 'Luckily your personal stylist is only a phone call away. Hurry up, get over here.'

In the end, Didi decided she wouldn't try so hard after all. She put the new dress back on. A moment later, she was bounding down the stairs two at a time. She'd better try to get past Mom quickly. Luckily, Elina looked like she was in a hurry, too; she was trying to gobble down a sandwich and put on her coat at the same time.

'Where are you going this late?'

'I promised Laura I'd go to her party.'

Elina swallowed a bite of her sandwich and Didi knew there was no escaping her mother's eagle eyes. She folded her arms across her chest and stood there, bracing herself for the criticism.

'It's a full moon tonight,' Elina said. 'When it's a full moon, you're always . . .'

'I'm what?'

'You always have a hard time sleeping,' Elina said.

'Right, so I may as well go to a party,' Didi said defiantly.

'I'm working the late shift. I can drop you off at Laura's.'

'I'll ride my bike.'

Elina followed Didi at a half-run, but then she remembered her purse and had to go back inside. Didi made it to the gate with her bike before she heard a window open and Elina call out.

'You won't stay out too late, will you, honey?'

'No, Mom,' Didi answered, without meaning it in the least. She waved, and a second later, she was out of sight.

It was a perfect end-of-summer evening: dusky but warm, and the heady scents of flowers and ripening apples mingled into such a heavy perfume that Didi could feel it on her skin and streaming off her hair. The tiff with Mom had seemed like it might develop into a full-blown fight, but now Didi was swaying in Johannes' arms on the dimly lit patio, and she thrust it out of her mind. Didi looked around for Laura, but her friend was utterly focused on smiling at her boyfriend. A few couples were moving along with Didi and Johannes in time to the gentle rhythms of the music. The rest of the guests were talking animatedly, helping themselves to food, clinking their wine glasses. And yet Didi and Johannes' expressions were grave. Suddenly Didi let out an involuntary gasp; the heavy clouds blanketing the sky parted, and the full moon gleamed above them, a pale disc. Johannes pulled her closer.

'What is it?' Didi asked.

She followed his eyes over to the side of the patio, where a few young men were shamelessly ogling Didi. Didi had been aware of how she had been drawing the attention of men all night. She was like a magnet. It was disgusting. She didn't want the men to look at her; it made her feel like there was something wrong with her. Tonight she wanted to concentrate on Johannes and Johannes alone.

The slow song switched to a faster one and Didi let Johannes twirl her a little further away. Both of them wanted to lighten the mood. Didi allowed her gaze to circle around to the other guests, the toasts, the people in their party clothes. The mood was buoyant, and with the help of the music, it rapidly infected Didi. She smiled at Johannes, and that made her feel bolder. It was easy to give in to the rhythm and not have to say anything.

By the time the song ended, Didi was sweltering.

'You want to go outside?' Johannes asked, his voice hoarse.

Before Didi could answer, he had grabbed her hand and was leading her back out onto the patio, a little further away from the others. They found a bench and sat down, and Johannes wrapped his arms around Didi. The party, the music, Johannes so close to her ... The moment was absolutely everything Didi had dreamed of.

Didi looked up, and now her eyes met Johannes'. She pressed

herself against him. Johannes didn't need to say a word; he could tell Didi felt what he was feeling.

'I want to be together, you know, really be together,' Johannes said right at the base of Didi's ear.

Didi ran her fingertips across Johannes' throat. Her skin touched his, and for an instant Didi expected to be surrounded by flying sparks. They looked deep into each other's eyes. *Wow*, Didi thought, relieved. *This is the feeling I've been waiting for*. Her belly felt hot. Johannes' hand moved lower, to her thigh, and her heart almost leapt out of her chest. She would never be more ready.

Laura's knowing glances followed Didi and Johannes as they discreetly made their way out of the party. Laura mimed that she would be expecting a full report from Didi later, and Didi acknowledged her with a noncommittal nod and a wave.

Now she and Johannes were sitting on the seats of their bicycles. The cooling air caressed Didi's face, offering momentary relief from the burning she was feeling inside. Their tires hummed steadily down the asphalt as the branches of the trees overhead reached across and grasped each other. Didi held out her hand, too, and Johannes did the same.

Didi burst into peals of laughter, the sensation was so indescribably right. At that instant, she loved Johannes, she loved this evening, and she loved the anticipation that would soon be rewarded. They rode the rest of the way hand in hand, and didn't let go until they curved into Didi's yard.

They walked through the dim house and upstairs to Didi's room, and Didi's self-confidence immediately evaporated. She had been so certain of what she wanted. Now her head was overflowing with Laura's practical instructions, the theoretical lessons from health class, and Mom's endless sermons and warnings. She stole a peek at Johannes and went over to sit on the windowsill to collect her thoughts and win some time.

The moonlight struck her face, and she felt her body tense as she took off her coat. She took a deep breath. *I need this, it needs to happen now*, she said almost out loud. A warm sensation rippled through her, surging into a larger wave. All it would take would be a single touch from Johannes, and the wave would crash over and engulf her.

Johannes came over next to her and tentatively stroked her cheek. Didi guided his hands to the straps of her dress, helped him lower them. Her dress fell to her waist. Didi shivered.

'We don't have to,' Johannes said, but the hoarseness in his voice spoke a different language as he drew Didi in to his body. 'There's no wrong way of doing this.'

'And this is just our first time,' Didi said.

Didi leaned into Johannes' inviting smile, inhaling both the potent high summer pouring in through the windows and Johannes' fresh, masculine scent.

'You smell nice,' Didi whispered, her breathing growing heavier. Now she was back to knowing what she should do. She slowly unbuttoned Johannes' shirt, until she saw his broad, bare chest. She rose gracefully from the windowsill, and Johannes couldn't take his eyes off her as she stepped into the middle of the floor and pushed her dress all of the way down. It slid to the floor with a soft rustle, and then she was standing in its pool, like a flower that had relinquished its petals.

And at that moment, all of her timidity fell away. She enjoyed the way Johannes' eyes lingered over her, full of longing and expectation. He took a couple of slow steps towards her and wrapped her in his embrace. They kissed.

As Didi continued to unbutton Johannes' shirt, he pulled off his belt. Their movements melted into one. Hot flesh pressed into hot flesh. Didi was panting by the time she led Johannes over to the edge of the bed. She flung her stuffed animals aside.

Didi wrapped her arms around Johannes' neck. Even though

her desire was insatiable, she wanted to experience every inch of Johannes' mouth, chest, throat, waist. She wanted everything to happen in such a way that she would never forget a single second of this.

'Let's take our time, OK?' Didi whispered into Johannes' ear, and she could see the shivers run up and down his spine.

'Didi . . .' Johannes started to say, but Didi wasn't interested in listening to silly words any more.

Didi settled into his arms, soft and warm, and slowly unclasped her bra. She lifted his hands to her breasts and moaned as he curled his lips around one of her nipples. She was afraid she would completely melt into a puddle. She tilted her head, and her lips searched for Johannes' mouth. Their tongues toyed with each other for a moment, and then their kisses grew greedy.

Didi was on fire. She and Johannes were in each other's arms, and she leaned back on the bed. Johannes was tender and passionate at the same time. Didi had no idea how good another pair of lips could feel as they nipped lightly at your stomach and your inner thighs. Or how wonderful the weight of a man's body could feel against hers. Her senses were so heightened that she felt like she had been drugged; the world fell away. Most of all, she was aware of Johannes' scent. He smelled clean and masculine, and his aroma entered her nostrils and traveled deep into her chest, and then lower down. Didi pulled Johannes up, pressed her face against his throat, and licked it so long and hard that he groaned out loud.

Johannes worked his way between her legs and caressed the curve of her buttocks with one hand before slightly raising her hips.

'I'll be careful,' Johannes whispered, pulling a condom on with a practiced hand.

'Let's stop talking,' Didi said.

The tile under Didi's cheek was cold and cruel. Her skin no longer tingled with joy, and the only smell she could make out was the faint whiff of disinfectant. She curled up into an even tighter ball on the bathroom floor. She was cold, but she was incapable of getting up. All she wanted to do was keep her eyes closed and wait for someone to come take her away, to say something that would dispel the horror.

A car drove past, and she could hear partygoers laughing. Of course. It was a perfect night for carefree fun. A tear rolled down Didi's cheek. She didn't dare to give in to the emotion, because that would make her start crying uncontrollably and hysterically, and insanity would take hold of her.

Then Didi felt the gleam of the moon and slowly opened her eyelids. Through the window, she could see the silvery sphere slip out from behind the clouds, bathing the room in a pale light. The light called to her, and, shivering, she rose. She pulled a bathrobe from the hook and wrapped it tightly around her, but she felt like she would never be warm again. Didi slowly walked back to her room and gazed at the moon, as if it could offer her advice. But none came, and Didi had to fall back on plan B. She groped for her cell phone.

'Laura?' Didi sobbed.

'Well, how did it go?' Laura was giggling. 'Tell me everything!'

Didi heard the chattering and the clinking of glasses from Laura's party in the background. Just a little while ago she had been there, too, but now that felt like another reality.

'Did you finally lose your virginity? Things looked pretty promising when you guys left,' Laura said.

A wail escaped Didi's lips.

'What's going on?' Laura seemed to sense that something was seriously wrong. 'Did he do something to you? Wait a sec, I'll go in the other room.'

Didi stared at her bed, and once again her limbs were paralyzed in horror.

'Is everything OK?' Laura asked a second later, this time with no background noise. 'Didi?'

'Johannes . . .' Didi didn't know if she would be able to say it out loud. She raised her eyes and saw Johannes lying naked on the bed. Johannes was smiling. But Johannes wasn't breathing any more. 'I think Johannes is dead.'

Even Laura didn't have a response to that.

And from somewhere, the faint drone of a bee carried into Didi's consciousness.

CHAPTER 3

Didi opened her eyelids and saw a pair of gentle eyes, familiar and yet unfamiliar. *Johannes didn't die after all*, she thought, exhaling. Her relief was immeasurable. It had all just been a bad dream. Soon Laura would be laughing heartily at Didi about the pressures of losing her virginity.

'Didi, is that you?' asked a voice. But it wasn't Johannes'. 'Did that bee sting you?'

And the eyes weren't Johannes' either; they were blue-green and steady and Didi had seen them countless times. The expression in them was familiar from years ago. Didi had just jumped off the deep end of the dock for the first time, and suddenly she hadn't been sure which way was up and which way was down. The feeling she was experiencing right now was exactly the same, and just like back then, she found herself gazing into a calm but concerned pair of eyes.

'Samuel?' Didi was completely bewildered. 'Where am I?'

'Outside the hospital,' Samuel said. 'I told your friend to go in and get you some water. A bee was buzzing around you and you freaked out. I brought you into the shade. Bees only like the sunlight.'

Didi looked around. She saw a large, pale building, people walking in and out of a broad set of sliding doors, and a green lawn. She gradually realized where she was.

Then her gaze shifted back to Samuel, who hadn't taken his eyes off her this whole time. He was wearing a white lab coat. His hair was brown and shaggy, just like when they were kids. Samuel was no little boy any more, but he still looked like he'd have no trouble doing a flip off the edge of the dock.

'Are you already a doctor?' Didi asked, as the pieces of her memory began to click back into place.

'Not quite yet,' Samuel said, sitting down on the bench next to her. 'I'm here filling in for a couple of weeks. I'm staying with Mom out at the stables, so I get to see a little bit of her. Then I'll be headed back to Helsinki.'

Suddenly Didi remembered why she had come to the hospital. Johannes had been brought here, and she hadn't known what else to do besides come along and wait for information. Whatever it was that had happened to Johannes, she felt deep within her heart that she was to blame. She began to shiver again, and Samuel instantly wrapped his arms around her.

'Are you cold?' Samuel asked. 'Do you want to go back into the sun?'

Didi managed to shake her head. She didn't want to go anywhere. She felt safe there at Samuel's side for the first time since . . . She didn't even want to think about it; she just lowered her head against Samuel's chest. If only she could stay there, nothing bad would ever happen to her again.

'You've grown up since the last time I saw you,' Samuel said softly.

'I don't want to grow up,' Didi replied, and Samuel held her even more tightly.

Didi remembered how the laces on her first pair of tennis shoes always used to come untied and flop around her ankles; one time she tripped on them and got a nice big scrape on her knee. Samuel, who was older, had first cleaned the cut and then put a Band-Aid on it. And when he was done, he had knelt down in front of her and tied her laces into double knots.

'When you're big, you'll know how to do this yourself,' Samuel had promised.

'I won't need to know, because I have you,' Didi had answered. And for years she had believed it. Samuel had always been there when she needed something. Then their age difference had grown more distinct, and they had drifted apart in other ways, too. Still, sitting next to Samuel now felt comfortable.

'What are you doing here, anyways?' he asked.

Didi was jolted back to reality, and she didn't know what to say.

At that moment, Laura rushed up with a bottle of water.

'This is Samuel,' Didi told her, relieved that she didn't have to go on explaining things to Samuel. 'He lived next door when we were kids.'

Samuel introduced himself: 'Samuel Koski.'

'Laura. We came to visit a friend. That's why Didi's a little down,' Laura hastily explained.

'I'm totally fine,' Didi said. She would have continued, but Samuel's pager beeped.

'Good,' Samuel said. 'I have to get going, but it was great bumping into you.'

But Samuel didn't move. He looked at Didi, waiting for a response, and even though Didi wished more than anything that Samuel would stay, that they could see each other again, the words caught in her throat.

'See you,' Samuel said, and left.

Both girls watched as he hurried inside in his white lab coat.

'That guy used to be your neighbor?' Laura asked. 'Could you please knock me out, so he can give me first aid?'

Didi was grateful for Laura's attempt to lighten the mood, but she couldn't respond.

There was a wrenching in Didi's stomach as bits and pieces of the previous night's events came back to her. She remembered how badly she had been anticipating the evening, how happy she had been. How nice Johannes had felt. She remembered how she had sighed Johannes' name . . . Then she had seen Johannes dead. Johannes had died while they were making love.

'I guess they took Johannes off somewhere to be examined,' Laura said a moment later.

The morning sun hit the bench now, and it felt unfair to Didi that its warmth felt so good on her skin. She had never seen a dead body before, and now she had briefly held one in her arms.

'This is so totally wack,' Laura said. 'I'm the one who pressured you to be with Johannes. I thought he was totally healthy, but he must have had some disease. Young guys don't just keel over like that . . .'

'Laura, please stop,' Didi said.

Laura stopped talking and slid her sunglasses up onto her nose.

Neither of them noticed the tall, dark-haired, and extremely athletic woman whose gait slowed slightly as she passed them and then stepped in through the hospital doors.

CHAPTER 4

Hospital security is amazingly lax, Kati thought, and not for the first time. If you looked the least bit like you knew what you were doing and where you were going, no one asked any questions. And since it was impossible for Kati to look any other way, she had no problem getting her hands on a lab coat and a face mask. After that, all barriers to accessing any areas of the hospital had disappeared.

Now Kati banished the redheaded girl from her mind and concentrated on the task at hand. She had to be certain. An orderly conveniently happened to walk past, and Kati flashed a sexy smile at him. The plump fellow looked confused, and without waiting for a response, Kati grabbed him by the arm and shoved him into a closet. She knocked him unconscious by applying a deft touch to a pressure point and waited for him to slide to the floor. Then she searched his coat and trouser pockets and found the set of keys she was looking for. She cracked open the closet door and made sure that the corridor was empty before continuing on her way.

A moment later, Kati was opening the door to the autopsy room; she closed it behind her before turning on the lights. Then she stepped up to the metal table in the middle of the chamber and raised the green sheet. The young man's body didn't arouse any feelings in her one way or the other. Kati examined the boy's already-pale skin, looking for the telltale red and blue marks, the burst blood vessels and bruises. There were more than she had expected. Now that was something worth considering. His eyes were shut, but his lips were still smiling. There was no longer any question in Kati's mind.

She lowered the sheet, efficiently snapped off the latex gloves she was wearing and tossed them into the waste receptacle in the corner. Then she cracked open the door to the corridor. The only people milling around were a couple of nurses, so Kati continued on her way, pulling off her coat and casually casting it off through an open closet door. She shook out her raven hair and suddenly sensed a man's eyes on her.

Kati whirled around. An old man sitting on a bench was staring at her, unable to help himself. *It doesn't matter if they're seventy, they're still men,* Kati grunted to herself. And of course she was worth staring at. She was tall, hot, and dressed from tip to toe in black. She was wearing a black sleeveless T that hiked up to reveal flashes of her taut navel, a pair of black leather pants, and biker boots. She retrieved her favorite black leather jacket from the hook and started towards the waiting room, where she could already make out the crackle of the television.

'Places like this already exist in bigger cities,' the interviewee on the screen was saying. 'We believe that there's a demand for twenty-four-hour cafes. The doors would be open to all, with free Internet access . . .'

That was all Kati heard, because now her eyes were intently focused on the redheaded girl who was just rising from her seat and walking over to the candy machine. The girl was completely lost in thought. She already had her money at her fingertips, but she hadn't made her choice yet.

Kati walked right up to Didi, startling the younger woman. 'Nothing catch your fancy?'

Didi stepped aside from the machine. 'Go ahead. I can't decide.'

Kati nodded at her, shoved a bunch of coins into the slot, and chose a candy bar. It fell into the compartment, and Kati immediately handed it to Didi.

'You should eat this,' she said. 'It'll do you good. It's been scientifically proven.'

Didi stared at the stranger, completely confused. She was too surprised to turn down the chocolate bar, even though her head immediately filled with her mother's warnings about taking candy from strangers.

'Thank you,' she said, and suddenly she found herself consumed by an overwhelming craving for chocolate. She started to unwrap the candy bar.

'Go see your mom,' Kati said. 'She's waiting for you in her office.'

'How did you know my mom works here?' Didi asked.

'If anyone asks you about Johannes or this incident, don't answer. Not even if it's the police. Elina will tell you what our next step will be.'

Before Didi could ask any more questions, Kati stalked off, leaving Didi munching on her candy bar.

It felt to Didi like she was in a nightmare that just kept going on and on, but the chocolate was taking the edge off her nerves. She ate it all, licking the final crumbs from her fingers.

Mom's the last person that I feel like talking to about how I lost my virginity and killed a man, she thought. But Didi didn't know what else to do. She steeled herself for her mother's inevitable ranting and raving.

She turned down the familiar corridor, walked up to the door of her mother's office, and knocked tentatively.

Before Didi could even blink, Elina opened the door and pulled her daughter into her arms. All of the tension dissipated, and Didi burst into tears.

'I didn't do anything,' she managed to say through her sobs.

'Of course not, honey.'

'Aren't you going to yell at me? Aren't you going to tell me that's what happens when you let some guy into your pants?' Didi had already gone over this part of the conversation in her mind.

'Sit down. I want to have a look at you and make sure you're OK.' Elina disentangled herself from Didi and assumed a professional role.

Didi no longer had any fight left in her; she obeyed and let Elina wrap a tourniquet around her arm, draw blood, and lightly press a bandage to her skin. Elina worked skillfully and efficiently.

Didi looked at her mother, who as usual was dressed in muted earth tones and natural fabrics. Didi always put her down for wearing such boring clothes, but now their familiarity felt comforting. Didi looked at Elina more closely and reflected that she hadn't realized how her mother had aged. The odd gray strand stood out against her dark hair now, and she already wore glasses. Elina's face also looked strangely weary.

'How do you feel?' Elina asked.

'Fine,' Didi answered. 'I was a little out of it, and then this woman came up and gave me a candy bar. I felt better after that. Maybe my blood sugar was really low.'

'Was she tall and dark? Beautiful? I called Kati when I heard about Johannes.'

'Could it be something contagious?' Didi asked. She didn't even know what she should be concerned about. None of her friends had ever killed a boyfriend by going to bed with them.

'Of course not,' Elina said. 'And whatever Kati told you, you be sure and listen to her. Wait there, I'm going to have a look at your blood. Then we'll go home.'

'Mom?' Didi's voice made Elina stop. 'I don't have any today. Not a single bruise.'

Elina's smile was relieved but somehow forced: 'Isn't that a good thing?'

'But Johannes was covered in bruises after we . . .'

'Don't think about that now,' Elina said. 'I'll be right back.'

Elina slipped into the next room and stood there for a long time, just breathing. Then she placed the sample in the centrifuge and waited for it to generate the plasma measurements. She pressed a button for the device to spit out a printout of the results. She rapidly scanned it. Albumin levels . . . Everything was as it should be, or actually as Elina had feared. She quickly shoved the slip of paper into the shredder and the samples into the waste receptacle, and then she returned to Didi.

'Everything's fine. Let's go.'

CHAPTER 5

Nothing's fine, Didi's heart cried out, as she stared at the flames in disbelief. Her face was withering and curling up in old photos, year after year of her childhood was going up in smoke as the flames devoured them, old report cards fluttered around her in bits of ash. Not that there was much about the grades that deserved saving. That thought did cheer her for a moment. As the heat grew unbearable, Didi took a couple of steps backwards from the conflagration that was lighting up their yard. The fire ate into Mom's files, papers, photo albums; it devoured folders and melted the casing of the computer. The night was dotted with glowing red sparks, burning butterflies that rose higher and higher and eventually extinguished mid-flight.

And Didi would have stepped back even further if Kati weren't standing right behind her. Kati looked at her with a vague smile, then clicked her lighter shut and shoved it into the pocket of her snug, enviously well-cut leather pants. She nudged the bottle of lighter fluid aside with her foot, as if arson were something she engaged in every day, and strode back in the house. The other stranger, a woman whose demeanor communicated at least a hint of empathy, shrugged, indicating her powerlessness.

Didi measured the women with her eyes. While Kati was cool and unfeeling, the one who had introduced herself as Nadia made a gentle impression. Her voice was soft, and she was dressed in a pale, featherweight chiffon dress. Her long, wavy, dark brown hair framed an oval face and accentuated her large brown eyes. When they met, Didi had felt like backing up and running away, but Nadia had reached for her with her long, beautifully formed fingers, and her delicate but firm grip had proved strangely soothing. At least temporarily.

Now Didi's eyes turned towards her deathly pale mother, who was standing at her side. Neither one of them had gotten a word out. Since the first moment when the unusual pair of women had stepped in through their door, her mother had lost all of her willpower. Why wasn't Elina doing anything to stop this travesty? Didi stared at her mother until Elina managed to tear her eyes away from the raging flames. Their eyes met, and then Elina's turned back to the dancing fire. She shook her head as if trying to deny everything that had happened and was happening.

'Didi? Elina?' Kati gestured for them to step away.

Didi was on the verge of refusing, but her mother took her by the hand and pulled her in the house and led her into the living room. Didi was amazed that her decisive mother could succumb so easily to being ordered around by complete strangers.

Kati nodded at Elina, who went over to the sofa, patting one of the cushions to indicate that Didi should join her. Then Elina lowered her head into her hands.

'Kati and Nadia are here to help us,' she said in a barely audible voice.

'Why?' Didi didn't understand how burning every last thing that was important to her and her mother was a favor.

The second woman, Nadia, set a long box on the coffee table and pulled out a syringe.

'You don't understand this yet,' Nadia said calmly, 'but we truly are here to help you. Kati and I. And your mother, too.'

Didi glanced at her mother. She was understanding less and less, and wished her mother would say something, but her mother just sat there, clenching some pendant in her fist. Terror was welling up inside Didi.

Kati had not remained passive. She was emptying the living-room shelves and carrying out more belongings from the other rooms to destroy in the flames, and she was clearly enjoying herself.

'That's our stuff!' Didi shouted. 'You can't take that! What the hell are you trying to do to us?'

'Elina, tell Didi that this is nothing to get upset about,' said Nadia, gently touching Elina's arm.

Kati looked at them and paused for a moment.

'Everything might have happened surprisingly quickly, but you knew this was coming,' Kati said to Elina. 'And you know this is necessary.'

Then Kati's attention focused on the fairy pictures Didi had drawn when she was five and that her delighted mother had framed. They had tormented Didi throughout her teenage years, and she had heartily wished her mother would get rid of them.

'Mom, say something,' Didi said. 'Tell them they're mine.'

But Elina just nodded at Kati. She opened her fist and gazed at the pendant resting there. It was heavy and made of silver, and it bore three oak leaves. Elina picked up the worn leather thong, hung it around her neck, and pressed it to her breast. She took Didi by the hand.

'Didi . . .' For a moment, her mother was incapable of continuing; she looked like she couldn't breathe. 'Didi, since the moment you were entrusted to my care, I've known that the day would come when I would have to give you up. Now is the time for you to leave everything you've ever known behind. Your home and your friends. And me. Kati and Nadia are here to take you, and you must go with them.'

The imperious tone of her mother's voice cut Didi like a knife. Her temper instantly boiled to the surface.

'Fuck you! I'm not going anywhere. I—'

Nadia, who had been preparing the injection off to the side, took a couple of steps closer and jabbed it unceremoniously into Didi's arm. The syringe hissed until it was empty. Didi looked at it in disbelief, as her consciousness started growing hazy.

'Mom?' Didi asked, before fading away. Panicking, she turned to Nadia and Kati.

'Remember that I love you,' her mother said, and it sounded to Didi as if her voice were coming from the depths of a forest. 'Never forget that!'

Didi's eyes fell shut, and she lay there, never knowing that Elina held her in her arms, stroking her red hair.

CHAPTER 6

Two men were climbing up the stairs to police headquarters. The older, stouter one was breathing a little heavily, but a spark of enthusiasm glowed in his eyes. Detective Harju's shabby trench coat was such a familiar sight to the desk officer that he paid no attention to it. Nor did the over-tolerant desk officer acknowledge the younger detective, with his ever-present can of Coke, as he didn't consider the way Detective Hannula dressed appropriate for an officer of the law. To him, Hannula's shoulder-length black hair, jeans, oversized belt buckle, and leather jacket would be better suited to, if not exactly a rock star, then a roadie. Nor did Hannula's dark brows and straight nose do anything for a grandfather waiting to retire, although they did for many of the younger female officers.

Detective Harju trudged into his office with Detective Hannula at his heels and immediately started spreading more papers across his already-overflowing desk.

'It's probably been thirty years since the first time I saw the photo.' Harju waved Hannula over. 'Here's a man who died in Bulgaria in the 1970s. In the 1990s, an older man died in Portugal, and now eight days ago we have a death here. As our guy is young, on the surface it would seem more like a case for the medical examiner than for criminal investigators.'

Detective Harju whirled around to the other side of his office. He was so fired up he was about to jump out of his skin, and Hannula's coolness just poured fuel on the fire. The new case had surged through him like a voltage spike, and he was fully energized. He flicked the oldest photo with a finger to make sure his younger colleague was paying attention.

'When I was at the academy, this case was used as an example. I was young, but it stayed simmering here.' Now Harju's finger had moved up and was pointing at his own graying temple. 'Every detective comes across a case during their career that they can't forget. For me, this is it. Never solved, an Interpol case. Three of our colleagues met their end during the investigation. A woman was arrested, but she vanished into thin air.'

Detective Hannula lowered his can of Coke to the table and picked up the photo to examine it more closely, but he didn't have time to ask any questions before his more senior partner's litany continued.

'Europol, another unsolved case. A local reporter died during the investigation. And this is the latest case. It happened here a week ago. Cause of death unknown. For me, this is not a medical case.' Harju paused for emphasis and his finger rose to his temple once again. 'It is a continuation of the case that's been waiting here for thirty years.'

Detective Hannula lifted the latest photo closer to his eyes. The victim was a young guy, and seemed to be in pretty good shape for a corpse. He wasn't exactly sure how he should respond to Harju's enthusiasm. On the other hand, the old guy was rarely wrong.

'So, are we taking this case over from the local team?' Hannula asked.

'The local police are not investigating,' Harju growled, tossing the file to his younger colleague. 'Heikki, we're taking on a case that doesn't exist.'

Hannula studied another photograph of Johannes Metso, one in which the kid was still among the living and clearly enjoying the company of his girlfriend, Didi Tiensuu. The girl was pretty, redheaded, and flirtatious in an innocent way, with her slightly too-short T-shirt that revealed a tattoo under her belly button. The tattoo was of a knot.

Fuck me, Hannula thought, but he maintained his poker face.

The younger detective's thoughts took an immediate detour, but he threw a few routine questions Harju's way in order to demonstrate an appropriate measure of interest. Then he left his older colleague reclining meditatively on the sofa, which was at least as world-weary as the detective himself.

Hannula casually drained his Coke as if nothing were wrong, tossed it into the trash, and stepped into the corridor. But as soon as he was out of Harju's sight, he leaned heavily against the wall. The girl in the photo had the tattoo he had hoped he would never see. He pulled out his cell phone, but couldn't bring himself to dial the number just yet. He needed a minute to think about things. He knew he was just postponing the inevitable, but it still might be smartest to call from somewhere a little more private.

Mitchell was gazing out the window, taking in the view of London sprawling beyond. Big Ben felt like it was so close he could reach out and touch it. The glass reflected back women in cocktail dresses, men in suits that cost as much as the average working stiff made in months, waiters serving champagne and hors d'oeuvres. You could practically smell the money. Even though he was no fan of conservative clothes, Mitchell melded perfectly into the crowd in his tightly cut midnight-blue suit. On the street, someone might have mistaken him for an extraordinarily clean-cut British pop star. He was a dandy, and he was perfectly happy to admit it. He glanced at his reflection in the window, supposedly unintentionally.

Mitchell was ready to rejoin the revelers when he felt his cell phone vibrate in his pocket. He took a discreet glance at the screen and answered.

'Saltmann and Saltmann, this is Mitchell Brannegan.'

It took a moment before the person at the other end said anything. Then he heard a nervous male voice. 'Hello. This is Detective Heikki Hannula from Finland.'

Mitchell's eyes narrowed slightly as he signaled to Lucas, who was always within arm's reach. Lucas was instantly at his side. He lowered a hand to Mitchell's shoulder, examining Mitchell's expression with interest.

'Do you know who I am?' Hannula asked.

'You said you were a detective.'

'One of you helped me once.'

Then the line fell silent again. But Mitchell could afford to wait.

Eventually Hannula went on: 'I was told to call this number if I saw anything. Or actually, I was ordered. A young man died here ... The mechanism of death will interest you.' By now, Mitchell's curiosity was definitely piqued, and handsome, blond, modelesque Lucas moved in closer to hear for himself.

'Had the person in question recently engaged in sexual intercourse?' Mitchell asked.

A smile spread across Lucas's face as he stroked his perfectly groomed stubble.

'Probably,' the voice answered. 'I have a photograph of the girlfriend.'

'Good. Send it to me.'

Mitchell hung up and accepted the champagne flute Lucas held out to him. He sipped it, trying to look as cool as could be, but a wait of even a few seconds felt too long. Finally his cell phone binged. Mitchell immediately opened the message, and a glance was all he needed.

'Lucas, book us a flight. We need to get to France.'

And at the same moment, Detective Heikki Hannula was sliding to the cold linoleum floor of police headquarters, wiping the icy sweat from his brow. He had known that some day the time to repay his debt would come, but he hadn't wanted to think about it. And now he had done the irreversible.

Hannula heard the voices of the officers returning from patrol, and it wouldn't do any good to sit there brooding over his actions. He rose and stepped slowly over to Harju's door. The older detective was lying on the couch with his eyes closed, but Hannula knew from experience that he was far from asleep. The wheels in Harju's head were churning steadily, eliminating potential scenarios, weighing up probabilities. The old guy annoyed him, and sometimes a hell of a lot, but he was by far the most consistent detective Hannula knew.

'You want to go for a beer?' Harju asked, without opening his eyes.

'I thought you'd never ask,' Hannula replied.

CHAPTER 7

It was the cooing of a dove that made Didi finally open her eyelids. The bird was strutting and fluttering its wings somewhere nearby. Where was the sound coming from? Didi realized she was lying in the fetal position on an old cot, but it was a minute before she dared to move. She didn't know where she was or whether she was alone – let alone how she had ended up there.

Didi allowed her gaze to circle the space, which apparently was an attic. She saw massive old beams and brick walls. The sounds of the doves were carrying in from outside. Didi slowly sat up and realized that she wasn't even wearing her own clothes: someone had dressed her in a pastel dress that was a little old-fashioned. She pulled up the blanket to cover her bare shoulders. The thought that she had been naked in the hands of some stranger gave her goosebumps. The red needle mark was still visible on her arm, and she remembered how the syringe had emptied with a hiss, draining her of her will to fight.

'Hello?' Didi called out, looking around. From the cracks between the boards that covered the windows, she could make out the crescent moon. The room was strewn with old furniture, dust-covered cardboard boxes, and other items that had clearly been left forgotten there ages ago. The sounds of the city, the hum and squeals of cars and trams, carried in from somewhere down below. *At least I'm not out in the middle of nowhere*, Didi thought. *Brilliant conclusion, Sherlock.*

Then Didi's eyes struck on a door, and she rose from her cot. It took her only a couple of strides to reach it. She immediately started fiddling with the lock, but in vain. She pushed the door with her shoulder, but it wouldn't budge. *I told you you should have come to the gym with me*, Laura probably would have laughed.

Didi was suddenly overwhelmed by panic. She was being held behind locks, imprisoned in a strange place, wearing strange clothes. Johannes had died, and then strangers . . . The two women who had forced their way into Didi's and Elina's home flashed across Didi's mind. The women who had subdued her always-so-strong mother as if she were a child. If they were capable of that, what were they capable of doing to her? What had they already done? Didi shoved the door with all of her might.

'Open up!' she screamed. 'Let me out! Fuck!'

She kicked the boards covering the windows, but they didn't give. And it wasn't as if Didi was fighting against boards and walls alone; she was fighting against everything that had happened. Flashes of memories of Johannes and Mom caused a huge lump of grief and pain to form in her throat. She kicked and raged with all her strength, and then she kicked again. But it was no use; eventually she collapsed to the floor, her red hair in tangles. She cried as long as the tears came. When they finally dried up, her head ached the way it did when she ate too much ice cream. Ice cream . . . Didi instantly felt an intense growling in her stomach. She noticed a mound with a tarp tossed over it, and she crawled over and pulled back the tarp. Underneath, she found a cache of water canisters and piles of canned goods: olives and pineapple and duck preserves. A can opener and a fork had been thoughtfully left out nearby. As had a slip of paper. She reached for it with trembling fingers.

'Don't worry,' Didi read out loud, with a hollow laugh. 'Great. I won't.'

For a second she tried to think of ways she could use the can opener and the fork to break out. But maybe it would be best to eat and drink something first. She opened one of the canisters of water and drank so greedily that it soaked the front of her dress. Next she opened a can of duck and a can of pineapple and attacked them with the fork. *Screw it*, Didi thought, tossing the fork aside and shoveling the food into her mouth with her fingers.

Didi had lost her sense of time. She could make out changes in the time of day through the light that penetrated the boards covering the windows, but she no longer had any idea of how long she had been in the attic. She'd examined every nook and cranny of her prison, and fortunately had found the toilet. She'd rifled through the old belongings, searched for escape routes and had eaten and drunk. The only thing that indicated approximately how much time had passed were the empty cans, and she would be running out of water soon, too. What would she do then?

The only real find had been a three-foot metal pipe she had discovered under the cot. Now Didi grabbed it and began banging it against a ventilation pipe. Someone was bound to hear.

'Does anyone live here?' she yelled with all her might. 'I've been kidnapped! Let me out!'

Didi only had enough strength to make noise for a few minutes before giving up. Her grip slipped, and the pipe clattered to the floor. She sat down on the cot and popped olives from a can. Then she picked up the last water canister and poured the final drops into her mouth. That was that. She hurled the canister against the wall and flung herself down on her bed. She felt sated, and for a little while she watched a bee dancing around the edge of the empty tin of pineapple. Its droning made her drowsy . . .

She was back in her own room. It was dim, but she could make out the retro wallpaper Mom had picked that Didi had loved as a child and hated as a teenager. And she wasn't alone; she was sitting, naked, in Johannes' arms. Johannes was so warm, slick with sweat and he was looking her in the eye as if he had just been given the best present in the world. Didi knew exactly how to move and find the right position, slowly, pleasurably. Johannes' breathing grew more intense, and Didi also felt like she was an explorer on the cusp of reaching the goal of her first expedition. Some sort of energy from Johannes flowed into her, she felt her skin glow in the night and she was fully prepared to give in to the moment, to cum. And at that moment, Johannes' head dropped slowly and heavily to her breasts. She was eager to keep going; she tried to kiss Johannes, but he just smiled at her, eyes wide. His eyes no longer saw anything. And then Didi noticed the familiar bruises, except they weren't on her skin, they were on Johannes' . . .

Didi snapped out of her stupor into a state of complete alertness. Dusk had already fallen. There were voices at the door. The bolts of the lock twisted open one at a time with a metallic screech. Didi jumped up fast as lightning, snatched up the metal pipe, and rushed over to the door. Whoever was entering was in for a big surprise. Didi could make out two human figures in the darkness. The beam of light from the flashlight held by the first figure circled the attic. The instant the light fell on Didi, she attacked, hitting the first intruder in the abdomen with every ounce of strength she had.

The intruder buckled over, and in a final effort Didi pushed the intruder so hard that they crashed over onto the old cardboard boxes, cradling their ribs. The flashlight rolled across the floor, and during the brief blaze of light, Didi caught a glimpse of the women who had paid a visit to her and her mother. That was all it took. She sprinted off.

'Didi, stop!' Nadia yelled after her, but nothing was going to keep her from running now.

Nadia turned to Kati, who was slowly picking herself up from the floor. She was on her knees, holding her stomach and breathing heavily.

'You wait here. I'll go,' Didi heard Kati say. The joy in the dark-haired woman's voice at the unexpected opportunity to give chase struck terror into Didi's heart.

Didi headed for the stairway as fast as her legs could carry her. She knew that Kati was already after her, but she ran on, praying that she could make it out to the street before the other woman caught up to her. Surely Kati wouldn't do anything to her if there were other people around. Didi was panting heavily, but Kati moved with a steady effortlessness. Didi made it to the lower door and fumbled with the lock, finally managing to open it. And then she was outside, in the courtyard of an old stone building.

Didi looked around. She dashed out the building's portico and found herself in a narrow lane. She might make it. She heard footfalls behind her and glanced over her shoulder, even though the cobblestones were uneven. She saw Kati smile smugly, and at that instant Didi staggered. Her ankle twisted beneath her, she stumbled and howled in pain as she collapsed against a wall. In a flash, Kati was bending over her.

'Stop being such an idiot,' Kati said, glancing up and down the alley to make sure no one had seen them. 'There's no point trying to run. Just relax.'

Didi bent her knees and held her ankles as if trying to protect herself. She looked at Kati, eyes wide. She was heaving, out of breath, and dripping sweat, while Kati looked as cool as a cucumber.

Then Kati whipped out a stiletto, and Didi flinched and tried to back up. Kati's eyes were steely as she slashed the hem of her shirt and ripped off a piece of fabric. She bound Didi's ankle with sure movements.

'Does it hurt?'

Didi couldn't get a word out; she just let Kati manhandle her as if she were completely paralyzed. It's not like she would have been able to escape on her injured foot anyway.

'Have you noticed how men look at you?' Kati asked as she firmly wrapped the bandage around the ankle, topping it off with a playful bow. 'Why is it that once a month, you get this strange sensation here, and here?'

Kati pressed her hands to Didi's breasts and below her belly, but this time Didi didn't pull away. Something about what Kati was saying sounded so familiar that, against her will, she felt compelled to listen.

'You've noticed that you're not like other people. You're not some ordinary girl.'

'What's wrong with me?' Didi asked, because that's how she had always felt.

'You have nothing to fear from us,' Kati said, helping Didi up. 'We've been through exactly the same thing. That's why you need to come with us and let us help you.'

'I don't even know you,' Didi protested.

For the first time, Kati's expression communicated a hint of empathy.

'But we're like you.'

'And what am I?'

'A nymph,' Kati said.

CHAPTER 8

Vigorous, dark-haired Erik Mann hurried from the lecture hall to his sumptuous chambers near the university in Montpellier. He had performed his teaching duties by rote that day, oblivious to the admiration of his students, both female and male. On the surface, everything about the professor was controlled. His black hair and beard were trimmed with millimeter precision; his wool sport coat, cut like an old hunting jacket, was tailored to fit like a glove; even the way he walked was deliberate. He wholly concealed the excitement that had been growing stronger and stronger within him since receiving the photo that Mitchell had sent to his phone the previous evening. Now he was waiting for Mitchell and Lucas to show up and provide him with further details on the situation.

Erik walked into his study, sat down at his desk and pressed his fingertips together into a pyramid. He had to find some way of passing the time, so he signaled to Nicoletta, who was waiting in the doorway, and before long she ushered in a young couple, completely nude. Erik pulled a sketchpad out of the drawer of his baroque writing desk and nodded. The couple settled onto the chaise longue that stood before him and started making love. Erik studied them for a moment and then began to sketch their intertwined bodies. He pictured the painting that he had been imagining for some time; its composition, the colors. He wanted to calm down, but inside he was seething.

Apparently Albena, the dark-haired woman in the loose white shift standing behind him, sensed it, because she brought a glass of ruby-red wine over to his desk and beat a hasty retreat. Erik inhaled the earthy Mourvèdre, sipped at it, but that was not going to be enough to satisfy his sensory cravings today, either. He tossed the sketchpad aside, and the couple gave him a questioning look, awaiting instructions. He raised a hand slightly to indicate they should continue.

Erik pulled his phone out of his pocket, deliberately prolonging the moment as he searched for the photo that Mitchell had sent. Red hair, translucent skin . . . Everything was as it should be. His blood started to flow more rapidly; even the acids in the wine felt more pronounced as they flowed over his taste buds. Nicoletta and Albena had noticed, no doubt. Perhaps they even caught the red gleam in his eyes, regardless of how he tried to control himself, because they both stepped back a few paces.

Erik was overcome by a sensation that he knew could only find relief if he was to allow his emotions to take control. But then there was a knock at the door. Mitchell entered, with Lucas immediately behind. The arrogance on Mitchell's face made it easy for Erik to deduce that Mitchell felt he had done a brilliant job carrying out his mission.

Erik held up the photo on his phone to Mitchell. 'Where did you get this?'

'Finland. Isn't she the one we've been looking for?' Mitchell's voice had an unmistakably victorious tone, and Lucas cast an admiring glance at him.

'Lucas, please,' Erik said, gesturing at the couple moaning on the chaise longue. Erik's interest in the fine arts had passed for the time being.

Lucas took a couple of steps closer. The young man and woman were wrapped in each other's arms, approaching climax. Lucas lowered a palm to the young man's bare chest. He spasmed fiercely, and an agonized shriek burst out from his lips. He went utterly limp. A hand-shaped mark smoked on his chest. Mute with terror, the woman started to wriggle free, but she experienced a similar fate.

Human life is so easy to cull, Erik thought. It was so easy to control. And yet doing so brought him no peace on this day, the way it sometimes did. As he rose from his chair and walked over to the window, his eyes blazed with a brilliant red flame.

CHAPTER 9

Didi had been too flustered to resist when Nadia and Kati had carried her from the street to the car and from there to the apartment. She was also in too much pain to be able to resist. Kati had lifted her lightly from the back seat of the car and up to the apartment, where she'd lowered Didi onto the couch. Now her aching ankle was resting in Nadia's lap. And yet, in spite of the other woman's gentle ministrations, Didi was on her guard. Kati had taken a seat on the sofa's armrest.

Didi looked around and temporarily forgot how desperately she wanted to escape. The apartment, which was in an old art nouveau building, was stunning. The ceilings were high, the windows were decorated with stained glass in the style of the era, and the parquet floor had a lovely patina. But the home was only partially furnished and echoed emptily. Nadia's touch took Didi back to what she had just experienced.

'I'm sorry,' Nadia said, exploring Didi's foot. There was a small contusion on it. 'We don't have time to let you get used to the idea. We're already in a hurry.'

'Hurry to what?' Didi said. 'You guys kept me locked up in that attic forever.'

'We had some things to arrange,' Kati said. 'Like find this place.'

'Why should I believe you?' Didi pulled her leg away, and

grimaced in agony. 'You kidnapped me, you stole me from my mom. You could be anyone and tell me whatever you wanted.'

'Does it still hurt?' Nadia asked.

'What do you think?' Didi said, but Nadia had already leaned over Didi's ankle and lightly pressed her lips to it.

Didi's first thought was that she was in the clutches of some bizarre lesbian cult. Then she looked at her ankle. The bruise had vanished, as had the pain.

'There's no way,' Didi exhaled, at first grateful, before remembering where she was. 'You drugged me. What exactly was in that shot?'

'Just a sedative,' Kati said. 'You're safe, and everything's fine. Stand up.'

Didi did as she was told, sure that she wouldn't be able to put her full weight on her foot, but there wasn't anything wrong with it any more. She could run away if she wanted. But she had to wait for an opportunity; Kati's astounding athleticism was still fresh in her mind. Besides, she wanted to know more about these women, and herself, too. The more Didi had thought about what Kati had told her, the dumber the whole thing sounded. A nymph! Nymphs were like fairies or something that frolicked in meadows with wreaths of flowers on their heads. Maybe Nadia was into some sort of hippie-dippie crap, but Kati was far from some delicate little creature with fairy wings.

Oddly enough, even though Didi had her doubts about the women, she still felt a strange camaraderie with them. Being in Nadia and Kati's presence was somehow effortless, and she found their closeness on the sofa somehow appealing. *Even though I'm not a dyke, and I'm definitely not some goddamn fairy*, Didi thought.

'You need to take a shower and put on some clean clothes,' Nadia said, interrupting her train of thought.

When she finally got into the shower, Didi took her time. She washed off the dust and the sweat and allowed the water to refresh her, pamper her. Nor was she bothered in the least by the thought that she was making the other women wait. When she finally felt clean, she wrapped herself in a plush waffle-weave towel and went back out to join the others. There wasn't much else she could do. Nadia handed her something to wear. Didi would have rather put on her own clothes. But she pulled on the panties while still wrapped in the towel, and eyed the terracotta-colored chiffon dress that had probably cost more than all of her rags from H&M put together. It occurred to her that she never would have picked out a color like that herself, but it set off her red hair perfectly. She also realized that it was impossible for her to get dressed while swathed in the towel, so she let it drop to the floor. She pulled on the dress, oblivious to how Nadia and Kati exchanged meaningful glances as they examined the knot tattoo on her stomach.

'Kati's going to help you get some new clothes,' Nadia said. 'Until then, you can borrow these from me.'

'Oh, so you guys were smart enough to grab me but not my stuff,' Didi said, in a barbed tone. But the chiffon *did* caress her skin.

'It doesn't exist any more,' Kati said. 'Nothing of your past must remain. Let's go into the kitchen. There's food in there.'

'Sure, why not,' Didi said, following.

Kati was standing at the kitchen island, where the cutting board was spilling over with herbs and nuts. She started chopping them with a skilled hand, but the doorbell rang, and Kati just wiped her hands against her black pants as she went to answer. Nadia and Didi walked into the living room and settled onto the sofa. Nadia was carrying a fistful of nuts and she offered some to Didi, who cautiously took one.

A moment later, Kati came in, followed by two young men in overalls carrying a large bed. 'Nadia's going to show you where it goes. I'm not responsible for the decor.'

Nor did she look anything like a hausfrau in her black clothes, one hand still clutching the sturdy knife.

The bed was cumbersome, but the men's eyes lingered a little too long on the three stunning women. Nadia gave them an evaluative look, her eyes narrowed into slits.

'Put it in the corner room,' she said a moment later, turning back to Didi. Didi's eyes had followed the well-built men. 'It's for you. Some of the landlord's old furniture is still in there. We'll get you some new things once you know what you need.'

But Kati's words continued to nag at Didi. 'Why did all of my old things have to be destroyed?' she asked in a barely audible voice.

It had grown apparent to Didi that she was being monitored. For the most part, she stayed in her room by herself, digesting everything she had been told. She had asked the women – the nymphs, she supposed she should call them – once more about it all. She just couldn't wrap her brain around the idea that she couldn't continue her former life. Johannes had died, but there's no way it really could have had anything to do with her. She didn't feel like some sort of fairy creature with magic powers.

'Hey guys, I can just go home,' Didi had said. 'I won't tell anyone about you. I'll just live a totally normal life.'

'That's out of the question,' Nadia had answered. 'You're in danger now.'

'Who would want to hurt me?'

Nadia had been on the verge of saying something, but Kati stepped in. 'Humans. Before long, someone will realize that you're not like them. And what do humans do to those who are somehow different, out of the ordinary?'

'Besides, you don't know everything yet. You're not ready to know,' Nadia had said. 'You just have to trust us that your life is in danger, and from more than one direction. Your mother entrusted you to us so that we would protect you.'

Didi considered these words carefully, and it made her crave fresh air, so she went out to the balcony, which was really more of a terrace. It had been comfortably decorated with light-toned furniture and lanterns that bathed the evening in a soft light. The view gave on to a lush courtyard. Didi wasn't cold per se, but she still wrapped herself in a large wool sweater she had found in the closet. She gazed at the moon, which had by now tapered to a crescent. She didn't turn around, even though she heard soft footfalls behind her. Nadia was the one who walked barefoot; Didi presumed Kati even slept with her boots on.

Nadia held out a steaming cup of tea to Didi, and they both leaned against the balcony railing.

'Should I let my mom know where I am?' Didi asked. 'Let her know I'm all right?'

'Elina knows,' Nadia answered. 'And we can't be in touch with her. That would be too risky.'

'Why can't mom help me, if she knows I'm like you guys?'

Didi twirled the spoon around the mug, unable to drink a drop, even though the mellow honey-like aroma of the tea enticed her.

'Because Elina is not your mother,' Kati said behind Didi's back. She had approached the railing silently, and she paid no attention to Nadia's disapproving glance.

'Kati's right,' Nadia said a moment later. 'You're a nymph, and there's no way your parents can be human.'

'We have a plan for you,' Kati said. 'It's critical that you're patient and we move forward one step at a time.'

'You have three weeks to learn what you are and what that means.' Nadia pressed a hand to Didi's shoulder, and Didi felt a soothing warmth radiate from it.

'What happens in three weeks?' Didi asked.

'The next full moon will rise,' Nadia answered. 'You need to learn to face the changes it brings about in you. You're in danger, but you're also dangerous to humans. We will teach you how to hide and still express your true nature as a nymph. We have rules of our own. We have to have a certain kind of nourishment. Each of us has our own special gift. Once you find your gift, you need to learn how to use it. And above all, during every full moon you need to—'

'Nadia, let's go inside.' Kati's tone was cautionary, and she turned to Didi. 'You should rest if you can. Tomorrow is a new day, and you can ask us whatever you want then.'

Then the two women left Didi there alone. She gazed at the sky opening up overhead and the dark silhouettes of the buildings. The crescent moon gave off a wan light. She was genuinely starting to get a little cold now, but her tea had already cooled, and despite the honey it had a bitter tinge. Maybe Nadia would steep some more for her if she asked. She softly padded her way on stocking feet towards the kitchen, where, based on the clinking, it sounded like glasses and a bottle of wine were being set out on the table. The women were talking to each other, and Didi stopped to listen.

'Maybe we should tell Didi the truth about what's happening to her,' Nadia was saying.

'Not yet,' Kati replied decisively.

'She must be afraid.'

'Still. Not yet. Nothing will get through her head right now.'

'Why not?' Nadia asked.

'First comes shock, then aggression, and only after that, rejection of the truth. Then sorrow, and in the end, acceptance. The shock and the aggression have already passed.'

'Wow, you're up on your basic psychology, huh?' Nadia laughed. 'How is the rejection being manifested?'

'You'll see soon enough,' Kati said, and then she apparently took a long sip from her glass.

Didi was incredibly annoyed. In a split second, she decided she had had enough. Once more she was being treated like a little brat who didn't understand anything and who had to be watched every moment of the day.

And then Didi heard Kati's voice again: 'Go lock the door from the inside. Let's make sure it's not too easy to escape from here.'

That's what you think, Didi thought. She went back out onto the balcony and looked through the living-room window to make sure that Kati and Nadia couldn't see her from the kitchen. Let them sip away at their white wine; she had other plans.

She had already noticed the fire escape in the corner of the balcony, and now she started climbing up the ladder without a moment's hesitation. At her mom's house, she used to sneak out by climbing down, so why wouldn't it work this way, too?

In a flash she was on the roof, and she took a cautious glance at the ground far below. At that same instant, she felt the first raindrops fall lightly onto her skin. She opened her palm to receive them. The refreshing drizzle cooled her brow. She looked around and saw a door. And luckily, it was unlocked.

CHAPTER 10

Didi had rushed out onto the rainy streets barefoot, without a clue as to where she was going. She made it a few blocks but then started falling into despair. It was late; the streets were empty. Then she saw lights not too far in the distance. A little neighborhood cafe was open. Didi went inside, but her relief only lasted a second because she realized she had neither money nor a plan.

There was a group of young men in the cafe, drinking beers as the server wiped down the empty tables. People glanced at her bare feet and figure-hugging dress, but no one said anything. You never knew what you were going to run into in the city.

It didn't take Didi more than a second to spot the computer in the corner. She sat down at the screen without any clear idea of what she should do. The cold had finally seeped into her skin, and she was dreading the moment when she would have to go back out onto the unfamiliar streets. She needed help, but she didn't know anyone . . . But wait, Samuel said he lived in Helsinki! Didi tapped the name into the search engine with chill-stiffened fingers: Samuel Koski. A second later she had an address: Katajanokanlaituri Dock No. 4. *That's odd*, Didi thought as she looked at the map, but nothing was going to stop her now. The thought of Kati on the hunt lit a fire under her feet.

There weren't more than a few straggling drops of rain falling from the black sky by the time Didi found the address she was looking for and realized that it was an old wooden boat. There was a light beaming from the cabin, and she advanced towards it cautiously. She had just run into Samuel for the first time in years, and the realization popped into her head that she knew nothing about his life now. What if Samuel was there, spending the evening at home with his girlfriend? The thought stung unpleasantly. And why would Samuel even help her like this, out of the blue? On the other hand, she couldn't remember a single time when Samuel hadn't been prepared to help her. When someone at elementary school had laughed at her and called her carrot-top, Samuel had immediately intervened.

Didi saw the name *Robur* painted on the side of the boat, and it made her think of her mother. Didi knew that *robur* meant oak tree, and Elina had always been strangely attached to oaks. *I wonder why I never saw her wearing that necklace before?* Didi thought, before movement on board distracted her. She stepped right up to the window. It was Samuel. She remembered lying up against Samuel as a little girl, twirling her red braids as he read her the story of the three musketeers in a slow, steady voice.

She also remembered one time when their mothers had been in Samuel's kitchen, drinking coffee with grave faces. As always, Samuel's mother had been in her riding gear. Did she even have any other clothes? The conversation had made an impression on Didi, since it was clearly not meant for anyone else's ears.

'The children are growing up,' Elina had said.

'There's no reason to get upset about it,' Pauliina had responded. 'Samuel and Didi have enjoyed each other's company, but it's going to be time to separate them soon.'

Didi still didn't know what they were talking about, but afterwards something had started to nag at her, and she had run over to start boxing with Samuel, half in jest, half seriously.

Didi shook the incident from her mind and peered in through the cabin window. Samuel was there alone, watching TV on his computer. He started when he heard the knock at the windowpane. Didi waved, and a smile gradually rose to Samuel's face as he recognized her.

'Didi!' He immediately opened up the cabin door for her, and the warmth flooded out. 'What are you doing here?'

'Can I come in?' Didi asked. She didn't even know where to start explaining.

Before long, Didi was sitting in the cabin of the *Robur* with a towel around her shoulders. Samuel had evidently taken a hint from her expression and hadn't forced her to offer any explanations. She had simply asked to borrow Samuel's phone and he had obliged. The result was not the one she had been hoping for, though.

'The number you have reached is no longer in service,' said the operator recording.

Didi exchanged the phone for the mug of tea Samuel was holding out. 'I don't get why Mom isn't answering. Can I make another call?'

'Of course,' Samuel said, considerately stepping aside to give Didi some privacy. Didi tapped in a different number and luckily, this time there was an answer.

'Laura Maasalo.'

'I didn't wake you up, did I?' Didi asked.

'Of course not,' Laura answered. 'Where are you?'

'I can't get a hold of Mom. She's not answering her cell phone,' Didi said, dodging the question.

'There's no one at your place, either. I've been by a few times and knocked on the door.'

Didi's heart was seized in a cold grip. Mom couldn't disappear just like that, leaving Didi to fend for herself. After all, she hadn't been that bad a daughter. And there were other unresolved issues, too.

'Have you heard anything?' Didi spoke quietly, so Samuel wouldn't hear everything she said. 'About Johannes.'

'It was supposedly some circulatory thing, even though I still don't get it,' Laura said. 'The funeral's tomorrow. You'll be there, won't you? Where are you, anyways?'

'I just had to get out of there,' Didi said. She didn't want to lie to Laura, so it was better to cut things short. 'I'll tell you some other time. Maybe I'll see you tomorrow.'

Didi hung up and squeezed a generous helping of honey into her tea.

'What now?' Samuel asked, anxious not to pry into Didi's affairs any more than she was prepared to reveal.

'I have to think a little,' Didi said. 'Can I sleep here for a couple of hours?'

'When you were a kid, didn't I promise I'd always rescue you?'

'Yeah, and then you said I was ugly,' Didi replied. By this time she was laughing.

'That was only after you'd punched me on the nose,' Samuel said. But he quickly regained his composure. 'Seriously though, is there anything I can do for you?'

'You can take me home in the morning.'

CHAPTER II

The neighborhood was still asleep. Didi thought about all of
those people, the families with children and pets that she had
greeted almost every day. It felt strange to think that after she
had left, their lives had gone on the way they always had. Before
long, they would be waking up, eating breakfast, going about their
daily routines. That was not the case in the familiar house with the
mansard roof. Samuel pulled his car into the drive. Even though
she had been anticipating this moment, Didi found herself unable to
climb out of the car right away. She had imagined running up the
stairs to the porch and rushing into a place where everything was safe
and familiar. But now the house looked foreign, lifeless. She turned
to Samuel.

'When I was ten, I thought you were the nicest boy in the world.
You just thought I was the funny little girl next door.'

'You were the funny little girl next door,' Samuel said.

'Did you ever think that there was something wrong with me?'
Didi asked.

'Never,' Samuel said. 'Everything is perfectly right with you.'

'Why did you agree to help me again?'

'Because you asked me to,' Samuel said, as if the answer were
self-evident.

Didi wanted to cuddle up next to Samuel, but it felt somehow
forbidden. Samuel turned away, too, and looked straight ahead.

But Didi had come here to look for clues, some tiny trace of her mother. She already sensed that that's not what she would find in the house; nevertheless, she felt like she would find something there. Following Samuel's lead, she stepped out of the car, walked up to the door, and knocked. No answer, just as she had thought. *On to plan B*, Didi decided, snatching up the first rock that looked like it would do and marching up to one of the first-floor windows.

'You're not going to break it, are you?' Samuel asked, but the glass was already shattering.

'This is my house,' Didi said. 'It's not like I'm breaking in.'

Samuel scanned around, but no one seemed to have heard the smashing glass. Didi had already slipped in through the window, and she came right around to open the front door for Samuel. They walked into the living room together.

Didi looked around her old home in the morning light, but the instant the glass shattered, she had known that something else was already broken. The old wooden house was nothing more than a shell for that life that she and Elina had shared in it. There were still some familiar details around the place, like the exercise bar hanging from the ceiling and the dark spots on the wallpaper where photographs and pictures had hung. A few pieces of furniture were left, although they were covered in sheets. This was a house where no one lived any more.

'Where's your mom?' Samuel asked. But Didi was already on her way upstairs.

The stairs creaked the way they always had, but now that the house was deserted, the sound was somehow different. Didi arrived at the door of her room. The only things left were the bed frame and her old dresser. Didi walked right over to the dresser. She wanted to find something, anything, no matter how insignificant. She especially wanted to retrieve her diary, the book in which she had recorded her dreams and feelings. She didn't want anyone else to ever read it.

She always conscientiously hid it under her tops, at the back of the drawer that jammed. She gave the drawer handle a firm tug. It didn't budge. She tried a few more times without success.

'Let me help,' Samuel said, rushing over. Didi tried to stop him, but Samuel had already grabbed the handle.

'It's OK, I got it,' Didi protested. And at that moment, her elbow smacked Samuel right in the chin.

'Goddammit!' Samuel yelled.

'I'm sorry. Does it hurt?'

'A hell of a lot,' Samuel moaned.

Didi leaned in to examine her handiwork. There was a cut in Samuel's lower lip, and a couple of drops of blood were dripping down from it.

The wound wasn't too big. *Men whine about the tiniest little things*, Didi thought, but then an idea popped into her head and made her smile.

'What's so funny?' Samuel asked, annoyed.

'Nothing. Did you have to get in the way?'

'I was trying to help. And got punched in the face for it,' Samuel said.

Didi raised a palm to Samuel's lips and their eyes met. For a moment Didi was awestruck by Samuel's eyes in the blue-tinged morning light: just a second earlier they had looked cool, but now they were almost electric. How could they always be so sincere, even at a moment like this? She was standing just a few inches away from Samuel, and she could make out every stitch of his dress shirt, how the fabric draped around his neck. The idea that had occurred to her a moment ago returned. If she actually were a nymph, and Nadia had been able to heal an ankle that was basically broken with a single brush of her lips, then what if she could . . .

Didi gulped and disentangled herself from Samuel. 'All I do is hurt people.'

'It was an accident,' Samuel said, taking her by the hand.

The gesture was so comforting that Didi didn't want to move a muscle. Samuel radiated a warmth that she needed right now.

'Can I try one thing?' Didi asked a moment later.

Samuel didn't say no, so Didi quickly leaned in and laid a light, soft kiss on the wound that could be seen on his lower lip. Samuel was stunned. Didi looked at him expectantly.

'What?' Samuel asked.

Didi examined his lip. There was no change. This whole thing about nymphs was a bunch of crap, just as she had suspected.

'Don't take that the wrong way,' Didi said in a hurry. 'I didn't mean anything by it—'

She didn't have time to continue. Samuel leaned in towards her, and Didi raised her face, expecting another kiss. But Samuel just stared at her, a glazed look in his eyes. Then his eyes rolled back in his head, and he crashed to the ground, limp.

'Samuel?' Didi whispered. She was gripped by a sudden chill, and her heart started to hammer. In a flash, she was on the floor at Samuel's side, helping him, but now she didn't even dare to touch him. She crawled back in a panic. She had no idea what to do. Samuel's chest was rising feebly, but his breathing sounded labored.

'Samuel!' Didi shouted at the top of her lungs, and in that instant, she heard the sound of a car.

A moment later, footsteps were clomping up the stairs, and then Didi saw Kati and Nadia in the doorway.

'Did I kill Samuel?' Didi asked, as the first tears welled up in her eyes. 'I accidentally elbowed him in the lip and I tried to heal it.'

'What did I tell you?' Kati said to Nadia, ignoring Didi's panic. She looked around the room to make sure there was no one else there and then she climbed up on to the dresser to sit and wait. 'Little kids always run home to their mommies.'

Didi refused to move out of the way as Nadia bent down at Samuel's side. She was terrified. Samuel was unconscious. What if the other nymph's touch ended his life completely?

'Don't you dare touch him!' Didi shouted, surprised by the hint of jealousy in her voice. She sprang up, intending to pull Nadia away, when the other nymph exerted unexpected force and held Didi against the wall. Then Nadia gently stroked her cheek, and her feather-light fingers acted like an invisible barrier.

'Didi, I'm not going to hurt him, but you could kill him,' Nadia said, her eyes nailing Didi in place. Nadia waited until Didi's resistance faded. Didi found herself powerless to do anything but stare at Nadia, whose tender voice was nothing but hypnotic.

'Listen,' Nadia said. 'I was born in Naples in 1756. When I turned eleven, I had my induction into *come essere una ninfa*, or how to live like our kind.'

'What does that mean?' Didi gasped.

'I needed to learn to hide from the humans who had burned us as witches for hundreds of years. Or killed us for sport, or out of fear. Now you have two weeks to learn all of the skills you need. If I were you, I'd want to learn them. Look at your friend. This isn't what you want, is it?'

Didi shook her head, and Kati nodded to indicate that now it was time to continue.

'I can still help him,' Nadia said. 'You would not have been able to.'

'In the worst case, you could die yourself. Nadia and I are the only ones who can help you survive,' Kati said. 'You have to trust us.'

Nadia bent down over Samuel again, this time pressing her lips firmly to his. Nothing happened. Didi stared at Samuel, slowly shaking her head. This couldn't be happening again.

Then Samuel opened his eyes and looked at Nadia, bewildered, and then at Didi, and last of all Kati. He sat up, and Didi felt herself start breathing again.

'You're OK,' Nadia said to Samuel. 'You fainted. Didi's elbow hit you pretty hard.'

'I guess,' Samuel said. Kati pulled him up from the floor as lightly as a little child.

'I'm going to walk you to the car,' Didi said, even though the nymphs tried to indicate that this wasn't wise.

When they were outside, Samuel stopped Didi.

'Who are those women, anyway?' he asked.

'Some friends of Mom's,' Didi explained. 'They promised to help . . . As it turns out, I guess Elina wasn't my biological mother after all. I don't even know everything that happened. There's some sort of family drama going on and I can't really talk about it.'

'I heard you mention a funeral last night,' Samuel said. 'Is that where you're going?'

Didi shook her head. Then she hugged Samuel. 'Thank you.'

'Come get me if you need any help,' Samuel said. He stood there for a second, but since he didn't get the reciprocation he was hoping for from Didi, he climbed into his car.

Nadia and Kati came out into the yard before Samuel pulled out of the drive and onto the road.

'Come on, Didi, let's go,' Kati said.

Twenty people in dark clothes were standing around the open grave. From the back seat of the car, Didi could see how the eyes of some of the attendees were red from crying. All of this was her fault. She had taken a human life.

Didi saw Laura, looking miserable, and she slid down lower in her seat. Tears were welling up in her own eyes, too.

'It's not your fault,' Kati said. 'You didn't know anything about this. You couldn't know that that boy would die.'

Didi wiped her cheeks. She had witnessed something she never could have believed. And to top it all off, she was alone. She had no choice but to trust these two women she barely knew.

CHAPTER 12

Kati started awake. She looked out and saw that dusk was falling. She must have dozed off for a moment, and for the first time in ages she had had the old dream, where she could hear the pounding of the horses' hooves, smell their sweat. She was being ridden down, her long, wet hair whipped against her cheeks in the wind . . . She was perturbed that the dream had come back to torment her at this particular time.

She stretched out her long limbs and listened to the chatter from the kitchen. She craved nuts and avocadoes now, and all the other perfect foods and drinks for nymphs.

She went into the kitchen, poured a healthy splash of cold white wine into a stemmed glass that immediately misted over, and grabbed a fistful of Brazil nuts. Nadia and Didi were sitting at the table, where Nadia was lightly scraping Didi's skin with a little knife. She carefully collected the sample into a plastic bag. Didi looked suspicious.

'We have a love-hate relationship with the moon.' Nadia ran her fingers down Didi's arm to indicate she was done and glanced at Kati. It was time to tell Didi.

'What does that mean?' Didi asked.

'The moon has a certain way of tormenting us.'

'You slept with Johannes,' Kati said. She didn't understand all this beating around the bush. It would be best to give it to the kid straight. She jumped up onto the island and refilled her glass. 'Which is why you have to be ready for the fact that the next full moon is going to have an even stronger effect on you.'

'Before, all you used to get were bruises,' Nadia explained in a softer tone. 'Now your skin is starting to dry. Your vision will grow weaker, your hair will become brittle, your joints will stiffen. And your breasts will wither, too.'

'Don't soften the blow, tell me now,' Didi said.

'But that can all be prevented,' Nadia continued. 'Remember the pain you used to feel, the slight gnawing in the pit of your stomach, the wrenching. That will all become a million times more intense if you don't do the right things.'

'So what do I need to do?'

'Be with a man,' Kati said.

'What if I don't want to?' Didi asked. The whole thing sounded completely ridiculous.

'Every time there's a full moon, a nymph has to be with a man,' Kati said. 'Think of it as regular self-care. Like getting a Brazilian, except it doesn't hurt as much.'

Didi had heard girls talk about sex in a casual tone before, but for her the notion was completely foreign, impossible. Besides, you always heard cautionary tales about how boys took advantage of girls. And now she was going to be doing the opposite?

'Is that what you do?' Didi asked.

'Of course,' Kati answered.

'You can't negotiate with the moon.' Nadia was labeling the sample, but she still cast a warning glance Kati's way. 'Pheromones lure men. I'll take a look at this sample. We'll try and figure out what pheromones you're giving off.'

'The tiny motes of your skin attract men like pollen attracts bees,' Kati said.

'And what happens to the man, then?' Didi asked, but neither nymph answered. 'The same thing that happened to Johannes? So I kill the man who keeps me alive?'

Kati jumped down from the island. 'I think that's enough for one evening. I'm going to hit the sack.'

Kati could feel Nadia's eyes on her back and knew that her fellow nymph had wanted to approach the matter cautiously and circumspectly, but Kati really wasn't in the mood. Didi got everything pre-digested, served to her on a silver platter. She and Nadia had done all the work. Didi was masquerading as a university student. They had arranged new papers for her, an apartment, put themselves at risk. And now on top of all that, they were supposed to hold her by the hand and teach her how to stay alive. Didi had no conception of what to do. She had lived with Mommy up till now and enjoyed the easy life.

When was the last time my life was easy? Kati thought, as she lowered her head to her cool pillow.

Kati leaned in to the horse's neck. Her heavy cloak and leather vest shielded her body from the blows of the leafless branches, but they still whipped her in the face and tore at her hair. She didn't care. She was fleeing for her life. She could sense the satyrs closing in on her, hear the snorting of their horses. She looked for a good spot to hide or turn and fight, because her steed was inevitably tiring. He steamed ferociously in the cool air and wouldn't have the strength to keep up the pace for long.

Suddenly a spear whistled past out of nowhere. Kati tried to gauge the direction it had come from so she could dodge the next one, but instead she heard a heavy gasp behind her as it struck a satyr. He fell from his saddle and struck the ground, and Kati reined in. That proved to be a mistake, because a second satyr jumped from his horse and ran at her, brandishing his sword.

Maybe it's better this way, Kati thought. She dropped to the ground, too, and deftly drew her own heavy blade. She had never been one to shrink from a fight. The satyr was within striking distance. Their blades clashed as Kati's gaze met the satyr's blazing red eyes. Kati knew what would happen to her if the satyr had time to gather its strength. She could already see the tips of his horns emerging from his forehead. Kati struck with all her might, but the satyr didn't move. Kati drew her sword back with both hands and steeled herself to impale the satyr on it as soon as he moved in. But the satyr just stood there, smiling, before taking a couple of slow steps towards Kati. His smile kept growing broader. Kati was momentarily stunned when he toppled forward, an arrow in his back. She looked around. Where was the attack coming from? She was still primed to kill.

Then she saw a brawny man step out from under the eaves of the trees and walk up to the satyr without the slightest hesitation. He verified the kill with a stout knife made of bone. The man had long, light brown hair and was wearing fat leather cuffs. A fox pelt warmed his shoulders.

'Are you all right?' he asked Kati.

'I don't think you understand what you're getting mixed up in,' Kati answered.

'We have our disagreements with the satyrs, too.' Now the man was smiling at Kati, replacing the weapon back its sheath after wiping it clean.

'Who's we?'

The man didn't answer immediately. Instead, he started to concentrate on gathering firewood.

'Fire is the most effective way of ridding yourself of potential problems,' he reflected.

Kati helped him collect wood until they had formed a large pyre. Together they lifted the satyrs' bodies on top of it, and the man ignited the wood with a couple of brisk strikes of flint. Kati pulled her cloak around herself more tightly and then turned away, thoughtful. She couldn't afford to trust anyone, which is why it was better to apply nymph stratagems than take matters into her own hands. She felt so self-assured she couldn't help but smile. She'd survived such situations before. Besides, the man looked as strong as an old stump, and even though it wasn't a full moon yet, perhaps she could rest here for a bit. She had shaken the satyrs from her heels, at least for a while.

Kati walked up to the man and casually wrapped an arm around his neck, ready to give him a long, deep kiss. But the man wrenched her arm away with his powerful fingers.

'I'm not fool enough to let a nymph's lips touch mine,' he said. It took Kati a moment to release herself from his grip. Her powers of seduction rarely failed her.

'I would have survived on my own. Don't presume for an instant that I owe you anything.'

Kati jumped right back onto her horse, refusing to give the man so much as a glance, knowing that he was smirking in satisfaction. Kati vanished into the black forest, but she could not forget that gaze, the gaze of Janos' blue eyes . . .

Kati woke up, immediately alert. It was morning. Strange footfalls were echoing from the living room. In a split second she was ready to defend herself, but then she sighed.

It was Didi, of course. Perhaps she wasn't accustomed to the girl's presence yet, nor did she know how much she could trust her.

Kati quietly shifted the blanket from her long, bare legs, crept over to the door, and peered out. Didi had wandered out of the bathroom and into the sun-drenched living room, where she was gazing out the window. She started heading back to her own room, but then she noticed the laptop that someone had left under a throw on the sofa. Didi looked around and then tiptoed off to safety with her new-found prize.

Kati was patient enough to wait before silently edging her way to the door of Didi's room and slowly opening it a crack for a better look. Didi was sitting on her bed with the laptop, her back to the door, and Kati could see Didi's friend's animated face on the computer screen. Kati pulled back and decided she would eavesdrop. Apparently Didi had already revealed some details about her new life to her friend.

'Hey, I was the one who was supposed to go off to university and get a cool place to live,' Laura said, feigning irritation. 'Friends aren't allowed to steal their best friend's brilliant ideas.'

'I just had to get away from there,' Didi answered. 'And this isn't as much fun as you think, not by a long shot. Sometimes I don't even really know who I am. If you only knew all the things—'

Kati was on the verge of intervening, but Laura got there first.

'At least you have totally new problems. It's so boring and depressing here,' Laura complained. 'Screw this, I'm going to pack my bags and get out of here too. I'll tell Lasse, "Peace, I'm off to find someone better."'

'I'm not sure you want to do that,' Didi said, not saying out loud what she was afraid would happen to Laura if she did.

'At least it would be something new,' Laura went on. 'You knocked that Samuel guy off his feet, after all.'

'By accident.'

'Knocking him unconscious is better than hitting on him the normal way.' There was a pause; Laura was looking at the screen, checking if there was anything in her teeth. 'So do you have a plan for how to handle this Samuel?'

'I sure do,' Didi answered.

Now Kati pricked up her ears. This wasn't going according to script. She knew Didi would be careless.

'Keep my distance from him. The further, the better.'

OK, Kati thought. *This might work after all.* And when Didi came into the kitchen for breakfast, she was already there, busying herself with her knife.

Kati had been looking for a space for her small seamstress shop and found the perfect spot. It was a short walk from the apartment and it gave her the freedom to do as she pleased. It was almost noon, and she fumbled around in the pocket of her leather jacket for her keys; it was time to open for business. She came and went as she pleased. It was highly unlikely that she would have enjoyed working for someone else for long. She didn't understand Nadia, who slipped right into any new role or community, as she had at the genetic medicine clinic.

During the week, it was nice and quiet in the boutique. A few customers, a little sewing. Over the centuries, Kati had learned to repair saddles as well as garments, so the work suited her perfectly. Today she intended to take things easy. She let herself sink into the armchair behind the counter, kicked up her feet onto a stool, and cracked open a women's magazine.

Kati idly flipped through the stiff pages full of scantily clad women. She couldn't help smiling. Sales would come to a screeching halt if they said that seduction had nothing to do with lack of clothes, that all you needed was a sidelong glance or smile. And Kati couldn't get excited about the clothes, either. She had no problem putting together her own armor for any era she happened to be living in.

Kati's phone vibrated, and Didi's face appeared on the screen. Better to answer right away, although dealing with teenage angst this early in the day wasn't exactly Kati's idea of a good time.

'How did things go at the university?' Kati asked.

'Fine, I guess, even though this is all so weird,' Didi answered. 'I told them that I just moved here and my name was missing from the attendance list by accident. What if someone asks how old I am, or who I am?'

'What name did you give them?'

'Desirée Tasson.'

'Good. Using your old name would make it too easy for people to find you,' Kati said. 'And quit whining. Just stick to the story and everything's going to be fine.'

'Why did you guys give me a name that's so hard to pronounce?'

'The time may come when it will protect you.'

'Who's looking for me, anyway?' Didi asked.

'It doesn't matter,' Kati said. 'But you definitely don't want to be found.'

CHAPTER 13

Everyone at the Montpellier campus was used to Professor Mann's extravagant lifestyle and the occasional unusual guest. When they saw this particular guest, students reacted first by gawking at him and then moving out of his way. It was difficult to say if he was a punk rocker or a soldier. His massive green army coat did nothing to conceal his wiry build. His blond hair stuck straight up, and he had a steely, penetrating gaze. A heavy sailor bag traveled easily at his shoulder as he strode up the stairs to the professor's office.

The visitor was ushered into the professor's study to wait. His casual dress and demeanor were in complete contrast to the room's oak-paneled walls and heavy velvet curtains. He eyed his surroundings and fingered the fusty books and antique objects on the desk with a look of sly amusement.

Erik paused to observe him from the doorway. It had been a long time since he and his visitor had last met, and he wasn't sure how the latter felt about the invitation. Jesper looked the same as ever: a lithe, blond satyr. His mouth was always on the verge of spreading into a smile that could just as equally be playful as ice-cold, and his gaze was keen and curious.

Erik stepped into the room, followed by Mitchell, Lucas, and a nymph in a pale outfit. He offered his guest a subdued greeting.

'Have a seat.' Erik gestured to a chair and then at the dark-haired Albena, indicating that the nymph should pour them wine.

'It has been a while since we last met.'

'I came out of courtesy,' Jesper said, without accepting the glass that was served to him. 'But I'm not following anyone's orders. I respect you, so I'm giving you this one chance to tell me what's on your mind.'

Erik weighed up the situation. Albena stood skittishly off to the side. Initially the nymph had been an infinite source of pleasure to Erik, but now he was bored. Perhaps it was time to have a little fun. As far as dealing with Jesper was concerned, it was best to get right to the point.

'I want you to do some work for me,' Erik said. 'I asked for the best, and Gabriel Korda recommended you.'

'Work?' Jesper asked. He lifted a foot onto the coffee table to demonstrate that he hadn't shown up to take orders from anyone.

'The fugitives have been spotted,' Erik said. 'In some small city up north.'

'You'll need one of them for that job,' Jesper said, lowering his foot back to the floor. 'A huntress. If the rumors are true, then the huntress has been dead and buried for quite a while now.'

Erik gave a hollow laugh. At least he had managed to spark Jesper's interest. That gave him a little room to move.

'You shouldn't listen to rumors.' Erik opened his desk drawer and pulled out a large key. 'Yet it is true that she's trapped in the earth. Shall we go?'

Jesper, Mitchell and Lucas followed Erik down to the basement. Erik stopped in front of a massive iron-reinforced wooden door and held the key out to Mitchell so he could do the heavy work. The door opened with a groan.

A dim corridor opened up before them, or more like a dungeon. Lucas turned on the high-powered flashlight he was carrying and illuminated the space before them. Jesper's eyes followed the beam of light until it fell on a blonde woman chained to the wall. She had the figure of a young woman, but her hair was lifeless and brittle, and her skin was like thin, wrinkled vellum. She was no longer able to stand; she dangled from her chains. Her irises had lost their color and turned to milk. And yet defiance still blazed within them.

'This is what a nymph who escaped seventeen years ago looks like,' Erik said, as if introducing a specimen to a group of biology students.

As if in response, the nymph hurled herself against her chains with the last of her strength. Her struggling was in vain, however. Erik smiled coolly and turned towards Jesper.

'Mitchell and Lucas and their friends handled the monthly visits, so our little Frida has remained among the living. However, a few weeks ago I decided that there's a limit to everything and it was time for the torture to come to an end. But this nymph is exceptionally tenacious, and she just won't die.'

Lucas now aimed the beam of light straight ahead, directly into Frida's face. Her eyes blazed with hatred. Erik tipped up her chin.

'My friend Jesper Janssen has left his ascetic life in the woods to join us. He would like to ask you a couple of questions,' he said, bending closer to Frida's ear. 'Ekaterina and her fugitive friends have been found . . . As has the reason for your flight.'

Frida didn't answer, so Erik pulled out his phone, and a moment later the face of the redheaded girl appeared on the screen. Without hesitating, Frida spat on Erik's cheek, but he just smiled as he wiped off the spittle with his handkerchief.

Frida's voice was raw, barely louder than a whisper: 'If you want to find them, you'll need me.'

Erik looked at his companions, as if proud that Frida still had defiance and rage to spare.

'Remove these shackles,' Frida continued. 'Then bring me water and food.'

'Why on earth would we do that?' Erik asked.

He immediately received the response he desired from the nymph. 'Because I'm the only one who can bring you Kati's head.'

CHAPTER 14

Didi started hopping down the stairs of the university two steps at a time, but then she slowed down. She'd already spent a few days trying to meld into this gang. She followed the stream of students out and watched them chatting, exchanging books and notes, laughing. It all felt so foreign. In the first place, she didn't know anyone, and in the second, she was younger than everyone else. Still, she had to act like she was one of them. She pretended to concentrate on the contents of her bag as she shoved her cell phone into it, but she was discreetly checking to see which direction the other students from the lecture were headed. She walked slowly, following them to a nearby cafe.

As soon as she stepped in, Didi realized that this was the place she had come on that rainy night, the cafe where she had looked up Samuel's address. Samuel was the last person she wanted to be thinking about, so she spun right around to leave. But in doing so, she bumped clumsily into a server, knocking everything he was carrying to the floor. The glasses shattered with a crash, and an embarrassed blush rose to Didi's cheeks.

'Sorry, I didn't see you.' Didi bent down to pick up the shards from the floor.

'Don't worry about it,' said the server. He was average height and wearing a black pique shirt and a black apron bearing the restaurant's logo. 'I'll clean it up.'

'But it was my fault,' Didi said.

The server had already squatted down, and their gazes met. He was middle-aged and had clearly been around the block. He had short, dark hair and understanding brown eyes.

Didi straightened up and briskly placed the shards on the cafe counter. 'I want to pay for this.'

The man gave her an evaluative look, and Didi starting getting nervous about what the total damage might be.

'I'm Valtteri Vaara,' the man said. 'Owner, waiter, driver, baker . . .'

'Desirée,' Didi said, still getting used to the sound of her name. 'But everyone calls me Didi.'

'Are you looking for a job, by any chance?' Valtteri asked. 'No pressure, but I happen to be looking for someone with good people skills. You seem to fit the bill, and I usually trust my intuition.'

'I'm not sure,' Didi began, but she immediately reconsidered, realizing that this would be a great way of integrating her fake name into her new life. 'On the other hand, why not?'

'That's the spirit. I like people who take chances,' Valtteri laughed.

Didi took the rag from Valtteri's hand. 'When do I start?'

After a brief negotiation, Didi and Valtteri had settled on her hours and wages. She drank the cappuccino her new boss offered her and then she headed home. Didi smiled. Kati thought she was nothing more than a spoiled brat who was incapable of handling her own affairs, but she had gotten herself a job just like that. She could barely wait to get home and tell Kati.

Didi was so satisfied with what she had accomplished that she stopped at the candy store on her way home. God, how indulgent it would be to collapse in bed with a bag of candy. She entered the apartment and poked her head into the kitchen, but there was no sign of Kati brandishing her customary broad-bladed knife. Instead, she saw Nadia, who had lowered a mesh bag full of fruit onto the counter. The bragging and the candy would have to wait.

'Would you like some?' Nadia asked matter-of-factly. She had just sliced an orange in two and lifted it up, squeezing its golden juice to her lips.

'Sure, why not,' Didi said a little tentatively, but the aroma of the citrus flooded into her nostrils. She grabbed the other half of the orange and followed Nadia's example. Most of the juice dripped down her chin, and Nadia wiped it away.

'You need to learn how to find pleasure in life,' Nadia said.

Didi was immediately reminded of her ascetic, withdrawn mother. Elina would have never let her play with food, nor did she encourage her to have fun of any other sort. The candy stash that weighed down Didi's shoulder bag wouldn't have had Elina's approval either.

'Do you have any idea what the life of a nymph is like? You will be eternally young,' Nadia said, as she started preparing a meal of fruit for them. 'You'll never put on an ounce of weight, no matter what you eat. All of your senses will be sharpened. You'll smell and taste more keenly.'

Didi accepted the piece of mango Nadia was offering, and her lips immediately started sucking the ripe fruit's flesh from the skin. So far being a nymph didn't sound half-bad. *Maybe after this, I'll eat all the candy and then a quart of ice cream*, Didi thought.

'And there's no point being afraid of the full moon, either,' Nadia continued. 'It will arouse you, it will make you crave touch.'

Didi didn't have time to pull back as Nadia wiped her cheek with the back of her hand. A sensation that was simultaneously soothing and stimulating seemed to flow into her from Nadia's caress.

'You will yearn for the touch of skin,' Nadia said. 'Your desires will awaken. Once you let yourself go and give in to the pleasure, you will know what it means to be a nymph.'

Didi immediately remembered her earlier experiences and the fact that what she and Nadia were talking about here was not some romp in the hay. She had wanted to fall in love, to make love. Look how that had turned out. Now she was supposed to be with a man so she could stay alive, and take someone else's life while she did it?

'I don't want to be with some random stranger,' Didi said.

'That's how you feel now,' Nadia replied. 'You have to totally change your perspective. That random stranger should want to be with you. Go get undressed, there's a new robe on your bed.'

Nadia headed for her own bedroom, and Didi stayed in the kitchen, confused. She didn't have the slightest idea what Nadia had in mind. She had no reason to suspect that Nadia had bad intentions towards her. Nor had Didi been the most modest girl at school, even if she wasn't quite as free-spirited as Laura. On the one hand, she didn't want to do as she was told, but then on the other, it seemed like Nadia might be about to teach her something titillating. It was as if she were joining some secret society, being initiated into rites that the other women were already privy to.

Didi went into her room and saw that a soft linen robe had been folded up on her bed. She hesitated for a minute, but then her curiosity got the better of her. She felt like being bold. She stripped down and then wrapped herself in the beautiful, dusty-rose-colored robe.

'Didi?' Nadia's invitation carried in from the bathroom, and Didi headed towards her voice.

Water was splashing into the tub. The bathroom was white, but the tub had been decorated with turquoise bath-balls, blossom-shaped candleholders and fresh rose petals. Nadia had set the mood with the lighting, and the flickering of the candles shimmered against the mosaic tiles.

Nadia was wearing nothing but a short cotton shift. She didn't say a word. She stepped closer to Didi and turned towards her, so she could slip the robe from Didi's shoulders. Every gesture of Nadia's seemed simple, and it was as if nudity were the most natural state in the world to the nymph. She held out her hand, and Didi reached for it. Nadia helped Didi step into the tub. She waited for Didi to lower herself into the warm water and then sat down on the edge herself. She serenely rubbed something into her hands.

'This is Moroccan rose oil,' Nadia said, humming as the floral scent began to sparkle in the air. 'I don't have much left, so I use it sparingly, only on special occasions.'

Nadia pressed her softened hands to Didi's neck and then her shoulders. Moving languidly, she warmed Didi up and then massaged her. After a few minutes, Didi, who was tense to begin with, relaxed. Her senses stopped working, and the water numbed her into a state where she felt like she was being cradled, shielded from everything that had happened. Nadia poured warm water onto her skin from a shell-shaped bowl, and the drops streamed down her red tresses, which glowed amid the turquoise.

'Water nurtures nymphs,' Nadia said. 'Being clean makes us feel calm, secure. How do you feel?'

'Good,' Didi whispered, her eyes fully closed. She was in another world, at peace, and it felt as if Nadia were telling her a fairy tale.

'I'm a water nymph,' Nadia said. 'There are water nymphs, mountain nymphs, and nature nymphs. Kati is from the mountains, the Carpathians. If you feel a connection with water, you might be a water nymph. In that case, you could become a healer.'

'I tried to heal Samuel,' Didi said, utterly relaxed. 'I was afraid he would die. I don't think I have it in me to be a healer.'

CHAPTER 15

Harju walked down the hospital corridor, the bottom of his ancient trench coat swinging in time to his stride. He was following a stout brunette doctor, and he tried not to hurry despite his excitement. He had a tendency to rush when he discovered evidence that supported his hunches. The doctor, who had doubtless acquired her tan on a golf course, gazed at his shabby appearance from behind her spectacles with a vague distaste.

'You said you're from the National Bureau of Investigation?'

'That's right. Detective Harju,' he answered, digging deep into his pockets. 'I'm looking for the pathologist who performed the autopsy on Johannes Metso, who died a little over two weeks ago.'

'This is a small town,' the doctor laughed. 'We don't have any doctors who specialize in pathology. And autopsies are pretty rare.'

'But one was performed in this case, wasn't it?' Harju asked. 'Metso was a young man and the cause of death was unclear.'

'Yes, an autopsy was performed,' the doctor answered. She went over to the file cabinet, and after a brief search pulled out the patient file, which she handed to Harju. 'What's this about?'

Harju focused on the data for a moment. His face was thoughtful as he tried to assess what he was reading as precisely as possible, but the folder only contained a single, solitary page.

'Are you the one who performed the autopsy?'

'We were a little busy then,' the doctor answered. 'A colleague assisted.'

'I'd like to speak to him.' Harju set the folder aside; it wasn't of the slightest use. 'Is he here today?'

'As a matter of fact, she quit right after Metso's death.'

Harju picked the folder up again. His hunch had to be right. There's no way it could be a coincidence that the doctor who had performed the autopsy had slipped off somewhere. Harju rubbed his stubble-covered chin.

'Where can I find this Dr Elina Tiensuu, specialist in women's health?'

'Let's go get the address and phone number from the office,' sighed the doctor, whose thoughts were already on the golf course.

Detective Harju had speedily acquired the information he needed and driven straight out to the house. He didn't even have to knock on the door to know that the house was deserted. He'd been around long enough to be able to tell when the chickens had flown the coop. Luckily, he'd come well prepared and quickly picked the simple lock.

As a formality, Harju called out from the doorway: 'Is anyone home?'

He turned on his flashlight and explored the downstairs rooms. The furniture was covered in sheets, and he didn't find a soul, or anything else of interest. Then it was time for the second story. He opened the first door and could tell at one glance that the room belonged to a teenage girl. That made him pause; it was a sight that had grown unfamiliar. He didn't remember what a teenage girl's bedroom looked like. A couple of posters hung on the walls, along with a joke postcard and a bouquet of dried roses. Harju's heart was clenched in a cold grip, and he sighed. Other than that, the room was empty. There was nothing here that would advance his case.

Harju was turning around to leave and close the door, when the beam from his flashlight struck the floor. There was something there. Harju bent down and looked more closely. Dozens of dead, desiccated bees. Dozens and dozens. This was something to consider.

Harju's cell phone started blaring out the theme from *Hill Street Blues*. He answered.

'Find anything?' Hannula asked.

'Not exactly,' replied Harju, whose analysis was far from complete. 'Or can you remember a single case where there was absolutely no trace left behind?'

'The only thing that comes to mind is that there is no case,' Hannula said.

'Good night.'

Harju knelt down. He pulled a small jar out of his pocket and carefully filled it with lifeless bees.

CHAPTER 16

Nadia took one more look at the photo of the young man as it lay against the stainless-steel counter in her lab. Kati had said that Didi's first experience needed to be a good one. That's why they had narrowed in on Janne Malasmaa, and the young man had been called into the genetic medicine clinic for an examination at the request of registered nurse Nadia Rapaccini. At least in his pictures, Janne looked handsome and sympathetic. The next thing they would do was test his endurance. Nadia looked around to make sure she had all of her equipment ready. Treadmill, electrodes, oxygen mask ... They'd help her determine Janne's suitability for the task at hand.

Out in the waiting room, Kati had no trouble recognizing their young man, and in the flesh he looked athletic enough for their purposes, the picture of health. Janne was average height; he had brown hair, dark eyes with a mischievous gleam, and a goatee. He was clearly a nice guy and smart, but he had a flirtatious side, too. All the better. Kati pretended to be reading a magazine that had been thumbed through a million times before. Something about her compelled Janne to take a seat right next to her. *They're simply incapable of resisting us*, Kati thought, as she feigned a yawn of boredom.

'Excuse me,' Kati said to Janne. 'The magazines they have here are ancient. I've read all of them and they make me feel like I'm ancient, too.'

'You're not old,' Janne said.

'How would you know?' Kati asked coyly.

'I have eyes.' Janne appeared amused, too. The woman's flirtation was obvious.

'Thank you. There should always be handsome men at the genetic medicine clinic handing out compliments. It works wonders for the self-confidence. I'm Kati.'

'Janne.' The young man extended a hand.

Kati made a pretense of retreating into her own thoughts for a moment, offering Janne the opportunity to give her a proper once-over. Kati's sleeveless black T-shirt revealed her strong arms, and she had positioned herself so the sunlight accentuated the firm muscles of her shoulders. Her black hair gleamed, and she knew her broad, sensual mouth was attractive. She slowly stretched her neck from one side to the other.

'What's wrong with you?' Kati asked.

'Nothing,' Janne answered hastily. 'I was called in for stress tests. I'm a stem cell donor.'

'You don't look like someone who stresses much about anything.'

'No, a stress test is . . .'

'I'm just kidding,' Kati laughed in a low voice.

'How about you, what are you doing here?' Janne asked. 'Sorry, that was awkward . . .'

'That's quite all right,' Kati laughed. 'I'm not a patient here. I'm just waiting for my friend to get off work.'

Janne eyed Kati and was on the verge of saying something when the door opened and Nadia stepped out into the waiting room in her lab coat.

'Janne Malasmaa?'

'That's me.' Janne rose and walked over to her.

'Don't get too stressed, now,' Kati teased as he walked away.

'Never. I wouldn't want the good impression to go to waste.' Janne waved and smiled self-confidently at Kati.

Kati waited on the sofa. The candidate they had hand-picked for Didi was now in Nadia's capable hands. All they had to do was to be patient and see if Janne passed the test. For both her and Nadia, Didi was a still-unknown quantity; the girl had powers that they couldn't quite figure out. Kati had to admit that she had been caught off guard. But the important thing now was to help Didi get off to a sound start so she could survive the next full moon. If something happened to Didi, her identity as a nymph might be exposed. And if that happened, it wouldn't be long before the satyrs would be at their heels. There was no point telling Didi about that yet, though. It would be smartest to take things one step at a time.

Kati glanced at the large hands of the clock on the wall. Before long, thirty minutes would have passed. The magazines truly were ancient, and sitting around with nothing to do didn't suit Kati in the least. It was a relief to hear voices behind the door, indicating Janne's return.

'You're still here,' the freshly showered Janne said, as he took a seat at Kati's side. 'I was kind of hoping you would be. Is your friend coming? Or do you feel like hanging out?'

'Thanks, but I'm going to wait a little longer,' Kati said with a smile. 'I could probably grab a coffee tomorrow. Give me your number and I'll text you.'

Janne did as Kati suggested. 'I'll see you tomorrow.' Kati noted that Nadia had arrived at the doorway to the examination room and nodded. Evidently everything had gone well.

Kati waited until Janne disappeared out the door, then Nadia came over.

'Looks good,' Nadia said. 'A healthy young man.'

'At least for now,' Kati said.

CHAPTER 17

Kati wasn't exactly sure why the exchange with Janne had taken so much out of her. Maybe it was because something familiar about the directness of Janne's gaze aroused old memories that still lurked in the back of her mind. She would have loved to leap onto the back of a horse and let her hair stream out in the wind. Well, now she had short hair and nanny-state helmet laws to deal with, but at least her motorcycle mimicked the sensation. She raced along the long, winding asphalt roads outside town and allowed her memories to take her back to how she used to plunge through the forest towards the mountain hut . . .

She leaped down from the saddle and was tying up her horse when Janos threw back the doeskins that covered the entrance to his home. Kati was in his arms in an instant. It had been over ten years since their first meeting, and Janos was now a man in the prime of his life.

'Katya!' he cried.

'The trip always gets longer,' Kati whispered into his neck. 'Light a fire.'

'You can come back soon,' Janos said. 'The area is full of new generations of villagers now.'

Kati spoke her wish out loud, even though she already knew the answer: 'It would be easier for us to live in town together.'

'We would not be free in the city. Fear would be our constant companion. This is where we belong.'

'I belong to you,' Kati said. She grabbed Janos by the hand and led him into the candlelight.

Kati remembered exactly what the inside of the hut was like; where Janos kept the honey, the water, the flour. How he replaced the bone-carved *nomos* knife in its proper place. She remembered every single stone in the hearth. And she remembered what it was like to lie naked under the pelt, watching Janos carry in dry branches for firewood . . .

The fire crackled as Kati stretched out languidly. Janos set the wood down. The flames and shadows played across his face. In this memory, Janos was older. His temples had grayed, and there were wrinkles at the corners of his eyes. But Kati couldn't imagine anyone she would have rather had at her side.

'What are you looking at?' Janos asked.

'Come to bed,' Kati answered.

Janos rose slowly, and looked at his nymph lover.

'As the years pass, I can offer you less and less, Katya,' Janos said. 'I'm barely worth one man any more. This is not fair to you.'

'I didn't ask you here to sleep,' Kati said. She sensed Janos' melancholy and wanted to banish it.

He came and sat next to her, and she wrapped her bare arms around him, felt his brawny chest and the oak pendant hanging against it. She refused to think about how her human lover was aging.

'I may be old, but I'm not tired,' Janos growled, settling down on his side.

'I love you,' Kati said, wondering at how easily the words rose to her lips. 'Every little crow's foot at the corner of your eyes, every complaint in your joints only serves to deepen my love.'

'When my time comes, I want to die in your arms,' Janos said.

* * *

That instant had been recorded in every cell of Kati's body. She tilted her motorcycle as she curved around the next bend. And humans imagined they had it hard. Bitched and moaned about relationship problems and totally stupid things, Kati thought, now wishing she could ride off as far as possible and leave everything behind once again. But she had to go home. She and Nadia had a task to complete. They had accepted it, and they had no intention of giving up. That's why it was important for her to track Didi down right now. In her text messages, the young nymph had bragged about some job at a cafe, and even though Kati was in principle opposed, it also opened up some new possibilities.

Half an hour later, Kati was back in the city, parking her bike. She was pulling off her helmet when she noticed a good-looking young man in her rear-view mirror. His dress shirt was sharp and the boy could wear a pair of jeans. It was Samuel. Kati didn't move a muscle; she just watched as he took a seat on the terrace. And before long, Didi was scurrying out to see him. Kati moved closer to the wall, so she would remain out of sight but could still hear what they were saying.

'Order something,' Didi said to Samuel. 'I'm working.'

'Take fifteen minutes.' This was the older man in an apron. 'You need to give your feet a rest now and again, Didi.'

Didi smiled, thrilled, and sat down with Samuel. She picked up a pitcher and poured water for the both of them.

'I never would have guessed that you'd become a waitress,' Samuel said. 'Or that you'd move to Helsinki. You've changed somehow.'

'Life got kind of complicated,' Didi said. She rapidly changed the subject when she saw the books that Samuel had laid down on the table. 'What made you decide to study medicine?'

'I guess maybe I wanted to do it ever since Dad died.' Samuel looked away for a moment. 'No one could explain what happened, so . . .'

Kati had an urge to go over and pull Didi away. It was patently obvious to her that Didi and Samuel had spoken to each other before. Hadn't they drilled it into the girl's head firmly enough, how important it was to be cautious? But she restrained herself. This was a good opportunity to get some more information.

'What made you decide to study art history?' Samuel asked. 'Oh never mind, I guess you were always pretty serious for your age.'

'Maybe *The Three Musketeers* had an impact,' Didi said. 'The portrait of Cardinal Richelieu fascinated me.'

Kati listened as Didi and Samuel chatted about this and that, but it was clear that they had a common past. Samuel's gaze remained fixed on Didi, and Didi's cheeks were tinged with a faint yet constant blush of excitement. They laughed at some joke that was clearly private and leaned into each other more closely without realizing it.

Before long, Samuel took his books and went on his way. Didi knotted her apron more tightly around her waist and started work again. She took orders in a firm but friendly manner and appeared to be earning pretty good tips, too. *It's all fun and games until someone loses an eye*, Kati thought, as she hung out, waiting for Didi to get off work.

Didi was blissfully unaware of Kati's grim gaze on her back as she stepped out onto the street once her shift was over. She inhaled deeply. She felt surprisingly adult. She was studying, she had a job, she had met Samuel . . . They had reminisced over childhood stories, but Didi had also been profoundly aware of the fact that Samuel was a man. Nor had she ever felt so comfortable in the company of any other man. Samuel inspired a confidence in her – and some other sensation, too. There was something in it that reminded her of their little spats when they were kids, some essence of those tiny moments when they were close to each other and out of breath. Didi was completely lost in thought when a steel-hard arm sheathed in black leather suddenly grabbed her and pulled her around a corner, out of sight. She was about to scream in horror before she realized she was looking into Kati's flinty eyes.

'No one can find out about us,' Kati said sharply.

At first, Didi was startled into silence. Then she realized Kati had witnessed her interaction with Samuel.

'Are you spying on me?' Didi's emotions boiled to the surface, and she felt the same agitation she used to feel with her mother. 'And is Samuel who you're talking about? We've known each other since we were little kids.'

'Oh, like you and that Laura you were Skyping with this morning?' Kati walked over to her motorcycle and removed one helmet for herself and another for Didi. 'Nymphs can't trust humans, especially men.'

'How did you know to find me here?'

'I have to keep an eye on you constantly, because you don't understand how serious the situation is. You run off, you go to work, you don't make proper plans with us. Try to get this one simple rule through your head: you cannot grow attached to a single human being.'

Didi had no intention of putting on her helmet until she had an answer. 'Why not?'

'Because one of you will die,' Kati responded in her unsympathetic way, whirling around onto the back of her bike before Didi could see her tear up. 'All the stories about nymphs and mortals are tragedies. Promise me you won't fall in love with a human.'

'I have no intention of falling in love,' Didi said, climbing onto the bike behind Kati. 'Are you going to give me a ride home or not?'

Good lord, this is one annoying babysitting gig, Kati thought, as she rumbled off into traffic. Hopefully Nadia had had the sense to stock the fridge with plenty of white wine, because it was time to take Didi's training to the next level.

* * *

Evidently Nadia was a mind reader. Wine glasses, fruit and nuts had been laid out on the kitchen table in an appetizing arrangement. Kati marched right over to fill her glass, grabbed a fistful of nuts, and popped them into her mouth.

'You're not expecting me to spend some girls' night at home or something with you, are you?' Didi said, turning up her nose at the table. 'You don't even know me, and you still think you're going to get me to go along with some scheme you two cooked up. I don't need anyone following me around!'

Didi slammed her bedroom door behind her.

Nadia glanced at Kati, who had no desire to make peace with the young nymph.

'Didi will learn to take care of herself if we just help with the first few,' Kati said to Nadia. 'She's strong and smart. She'll learn the drill. It won't be long before the whole thing is running ahead on its own steam.'

'Are you OK?' Nadia poured herself a drop of wine to keep Kati company. They had worked together for so long that she had become extremely perceptive, and Kati was not herself right now. *We all have our pasts*, Nadia thought.

'We have to keep that boy away,' Kati said.

'Samuel?'

'Samuel.' Kati spat out the name as if it were a swear word before disappearing onto the dusky balcony. 'That's the one.'

Nadia wanted to defuse the situation. She thought for a moment, then she took a couple of women's magazines and went into Didi's room, where the younger nymph was furiously brushing her red hair.

'Let me help you with that,' Nadia said, gently removing the brush from Didi's hands.

Didi might have been intending not to give in, but Nadia's touch was difficult to resist. She barely had time to realize what had happened before they were lying on the bed, laughing at the tips for hitting on men they were reading from the women's magazine.

'"Look him in the eye,"' Didi read. '"The look has to last at least seven seconds, otherwise he won't notice. Men are cursed with tunnel vision."'

'That is so true,' Nadia said.

'"Don't jump into bed with him right away. The three-date rule is so eighties, the new standard is five."'

Didi looked at Nadia, who wasn't laughing any more.

'We still have some time before the full moon,' Nadia said, resting a hand on Didi's bare knee. 'He will stay alive if you know how to be careful.'

'How?'

'In the first place, you make everything too complicated. You don't have to think about how to seduce anyone any more. You're a nymph.'

Nadia looked at Didi, whose cheeks were now red, and she felt a profound compassion.

'It's all right to be afraid,' she continued. 'I know what it feels like to be in your shoes. But you've already experienced how the desire grows. It sweeps you along, and you want to experience it again.'

Nadia could see that she had struck a chord, and she lifted Didi's hand to her own heart.

'Can you feel it?' Nadia asked. 'This is the source of its power. The full moon takes over, and you have to give in to it. That's all there is to it.'

'I don't understand,' Didi whispered. 'What exactly am I supposed to do?'

'Nothing,' Nadia said. She decided that it would be best to lighten the mood. She rose from the bed and led Didi into the living room. A second later, the music began to play. Nadia took hold of the younger nymph as if she were the man and Didi were the woman and started to lead. 'Men like to talk a big game, but when it's just the two of you, all it takes is a single glance to have any man you want.'

'I've never thought about stuff like this before.' Didi was getting hot, both from Nadia's proximity and the thought of a man's embrace.

'Men have fought wars over us.' Nadia took a few more steps, bent Didi backwards, and pretended to be serious. 'Men! They've built cities and kingdoms for us. They've been lords and kings. And yet you can have everything you want if you just undo your red hair and look a man in the eye.'

Didi gave in to Nadia's frolicking, and they danced a polka across the living room before collapsing on the sofa in exhaustion. Didi was gasping for breath, and the question rose to her lips without any inhibitions.

'What was your first time like?'

'I was fourteen,' Nadia said. 'I had been trained since I was eleven. I was still scared to death of that night. I made love to a man, but I didn't kill him.'

Nadia looked at Didi and saw a glimmer of hope. She didn't tell the young nymph that the next morning satyrs had slain the man.

'Wait here.' Nadia went into the kitchen and returned with a glass of water that had a tablet bubbling inside it. 'This will help you sleep,' she said to Didi. 'You'll need your strength by the week's end.'

Didi sat up and obediently accepted the glass and drank it dry.

But if a restful night was what she was hoping for, the tablet didn't bring it.

CHAPTER 18

Love, suffer, and avenge, thought Frida as she allowed her fingers to play across the plush velvet upholstery of the antique armchair. The door to the study had been left ajar, and Albena was standing there in a pale chiffon dress, flower behind her ear. She was shaving Jesper's throat with a knife. What a slave. She had been entrusted with a blade, and she still subserviently performed her task. And yet Frida was also awaiting Erik's next command herself.

No one would have ever guessed that this was the same nymph who just a few days earlier had languished in the dungeon, on the brink of death. Her blond braids radiated an inner light, her skin was flawless and smooth, her body supple. She was dressed in brown wool knee-length trousers and a tight-fitting vest of the same fabric. The ensemble was complemented by a white blouse, a tie, and sturdy yet feminine laced boots. She looked composed on the surface, but her gaze was hard, and at her side there was a hunting bow to which she intermittently lowered her fingers, as if seeking reassurance that she had been truly and totally resurrected. The bow had always been part of her.

'Frida fled with the others,' Jesper was saying in the study. 'Why would she betray her sisters to help us now?'

'There are two good reasons to bring Frida along,' Erik answered. 'For one, she can track Ekaterina. Frida will catch the scent. And in the second place, our breaking of the fugitive will send a message to the other nymphs.'

'It seems like a unnecessary risk to me,' Jesper said.

Erik glanced at Albena, who had finished shaving Jesper and was patting his chin clean. Erik smiled at the nymph and bid her to come closer.

'I'll give you a little head start,' Erik said. The nymph's eyes widened in terror as the meaning of this simple phrase sank in. 'And if you make it out of Montpellier alive, you'll live.'

Albena was paralyzed.

'Go!' Erik yelled brusquely, and the nymph bolted from the room. Erik turned towards Jesper. 'You wanted to know if we can trust Frida. We'll know in a minute, but first we shall dine.'

The satyrs left the room, while Frida remained in the neighboring chamber. She stepped over to the window, opened it, and raised her nose to the wind. She managed to catch a final glimpse of Albena weaving through the crowd below, her coat wrapped tightly around her. The nymph was making for a narrow lane and kept glancing over her shoulder to see if she was being followed.

Frida had time. She knew she'd have no trouble finding Albena. She'd let the dark-haired nymph tire herself out looking for ways to escape, for places to hide. Frida picked up her leather wrist-guard and attached it carefully. She studied a map of the city for a moment. Then she gathered her gear and headed out.

The assignment was almost too easy. Frida knew that Erik wanted the incident to be as public as possible so it would serve as a warning to other nymphs and teach them what happened when you longed for freedom. Which is why she had plenty of time to stalk the streets of the old town.

In the midst of her suffering in the dungeon, Frida had thirsted for freedom, but now it didn't feel the way she had imagined it would. Her pain hadn't relented in the least, and her desire for vengeance had only grown. She had been forced to take the agony: the desire aroused within her by the moon, the repeated rapes at the hands of the satyrs, and the subsequent return to the shackles. These were agonizing memories. But before long, she would have the chance to put an end to it all. Maybe that would finally free her of the image of her beloved's face drawing her final breath. The gaze that radiated joy and defiance until the end.

When dusk fell, Frida honed in on the Montpellier bus station. The area was crowded with locals and tourists. She'd already scouted out the area and picked a good spot in a building on the square, and she had no trouble climbing out a window onto a small ledge. Frida pulled back into a corner where she was completely hidden, but still had a line-of-sight view of the station. She readied herself. Her wait was not long. The exhausted Albena appeared in the street below, moving slowly in her now-dirty coat. The bus was taking on new passengers, and Albena apparently believed she would make it on board with the other travelers, because she no longer had the sense to be afraid. Frida tensed her bow. She didn't feel an ounce of pity for her fellow nymph. Albena was trivial compared to the prize she sought.

The arrow zoomed into flight, and suddenly the young woman in the light-colored coat who had been waiting at the bus stop crumpled to the ground, holding her chest. It took the crowd a moment to realize what had happened, but then they scattered in horror.

Frida left the balcony soundlessly. The message that Erik had wanted to send to the fugitives had been delivered. She had shown Erik how deep her lust for vengeance was, and that she deserved a place in the hunting party. Now the time had come for them to travel to Helsinki.

CHAPTER 19

Didi set two large lattes down in front of Nadia and Kati. She was surprised at how glad she felt that the older nymphs had wanted to come see her at work. Just that morning, Nadia had especially picked out a fluid olive green dress with a scoop neckline that just barely licked her breasts. The apron wrapped across the front of it showed off her narrow cleavage.

'You're going to be a decent barista someday,' Nadia said, inhaling the strong coffee aroma.

Didi lowered her tray and took a seat in the booth. The nymphs had chosen one that was off to the side.

'So what do you guys think?' Didi asked.

'It's a nice place,' Nadia smiled.

Didi waited for Kati to say something, too, but the other nymph's eyes circled the tables before focusing on the door.

'Do you guys want anything else?' Didi asked. 'The brioches just came out of the—' Didi didn't have time to finish before Kati suddenly stood and waved at someone. A young, good-looking guy was standing at the door. He nodded at Kati and walked towards her. Apparently he didn't realize that Kati wasn't alone until he reached the table.

'Hey, Janne,' Kati said casually. 'These are my friends Nadia and Didi.'

'Hi,' Janne responded politely, even though Didi sensed a mild disappointment. Had Kati set up a date for herself at the cafe? Didi glanced at the black-haired nymph, who was smiling sweetly at Janne.

'Have a seat,' Kati said, conveniently arranging things so Didi and Janne were sitting right across from each other. 'I met Janne at the clinic while I was waiting for Nadia to get off work.'

Nadia said a few words to demonstrate that she remembered Janne, and Kati chatted about this and that. Didi looked at her, bewildered. Kati didn't seem anything like her usual self. Just then Kati got a text message.

'Oh no, I have to go take care of something,' Kati said, after reading her message.

'And I have to get to work,' Nadia chimed in.

'It was nice to see you, Janne,' Kati said. 'Let's do this again sometime.'

An instant later, the nymphs had vanished, and Janne and Didi were alone at the table. Didi was embarrassed. She had always been bad at making conversation. Apparently Janne sensed this, because he broke the ice.

'Does it feel to you like we were set up?' Janne asked.

Didi burst into laughter, relieved. 'Just a little. Can I get you a coffee and brioche to make up for it?'

A little later, they were talking freely. Janne told Didi about his work, and she told him about her studies. They compared notes on movies they had seen, and it turned out Janne was a total movie freak. Without realizing it, Didi kept him company for almost an hour, until Valtteri dropped by the table to tug at her sleeve and tell her it was time to get back to work.

'It was nice meeting you,' Janne said. 'Can I call you sometime?'

Didi thought about it for a second, but she had genuinely enjoyed herself. She gave Janne her number and then went back to waiting tables. She might have a word with Kati and Nadia later about their clumsy set-up, but the reality was she wasn't angry about it in the least.

That evening Didi was lounging around on the couch. She could feel the effects of a long day at work in her feet. Maybe Mom had been right after all. When Didi had expressed wistful dreams about getting a job at a clothing store and the attendant benefits, Elina had responded that it would be a good idea to go to university. Didi hadn't expected that a handful of lectures in art history and women's studies would have caught her interest. But now she was actually looking forward to more. Plus, she had been able to discuss them with Janne like an adult.

The doorbell rang, startling Didi. They didn't generally have visitors. She waited for a minute, hoping that she wouldn't have to get up from the sofa, but she didn't hear anyone else moving to answer it. She padded over to the door and expected to find some frumpy lady spreading the gospel when she opened it. She definitely didn't expect to see Samuel. At first Didi was pleased, but then she remembered the lecture Kati had given her.

'What are you doing here?' Didi asked. 'How did you know where I lived?'

'I told your boss at the cafe that you had forgotten your purse at my place,' Samuel said.

'And Valtteri believed you?' Didi asked.

'I have such an honest face.'

You are honest. You are trustworthy, Didi thought. *I could tell you everything. I'd love to wrap myself in your arms and tell you everything. But then you'd be in danger.*

'You can't come in,' Didi said, knowing she sounded completely silly. She was already trying to close the door so she wouldn't have to explain more, but Samuel blocked her way.

'Do you remember when we were kids and somehow I always knew when things weren't OK with you?' Samuel asked, and

Didi eased her grip on the door handle.

Samuel's words pierced her to the very core. She'd only experienced short periods of normalcy and happiness before all of these strange new things would start spinning around in her head again. She didn't understand anything about being a nymph yet, but the thought of the full moon filled her with dread. Her eyes pleaded with Samuel. They communicated two wishes: that Samuel would leave her right then, and that he would never leave her ever again. Then she came to her senses. She had wanted Johannes, and what had happened? If she cared one bit about Samuel, it would be better by far for him to keep his distance from her.

'Everything's fine,' she said. 'Please go.'

'No. Something's wrong,' Samuel insisted. 'At first I thought that it was none of my business, but then I knew I had to come see you. I don't want to think down the road that I could have done something, that I could have helped.'

Kati's voice carried out from the living room: 'Didi? Who is it?'

'You have to go,' Didi said urgently.

'Do you have roommates?' Samuel asked.

At that instant, Kati's powerful body thrust between them.

Didi tried to make introductions: 'Kati, this is Samuel.' But Kati took her by the shoulders and shoved her aside.

'I'm sure Didi already made it clear that it would be best if you left,' Kati said, pulling the door shut in Samuel's face. She gave Didi an icy look.

'I didn't invite him here,' Didi said.

Kati spun around and stalked off, but Didi stayed in the entryway. She pressed her hands against the smooth surface of the wooden door and could have sworn that she felt Samuel's warm hand on the other side.

CHAPTER 20

The flames from the funeral pyre were nearly licking the fringes of Kati's heavy wool cloak, but she could not make herself step back. She had erected the pyre with her own hands, and she had carried the man she had loved for decades to it and lowered him onto it. She had watched Janos grow gray, but in her eyes he had always remained the young man who had come between her and the satyrs, the one who hadn't allowed himself to be fooled with a kiss. No, a kiss had not sufficed: Janos had taken her heart.

The flames gradually died, and Kati doubled over in grief. She waited until morning, and then gathered the ashes into the casket that Janos had shown her. It had originally held a parchment.

'My ashes belong there,' Janos had said, pointing at an island marked on the map. The map indicated its name as Velanidia.

'Don't say that.'

'Katya, please release me,' Janos had said, and by this time his breathing was labored.

And so Kati had carried out his last wish. She had given Janos all of her love, wrapped him in her arms and let her lips feel how the life flowed out of him. Only then did she give herself permission to cry.

Kati gathered up her few belongings and saddled her horse. The journey would be a long one, but that made no difference to her. It would be best to get as far away as possible. She had no intention of ever coming back to this forest.

When she was finally approaching her destination, she realized she was too late. An ancient temple loomed in front of her, but it lay in ruins, and smoke hung in the air. Kati slowly rode into the valley and towards the holy edifice. Bodies in brown robes were strewn along both sides of the narrow path. Nevertheless, she continued until she reached the temple. She knew that was where Janos had wanted to go.

She got down from the saddle and was just about to take the small casket from the saddlebag when she sensed movement out of the corner of her eye. She was on the attack in an instant, but the figure she saw didn't pose any threat to her.

It was an old man lying in a pool of blood, and he laboriously raised a hand towards her. 'Nymph?'

'I'm sorry, I'm not a healer,' Kati said.

'Some traitor gave us away,' the old man whispered. 'They came at dawn.'

'Satyrs?'

'They destroyed us. They were looking for this.' The old man struggled as he reached into the folds of his robe, and Kati helped him fish out a small fabric pouch from a hidden pocket. An image of a knot had been embroidered on it in tiny cunning stitching. 'It is our secret. Hide it until the moment comes.'

Kati opened the pouch and poured out some of its contents. Seeds.

'What are these?' Kati asked, and bent down to listen to the old man's final words.

After that, the man closed his eyes and died. Kati sat at his side for a moment, but then she rose with fresh determination.

Kati put the seeds back into the pouch. She retrieved the casket from the back of her horse and carried it over to the broad, flat stone in the middle of the temple. She raised her eyes heavenwards and felt the ancient spirit of the place, the devotion that had gone into its care. In her heart of hearts, Kati felt that this was Janos' true home, and she knew she had fulfilled her mission. She pressed her hands to the cool, rough surface of the stone and bid Janos a silent farewell.

It had been the heaviest moment of Kati's life.

Now Kati was leaning against the gunwale of the *Robur*. As she thought about Janos and the risks inherent in relationships between nymphs and men, she grew increasingly certain that the story of Didi and Samuel needed to be nipped in the bud as soon as possible. As a nymph, Didi was still a novice. All of this new information was confusing her; she didn't understand the dangers. Kati felt that it was best to keep the reins in her own hands. Which is why she and Nadia had picked Janne for Didi. Once Didi's true nymph instincts were aroused, her interest in Samuel might fade. It wasn't the least bit difficult for Kati to understand what Didi saw in Samuel. He was a good-looking young man, with a clearly intelligent gaze. Plus he looked great in a pair of jeans. Of course they had a shared past, and Didi missed an anchor to her past life, but she couldn't cling to that now. The easiest thing would be to remove Samuel from the equation one way or another. If Samuel were to get a proper scare, he wouldn't be any more trouble.

Kati heard footfalls and pulled out her stiletto knife. In her experience, a steel blade generally got your message across more effectively than fancy words.

'I dropped by to repay your visit,' she said, stepping out from the darkness and right in front of Samuel. She held the knife casually in her hands.

Samuel was caught off guard and backed up a couple of steps, but Kati advanced.

'I just wanted to make sure that Didi was fine,' Samuel said.

Kati could have just as easily been making small talk about the weather or anything else: 'If you're really Didi's friend, you'll leave her alone.'

'Don't friends normally look out for each other?' Samuel asked, making a move to pass Kati and climb onto his boat.

Quick as a snake, Kati threw him against the side of *Robur*, grabbed him by the arm, and let her energy flow so that Samuel's limbs went numb. She pressed the knife up to where the boy's ear met his throat. 'Maybe you didn't hear me. Or did I mumble?'

Samuel slowly shook his head as much as he dared with the knife there.

'Good. Because you don't want me to come back again. I might not be in such a good mood next time.'

Kati slipped the knife back into her pocket, and before Samuel knew it, she had already sped off on her motorcycle.

CHAPTER 21

Didi looked at her reflection in the ladies' room of the restaurant, still not understanding how she had let things go so far. On the other hand, if she believed Nadia and Kati, the alternative would mean her own death. Besides, Janne had seemed like a nice guy back at the cafe, and now that they had eaten and chatted, her impression of him had only gotten better.

Didi undid her ponytail and fluffed out her hair. *Does this make any sense?* she wondered. First she been stingy with her virginity, and then she was supposed to pick up a new guy every month. Still, she had to admit that the hunger inside her had been aroused, just as the nymphs had promised. But she felt lost without Nadia and Kati. She had pointlessly asked them to join her as her wingmen.

'It's the full moon,' Nadia had smiled.

'We have our own plans,' Kati added.

The full moon. How exactly did it affect them? Was she imagining things, or was her skin a little clearer, her lips plumper and redder? Maybe she really could be a sexy seductress . . . Or not. Didi quickly snapped the elastic around her ponytail again and went back out to the table.

Janne looked handsome in his white shirt. *Hot bod*, Laura would have noted with approval, and the thought made Didi feel better.

'Would you like some dessert?' Janne asked.

'No thanks.' Didi didn't want to stare at him, so she looked around at everyone else.

'There's one problem with this date,' Janne said, closing his menu. 'I wasn't supposed to be interested in you, but now I'm totally hooked.'

'No, you're not.' Didi wasn't even totally sure what Janne meant.

'Yes, I am. I'm completely crazy about you. I've never felt this way before.'

'It doesn't necessarily have anything to do with me,' Didi said, because it was this precise power of attraction that the nymphs had told her about. She was irritated, that's all there was to it. Janne wasn't interested in her, he was just responding to the call of her pheromones. 'I have to go.'

Didi rose from the table and rushed towards the restaurant doors, leaving Janne standing there, stunned. It didn't take long before he was hurrying out after her.

'I'm not letting you go that easily,' he said in a low voice, pressing a kiss against Didi's lips. 'It's like you're from a painting or something.'

Didi's breathing immediately intensified, and she felt a throbbing in her chest. She pulled back in a panic.

'Don't you want me too?' Janne asked, and Didi leaned in a little closer, sensing his smell in her nostrils. 'Let's not end this evening yet,' he went on. 'Come back to my place; we'll have one last glass of wine.'

Janne's scent was too much for her. Didi wrapped her arms around his neck and kissed him, not caring in the least that the other customers' heads were turning around inquisitively in their direction.

'Let's go,' Didi said, and the tone of her voice told Janne everything he needed to know.

Outside, Didi could feel how the full moon sped her footsteps along, and a few minutes later they were at Janne's place. Nor did Janne resist when Didi started to unbutton his shirt. They fell into bed. Didi did manage to register that the apartment was small but tidy. There were a couple of movie posters on the walls and some barbells in the corner. Janne was an interesting guy all round. All Didi had to do was let the moon do its job, just like Nadia had said.

And what was strangest of all, Didi's modesty fell away completely. For a second she had been wary of the embarrassing moment of stripping, but now they were facing each other, caressing, nipping. Janne's arms were strong, his skin was hot. Didi was almost in pain, but there was something sweet about it too. She wanted Janne inside her. A couple of seconds more . . . Her gaze shifted to the window and out at the moon.

'Look this way,' Janne said.

At first Janne was a little too cautious, but Didi rolled over on top of him and soon Janne was slipping effortlessly inside her. Didi moaned. This is the way it was supposed to be. She pressed her palm against Janne's bare chest and felt the powerful thump of his heartbeat. They moved as one, and in the light of the moon Didi's skin started to glow. Janne's eyes were half-closed, and he was panting. Didi tensed. This was the experience she had been waiting for; she had been so close with Johannes, but now her skin was electric and she felt an enormous force burst inside her. She screamed out loud. She had never felt anything like it before.

She pressed herself against Janne and deeply inhaled his scent.

Kati was catching her breath on the black satin sheets in a boutique hotel. The man at her side on the king-size bed was unconscious but smiling. Kati gave him a couple of pats on the thigh, but she couldn't elicit any sort of reaction from him. Well, it was almost time to dress and slip out anyway. But her phone forced her out of bed sooner than she had wanted.

'Didi?' Kati asked.

The younger nymph's voice was faint: 'Kati? I messed up.'

CHAPTER 22

Jesper hated wearing a dress shirt and a tie, but now and again he was required to make concessions for his role. He stepped down from the black SUV and scanned the hospital parking lot. Mitchell had sent him a photo of Detective Hannula. He recognized the NBI agent right off and walked towards him. Hannula was just popping the ring off a can of Coke when Jesper approached him and allowed his satyr eyes to flare red for an instant. Hannula flinched. Then he slipped his police badge into Jesper's hand and continued on his way.

Armed with a broad smile and the badge, Jesper quickly discovered the location of Janne Malasmaa's body. The forty-year-old pathologist was in the middle of dictating the results of her examination.

'Capillaries broken due to constriction. Current theory is peptide-hormonal disturbance,' the woman dictated, before turning to Jesper with a questioning look. 'What are you doing here? You can't come in here.'

'Police,' Jesper answered, pulling the sheet back from the corpse. The pathologist was used to working with law enforcement, and the morgue wasn't normally a place she would find herself flirting, but the proximity of the blond detective and his inquisitive gaze threw her off balance. She was irritated that she had changed out of her new high heels into the sensible flats that were more comfortable on the job.

'Was it a natural death?' Jesper asked, as if he needed to know for professional reasons. The fact was, he had seen serene, bruise-covered corpses like this before.

'I've never seen anything like it,' the pathologist said, turning back to the smiling corpse. 'Perhaps the person he was engaged in sexual intercourse with could shed some light on what happened.'

'How so?'

'He had a very unusual erection,' the pathologist replied. 'There are bruises on the penis.'

Jesper drew the sheet even lower and took a look for himself. 'Who was his sex partner?'

'I just study medical phenomena,' the pathologist snapped. 'You might want to ask one of your colleagues about that.'

'You mentioned hormones,' Jesper said, leaning casually against the counter.

'Let's go over to the lab; they might have some more details by now.' The pathologist opened the door to the other room and held it open for Jesper. 'This is Nadia Rapaccini. She's interning here in clinical genetics while she studies for her RN license. Nadia?'

A woman had been standing at the microscope, and now she turned around. For several seconds, Jesper was unable to breathe.

'Nadia, this is . . . from the NBI . . . I'm sorry, I've forgotten your name.'

'Ninette,' Jesper said in a low voice.

'Do you know each other?' the pathologist asked.

'It's been a while,' Nadia answered. It was quite an understatement, considering that they had last seen each other on the shores of Lake Garda in 1806.

'Well, it doesn't look like you need me for anything more,' the pathologist said.

'No, we certainly don't,' Jesper said.

The door clanged shut behind the pathologist, and Jesper

immediately felt a sharp object in his groin. He cried out and looked at Nadia in shock.

'A couple of squirts from this needle, and you'll never have to worry about having kids,' Nadia said, calm as can be.

'As I recall, we were supposed to have children together,' Jesper answered.

'And you were supposed to be dead.'

'Ninette . . .' Jesper closed his eyes. He felt indescribable joy and bewilderment at the same time. 'I would never hurt you. I'm just as surprised as you are.'

Nadia considered the situation for a moment. She extended herself towards Jesper and sensed forest, solitude . . . She withdrew the needle from his crotch and circled around to the other side of the table to put some distance between herself and the satyr. Now she finally got a good look at Jesper. Their eyes met.

Centuries earlier, they had eyed each other across the bounties of Baron Savichny's banquet table. Wine was being poured into goblets, and the serving dishes were heaped with eel, herb-dusted pigeons, olives, polenta, eggplant salad, and crusty bread. The mandarin oranges imported from Canton spoke of the baron's wealth, and Nadia thought that she would never get enough of them. Now she raised her glass to Jesper as if to say: we have come this far, and soon our task will be completed.

The baron was good company, but his men had captured a frigate that, according to Mitchell, contained a small yet invaluable rosewood casket. Mitchell had sent Nadia and Jesper to retrieve it regardless of the consequences. The satyr and nymph had had no trouble making the acquaintance of the baron, and immediately received an invitation to dine with him.

'So you are betrothed to one another?' the baron asked, his eyes devouring Nadia almost more greedily than the plate that a servant had placed down before him. 'It will be a beautiful union of Holland

and Italy. Your heirs will be something in between. French, I'd wager.'

Jesper chuckled politely and took a healthy swig of luscious red wine. 'If Napoleon has his way, their mother and father may well be French before long, too.'

'No, no, gentlemen,' Nadia interjected breezily. 'My blood runs hot, red, and Italian. My betrothed's blood is as blue as the baron's. And since our children will be white, they will live as free, fraternal equals.'

'A lovely sentiment,' the baron said, but his thoughts were somewhere entirely different. He possessed a developed aesthetic sensibility, and Nadia had aroused his acquisitive instincts.

Jesper had also noted this, and when he and Nadia withdrew from the castle to the rooms that had been appointed to them for the night, he wrapped her in a close, passionate embrace the moment they heaved the heavy door shut. All Nadia had to do was graze his skin as she pulled off the neck tie that the Croats had invented and Jesper was fully hard. He lifted the layers of her petticoat out of the way, allowing Nadia to wrap a leg around him, and then he thrust himself into her.

'My love,' Nadia whispered heavily.

'When the next full moon rises, our child shall be conceived,' Jesper promised.

Since that moment, Nadia had never desired a child with another satyr, and conceiving with a human would have been impossible. She was standing in the kitchen of the home she shared with her fellow nymphs, gazing out the window with her hands on her belly, when Kati came in. The evening had passed and turned to night as Nadia considered what she would tell Kati about the day's events.

Kati clearly sensed something had happened. 'What's going on?'

'A police officer came by the clinic today,' Nadia said, turning towards her. 'I was assigned the task of investigating Janne Malasmaa's hormone levels.'

'Great. That gives you the perfect opportunity to cover them up.'

'I suppose you're right,' Nadia said.

'So what's the problem?' Kati asked.

'What's going to happen if Didi unintentionally sets something into motion that will have the police start searching for us?'

Kati had split an avocado in two, and now she struck the knife into the pit and wrenched it out. She dug the soft flesh out from the rind and downed it in a couple of bites. 'OK, I'll take care of that.'

Nadia wondered if she should tell Kati everything that had happened or keep it to herself. She looked out the window once more and knew that, somewhere nearby, Jesper was thinking the exact same thing.

Jesper dropped his business-appropriate dress shirt and sport coat on the floor of the hotel suite, knowing that the following morning they would be hanging in the closet, ironed and impeccable. It was easy to get lazy when you traveled with Erik, because his money provided every comfort imaginable. Jesper stretched out. That damn suit had been confining. He grabbed an open bottle of red wine from the console, pulled out the cork with his teeth, and drank long and hard. *I guess I can't complain. Erik doesn't skimp when it comes to best wines, either*, he reflected as he collapsed on the sofa.

Jesper sensed that Frida had walked up to the doorway separating his rooms from her side of the suite. He waited for a moment, and before long the nymph was stretched out on the sofa, under his arm. They might have been from enemy camps, but their intimacy was utterly natural, as it had been between satyrs and nymphs throughout the millennia.

Jesper was lifting the bottle to his lips for another swig when

Frida twitched restlessly. The nymph's eyes wandered around the room and then closed in on him.

'What now?' Jesper asked, but Frida lowered her nose to his bare chest, almost touching his skin. 'Knock it off.'

'I smell . . .' Frida started to say. But she was unable to complete her sentence.

Erik Mann had entered the room. His footfalls were deliberate and his movements were overly calm. Yet he emanated an agitated energy. Jesper wasn't afraid of Erik, but the other satyr's rage was palpable.

'What are you two doing here?' Erik enunciated each word with exaggerated precision. 'You are supposed to be on the hunt!'

'I just got back,' Jesper said calmly.

'Did you find the girl?'

'Not yet,' Jesper said.

Erik stared at Jesper and Frida for a moment, overcome with a thinly veiled rage. Then he stalked off to his own room. The slammed door was the only indication of how displeased he was. Jesper nodded at Frida, and they settled back down on the sofa in their original positions.

'There was something strange about that body at the pathology lab,' Jesper mused. 'Could that story about the redheaded nymph really be true?'

'Would that scare you?' Frida asked.

Jesper focused on tipping back the wine bottle to his lips again. 'I wonder if there's anything on TV?'

In his own room, an unbelievably irritated Erik was pacing back and forth like a starved, caged lion. He felt like he was so close to his goal that every moment of delay was agony. And yet he still had to calm himself. He could hear the faint rhythmic beat of the music channel and Jesper's and Frida's passionate dance from the next room. In a sense, everything was as it should be, eternal. Satyr and nymph, music, wine. But for Erik, that was no longer enough. The culmination of his grand plan was almost within reach.

Erik opened a folder and pulled out a photograph. Innocent, redheaded Didi Tiensuu in a cropped shirt, the knot visible for anyone to see. And at her side, the blissfully ignorant boyfriend. Erik's eyes bore into Johannes and the thought of the little upstart in the company of his treasure was too much. Erik grabbed the photograph and tore it in half. Johannes' half fluttered to the floor.

Now Erik's eyes rested on Didi alone.

CHAPTER 23

Didi had had a restless night. A pair of red eyes that burned in the darkness had been hunting her. She'd sought safety in Johannes' arms and closed her eyes to kiss him, but Johannes suddenly grew cold and smiled at her, his eyes glazed over. Didi ran to Janne, and he caught her up in his arms, carried her over to the bed, and lay down so she was straddling him. But at the same instant his skin broke out in tiny bruises ... Didi was grateful when the sound of clanging from the kitchen roused her from her sleep. Besides, she was hungry.

She was instantly wracked with guilt when she realized she was thinking about food after everything that had happened. Two people had died because of her. With Johannes, she had been innocent, but with Janne she had taken a risk.

Both a creeping sense of panic and the smell of an omelet wafting into her room prompted Didi to rise from her bed. The sensation she felt inside when she was with a man, right there under the knot on her belly ... She lifted up the hem of her cropped cotton nightshirt and stared at the tattoo. She had to get a better explanation for all of this.

Kati was at the kitchen table, just digging into her omelet, when Didi marched up to her and lifted her nightshirt again. Contrary to Didi's expectations, Kati didn't choke on her food, but just kept eating as calm as could be.

'Why do I have this?' Didi asked. 'Does it mean something?'

'No.' Kati reached across the table and helped herself to a slice of bread.

'Doesn't it mean that I'm a killer, not some healer?'

'You're not a killer. You've just had bad luck.'

Didi let the hem of her nightshirt drop and took a seat at the table next to Kati. Now that the older nymph was concentrating on her food, she had the perfect opportunity to pose the questions that were gnawing at her.

'Did you know my real mother? Where did I come from?'

'No one knows,' Kati said, wiping her mouth after eating her final forkful.

'How did you find me?' Didi continued.

'Stop asking pointless questions.'

'What questions wouldn't be pointless, then?' Didi asked sarcastically.

Maybe Kati would talk if Didi could find a way to provoke her enough.

'Oh, say, where are we going to get the money for rent this month?' Kati answered, waving a couple of bills in front of Didi's face.

'I killed someone!' Didi slammed her fist into the table so hard she scared herself. Saying it out loud made it more real.

'We're nymphs and we need men in order to survive. You can't blame yourself.'

'I'm blaming you. You chose Janne. You knew what would happen.'

'Nadia and I examined him. What happened shouldn't have happened. And it's not my fault we're nymphs.'

Didi was on the verge of jumping up and marching out in protest, but suddenly Kati grabbed her wrist in an iron grip and stared deeply into her eyes.

'You're going to have to accept realities, and fast, little lady. All this is part of your life.'

'I'm late for class,' Didi hissed.

* * *

This is studying, too, in a way. Didi was sitting in the university library, justifying her skipping class to herself. She had asked a librarian for help, and he had gradually piled a large stack of works on nymphs, Ancient Greece, symbols and heraldry in front of Didi. She had explained something vague about genealogy to the elderly male librarian and given him a winning smile. None of the books were leading anywhere, though. After a couple of hours, all the curlicues and foreign letters were turning into a huge mush in her head, and the dust from the moldy tomes was tickling her nose. She needed some fresh air.

Outside, it was just the right amount of windy, and Didi started walking towards the seashore. She sensed the saltiness of the sea long before she reached it. *Would I have smelled it this keenly before?* she wondered. Maybe not. Nor would the minute black seeds in the cone she bought at the ice-cream stand have tasted so intensely of vanilla. Before, she would have devoured the cone in an instant, but now her taste buds were heightened, and she took a lingering pleasure in the experience of eating it. Some things about the life of a nymph were worth valuing.

Didi stopped in front of a flower shop and gazed in through the display window. The large vases held exquisite arrangements, and for a moment Didi was disappointed that she hadn't paid proper attention when Elina had tried to teach her about flowers. Now the only blooms she more or less recognized were tulips and carnations. Suddenly she felt a powerful urge to smell the flowers. Maybe she could buy herself a bouquet and take it home. Kati probably wouldn't give two hoots, but Nadia would definitely be delighted.

Didi stepped into the shop and had to shut her eyes. She sensed sweet smells, the potent aroma of greenery. It took her a moment before she was able to simply look around without all of her senses being overwhelmed. When she finally opened her eyes, all she had to do was decide whether she wanted a bouquet of light-colored flowers or dark blooms, big or small . . . Didi's gaze fixed on the florist working at a tall table; she was constructing a gorgeous arrangement out of long-stemmed roses. All scents and colors immediately vanished from Didi's mind, and her hearing sharpened. She heard the metallic rasp of the scissors, and then the snap as the florist severed the stout stalk of one of the roses. Didi heard the snap as if it were a bullet being fired between her ears. There was another aspect to it, too – it was a cry of pain. The woman cut another rose. This time Didi shuddered. The blades were cutting fibers within her, the steel was slicing something open, the taste of metal rose to her mouth. The woman moved on to the third rose, and Didi couldn't take it any more. She lunged out the door and sought shelter in a porch, where she doubled over. It took several minutes for her breathing to level off.

More than anything, Didi wished she could drag herself home, but her cell phone reminded her that her shift at the cafe was about to begin. She considered skipping out on that, too, but for some reason deceiving Valtteri was much more unpleasant than deceiving Kati.

The instant she walked into the cafe, Didi regretted her decision to come to work. Samuel was standing in the middle of the coffee shop, clearly looking for her.

'I came in to buy you lunch,' Samuel said.

Didi tried to turn him down as she sidestepped him to reach for an apron: 'My shift is about to start.' But Samuel stopped her.

'Wait,' he said. 'It occurred to me that we've kissed, you've knocked me unconscious, and your friend has threatened me with a knife. Isn't it the part yet where we get a chance to sit down and talk?'

Didi had noted that several of the women sitting in the cafe were looking at Samuel in evident admiration, and now she started to smile as well. Samuel apparently took it as a sign of consent, because he snatched up a bouquet from a vase on the counter and held it out to Didi.

'May I buy you lunch, miss?' he asked.

'You stole those,' Didi answered.

'Of course I did. For you.'

'I might have a minute,' Didi said. 'Sit over there. I'll get us something.'

A moment later, they were seated together. Didi had brought Samuel a slice of ham quiche and a salad for herself.

'Why do women always eat salad?' Samuel asked.

'For men, silly,' Didi answered. 'We're so vain.'

'You don't need to go to any trouble for me,' Samuel said.

An awkward silence followed. Neither knew which direction to take the conversation in.

'Do you know how someone can find their parents?' Didi asked a second later. It's not likely she would get answers from Kati or Nadia, so she would have to take matters into her own hands. Samuel was older and might have some ideas about what to do.

'You want to know who your biological father and mother were?' Samuel asked. 'That's understandable.'

'It might make it easier to accept some things,' Didi said. 'And maybe plan for the future, too.'

She hadn't intended to be so open about her feelings, but Samuel held out his hand to her, and she gratefully took hold of it.

'I could help you look for information,' Samuel said, but he wanted to lighten the conversation a little, and Didi's mood, too, while he was at it. 'As long as you promise me that I won't end up in a dark alley with that black-haired amazon you live with. That's one scary chick.'

Didi laughed and released herself from Samuel's touch. Once again, Samuel was willing to help out of the goodness of his heart. But would Samuel have been so generous if he knew about the bodies that she had left behind in her wake?

Didi concealed her feelings, lifted the bouquet up to her nose and sniffed it, but what she experienced was anything but pleasant. There was something repulsive about the flowers. She tossed the bouquet back on the table and stared at it as if it were capable of attacking her. It took a moment before she realized that Samuel was staring at her, completely baffled, almost offended.

'There must have been a thorn,' Didi said.

CHAPTER 24

Nadia had just slipped the ampule and the syringe into her purse when there was a knock at the laboratory door. Whoever it was stepped in without waiting for a response, and she was instantly on guard. Two men stood in the doorway. She remembered having seen the younger one hanging around the hospital parking lot. The older of the two headed straight for her. These weren't satyrs, though; Nadia was sure of it.

'National Bureau of Investigation,' the older man said. 'I'm Detective Harju and my colleague here is Detective Heikki Hannula. Your name is . . . ?'

Nadia said her name softly: 'Rapaccini.'

Detective Harju smoothly continued right on, and looked around the workspace as if he belonged there. 'A young man named Janne Malasmaa came to this clinic. Apparently he saw you. You conducted tests on him to see if he would be suitable as a stem cell donor.'

Nadia didn't say anything. She didn't like the way Detective Harju had just waltzed into her territory. Besides, she wanted to hold back and get a better idea of what the detectives might know. In her experience, people felt a need to fill silence.

'Did Malasmaa visit you here?' Harju asked, not saying any more at this point.

'I'm just a nurse,' Nadia answered calmly. 'As far as I recall, I conducted some basic tests.'

'Which is unusual, because none of the doctors ordered them.'

'I don't know anything about that,' Nadia said. 'It was marked on my assignment sheet.'

Nadia went over and sat down and turned towards her desk to indicate that she was busy, but Detective Harju wasn't so easily put off. He twirled her chair around until she was facing him.

'Janne Malasmaa died,' Detective Harju said. 'So did another boy. About a month ago. Heikki, what was his name again?'

'Johannes Metso,' Detective Hannula said.

'The same identifying marks,' Harju continued. 'Metso had spent the evening with his girlfriend.'

'I don't know him, and I didn't exactly know Malasmaa either,' Nadia said.

'One thing is bothering me.' Detective Harju bent over and examined Nadia closely. 'Could it have something to do with bees?'

Now Nadia was surprised. She eyed each of the detectives in turn.

'I guess, if the victim were severely allergic,' Nadia said. 'I really can't say. I'm just a nurse.'

'Ahaa, OK,' Detective Harju said, pulling from his pocket a business card that had seen better days. 'Heikki, give her one of your cards too, just in case the little lady remembers something later.'

Detective Hannula did as he was instructed. The two policemen were already at the door when Detective Harju turned and looked at Nadia one final time.

'Oh yeah, both of our young friends had a taste for redheads,' he said, watching Nadia's reaction. 'Metso's girlfriend was Didi Tiensuu, whose mother conducted the autopsy. Both the mother and the daughter disappeared. And red hairs were found at Malasmaa's house. I was wondering where the girl might be. I assume you have no idea?'

All Nadia could do was shake her head. As soon as the door shut, she called Kati.

'Two detectives just came by,' she said, laying their business cards out on the counter before her.

'Senior Detective Harju and Detective Heikki Hannula. They're looking for Didi.' She heard the change in Kati's breathing, and she could almost hear the gears in the other nymph's mind fire up as she started to process the problem at hand. 'OK, come here, we'll think of something.'

'I can't yet,' Nadia said. 'I have to work.'

'Oh that's right, your human work,' Kati snapped and hung up.

Nadia lowered her head into her hands. Ever since Elina had gotten in touch with them, events had bounced off into a completely new orbit. So many things that she would have preferred to have forgotten had come back to life. Literally.

Jesper was holding a torch aloft, illuminating the path to the damp, dark cellars of the baron's castle.

'What does the casket look like?' Nadia asked. Spaces like this made her feel extremely uncomfortable, and she wanted to get out of there as fast as possible. She wrapped the blanket more tightly around herself.

'You'll know it as soon as we find it,' Jesper assured her.

They advanced slowly to the heavy door and thrust it open. Jesper stepped in first, holding the torch to light the way. Nadia cried out in terror. Two of the baron's soldiers stood before them, weapons drawn. They instantly knocked Jesper to the ground, and a second later Nadia was lying there next to him. Then she and Jesper were being dragged off to a cage deeper in the dungeon.

'No.' Savichny's voice came from further off. 'The woman comes upstairs.'

The men started lifting Nadia off the ground, but she wriggled free and knelt at Jesper's side.

'I'll tell the baron the truth about us,' she whispered urgently. 'I'll get him to free us.'

She felt Jesper shove something into her hands. It was a ring.

'At the lunar eclipse, we'll be each other's forever,' he told her. 'Unless you tell him who we really are. That would be a violation of all our laws, and the satyrs wouldn't allow it. It would be suicide. You have to flee.'

'I won't abandon you here,' Nadia said as she was dragged away. That had been the last time she had seen Jesper alive.

Not long after, Nadia was lying on the floor of the baron's sumptuous bedchamber. She made no attempt to rise; she simply surveyed her surroundings. There might be a suitable weapon somewhere. She didn't have the least compunction about killing Savichny. She heard him walk up to her in his fine calfskin boots, and braced herself for the blow.

'I need your help,' the baron said. 'Follow me.'

Nadia warily picked herself up. The baron had paused at one of the doorways leading from his room and waited for her to follow.

The door led to a dimly lit chamber, where the baron's twelve-year-old son and heir lay on the bed. All of Nadia's violent instincts instantly softened; the only things she could perceive were the baron's dismay and the boy's fear. She walked up to the bed and bent over the child. She felt his limbs and let her own warmth move into his body.

'I don't know exactly what you are,' the baron said. 'And yet somehow I sense that you can help him.'

'Did you fall from a horse and onto your neck?' Nadia asked the boy.

'He was careless. He tried to jump over a fallen log,' the baron spat out, palpably angry, before lowering himself to a chair. His entire body was tense.

Nadia called over a timorous-looking servant and told her to bring heaps of orchids, carnations and freesia. Once she had them, Nadia covered the boy in the petals, pressing them to his body with her hands. She was searching for the point where the boy's body and spirit no longer found each other.

The baron had begun to pace back and forth impatiently.

'Is this magic or some other sort of tomfoolery?' he asked Nadia. 'I don't hold with such nonsense.'

'You're not losing anything by letting me try,' Nadia said, escorting him back to his seat. She knelt down before the baron. 'Allow me to do my work and then remain in your service. Hundreds of years ago that was the custom. Many great families wanted a nymph of their own because of the skills we possess. I will care for you and your family. But only if you free my betrothed.'

The baron looked at her, and for the first time, he allowed his feelings to show. 'If you heal my son, I will grant your request,' he answered, his eyes growing moist.

'Wait until morning,' Nadia said.

She settled herself onto the bed next to the boy and kept her hands on his body throughout the night. From time to time he would wake and then drift back off to sleep, soothed by Nadia's touch. When dawn came, Nadia rose. The baron did not take his eyes off her for an instant as she bathed the boy with fresh water and then pressed her lips first to his brow, and then to his heart.

'Try to sit,' Nadia said. 'Take your time.'

She supported the boy's back as he slowly sat up.

'That's impossible,' the baron sobbed.

'I kept my word,' Nadia said. 'Now keep yours.'

The baron held his son for a moment. He nodded at Nadia and left the room, but immediately locked the door behind him. Nadia lunged for the door and pounded on it, but in vain.

'Whatever that creature is, it must be executed,' Nadia heard the baron say to someone, and a cry of terror tried to escape from her lungs. 'Destroy the body.'

She turned to look at the boy on the bed, who was now smiling tentatively at her. She didn't want to frighten her patient, who was still in a fragile state. She knew that struggling against doors and locks would be in vain. What she needed now was patience.

That night she took the baron into her bed, and in the morning she closed the dead man's eyes before searching his room for the rosewood casket. Weeping, she fled the castle in the gray light of dawn, and journeyed to the place she and Jesper had agreed to meet Mitchell in Naples.

When she finally arrived, she was spent and half-dead from hunger.

Mitchell laid a chalice of wine and a plate of food before her, and she began to eat. The coffer stood on the table between them. Mitchell gazed at it for some time, then he picked it up with both hands and hurled it into the fire.

'Why are you burning it?' Nadia barely had the strength to form the words. Jesper had sacrificed his life for that casket, and now it was turning to ash before her eyes.

'The knots can destroy us,' Mitchell answered, staring into the flames. 'All of us. Ninette, you broke one of our longest-lasting laws by revealing yourself to a human. You know that punishment must follow. But I will speak on your behalf and try to save your life, since you brought the coffer to us.'

'Thank you,' Nadia gulped.

Now Mitchell turned to her. 'Give me the ring.'

'What happened to Jesper?'

'The baron's soldiers took his life,' Mitchell said coldly. 'We killed the soldiers and covered our tracks, but you can no longer bear the ring of a satyr.'

Nadia looked at the only memento she carried of the love of her life, removed it from her ring finger, and handed it to Mitchell. What difference did it make any more? She was completely numb, as good as dead herself.

CHAPTER 25

Jesper unwrapped the towel from his waist, tossed it in the corner, and walked over to his closet. Erik was in the hotel restaurant, entertaining his business partner Roland Gyllen with lengthy anecdotes and healthy pours of wine and cognac. Jesper had taken advantage of the free time to work up a proper sweat in the hotel gym, while women looked on in admiration and men in envy. He had needed the self-torture. He had seen so much over the course of his long life as a satyr that he didn't think anything could faze him, but when the woman in the white lab coat had turned around and Ninette's eyes had looked directly into his own, he had felt as if his legs would give way. How could he be experiencing the exact same sensation he had felt centuries before? It was beyond his comprehension. Nor did it matter. The only thing that mattered was that they were both alive.

Jesper retrieved his well-worn backpack from the depths of the closet and unzipped it. A moment later, he pulled out a little box, and from the box, a ring set with a garnet. He had a precise memory of being at the kitchen hearth of an Italian inn, tending to the deep wound in his belly, when Kati had handed him the ring and informed him that Nadia had died at the full moon. He remembered how his wound had pulsed, but the pain was nothing compared to the grief that tore at him with its teeth like a gray wolf, and ripped him apart piece by piece until nothing was left.

He had feared for Nadia's life when he turned towards the baron's soldier and the sword had pierced him. The soldier had had no idea that a stab wound would simply serve to goad the strapping satyr and act as a little foreplay before the battle proper. Jesper's eyes had immediately glowed red-hot, and soon he was growling in pain and rage. The horns had thrust forth from his forehead and he had used them. The soldier hadn't lived long.

Jesper heard Frida's movements in the next room and he replaced the ring in his pack. Then he stepped into Frida's room without bothering to wrap the towel back around his waist. Frida was standing in front of the mirror in a skintight dress, fixing her lush blond tresses.

'Let's continue the hunt, shall we?' she said. 'I'll check the restaurants near the university. They're sure to be trawling for men down there.'

'Good, let's do it.' Jesper leaned against the wall, but didn't move a muscle.

Frida eyed the long scar on Jesper's stomach. Then she stepped in closer so she could see Jesper's eyes. 'I can tell when someone's lying.'

'Not telling everything isn't lying,' Jesper said with a cool smile. 'I told a nymph everything once and I learned my lesson.'

But Frida had already wrenched his arm behind his back and pushed him against the wall in an armlock. She pressed right up against him.

'Have you forgotten that we're on the same side?' Jesper said.

'I've been dangling from chains for seventeen years,' Frida hissed in Jesper's ear. 'Believe me, I won't forget that I can't trust anyone.'

Frida gave Jesper's arm a hard twist, and he gasped. Then she released him and resumed fixing her hair.

'I'll go have a look at a couple of other places where fugitives might turn up,' Jesper said, knowing that Ninette was almost certain to be waiting for him in the same place they had last met.

He went to his room and put on a pair of jeans and a jacket, and then he took the elevator to the hotel restaurant. The laughter of Erik's companion, the elderly Mr Gyllen, could be heard all the way to the elevator lobby. Erik certainly knew how to entertain his guests. He had already charmed the waitress, who was flirting with them. An expensive bottle of cognac stood on the table; Erik enjoyed playing the host. But as Jesper approached, his brows furrowed.

'I caught scent of the redhead,' Jesper murmured in Erik's ear.

'What the hell am I going to do with a scent?' Erik said, still smiling broadly at his guest.

'I'll bring you the girl, but first I need you to tell Frida to stop breathing down my neck.'

Erik raised his glass of cognac to Gyllen. 'You can do whatever you want with the nymph. Dismissed.'

Jesper moved soundlessly down the hospital corridors and had no trouble finding the right door. He knocked on it softly and entered without waiting for a response. Nadia was sitting on the examination table, and right away Jesper felt like he could drown in her brown eyes.

'I came to warn you,' he said from the doorway. 'I can't hide anything from Erik.'

'You can't?' Nadia asked.

'You broke one of the most fundamental rules. You fled, you betrayed your covey. You betrayed your own.'

Nadia tilted her head slightly, but she didn't say a word. Jesper went over to her.

'I know you believe in that fairy tale about the knot, but I don't,' Jesper said. 'No one with any sense does.'

'Then I don't have any sense,' Nadia said. 'And I'm free to believe whatever I want.'

'Run while you can,' Jesper said, grabbing Nadia by the hand. She didn't pull it back. 'That redheaded nymph will not escape, but because of our past together, I don't want to take your life.'

Nadia's eyes softened, and for a moment Jesper believed that she would give in and give up. But at that instant, he felt the sharp tip of a needle in the crook of his arm.

Jesper tried to sound casual: 'Come on, let's stop playing these games.'

'This time the syringe contains a substance that will put an end to our shared past,' Nadia said. 'Unless I can be sure that you won't reveal us to Erik.'

'What exactly are you intending to do?' Jesper asked.

'I've lived freely for seventeen years now,' Nadia answered. 'I will not betray Kati. We found Desirée Volanté Tasson, and I will not leave her to the mercy of the satyrs as long as I can wake up every morning with hope in my heart. The prophecy will be fulfilled. Desirée can change our lives.'

Jesper was emphatic: 'Erik is looking for you.'

'And you are indebted to me,' Nadia said.

Jesper turned away from Nadia. This intimacy was too much for him, not to mention the nymph's expression, equal parts determination and pleading.

'You're asking a lot of a satyr,' Jesper eventually said. 'But fine, I swear.'

'Thank you.'

CHAPTER 26

Kati had been following Detective Hannula for a while, trying to figure out the best way to approach him. Now Hannula had returned to police headquarters, and Kati decided to take the next step. She was wearing black hip-huggers, a white blouse and a black boyfriend vest. She finished her look off by biting her lips so they would be as full as possible.

She walked in and could see Detective Hannula in his office a little way off. She sashayed towards him, deliberately taking her time. The detective must have registered her out of the corner of his eye, because he turned to look. And he took a good, long look. He had been drinking Coke out of a can, which he now dropped in the trash. Kati was getting a kick out of the situation, but she didn't let it show.

'I've been robbed,' Kati said, looking nothing like a victim.

'Really?' Hannula said.

'Someone took my bike,' Kati explained, tilting her head coyly and making Hannula's pulse rise even higher. 'It sounds a little silly, but that bike meant a lot to me.'

'They can help you fill out a report at that counter over there,' Hannula said. But he didn't make a move, and Kati knew she had him hooked.

'But those papers always get lost in the shuffle and I'll never see my bike again,' Kati said. 'Can't you help me?'

'All right, why don't you join me over here,' Hannula said, and he stepped away to retrieve the forms.

Kati discreetly crept over to Hannula's desk. The folder lying on it was labeled *Johannes Metso*, and photos of Janne and a couple of other men were tacked to the wall. All she needed was to cause a little distraction, and she'd find out how far along the investigation was.

'Let's get these papers filled out,' Hannula said as he returned.

Kati started describing her stolen bike, and Hannula jotted it all down.

'What happens now?' Kati said a moment later. 'I want to get my bike back so bad.'

'Wait here, and I'll go ask around a little,' Hannula said. 'Even though this isn't exactly NBI business.'

As soon as Detective Hannula left, Kati started rifling through Johannes' folder. She quickly sifted through the documents and then moved on to the photos on the wall. By the time she finished, she had a good idea of where the detectives were in their investigation. The bad thing was that Johannes was smiling with Didi in one of the shots.

Then Kati heard Hannula's voice call out behind her: 'Come have a look!'

She went out into the corridor. Detective Hannula was standing there with a red bike in front of him and a satisfied look on his face. Kati looked at him, eyes wide as plates. Evidently Hannula misinterpreted her expression.

'Not bad, eh?' Hannula said. 'Another crime solved by yours truly. The rear reflector is broken too, just like you said.'

'There's just this one problem,' Kati said. 'I don't even own a bike.'

'You made that whole story up?' Hannula asked. 'Why?'

Kati tried to look coy. 'I noticed you out on the street . . . I don't usually do things like this, but I wanted to get to know you, and the only thing I could think of was a stolen bike. I'm so sorry.'

Hannula chuckled.

'To be honest, there was one bike back there that more or less fit the description, and I gave that reflector a little tap with my shoe,' Hannula said.

'Can I take you to coffee?' said Kati, thinking: *Step into my parlor, said the spider to the fly.*

It was late by the time Kati got back to the apartment, and she would have gladly spoken with Nadia alone, but Nadia and Didi were both out on the balcony, sitting in the lantern light. Didi looked pale.

'What's the matter?' Kati asked. 'We're not out of white wine, are we?'

'Didi had a reaction,' Nadia explained. 'In a flower shop.'

Kati listened quietly as Didi recounted what had happened.

'Did you react to the cutting of the flowers reflexively, or was it more like a pain?' Kati asked.

'I guess there was a little of both,' Didi said, shivering. She could still remember the sensation.

Kati considered what Didi had just told them, but Nadia sat still, gazing into the steady flame of the lantern.

'Isn't this good news?' Kati asked Nadia.

'Yes.'

'How so?' Didi asked. She didn't understand how pain could be a good thing.

'You're not a water nymph or a mountain nymph,' Nadia said in a faraway voice. 'You felt what those flowers felt. That means you're a nature nymph.'

'What's wrong with you?' Kati asked Nadia. This should have been critical information for the other nymph, but she didn't seem to be registering it in the least.

'Nothing,' Nadia answered, gradually coming out of her reverie. 'I just have a lot on my mind.'

'Because of the police?' Kati asked.

'Precisely,' Nadia said.

Now it was Didi's turn to ask a question: 'What about the police?'

'Never mind.' Kati wheeled around and headed for the fridge. What she needed now was a glass of white wine and some criminally rich cheese. 'I took care of it.'

CHAPTER 27

Didi looked at the book lying in front of her and blew on its cover. A cloud of dust rose into the air, making Samuel sneeze.

'Thanks a lot,' he said as Didi laughed.

'Don't mention it,' Didi said. She felt like wiping the dust from the tip of Samuel's nose.

Didi had called Samuel and asked him which library would have historical works or old books. Samuel had told her and promised to join her. Which is exactly what Didi had been secretly hoping for. The library felt like the perfect environment to spend time safely with Samuel.

The patient, elderly librarian had carried book after book over to them, and Didi and Samuel studied them, their heads pressed together. They had come across lots of interesting things and giggled together at the old-fashioned expressions, but Didi didn't feel like she was any closer to her roots.

'What's this?' she asked Samuel. She was starting to tire out. They had been having a good time, but even Samuel must have limits to how willing he was to help.

' "*Procurements from Tammisaari Manor from the 1940s*",' Samuel read, and for a second he didn't even get why the librarian had brought them the book. Then he wiped the cover. 'Hey, look, this is the same knot you have tattooed on your stomach!'

'You still remember it?' Didi was surprised, but she still grabbed the book. Suddenly she'd got a second wind.

'I always wondered about it whenever we were at the beach. You explained that your mom wanted to make you special.'

'That's what Elina told me whenever I asked about it,' Didi said. 'It's an Ancient Mesopotamian knot. I found it in this book on symbols.'

They browsed through the procurement catalog, examining the pages filled with an ornate script.

'What on earth are "queen-of-the-night seeds"?' Didi wondered out loud.

'If it was one of those grand old manors, then maybe they had some old greenhouses,' Samuel said, re-opening his laptop. 'I've seen pictures . . . Here, I found it online. The manor has been in the same family for generations. The current owner is Matias van der Haas.'

Didi stared at the screen. She immediately knew what she wanted to do. 'I need to visit this place.'

'Let's take a trip out there this weekend,' Samuel suggested.

'Right now,' Didi said.

'Maybe we should do a little planning. I don't really think you can just waltz right in there without letting them know,' Samuel said.

'Don't worry, I can go alone.' Didi was already packing her shoulder bag and getting ready to walk out.

'No, I'll take you,' Samuel sighed. 'I guess I can't really let the funny little girl from next door wander around on her own.'

The drive to Tammisaari was smooth, and they arrived about an hour and a half later. They found the manor pretty easily, too. But evening had already started to fall, which roused Samuel's cautious side again.

'Didi, I'm sure we're going to find some things out,' he said. 'But maybe you should think about it for a second. There might be things that you don't want to know.'

'I have to know,' Didi said, climbing out of the car.

They left the car at the wrought-iron gate and eyed the massive house looming at the far end of a lane of old oaks. Didi started marching down the drive purposefully, and now her desire to make progress in the investigation infected Samuel, too.

Didi was the first to make it to the stone steps of the mansion. She peered in through the porch windows, but all she could see were a few pieces of furniture covered in sheets. The fact that the house looked deserted was a disappointing blow to Didi. But she couldn't break into this place, like she had into her own home just a few weeks earlier. A dog barked somewhere off in the distance.

Samuel and Didi were circling the house to get a better idea of it when they saw light in the nearby forest. They stopped and waited, and before long an old woman approached, accompanied by two German shepherds. The woman was carrying a flashlight.

'Hello.' It was impossible to tell exactly how old she was. Her back was still straight, and her gray hair was gathered in a bun at the nape of her neck. 'What's your business here?'

'We're looking for Matias van der Haas, but the house looks empty,' Didi said.

'It is, and the family won't be back this year. What is it you're needing?'

'I'm Desirée Tasson,' Didi said, making Samuel's eyebrows rise slightly. She had decided to use the name the nymphs had given her in the hope it would elicit a reaction of some sort in the woman. 'I was hoping that the owner of the house, Matias van der Haas, might know something about my parents.'

'I have no idea where he and his family are at the moment,' the woman answered.

Didi fumbled in her pocket, pulled out a piece of paper, and showed the symbol of the knot to the old woman. Maybe she was just imagining things, but she thought she saw the elderly neighbor's eyebrows rise a touch.

'Do you have any idea what this might be? It has something to do with me, and with this manor, too.'

Didi's voice may have been imploring, but it had no effect on the old woman, who had already turned away.

'I don't know,' the woman said over her shoulder. 'You need to leave. This is a private property and the neighbors around here keep an eye out for each other.'

'We didn't mean to cause any trouble!' Samuel called out before darkness swallowed her.

Didi reluctantly followed Samuel back to the car. She sensed that the house contained a secret that had something to do with her. She had driven out here fired up with enthusiasm and expectation. She had been absolutely positive that she would discover something, but instead she had run into a wall. She wanted answers! Someone on this earth had to know who she really was. Frustration was tossing her around like a gust of wind.

'I can't take this any more,' she suddenly said. They were already in the car, driving back to town.

'We'll keep looking,' Samuel said encouragingly. 'We'll find out where this Matias is.'

'I don't want this!' Didi shouted. 'Goddammit, I don't want this! Stop! Right now!'

Samuel heard such profound panic in Didi's voice that he didn't ask any questions, he just pulled over to the side of the road. Didi bolted out of the car and plunged into the woods.

'Didi! Where are you going?' Samuel shouted. Didi didn't know herself. Something was urging her on, even though her chest was heaving painfully as she ran. She remembered the statue from her dreams, the one that seemed to know much more than she did, the man with red, glowing eyes, titillating and terrifying. She wanted to escape from it all. Her heart was hammering. She saw something shimmering up ahead and stopped short.

The surface of the small forest pond was still. She could make out a few water lilies in the darkness. She raised her face to the rapidly cooling night air. Her breathing grew steadier. She could hear Samuel's footfalls behind her, and a moment later he was at her side. She leaned over the surface of the pool, washed her face with the refreshing water, and scooped up some into her mouth.

'What are we doing here?' Samuel huffed. 'Why did you call yourself Desirée or whatever?'

Didi stood up and looked at Samuel. Suddenly she was absolutely clear about some things. 'We shouldn't be together. Our mothers knew something and that's why they separated us.'

'How did they supposedly separate us?' Samuel asked.

Hot tears welled up in Didi's eyes, and Samuel stopped questioning her. He tried to wrap his arms around her, but she dodged him.

Didi started walking along the edge of the pool, with Samuel following her.

'You haven't changed since those days,' Samuel said. 'You were spunky and cute back then, too . . . When we were kids, you got me to do all kinds of stupid things. I was so in love with you. And when I suddenly saw you again there outside the hospital, you looked so beautiful I was instantly hooked again.'

Didi stopped. She was afraid that she wouldn't be able to help herself if she turned to look at Samuel. Even though Samuel had been absent from her life for years, her trust in him hadn't gone anywhere. She felt the same tenderness and solidarity that she had felt as a child. Samuel was good, but she wasn't good for Samuel.

Didi looked at her feet. She was standing on a bed of moss, like the statue in her dream. The statue beckoned her to touch it, as if human hands could bring it to life. Didi simultaneously hoped and feared that Samuel would touch her. She had to keep her feelings under control, because desire was mixed up in them. If she gave in to it for even an instant, she would be lost in it for good. She had to admit that to herself, here in the shade of these dark woods, surrounded by the fragrance of moss. Didi felt how genuinely similar she and the statue were, hot and cool at the same time. And she knew that Samuel was waiting for an answer.

She slowly turned around and gradually dared to raise her eyes to Samuel's face. She saw how worried he was. And she could feel how badly he wanted her. Some sentiment rose to her lips, but she was unable to utter it out loud. The air between them tingled. But Didi didn't dare to allow her face to move any closer to Samuel's; she placed a hand on his chest to maintain the distance between them.

'There's no rush, Didi,' Samuel said gently. He covered Didi's hand with his own, and Didi could feel the steadiness of Samuel's heartbeat. Then his smile faded. At first he fell to his knees, and then to the ground. He was gasping for breath.

'What have you done?' he choked out, his voice a whisper.

'Samuel?' Didi asked, but by this time he was completely unconscious. Didi looked around frantically. 'Help!'

CHAPTER 28

Didi glanced at Samuel once more from the doorway of the hospital room, where he was being examined by a doctor. She would have loved to stay there, both to hear the results and to hide from Kati, who was sitting in the waiting room in her black leathers. At the moment of her greatest panic at the edge of the forest pond, Didi hadn't known who else to call. She barely knew where she was. Luckily she could trust Kati's hunting instincts, and less than an hour later Kati caught up with them – in a stolen car, which she had driven into the brush to hide – and then she drove them to the hospital in Helsinki. They hadn't exchanged a single word during the trip, but now it was time to talk.

'What happened back there in the woods?' Kati lowered a foot from the waiting room coffee table and eyed Didi sternly.

'I just put my hand on Samuel's chest.'

'And that's all?' Kati asked. 'You didn't give the hospital any personal information, did you?'

'Of course not,' Didi answered. 'I'm not a complete idiot.'

'Are you going to stay here?' Kati asked, as if reading Didi's thoughts.

Didi nodded. 'They're keeping Samuel overnight to monitor him, and it's my fault he's here.'

'Be careful about what you say,' Kati said. Then she stood up and stalked out the door, without giving Didi so much as a backwards glance.

A moment later, the doctor left Samuel's room, and Didi slipped in. Her heart immediately leapt with a mixture of joy and anguish. Samuel was so pale. She went over and sat next to his bed. She didn't dare to even stroke the blanket that covered him; she just pressed her forehead to the edge of the bed and closed her eyes. The night had drained every last ounce of her strength.

'I'm alive.'

Didi snapped awake to the sound of Samuel's voice. She had fallen asleep, and the room was already bathed in the light of dawn.

'How are you?' Didi asked urgently. 'Should I call in a doctor?'

'No need,' Samuel laughed. 'And I'm a doctor, too.'

'No you're not, not yet,' Didi said. She felt like hugging Samuel, but after the previous night's events, she didn't dare to so much as lay a finger on him. 'Could they figure out what was wrong with you?'

'I told them I've lost consciousness a couple of times recently, but at least right now, my heart and blood pressure are totally fine.' Samuel sat up in his bed. 'They think it might have been some severe allergic reaction. Anaphylactic shock. Maybe I was stung by a bee.'

'A bee?' Didi asked. 'Out there in the woods?'

'Yes. What were we doing there, anyways?'

'Don't you remember?'

'I remember that you freaked out because we hadn't found anything at the manor,' Samuel replied. 'Then suddenly you wanted to be in the forest.'

'I just felt like the forest could calm me down,' Didi said, just now making the connection herself. 'Let's talk about that some other time.'

'Did I tell you out there in the woods that I'm falling in love with you?' Samuel asked. 'That you knock me off my feet? Literally, apparently.'

'You did mention something . . .'

'Maybe I've always loved you, Didi,' Samuel said. 'I don't know all about what's happened to you since we were kids, but it doesn't matter. I just want to be with you, and if you want that, too, then everything else will be all right.'

Didi thirstily drank down Samuel's words. She had never wanted to hear anything so badly; with every cell of her being, she craved the comfort and certainty that could be heard in Samuel's voice.

Then she realized that Samuel's hand was reaching for hers. Her mind was immediately overwhelmed by fear, and she quickly snatched her hand back.

'I can't, Samuel. My whole life is in knots.' *Starting from that tattoo on my stomach*, Didi thought, trying to make eye contact with Samuel so he could read her emotions.

But Samuel turned away.

'I wish I could, but . . .'

The room was charged with unspoken feelings. Didi felt an overpowering urge to start from the beginning and tell Samuel everything, so he could understand why even a simple touch between them was too much right now. She leaned in a little closer, but Samuel closed his eyes.

'Fine,' Samuel said softly.

'I'll stay with you and wait for them to release you, and then I'll take you home,' Didi said.

'I'd rather you didn't. Please go,' Samuel said, turning his back on her. 'I'm tired.'

And after a moment had passed, there was nothing Didi could do but stand up and leave. She stopped at the door to give Samuel the chance to say something, but he was pretending to sleep.

In a flash, all of her tender feelings for Samuel flipped inside out. If Samuel could have just been satisfied with what she was able to offer at the moment, then maybe she could have . . .

Didi slammed the door behind her. *Go ahead and sleep, then!* she thought. At first the guy confesses his love for her, and then he supposedly falls asleep.

Didi searched out a shady spot under a tree and sat down to give her feelings a chance to cool off. The sturdy bark warmed her back, and she reflected on everything that had happened over the past twenty-four hours. At the Van der Haas manor, she had felt like she was on the verge of a major revelation; she had been positive she would discover something momentous about herself. She had seen the wisdom in the old woman's eyes and waited for an answer, for the words that would explain where she came from, why she was the way she was . . .

Didi was roused out of her reverie by a tickling sensation on her bare shoulder. She was about to brush it away, but realized that she was looking straight into the eyes of a bee. The bee's proboscis was sensing its way around her skin, and the urge to shoo it away instantaneously faded.

Nadia was arranging flowers in a vase when she heard Didi finally come home. The younger nymph kicked her tennis shoes off, sending them flying across the entryway, and stared at Nadia defiantly for a moment before stomping off to her own room. Nadia had been on the verge of saying something to Didi about keeping the apartment tidy, but Didi had looked so miserable that she turned back to her flowers, even though she was consumed with curiosity about the previous night's events. It would be better to wait for a moment when Didi was ready to talk. Besides, Nadia was the last one to be telling anyone that they couldn't be keeping their own little secrets right now.

Nadia lifted the delicate blue cornflowers closer to her face. It was the willpower they bestowed that she needed now. There were secrets she had to carefully guard, especially from Kati. In the past, that would have bothered her. But Jesper's resurrection from the dead had made Nadia realize that hundreds of years ago at Garda,

Kati had known more than she had revealed. Kati had been in on the plot to keep her and Jesper apart.

Maybe I should have gotten some honeysuckle, too, Nadia thought. *It would clear my mind of the past, and I'd be able to concentrate better on the task at hand.* With that goal in mind, Nadia began to prepare their evening meal. She had heard Didi lie down for a nap, and Kati's expression indicated that the previous night had been an intense one. Nadia knew just the thing for that. She drizzled a thick emulsion of olive oil and mustard over an avocado salad, chopped up some fat brazil nuts and tossed them in, and put the white wine in the fridge to chill. She set the perfect cheeses out on the flat platter, a crumbly *pecorino sardo* and, to complement it, a gorgeous and mild *caciocavallo*. All of these foods would soothe the mind, and she could get Didi to listen.

Nadia took her time washing and moisturizing her skin. She picked her favorite cream-colored tunic and brushed her thick dark hair before wrapping it into a casual knot at her neck. She sat down and pulled her trusty guide to herbs from the shelf. She could always lose herself in the book. All she had to do was wait.

Early that evening, Nadia heard Didi moving around and taking a shower. She laid out the meal on the coffee table in the living room and lit the candles. And when Didi emerged from her room, Nadia poured her a glassful of the lightly sparkling white wine.

Didi raised an eyebrow in question.

'What I need tonight is a quiet night at home,' Nadia said, as if Didi were doing her a favor. After all, there was no rule that said a healer nymph couldn't be devious.

Nadia took pleasure in seeing Didi's appetite roused and her guardedness slip away. They chatted about Didi's studies, clothes, and the way the cheeses tasted, until Nadia sensed Didi was relaxed enough.

'So you and Samuel were together in the forest and you touched his chest,' Nadia said. 'And Samuel lost consciousness.'

Didi nodded and took a big swig from her wine glass.

'Are you in love with Samuel?' Nadia asked.

Didi shrugged. 'Of course not. We just—'

'Take a look at this,' Nadia said, and let out a tinkling laugh. She picked up an invitation from the table. 'This arrived at the perfect time. There's going to be a huge Venetian ball at the university. Nymphs are known for their love of such affairs throughout the ages.'

Nadia held out the card to Didi, who examined it in confusion.

'How is some party going to help me?'

'Twelve days from now you'll be at the mercy of the moon again,' Nadia said gently. 'We need to find someone who won't faint from a tiny smooch.'

'I can't do it any more,' Didi said, and suddenly the food didn't taste so good. 'It might be totally normal for you and Kati, but not for me.'

'You've had bad luck,' Nadia said. 'You don't need to kill anyone. I haven't killed anyone in decades.'

'I can't,' Didi repeated.

'Didi, you have to trust us,' Nadia said. Didi was standing up now. 'We'll make a better choice this time. This masquerade is the perfect opportunity. You don't know what it feels like to wither. You'll die.'

'I have a test. I have to go study,' Didi said, leaving Nadia alone in the living room.

Nadia stretched out her back and her neck and freed her long hair from the knot. She plucked a few nuts out of the salad bowl and munched on them as she thought. She had no intention of pressurizing Didi. At least not so that Didi would notice. Nadia turned her dark eyes towards the dim entryway.

'Were you eavesdropping on us?' she asked Kati, who thought she had entered soundlessly. 'It's hard to stay undetected if you smell like a smokehouse.'

Kati crossed the living room with a few strides and collapsed on the sofa. She was still in her full leathers. 'I knew Didi would put us all at danger over that boy,' she said. 'We have to put a stop to it. You do agree with me, don't you?'

'Didi will never forgive us if we hurt Samuel,' Nadia said.

'Which is why we'll let Didi do it herself.'

'How?' Nadia asked.

'Let's get them together during the next full moon,' Kati said. 'A nymph can't help her nature.'

CHAPTER 29

Kati had been busy since the previous night, when Didi had called her in a complete panic from somewhere out in the boondocks. There had been no time for her to come up with a good plan; she had simply stolen the first suitable vehicle and raced out to Tammisaari as fast as possible until she saw Samuel's car at the side of the road. Then she had followed the footprints to the pond, to the scene of the great teenage drama, where she picked Samuel up in her arms. She carried him to the car, and then from the car into the hospital once they got to Helsinki.

Kati had observed Didi's body language at the hospital, and to Kati there was no question about how she expressed herself around Samuel. The kid could deny it all she wanted, but Kati had seen first love before. She was already concocting a plan, when a phone call from Detective Hannula interrupted her. She had kicked off a successful flirtation with the police officer. Maybe he wanted to move deeper into the trap.

'Miss me already?' Kati asked, a smile in her voice.

'In a way,' Hannula answered. 'My boss saw your photo on some surveillance camera footage, and it caught his attention. You mind coming down to the station?'

'Wow, an invitation like that is hard to resist,' Kati said. 'I'll be there in fifteen minutes.'

Detective Hannula was waiting for Kati outside the stationhouse when she pulled up on her motorcycle. She took off her helmet and shook out her raven hair, giving Hannula a shy smile.

'Did you find me a new bike?' she asked. Hannula didn't answer; he just escorted her into a small office where an older detective was already sitting. He introduced himself: 'Detective Harju.'

Harju had gone over the surveillance camera footage again and again until his eyes ached. He was about to invite Kati to take a seat, but she had already settled into the most comfortable chair. 'I was reviewing the surveillance footage from the genetic medicine clinic here. You were walking down the corridor there with a certain Janne Malasmaa. Heikki here ID'd you.'

'Heikki and I just met not long ago,' Kati said, taking off her leather jacket. All she was wearing underneath was a black sleeveless T-shirt, but apparently Detective Harju didn't let the sight distract him.

'Does the name Johannes Metso mean anything to you?' Harju asked, holding out a photo to Kati.

'A beautiful boy,' said Kati.

'A dead boy.'

Kati didn't react to this news in the slightest; she just handed the photo back to Harju. He exchanged it for a photo in which Kati was walking down the clinic corridor with Janne.

'What did you do with Janne Malasmaa?'

'What does one do with beautiful boys?' Kati asked, making eyes at the clearly disconcerted Hannula from behind her long lashes.

'Did you two have a relationship?' Harju asked, pressing on.

'You mean, did I screw him? Unfortunately not.'

'Where were you when Malasmaa died?'

Kati sensed the trap: 'When did he die?'

'The night between the fourth and fifth of June,' Hannula said. 'On the night of the full moon.'

Kati smiled sweetly at Hannula and then at Harju. Then she dug a small wallet out of one of the pockets of her leather jacket and pulled out a card, which she handed to Detective Harju. He fumbled around for his reading glasses and put them on.

'What's this?' he asked.

'I remember that night very well,' Kati said. 'And I'm pretty sure the person who gave me that card does too, even though I've heard that rough sex can lead to memory loss.'

Detective Hannula asked the next question: 'You have an alibi?'

'Maybe the bastard will admit to the police what he wouldn't admit to his wife,' Kati said, already more than bored with the conversation. 'I guess it's my own fault for getting mixed up with a married man. Are we done here?'

'Don't be surprised if you hear from us again,' Harju answered.

Kati tossed her leather jacket over her shoulder and took her time walking out. As soon as she made it outside, she had to stop to think. She didn't like the feeling that someone was at her heels. She didn't like it one bit. Harju might look like he was on his way out, but Kati had noted the effectiveness of his techniques. The nymphs would have to be careful now, because if the police were after them, it was also probable that Erik would catch wind of their location. The satyrs' influence reached to all levels of society.

And there was another obvious problem: Didi. The girl was putting herself and others in danger by denying what she was. Kati and Nadia would have to set up an appropriate encounter for Didi to realize her true nature. But before any of this could happen, Kati had to be able to relieve some tension herself, even though it wasn't the full moon. Sometimes a nymph liked to have a good time just for the fun of it.

A few hours later, Kati was gazing out at the view of Helsinki that opened up beyond the windows of a stunning penthouse. She bent down to listen and make sure that the tall, dark, handsome man at her side was breathing, and then she poured herself more cognac into a snifter. Now she had to decide how she would handle things. If the nymphet had been anyone else, Kati wouldn't have lifted a finger to help the little brat, but it was Didi . . . Kati's thoughts instantly went back to a time almost twenty years earlier, in London. She had been so happy as she embraced her sister in the shadows of Westminster Bridge. But the feelings of reassurance and relief had been short lived.

'I need your help,' Rose whispered as they hugged. Her red hair was so bright it glowed in the dusk.

'Everyone's worried,' Kati said. 'Erik's worried. Everyone's looking for you.'

'Listen to me, sister . . .'

'I'm here now. I'll protect you,' Kati said, her heart about to burst. 'I'll bring you back safely.'

'I'm not coming back,' Rose said. 'I've met someone.'

'A human?' Kati stared at Rose, unable to believe her ears. 'That's not going to fly. I'm taking you back, and I'll fix everything. Erik is waiting for us at Nesebar. I won't let anything happen to you.'

A couple out for an evening stroll passed by, and the sisters stopped talking for a moment. But Rose's smile didn't fade for an instant.

'You don't understand,' Rose said when they were alone again. She took Kati by the hand and pressed it to her belly. 'There's no way. I really can't go back. Nor do I want to.'

It took Kati a second to grasp what Rose meant.

'You can't be pregnant,' Kati said. She yanked her hand away in shock and turned towards the river. 'I already made up a story. I told Erik that you had managed to infiltrate that banking company like he ordered, but some men discovered you were a nymph and they—'

'There's no way he'd ever expect anything like this,' Rose said. 'It's impossible for me to be impregnated by a human. But I'm carrying a child.'

'Rose, I swore on my life,' Kati said, brushing Rose's red tresses away from her face. 'If Erik even suspects . . . Think about your child at least, if you refuse to think about yourself or that human.'

The sisters gazed at each other for a moment, and Kati knew full well that she would never convince Rose to return to Erik. At least not forever. That's why they had to play for time. They had to come up with the perfect diversion that they could use to help Rose disappear. Maybe forever.

'First off, you have to come back,' Kati said. 'When will you start to show?'

'Two or three months from now,' Rose answered.

'So that's how much time we have to figure out how to keep you and the child alive,' Kati said. 'It's lucky that I'm the one you called on for help, sister dear.'

Immediately afterwards, in a show of deference, Kati had informed Erik that she and Rose were about to head back to Nesebar. She needed a few days to arrange the trip and tend Rose so she would be well enough to travel. Erik had reluctantly agreed.

Kati succeeded in delaying their departure for a week. She had time to come up with a scheme, make the necessary purchases, and prepare Rose for what lay ahead. Rose refused to say a word about the father of her child, but other than that, she put herself wholly in Kati's hands. She knew that a watertight plan would be necessary for their ultimate escape to succeed.

Kati and Rose flew to Bulgaria, and Erik's satyrs picked them up from the airport. Up to this point, all went according to script. But at the Nesebar manor, it was another story. Erik had been waiting for Rose, and he was in no way prepared for the fact that she would agree only to sleep at his side, nothing more.

'There is a line of nymphs the other side of that door prepared to do anything in their power to claim your place in this bed,' Erik shouted at Rose, fully aroused and eyes red with lust.

'So take one of them. Take a few,' Rose said quietly, before turning her back on him.

'You're mine,' Erik said, knowing that Rose was the key to controlling Kati, too. 'It is your duty to keep me satisfied.'

'You know what happened to me in London, when I was carrying out your orders,' Rose answered, just as Kati had told her to.

'Ekaterina killed those men,' Erik growled. He was stroking Rose's neck and hair, but his touch lacked tenderness. He wanted to demonstrate that Rose was utterly and completely his property, his and his alone. 'And that's nothing compared to what I will do to you if this continues.'

'I'm trying,' Rose said.

'Try harder,' Erik said. 'Go. I will not stand for this tomorrow.'

Rose slipped out of the bed and wrapped a robe around her silk lingerie. She glanced behind her as she walked down the corridor to make sure no one was following. And then she ran soundlessly to the library, so she could be in peace. She had always liked it in there. The old books emanated tranquility, and the large windows gave onto a pretty garden. Sheaves of old, yellowed paper lay on the writing table; they had been inscribed with a quill in an unknown language. An unusual knot pattern adorned the leather cover of a heavy, hand-bound book. Rose ran her fingers across its curves. She sighed. The pregnancy tired her. She was settling in, preparing to spend the night in the armchair. She hoped that by morning her sister would have a plan ready for her.

Suddenly the floor lamp in the corner of the library flashed on, making Rose jump. Kati stepped into the light, and Rose exhaled.

'You've come up with a plan, haven't you?' Rose asked. 'I can't hold Erik off.'

'Don't hold him off,' Kati said laconically, eyeing her ink-stained fingertips.

'Erik is a satyr, the child is human. I'm afraid if I allow Erik inside me, something will happen to the child.'

'We already have enough problems,' Kati said. 'You'll have to

submit to Erik while your belly doesn't call any attention to itself. I
have a plan, but we need more time.'

'Does it have anything to do with this?' Rose asked, pointing at
the old book lying on the table.

'I'll explain later,' Kati said, tickling Rose's chin with the quill.

Rose, Kati thought now. Her stubborn sister. And the task that Rose
had charged her with. That's why she needed to act now. She emptied
her cognac glass and took a final look at the muscled glutes of her
strapping companion. Kati would have been perfectly happy to
continue playing, but you don't always get what you want. She rose
and dressed, and then she shoved the cognac bottle under her arm
and left.

It didn't take more than a blink of the eye for Kati to make it to
the marina on her motorcycle. Samuel's boat was there right in front
of her like it was being served to her on a silver platter. Kati calmly
walked up to it and looked into the cabin. She didn't see anyone. It
only took a second before the lock on the door was broken, and Kati
stalked in. Her gaze lingered on the old photographs on the wall.
Samuel was a lot younger in them. They had been shot with his
mother and father against the backdrop of the Greek islands. She
looked for something that would tell her anything about Samuel,
about his strengths and weaknesses, but the old wooden boat was like
some ancient relic. Samuel may have been living there, but it felt
more like a museum, a monument.

Oh well, Kati thought. *Nothing lasts forever.* She opened the bottle
of cognac and drained it over the bed, where she had already tossed
a heap of newspapers and old books. She pulled her old lighter out of
her pocket, and before long the bed was in flames. Kati stared at
the fire for a second. She had left a final swig in the bottle for herself,
and finished it off before she climbed back onto the dock. She didn't
look behind her, even though the blaze was lighting up the night sky.
Step One of her plan had been executed.

* * *

When she made it home, all Kati wanted to do was kick off her boots and fall into bed, but she heard Nadia and Didi talking. She knew how persuasive Nadia could be, and under other circumstances she may have even had the patience to wait for Nadia to achieve her goal, but time was of the essence now. That's why the easiest way to handle things was to bring Didi and Samuel together.

'Is that your plan?' Nadia asked.

'What reservations do you have?' Kati said.

'I want to take some copulin samples from Didi,' Nadia said. 'I've racked my brains trying to figure out what happened to Janne. He should have survived.'

'Aren't nymphs always at their most powerful when they're just coming into their own?' Kati said. 'Besides, we *want* Didi to take the next victim's life.'

Sometimes Kati's cynicism went a little too far for Nadia. If she hadn't prioritized this task above all else, she would have given Kati a speech in defense of humanity and freedom. It was freedom that was the crux of everything right now. Nadia looked at Kati, and she could tell from the other nymph's face that the wheels were already spinning.

'What have you done?' Nadia asked.

'What had to be done,' Kati said. 'And now Samuel's homeless.'

CHAPTER 30

Didi wiped down the cafe table, deep in thought. A group of three young women, clearly students, walked in, ordered coffee and panini, and made space for themselves. Didi was envious of how carefree they were, how *free*. They could come and go as they pleased, study, meet their friends. Have sex or not have sex. Didi was still thinking about what Nadia had said about the next full moon. She just couldn't wrap her brain around the idea that her life depended on it. Of course when she was in high school she had had crushes on boys and imagined she would die if they didn't show any interest in her, but she couldn't fathom that now she really would die without sex. No one died because they couldn't get laid.

Why can't my life be simple? Didi thought. Like for those girls, who were gossiping about tests and clothes. I could fall in love with whoever I wanted, date whoever I wanted. When her best friend Laura found Lasse, Didi had initially been a little jealous. Then bruises started to appear on Laura's arms, and sometimes she'd have a split lip . . . That wasn't freedom, or love, either. Didi couldn't understand how someone as sensible and decisive as Laura could let herself be treated so poorly. *Samuel would never do that to me,* Didi thought, as she carried dirty dishes into the kitchen.

She returned to the dining area and was headed over to take out the trash, when her eyes fell on Samuel. The first thought to cross Didi's mind was the rude way Samuel had chased her out of the hospital, but then she saw the completely lost expression on his face. She steeped a cup of chamomile tea and took it over to him.

Samuel looked at her with red eyes, unable to say a word. Next to him on the bench there was a bag full of random, soot-covered stuff.

'What happened to you?'

'Someone burned *Robur* last night,' Samuel said, as matter-of-factly as if he were discussing the weather. 'The police are investigating it as arson.'

'Can I get you something to eat?' Didi asked.

'Nah, I'm good,' Samuel said. 'I just need to come up with a new home right away. Or at least somewhere to sleep.'

Didi reached across the table and pulled a scorched picture frame from the bag. She gazed at the photo of Samuel's mother it contained.

'That's all I have left,' Samuel said. 'It's a pretty weird feeling, not owning a thing in the world.'

Didi looked at Samuel and waited for him to fall apart, but somehow Samuel managed a smile.

'How are things here?' Samuel asked.

Didi ignored the question: 'What are you going to do?'

'I don't know.' Samuel shifted his gaze to the window, but it didn't look like he was seeing anything. 'The clothes and all the rest of my things were just stuff, but Dad left me the boat when he died. *Robur* was mine. I took good care of it.'

Didi slid into the seat next to him. She took his hand, wanting to hold it in her own, but she suddenly jerked and pulled her hand back.

'What now?' Samuel asked.

'You're hurt,' Didi said. 'You're truly in pain. The memory of that boat causes you physical pain.'

'Of course,' Samuel said. 'It was the only thing I had left of my father.'

Didi stared at her burning hand, but then she remembered that she was the one who was supposed to be comforting Samuel. She made an effort to smile empathetically.

'I'll bring you some soup,' Didi said. She couldn't think of what else to say.

'Don't bother,' Samuel said, gathering up his belongings. And with that, he was gone.

That evening, Didi dragged herself home, exhausted. She wasn't tired so much from work or from studying, but from thinking too much. And no matter how much she thought, things didn't make any more sense to her. Everything just got more and more confusing. She found herself hoping that Nadia had decided to pamper her again with something good to eat and a nice girls' night at home. Instead, Didi ran into her roommate in the stairwell.

'Hey,' Nadia said. 'I have to go back to work, but Kati's at home. I probably won't see you until morning.'

But the apartment was empty, and no one responded to Didi's hellos. She went out onto the balcony and watched as evening fell. Then she started climbing up the fire escape to the roof.

She found Kati there, melting into the dusk in her dark clothes. 'How did you know to look for me here?'

'A mountain nymph and a roof, it's a pretty simple equation,' Didi said.

'That's just a stereotype. Not that it isn't true.'

Didi joined her on the roof. The cooling air on her bare shoulders instantly made her feel better, but the crescent moon in the sky reminded her of what lay ahead.

'What kind of nymph am I?' Didi asked.

'You felt the urge to escape from Samuel's car, to run deep into the forest.'

'So I'm a dryad, then.'

'You've been reading up,' Kati smiled, perhaps remembering something else.

'You guys are the ones who enrolled me at the university,' Didi said, but she was still thinking about her tingling hand, how Samuel's pain had shifted to her. 'A nature nymph, *as unpredictable as the weather, like the changing of the seasons*. Those mythology books are like horoscopes or something.'

'There might be a grain of truth in them,' Kati said.

'And truth is stranger than fiction,' Didi retorted. 'Tell me another cliché, why don't you.'

'Didi, no matter what kind of nymph you are, you're still yourself.'

'Nadia knows how to heal. What does a mountain nymph know how to do?' Didi was clearly throwing down the gauntlet.

'Maybe someday you'll find out,' Kati answered.

'Samuel's boat was burned last night,' Didi said a minute later.

'You're kidding.' Kati feigned the appropriate amount of interest. 'Maybe you should invite him to come live with us.'

Didi lifted her head and looked at Kati in surprise. 'Wow, where did that come from?'

'I've been doing some thinking,' Kati said. 'And you're right. It's time for me to start trusting your instincts. The life of a nymph is still totally new to you, so maybe you should have some contact with someone from your old world. Samuel could offer you something that you can't get from me or Nadia, at least not yet.'

Didi was in a rush to convince Kati, now that she seemed to be open to the idea for once: 'Samuel and I never—'

'Of course not. I trust you now,' said Kati. 'Besides, that poor kid needs help.'

'I'm going to call him right now,' Didi chirped happily, and she walked towards the fire escape.

'Watch your step,' Kati called out. 'And I mean that in every aspect of life.'

'Yeah, yeah,' Didi said, disappearing over the edge of the roof.

It wasn't long before Didi had presented the idea to Samuel, too.

She had expected him to be immediately pleased, but Samuel didn't think it was such a great idea after all.

'Move in with you guys?' Samuel asked. 'Isn't that going to cause a little unnecessary confusion between us?'

'We've been friends since we were kids,' Didi said, trying to sound casual. 'Why wouldn't it work now?'

'I don't think it's a very good idea,' Samuel said. 'But thanks anyways.'

Didi put down the phone. Why was life such a roller-coaster? Just a minute ago she had been ecstatic, but now Samuel had dumped a bucket of cold water on her. Next Didi dialed Laura's number. She would start off by telling her friend a few choice words about men.

Nadia looked into Jesper's eyes, as clear as a woodland spring, and she felt embarrassed that she had actually run the last few steps to the clinic, knowing that he was waiting for her there. Now the satyr was sitting self-confidently on the examination table, and Nadia was unspeakably irritated. She quickly yanked the curtain around them to conceal them.

'Oooh, so now we're hidden?' Jesper asked playfully.

'I don't even want my coworkers to see us,' Nadia said.

'You talk of humans as if they were your fiends,' Jesper remarked. 'Living with them for seventeen years works wonders.'

Nadia had no intention of moving a single step closer to Jesper. 'What's your decision?'

'Frida might know about us.'

'What do you mean?'

'Frida smelled you on me,' Jesper said, and the hoarseness of his voice was like silk on Nadia's skin. 'I could lose my head because of you. You're dangerous for me.'

'And you're dangerous for me,' Nadia answered, feeling the truth of what she was saying in so many ways.

Jesper stepped down from the examination table, searching

Nadia's face. He lowered his head a little so they were looking straight into each other's eyes. 'I have to tell Erik the truth sooner or later.'

Nadia raised her palm to Jesper's chest, and her breathing accelerated. Jesper bent in even closer, and now their lips were only a few millimeters apart. And yet Nadia suddenly backed off.

'This is wrong,' she said. 'I have to tell Kati.'

'Fine,' Jesper said, a broad smile rising to his face. 'I'll tell Erik and you tell Kati.'

'OK,' Nadia said, but neither one of them made a move to leave. 'When will you tell Erik?'

'Not just yet,' Jesper said, drawing her into his arms.

CHAPTER 31

Erik steered his SUV along the city streets confidently. He had instructed both Jesper and Frida to climb in the back seat, so he could sit up front in lofty solitude. He had always loved driving, and he still remembered his first automobile, the combustion-engine model that he had procured from Karl F. Benz himself. The graphite-gray beauty he was driving at the moment was one of his favorite rides. But for some reason, driving wasn't calming him the way it usually did. He had made the mistake of staying in town when he should have headed for the highway. He would have been able to fly down the asphalt instead of being trapped in stop-and-go traffic. That redheaded nymph was tormenting him, and the thought of her proximity made his blood boil.

Erik noticed a light turning red up ahead and came to a steady stop, even though his instinct was to step on the gas. But he didn't need to attract any extra attention to himself.

At that instant, the SUV shuddered and the rear lights broke with a loud crash. Someone had rear-ended them. Erik jumped out of the car fast as lightning. Jesper didn't have a chance to intervene before Erik, in one smooth movement, wrenched the driver of the car behind them out of his vehicle and into the road.

'It doesn't look like you have a very good understanding of your tires' wet grip capacity,' Erik hissed, hunched over the young man. 'Permit me to give you a lesson.'

Erik slapped him across the face, rose up to his full height, and gave him a swift kick in the abdomen. He would have continued, but Jesper lunged in between them. People were reaching for their cell phones. Erik straightened his jacket and allowed Frida to lead him back to the shelter of the SUV's tinted windows.

Jesper shoved a wad of cash into the young man's pocket. 'I think we're square now, wouldn't you agree?'

'I'm going to call the cops! Who the hell is that fucking nutcase?' the man whined. 'I already have your license plate number.'

Jesper snatched the cell phone from the man's hand and stomped on it, smashing it into the ground. Next he reached into the man's breast pocket and pulled out his driver's license. He took a moment to compare the man and the photo.

'And now I know who you are, too,' Jesper said. 'If we hear anything from you, I will personally come and rip that face off.'

Jesper took a few strides and climbed back in the SUV, and they continued on their way. It only took a moment for Erik to collect himself. Once again he looked the part of impeccable businessman. Not a single hair was out of place.

'This godforsaken hellhole is wearing on my patience,' Erik said.

'Jesper will deliver the fugitives to us,' Frida said from the back seat, as she pressed a hand against Erik's chest. 'Won't you?'

Frida had to give Jesper a meaningful look before he answered.

'Of course,' Jesper said. 'I've already promised.'

'And when we get back to the hotel, I'll help you calm down,' Frida said, rubbing Erik's shoulders in a soothing massage. 'I'll make sure your satyr's horns stay hidden. You don't want to endanger your own operation, do you?'

Up in the suite, Erik let Frida work her magic. He was lord and master, and Frida was alive due solely to his magnanimity. Yet she was nothing more than a substitute for what he truly desired. When Frida straddled him and lashed him with her long blond hair, he imagined Rose's lush red curls, how they spread, radiant, across the pillow like the petals of a flower, how Rose's body curved into an arch the moment before she came.

As Frida rocked back and forth on top of him, Erik turned his eyes to the photograph on the wall. If he squinted slightly, he could see both Rose and the young nymph in her, and Frida knew that he would cum ferociously a moment later. She took it for all it was worth.

Once the satyr was sated, Frida rested on top of him for a moment, and then rose to go back to her own room.

'Order me something to eat and drink,' Erik told her, stretching before rising to take a shower. Frida had indeed released the tension from his muscles.

After his shower, Erik wrapped himself in one of the plush black hotel bathrobes and stepped back into the suite. A pretty waitress who had already caught his eye in the restaurant was setting out the food and red wine that Frida had ordered. Erik was prepared to give her a princely tip, but there was something delicious about her, and the scent of the food had stimulated his senses again. He grabbed the remote control and the soft rhythms of a *cumbia* flooded the room.

'May I . . . ?' Erik said, looking at the nametag at the blonde girl's breasts, '. . . Anna?'

'Unfortunately I'm not allowed to dance with guests,' she said, but she clearly wasn't offended by his asking.

'Is there a rule somewhere that says that hotel employees can't have any fun?' Erik grabbed Anna by the hand, and his animal magnetism lured her into joining his smooth footwork.

Erik whirled Anna around a few times, and she was already beginning to relax under his lead, but with the next twirl, Erik's eyes lit on the framed photo of the redheaded girl, and he flung Anna violently onto the bed. In the blink of an eye, Anna understood that this was no longer a game. There was something bizarrely threatening about the dark, handsome man now. A scream of horror rose to her lips, but it caught in her throat when she saw his gleaming blood-red eyes and the horns thrusting forth from his forehead.

'I'm sorry,' Erik said softly. 'You weren't supposed to see this.'

CHAPTER 32

Detective Harju was lying on the sofa in his office. His eyes were closed, and he was using his trench coat as a blanket. He was supposed to be thinking about the case, but he was thinking more about the existence of young women. They had their futures ahead of them. They were radiant, hungry for life, full of joy . . . And the same went for the young men he had seen in the morgue, too. Harju realized that he had entered dangerous terrain and struggled to stand up. He wandered over to the photos and information that covered the wall. Everything had gradually come together, and now it was time to make a move.

He yelled out into the corridor: 'Heikki, I need you!'

Harju's younger colleague slowly trudged in, the eternal can of Coke in one hand, but his attention immediately focused in on the pictures on the wall. When Harju saw the bewilderment on his partner's face, a satisfied grin spread across his. The older detective stepped over and tapped Nadia's passport photo and the shot of Kati in the hospital corridor.

'These two women have two things in common,' Harju said. 'Both of them met Janne Malasmaa, and they both live at the same address. They live together.'

'Is that our new line of investigation?' Hannula asked.

'Not exactly.' Harju took the new photograph sent over from the university and tacked it to the wall near the other photos. 'According to the building's register, a third woman lives in the apartment, too. A redheaded girl.' Now they were looking at a lineup of three very different-looking women. Harju backed up a little so he could see all of them at once.

'Desirée Volanté Tasson looks quite a bit like Didi Tiensuu from that small town, don't you think?' Harju asked. 'That is our line of investigation.'

'So what's our next step?' Hannula asked, trying to hide his agitation by taking loud slurps from his can. He wasn't the least bit happy about this turn of events. It was going to make life a lot more difficult.

'I want you to discreetly look into what these ladies are up to,' Harju said.

'What do you suspect?'

'Tiensuu's mother is a doctor, Rapaccini works at the genetic medicine clinic,' Harju said, but he still wasn't getting any sort of response from Hannula. 'Do I have to spell it out for you? Let's start by, say, investigating the illegal trafficking or abuse of prescription drugs. That will have to give us something.'

Harju stared at Hannula for a second before going back over to the couch and making himself comfortable. 'Now get to work. I have things to think about.'

CHAPTER 33

Kati smiled, watching Didi and Nadia giggle as they plundered the shopping bags she had brought home. The two nymphs were pulling out richly painted and skillfully decorated Venetian masks, feathers, baubles and headdresses. Kati had emptied the stores of everything she came across that was appropriate for the occasion. She tilted her head and gazed at the reflection in the window. The three of them looked like a happy family gathered in the living room. *Was such a life even possible?* Kati wondered.

Didi and Nadia tried on different ensembles and took turns preening in front of the mirror. Kati joined in the fun as best she could, but she kept pricking up her ears and glancing over at the front door. She wasn't sure Samuel had swallowed the bait when she dropped by his job and claimed to have Didi's best interests at heart.

'Don't you have the guts to move under the same roof with me?' Kati had asked, smiling reassuringly.

'It doesn't have anything to do with you,' Samuel had said, trying to step around her. Kati had firmly blocked his way.

'Good. Because I'm actually here for Didi's sake,' Kati had said, and that had caught Samuel's attention. 'Didi's life is in turmoil. You've known her since childhood. You're a connection to her past. Your presence could help Didi.'

'Maybe Didi doesn't want me nearby.'

'The amount of time humans get to spend walking the face of this earth is pretty short,' Kati had said. 'You might want to think about how you spend it.'

At the time, Kati had decided that that had done the trick. She sensed that a guy like Samuel would never do anything he felt pressured to do. But maybe she should have tried to entice him a little more after all.

Regardless, now she had to take advantage of the current situation and educate Didi about her roots.

'Nymphs attended masquerade balls whenever they had the chance,' she explained to the young nymph.

'Late seventeeth century Venice was a golden age for us.' Nadia shot Kati a glance to indicate that she was in on the plot. 'Back then, you could use masks from October to June. It was easy for a nymph to hide behind a mask, a tricorn hat and a cape.'

'And then they started cutting back on the period when masks could be used,' Kati said. 'Too many young men started turning up dead.'

The smile had faded from Didi's lips. She lowered a mask embellished with blood-red rhinestones from her face. The history of her fellow nymphs both fascinated and frightened her. She barely dared to ask the question: 'Did you kill men, too?'

'A few. There were a lot of us then,' Nadia answered frankly.

'How many?' Didi asked.

'Maybe twenty.'

'How many of us are there now?' Didi continued.

'Not as many,' Nadia said.

Kati sensed that the conversation was headed in an overly serious direction. It would be better to keep the mood relaxed.

'Parties these days are nothing like the balls of Venice. Back then, we always—' Kati was interrupted by the sound of the doorbell.

'I'll get it,' Didi said, jumping up. She didn't notice the way Kati and Nadia moved closer together, the alert look in their eyes, or the knife that had appeared in Kati's hand. They couldn't be certain who was on the other side of that door. When they heard Samuel's voice, they relaxed, and a moment later Didi was walking back into the living room, smiling happily.

'Is it all right if Samuel moves in with us until he can straighten things out again?' Didi asked, a little shyly.

'Of course. Join the club,' Kati said, casting a suitably grateful glance Samuel's way and scooting over to make room for him on the sofa. But Samuel stayed at Didi's side.

'Now this is worth celebrating,' Nadia said, rushing into the kitchen. She had to get the ice crushed as quickly as possible. 'We're going to toast with real champagne and have a feast!'

A pulsating soul beat started floating through the apartment, and Nadia conjured up antipasti in a flash, followed by fresh ravioli. The air was redolent with basil, lemon, and bacon. After a couple of glasses of champagne, Samuel had been lured into the living room to dance. Didi was twirling on the floor in the terracotta dress with the spaghetti straps that showed off the paleness of her skin. All her cares had evaporated.

For her part, Kati made sure that no one's glass remained empty for long. She had to admit that she was enjoying having a relaxing evening, too. She inconspicuously made her way to the windowsill and took a seat. She and Nadia exchanged glances. *We are irresistible*, Nadia's eyes said to her, and Kati nodded. Kati pointed out the window, where the moon shone, almost full. Nadia understood, and she also came over to the window to watch along with Kati as the unsuspecting Didi and Samuel frolicked.

Love makes us do all kinds of things, but most of all it causes trouble, Kati reflected, and her thoughts inexorably returned to that night at the manor at Nesebar.

Kati was sitting in the library, exhausted from her efforts. She much preferred physical labor to diddling around like this, but she was prepared to do anything on behalf of her sister. Rose looked at the ancient opus that lay open on the table before her.

' "When the moon goes dark above the pale hills, a nymph will be born in the forest eaves," ' Rose read in a soft voice, staining her fingers in ink that hadn't had a chance to dry properly yet. 'What is this, Kati?'

'Plan B,' Kati said, casually flinging down the quill. 'It won't be long before we can escape.'

'Why did we come back if we're just going to run for it now?' Rose asked.

'We need to be able to escape for good,' Kati answered. 'We're going to disappear from the face of the earth.'

'And how are we going to manage that?'

'With this.' Kati indicated the book. 'And if it doesn't work, Erik will have every single one of us killed. Including you and . . .'

Kati was almost angry with herself for her rash words, when she saw how terrified Rose was at the thought of losing her child. She didn't care about her own life that much. *Love makes us do all kinds of things*, Kati thought, not for the first time, or the last.

Kati calmed her sister. 'This legend is our life insurance. It will keep the baby alive. Sit down and help me.'

Kati retrieved the quill and dipped it into the bottle of ink.

Rose looked at her trustingly.

Kati and Nadia discreetly stepped out onto the dim balcony. The soft, soothing music carried out faintly, and they stood there for a moment in silence, gazing at the moon.

'So what do we do now?' Nadia asked.

'Now we just sit back and let things take their course,' Kati said.

CHAPTER 34

All Nadia had to do was take two steps towards the hotel bar and the young bartender was rushing over to take her order. The attention of the other men also focused in on her, regardless of whatever companions may have been at their side. Nadia's dark hair and pale, ethereal dress were a dazzling combination, but many of the women in the bar sensed that she radiated something else as well.

A cool-misted glass of Pinot Grigio had just been set down in front of her when her cell phone rang.

'Where are you?' Kati asked. 'Weren't we supposed to go out together?'

'I already set something up,' Nadia said, gracefully skirting the truth.

'It wouldn't happen to involve a handsome man with blond hair, would it?' Kati asked. 'Say, someone who looks a little like Jesper?'

'Actually, he looks so much like Jesper it's criminal,' Nadia answered.

'You need to start getting over that fixation,' Kati ordered. 'Go for someone with dark or sandy hair once in a while . . .'

'Maybe next time,' Nadia said and hung up, as Jesper walked over to her. Words were no longer needed. They kissed each other as their hands searched each other's bodies.

Jesper glanced around. They were calling attention to themselves, but he didn't care. He took a sip of wine from Nadia's glass and wrapped his arms around her waist. 'Is it worth it? Living according to the constraints of mortals?'

'It's the best thing that's ever happened to me,' Nadia whispered in his ear.

Jesper grazed his fingers against Nadia's collarbone and thought about all the years that had passed, about everything he had lost.

'I've been living the life of a recluse,' he said to Nadia, as if confessing a sin. 'I answered the call if it came, but couldn't go back to living in a band of satyrs.'

Nadia cast an expectant glance his way. She didn't know any other satyr who would have done what Jesper did.

'You want freedom,' Jesper continued. 'You could be free with me.'

'What do you mean?'

'The most likely scenario is that this story of ours is going to come to a sad ending,' Jesper said. 'I'm trying to think of a way of preventing that.'

Nadia felt a hot current building up in her belly. Her gaze met Jesper's again. Freedom was the last thing on her mind.

'Let's go,' Nadia said. 'I reserved us a room upstairs.'

Kati hung up her phone and started concentrating on her eye makeup. She had attended countless masquerades, and even though a student party was no doubt going to be less opulent than that of a Venetian noble, she had every intention of enjoying herself. People were different at masquerades. They loosened up, dared to break the rules. That was good for a nymph.

Kati looked herself over in the mirror. This is what she had been missing: a change, a little playfulness. She wanted to be mysterious, overtly sexy. Black fishnet stockings, micro-shorts, a corset, a hooded cape that brushed the ground, and a mask adorned with pearls and feathers. *Yes*, she thought, as she prepared to make a quiet exit. But at that moment Didi stuck her head into her room.

'Where are you going?' Didi said. 'I'm not dressed yet. We were supposed to go to that party together.'

'I have an errand I have to run first,' answered Kati, whose plot was moving ahead nicely. 'I'll pick you up at eleven. You and Samuel just enjoy yourselves.'

'Samuel's studying for a test,' Didi said sullenly, but Kati had already walked out the door.

Didi hung around the apartment by herself. She didn't want to believe what the nymphs had told her about the effect of the moon, but just to be safe, she decided to draw the curtains across the windows. Then she went into the bedroom she shared with Nadia now that Samuel had moved in with them. She started feeling restless, so she went back out to the kitchen and drank a glass of water, but it did nothing to settle her agitation. She flopped down on the couch and seriously considered channel-surfing, but that didn't sound appealing either. Her eyes kept wandering back to the door of Samuel's room, which was ajar. Maybe she could peek in, see if he was hitting the books hard, or pretend she needed one of her own books, or maybe that little lace bra from the upper drawer . . .

She silently crept up to the doorway and looked in. Samuel was lying on the bed on his stomach, breathing heavily. One hand was resting on his textbook. Didi knocked on the door, maybe a little too loudly, and Samuel snapped awake.

'For a second I thought I was back in the hospital,' Samuel said, a little out of it. 'You know how you wake up in a strange place and don't know where you are.'

'I wake up feeling that way almost every day,' Didi said. She sat down on the bed at Samuel's side. 'I try to trust that everything will gradually fall into place, and that all this new stuff is better than my old life.'

'Is it?' Samuel took Didi by the hand, but she quickly pulled it back.

'I'm lousy company. All I do is cause problems for everyone,' Didi said, leaving out that her company was so lousy it was downright deadly.

Samuel sat up. They were so close to each other now that he felt an irresistible urge to say all the things that were mulling around inside his head.

'Out there in the woods . . .' he began. 'Out there in the woods, for the first time in my life I felt what it feels like to be in love.'

Didi's steady gaze remained fixed on Samuel, and he took it as an invitation. He placed one hand gently on Didi's neck and drew her in. Their lips were only a millimeter apart from each other, when Didi suddenly felt so agonizingly hot that she pulled back, on the verge of panic. She had felt this sensation before, and she knew what would follow. She sprang up and left Samuel sitting alone in his room, completely bewildered.

Didi couldn't see the moon, but she could feel it. She was almost doubling over in pain by the time she made it to the sofa, fumbling around for her cell phone. First she called Nadia, not knowing that the other nymph was panting hotly against Jesper's neck at that very moment. The other alternative was Kati. And Didi had no idea that Kati was the one who had plotted to arrange things so Didi would be alone with Samuel in the first place.

Didi cursed. First the other nymphs watched her like hawks, and now when she needed their help, they were nowhere to be found. Her forehead was glistening, she was sweating in agony, and she tried to make it out to the balcony, into the fresh air. She pushed aside the curtain that covered the door and was just about to step out when the moonlight struck her. It surrounded her entire being with an electric, tingling warmth. Her skin quivered, and she could have almost sworn that she was glowing in the dark. At first the feeling was like a soothing wave, but then a heat flowed down through her, filling her, making her spasm, taking her breath away. Her hands involuntarily clenched into fists and her irises flickered milky white.

'Didi?' Samuel's voice asked behind her.

Didi stretched her neck and felt her body's balance being restored. She turned to Samuel, took a couple of steps towards him, and pressed up against him. She could immediately feel how badly Samuel wanted her.

'You're right,' Didi whispered in a hoarse voice. 'I feel exactly the same way you do. Let's not fight it.'

Without further ado, Didi grabbed Samuel's buttocks with one hand and his crotch with the other. But Samuel was already trying to pull back. His desire had been aroused, but he didn't know this girl at all.

'What's wrong with you?' Samuel asked.

'This is what you wanted,' Didi said, leaning in towards Samuel's lips. She could already feel Samuel's impassioned breathing and was certain of victory.

And indeed, Samuel was incapable of resisting her any more. Didi took him by the hand, led him to the bedroom, and threw herself onto the bed on her back, letting him pull off her pants. She unbuttoned her top and saw the bruises that had appeared on her skin. But there wasn't a force on earth that could stand in her way now. She pulled Samuel on top of her and then rolled over on top of him in nothing more than her underwear. Soon Samuel would be all hers ... She opened her eyes slightly and saw her reflection in Samuel's eyes. Except it wasn't her, it was a stranger. Not a woman, not a beast, but something in between. Some pitiless creature that cared about nothing, no one.

Didi started as if she had been woken up from a trance. For a moment she didn't even realize she was on top of Samuel. Then she quickly jumped off.

'No, this can't happen,' Didi said. Her body was trembling all over. A second ago, she had felt desire, now she felt pure dread at how the power had taken her over. It made her evil, a ruthless predator that she didn't recognize as herself.

Samuel tried to reassure her: 'Everything's fine.' But Didi could tell from his voice that he also considered her unnatural.

Didi gathered up her clothes from the floor and ran into her own room.

'Where are you going?' Samuel called after her.

'Leave me alone!' Didi yelled back as angrily as she could, so Samuel would stay as far away as possible from her.

She was already wracked by fever as she pulled on the long, petrol blue dress she had picked out as her masquerade gown. She slipped her feet into her heels and ran out the door. She managed to register that Samuel was following her in a daze.

Didi made it out into the cool night air and stood for a moment under a street lamp. She had a vague idea of the direction she should head in, and an agonizing urgency forced her onwards. Her strength was ebbing with every step, and she was panting heavily by the time she finally made it to the masquerade venue. A stream of people dressed in old-fashioned clothes and masks was flowing out, pushing back against her. Some looked at her in astonishment, others in admiration.

'Nice legs,' said a man in horns, and Didi cried out in alarm.

She stumbled inside. She had to find Kati or she would die. She felt like she was in a sea of men, and all of her senses were in overdrive. The masculine aromas surrounding her formed a fog through which she wandered blindly. And at that instant she recognized Kati, who was laughing heartily at a young man's stories. Didi staggered over to her. The throbbing music was nothing but a blur in Didi's ears.

'Kati . . .' Didi mumbled, almost falling into the other nymph's arms.

'You don't do anything the way you're supposed to,' Kati said, as she took hold of Didi.

'You left me alone with Samuel on purpose,' Didi said. Then the realization grew clear in her fog-addled brain: 'You're the one who burned Samuel's boat.'

Kati started dragging Didi aside and helped her sit down. She picked up a mask that had been left behind and pressed it to Didi's face.

'Try to stand it a little longer,' Kati said. Her gaze was already fixed on a young man leaning against the bar. 'You need to eat.'

CHAPTER 35

Nadia closed Didi's door after taking a peek into the dim room. Didi lay there mutely, curled up under her floral blanket. *At least the girl's alive*, Nadia thought, but that was the only positive thing about the current circumstances. Nadia went out on the balcony and joined Kati, who was leaning against the railing with false nonchalance.

'Did you have to kill the other boy, too?' Nadia asked.

'We might have been exposed if I hadn't. It was a purely practical consideration.'

Nadia knew Kati well enough to know that it would be impossible to talk to her right now. She turned back towards the kitchen, where she had already started to prepare a nutritious and nourishing meal for Didi.

'If you have some idea of how to handle this better, I'm all ears,' Kati called after her.

Nadia turned to look at her friend's face and tried to divine what exactly was going on, but Kati's eyes were inscrutable as ever.

'For me, the heart of all this was that we would be honest with each other,' Nadia said. 'We knew that freedom had its price, and for all these years, the only thing I've been afraid of is the satyrs. Do I need to be afraid of you, too?'

'Don't you worry your pretty little head, you just go ahead and cook up your little broths,' Kati snapped. 'I'm the one who gets to deal with all of the big messes!'

Nadia had already turned around and didn't glance back at Kati. She swallowed the bitter words that were forming in her mouth, knowing that they wouldn't be of any use right now.

She picked up a fistful of herbs in addition to the nuts she had already chopped and minced them finely, to find comfort in their essential oils. The kettle whistled, and she poured the steaming water into the cup, adding a few drops of an essence she had distilled.

'What's in that?' Samuel asked, coming into the kitchen.

'I call these my clear-your-mind drops,' Nadia answered. 'That's what Didi needs now.'

'Everyone at the university is talking about what happened at the masquerade ball,' Samuel said. 'A janitor found two guys dead the next morning in the basement. Didi's probably really freaked out, just like everyone else.'

'Maybe that's a subject we should drop for now,' Nadia said, handing him the cup. 'Could you take this in to Didi?'

Samuel felt like asking Nadia if she thought Didi might have known the boys or any of their friends, but Nadia clearly was in no mood to talk. He took the mug and went and knocked on Didi's door. There was no response, so he quietly snuck in. He sat down on the edge of the bed and placed the cup on the nightstand.

'Nadia made you something to drink,' he said. 'She says it will make you feel better.'

Didi had peered at him from under the corner of the blanket, but now she drew a pillow over her head. 'I don't want to feel better.'

'It sure is creepy. No one knows what happened,' Samuel said, stroking Didi's shoulder.

I know exactly what happened, Didi thought. *I smiled at the guy with the lighter hair and he started following me. By that point he no longer stood a chance. When I put my arms around his neck and wrapped my legs around his waist, he was already dead, even though he didn't know it. And I loved every minute of it.*

The euphoria had continued to flow through Didi's veins on Sunday, too. She climbed out of bed when evening fell and admired her glowing skin and red lips in the mirror. Her hair gleamed, and she felt like she could conquer the world. On Monday morning she was excited about her art history lecture, but she only made it a few feet past her front door before the tabloid headlines punched her in the face.

TWO STUDENTS BRUTALLY MURDERED! She had no trouble identifying the young man from the photograph, the young man whose name hadn't even interested her, overcome as she had been with lust. She tried to hurry past the headlines, but it was even worse at the university. Some people were crying, others were gossiping, but the air was thick with the aftermath of the masquerade ball. Didi had sat in her lecture for a little while, but then she had been forced to run back home.

Now the fragrance of the herbs was rising to her nostrils, and she slowly sat up. The drink Nadia had prepared for her had cooled a little, so Didi sipped it, eyes closed. She might be a wreck, but one thing was for sure: this would never happen again. She had to get her nymph urges under control or rid herself of them completely.

Didi hadn't made any real friends at the university, because she was afraid of being caught. Plus, she was also jealous of the other people's mundane problems compared to her own. Her mother was lost or dead, she was a killer, and she lived with two make-believe creatures . . . Didi lowered the nearly empty mug back to the nightstand and pulled the laptop onto her lap. She needed someone to talk to, someone to cheer her up.

It didn't take long for Didi to reach Laura, and her friend's smile and warm eyes were more effective at calming Didi than Nadia's soothing drink. Then again, Laura didn't look very happy. *It's that asshole Lasse*, Didi thought, but she didn't say anything out loud.

'I'm sorry I've been such a bad friend lately,' Didi said. 'I've just been going on and on about all my own problems, and I haven't been listening to you at all.'

'I love hearing about your classes and all the exciting stuff you're doing,' Laura answered. 'Who are you going to tell all that stuff to, if not your friends? We've never kept any secrets from each other.'

'No, we haven't,' Didi said, even though she almost choked on the lie.

'I don't even have anything interesting to tell,' Laura said. 'Things are going well with Lasse, at least eighty-five percent of the time.'

'And the other fifteen percent is a total hell,' Didi said, knowing that her friend was lying and keeping secrets of her own.

Now Laura was on the defensive. 'Just because you're going through problems doesn't automatically mean everyone else's life is a mess. If you're not happy, do something about it.'

'You're right,' Didi slowly said, her thoughts growing clearer. Maybe Nadia's elixir really did work. 'I don't like myself this way. And I'm going to put a stop to it.'

CHAPTER 36

It was easy for Didi to skip lectures without feeling any pangs of conscience, but work was a different matter. In the first place, Didi didn't want to leave Valtteri in a bind, and in the second, the cafe gave her other things to think about. It felt good working with people, pretending she was one of them. The simple sensation of holding a dishrag in her hand brought her satisfaction. A new customer, a middle-aged man with a gentle, bear-like demeanor but a keen gaze sat waiting for a couple of minutes before Didi managed to make it over to him.

'Are you ready to order?' she asked with a sunny smile.

'Coffee,' the man said, spreading out his paper. The front page was calling for a hunt for the masquerade ball murderer. Didi shivered. She had forgotten all about it for a second.

The man clearly noted her reaction. 'Pretty strange case. But I guess there's all kinds of Satan worship and stuff going on these days. It was a full moon that night.'

'Was it?' Didi managed to squeak out. 'Anything else, or just the coffee?'

'Desirée,' he said, focusing his analytical eyes on her. 'Detective Harju, National Bureau of Investigation. Why don't you have a seat?'

Didi slowly sank into the bench across from the man. The fear that she would be caught was paralyzing. For once she wished she had Kati with her.

'Why don't I help you get started,' the man said, after waiting a second for Didi to say something. 'You were a normal schoolgirl from a small town. Everything was fine: you had friends and you lived with your mother, who was a doctor. And doctors prescribe medication.'

Now Didi raised her eyes to look at the senior detective. She wasn't sure where this anecdote was heading, but she tried to pay attention so she could cook up an explanation for everything he said.

'You had a boyfriend, Johannes,' Harju said.

'Johannes died.'

'So you moved away, changed your last name to Tasson, forged papers and started studying art history at the university.'

Didi was completely blown away. How could a man she had never met before know so much about her? Nadia and Kati had assured her that their cover was airtight and no one would find them.

'Shall I continue?' Harju asked, and Didi nodded. 'Then your mother packed her bags and took off for Ecuador just like that.'

Harju dug into his pockets and pulled out a slip of paper, evidence to support his claims. It was a copy of a plane ticket. Didi grabbed it with both hands and tried to digest the news she had just received. She was incapable of hiding her shock. The old detective had completely thrown her off.

'I guess you didn't know that bit,' Harju said. 'Your photograph has come up in the investigation of the murders of four young men. I'm sure you can help us.'

Didi took a deep breath. Now she had to stay calm. Harju might have more critical information for her to gain, but she must not reveal anything to him, even by accident.

'Why are you saying Johannes' death was a murder?' Didi asked. She started shoving the slip of paper into her apron pocket, but Harju pulled it out of her hands.

'Were you at the masquerade ball on Saturday night?'

'No,' Didi said, steadily eyeing Harju, who suddenly seemed to warm to her.

'There's nothing for you to be afraid of. You can tell the truth,' he said. 'But this isn't the place. Come to the police station at eleven AM tomorrow and we'll talk some more. Will you be there?'

Harju handed his calling card to Didi, and she nodded. Then Harju shoved his paper under his arm and left.

Didi sat there for a moment longer. The day that had started so well was now heading in totally the wrong direction. But at least now she had some information on Elina. And at least Elina wasn't dead. That was an immense load off Didi's shoulders. Somehow she didn't feel so alone in the world any more. Ecuador was a long way away, but now she had some way of contacting her mother. Didi still couldn't wrap her brain around the idea that Elina wasn't her mother. During their arguments, Didi had always wished that Elina would disappear from the face of the earth, but then when she finally did . . .

Didi worked the rest of her shift, completely numb. She smiled at people when she was supposed to and brought orders out to the tables, but it was like she was a robot. She couldn't understand why Elina hadn't been in touch, even just to tell Didi that she was fine. What hurt her even more was that Elina hadn't asked Didi how she was doing. She was the one who had been left in the care of strangers, after all!

Besides, Elina owed her a lot of explanations. The list was a long one: How had Didi ended up with Elina? Who was her real mother, let alone her father . . .

But despite all the anger that Didi wished she felt, the primary emotion she experienced was longing, the desire to see Elina again. An idea started to simmer in her mind.

The work day was finally coming to a close, and Didi wanted nothing more than to take off her apron and sit down and enjoy a large café au lait, when one of the tables called for a waiter. She looked at the couple. They had already ordered all kinds of things: wine, coffee, croissants, macaroons. The woman was young and very blonde. Her hair was plaited in an intricate braid and, despite her casual clothes, she looked as sinewy as an athlete. The man, on the other hand, was very dark, and his nearly black hair gleamed. He was wearing a black sport coat that was cut a little longer than usual and had an old-fashioned collar. The eyes of many female customers were glued to him.

Didi straightened out the hem of her apron and approached the table. The woman gave the man a look full of meaning, and he turned around. His mouth cracked open slightly and he lifted his chin, which was covered in a short, groomed beard.

'What can I get you?' Didi asked, trying to avoid his intense dark eyes.

'May I look at you for a moment?' the man asked, without a trace of shame.

'Staring isn't exactly polite,' Didi said. Oddly enough, she was starting to blush at the throat.

'Aah, but it would be a waste not to look,' the man said in a low voice. 'I would never forgive myself if I didn't take advantage of this opportunity.'

He spoke in a slightly antiquated tone, and Didi felt as if she were the butt of some joke, but then the man held out his hand. Didi didn't know what she was supposed to do. The woman just sat there, her lips arched in a faint smile. The man was handsome and by no means unpleasant. On the contrary, there was something magnetic about him. *Debonair* was a word that used to appear in old novels sometimes. Almost involuntarily, Didi held out her hand, and the man took it. And did not let go.

'What do you feel?' the man asked.

Electricity surged from the man into Didi, and a thousand images flooded her mind, sounds, rhythms, something inexplicable. Didi had to use all of her strength to wrench free.

'He does that to everyone,' the woman laughed. 'Don't let it bother you. Could you please bring me another glass of red wine?'

'Of course.'

Didi was infinitely grateful for the opportunity to escape. She rushed into the back room and flung her apron on the chair. She had no intention of serving anything to the table any more.

Erik's satyr breast had been filled with turmoil a moment ago, but now an utter calm took over. Frida had arranged a happy surprise for him. He was so close to his goal. Goddammit, he had already touched the redheaded nymph of legend. Nothing could stand in his way now.

'Thank you,' Erik said to Frida.

'Don't thank me. Promise me,' Frida answered.

'You will not dictate conditions to me,' Erik said, even though now he was in an accommodating mood.

'I want Kati.'

'Revenge arouses powerful emotions,' Erik said, shoving the last bit of croissant into his mouth. His hand was still tingling, but there was no way he would be revealing to Frida all the thoughts that were going through his head. Yet perhaps it would be best to keep the huntress satisfied. 'All right. You can have Kati. You have until the next full moon.'

Frida emptied her glass and sat there musing, pondering whether she would take Kati's life quickly or very, very slowly.

CHAPTER 37

Frida and Ana-Claudia had experienced countless hot summers together, but for some reason the summer of 1994 in Nesebar felt like the hottest ever. The satyrs had been away from the manor for an extended period and were not expected back for a while still. Which is why Frida and Ana-Claudia could loll in the sweat-drenched afterglow of their lovemaking and allow their breathing to even out in peace.

'I never want this to end,' Ana-Claudia said, stroking the white flesh of Frida's thigh.

'It won't.'

Frida tenderly took hold of Ana-Claudia's hand and guided it upwards. But suddenly she stopped; their languid world was under assault. Ana-Claudia also heard the gravel crunching out in the court-yard of the manor, and an instant later there was a knock at their door. The nymphs held their breath and looked each other in the eye. Ever since their first moment together, they had feared being caught. The satyrs did not countenance relations between nymphs, and the punishment for the crime was monstrous enough to keep most nymphs in line. But for Frida and Ana-Claudia, love surpassed their fear.

Kati's low voice carried in from the corridor: 'Ana-Claudia? Frida?'

Frida rushed to the door and cracked it open as Ana-Claudia frantically collected their gauzy summer garments from the floor.

'Mitchell's back early,' Kati said. 'Lucas, too. Something's going on. Clean up and get dressed, I'll head them off.'

Kati didn't need to explain to either of them what would happen if Mitchell caught wind of the carefully guarded relationship between the nymphs. Let alone Erik.

Kati hurried to the foyer, where Mitchell and Lucas were leading a third man into the study. There was a tattered bag over the man's head, and his hands were bound. He was cowering in pain and fear. Kati watched the satyrs and allowed them to sit the man down in a chair. Then they all waited on Erik's pleasure. The lord and ruler of the manor would show up when he felt like it. Kati's neck hairs rose in exasperation.

'Such oppressive weather,' Erik said, even though he was wearing a sport coat of dark wool. The heat didn't appear to bother him in the least. 'I wish it would rain, that would make it a little more pleasant. Wouldn't you agree?'

Erik drew the bag from the man's head and skewered him with his penetrating stare, waiting for an answer. The quivering prisoner managed to produce something resembling a nod. Erik waited for a moment and then gestured for Kati to approach, indicating the leather thong visible beneath the man's shirt. Kati drew it from the man's neck and held the pendant aloft for all to see. The silver oak leaves gleamed faintly.

'It's not mine,' the man protested weakly.

Erik dropped the pendant into his pocket and took a leather cylinder from the table. He held it right up to the man's eyes and waited for an answer, without saying a word.

'I don't know anything about that,' the man said. 'Some woman gave it to me.'

Mitchell stepped in closer to them. He wanted to take a little more control of the situation. After all, he was the one who brought in both the man and the cylinder.

'He was right where Rose said he would be,' Mitchell said. 'There was also one queen-of-the-night, but it hadn't had time to flower yet.'

Erik opened the cylinder, removed the scroll of parchment within, and scanned it.

'You don't even need to tell us about this,' he said to the man. 'The document speaks for itself.'

For a second, the man appeared relieved, but Erik immediately pressed a palm to his chest. The man flailed for a moment and died with a hoarse moan. Erik stood up as casually as if he had just completed some mundane task and handed the scroll to Mitchell. He glanced at Kati, whose face hadn't so much as quivered this whole time.

'I thought we had killed off the entire Oakheart family,' Erik said. 'Find this place and whatever it is that this Oakheart has hidden there. And Kati, could you clean up this mess?'

The satyrs left, and Kati remained in the room. Even though she was no stranger to violence herself, Erik's deed repulsed her. She had resorted to force on many occasions to save herself or one of her sister nymphs. Yet she found Erik's way of using his might and his powers repugnant. But for the moment, she knew that it was wisest to play docile and obey. *Even a little annoyance is still an annoyance*, she thought, as she dragged the body across the floor and rolled it up in one of Erik's expensive oriental carpets. Erik valued his fine possessions, so maybe next time he'd think twice about who he left with the cleanup job.

Kati carried out her duties quickly, but she waited until evening before calling the others together in one of the nymphs' bedchambers. She had invited Nadia, Rose, Ana-Claudia and the already reluctant Frida. She had explained to them what had happened and waited for a moment for them to digest the situation.

'What was on the parchment?' Frida asked.

'Our names,' Kati answered. 'That's why they will slay us at the next full moon.'

Frida would not relent. 'And why should we believe you?'

'Why would I make anything like this up? The satyrs believe that they have discovered a legend, and they intend to kill anyone who knows about it.'

'It's a fairy tale, nothing more,' Frida said disparagingly.

Now Rose chimed in. 'But what if it's not? The next lunar eclipse is two months from now, in France.'

'And the satyrs believe that the nymph of the legend will be born then,' Kati continued. 'They have to kill me, Nadia, Ana-Claudia and Rose.'

'Why wasn't my name on the list?' Frida asked.

'Because it's just a fairy tale to you,' Rose whispered.

Kati made an impressive sight, standing in the middle of the room in her tight trousers and tall boots. She wanted to take charge of things, because she had one goal, and now was the moment to announce it.

'There's only one way for us to survive. We must flee.' Kati's steely gaze circled the room, looking each of the nymphs in the eye. 'Nadia, your love was taken from you because of the legend of the knot. My sister Rose, they want to fetter you to die under the moonlight, because you know too much about the knot. Ana-Claudia and Frida, it is only a matter of time before your love is exposed to the satyrs, and that will be your end. Flight is our salvation, but it will bring us an even greater prize: Freedom.'

Ana-Claudia had taken Frida's hand, and Kati knew she had convinced the darker nymph. That was all she needed; Ana-Claudia would surely bring Frida round. Nadia was prepared to do anything in the name of freedom, and Rose . . . Kati took a deep breath and tried not to think about the life growing inside Rose, the life that had put them in death's way. She couldn't even imagine the magnitude of Erik's fury if he somehow discovered that Rose was pregnant, and of all things, to a human.

The nymphs conferred for a moment longer, and then the others exited, leaving only Kati and Rose.

'Why does Frida have to be so aggravating?' Kati snapped as soon as she and her sister were alone.

'She's exactly like you are,' Rose answered.

'Yeah, right!'

'Strong, decisive, capable,' Rose said.

Kati hugged her sister and they held each other for a moment. The future might be frightening, but there was no room for fear.

Later that night, Ana-Claudia listened carefully to make sure Mitchell was truly lost in a deep slumber before unwinding herself from the sheets and creeping out of the room. The corridor was empty, and before long she was in Frida's room. She slipped into the bed next to her beloved.

'Let's leave with the others the night after the full moon,' Ana said.

'Earlier you just wanted things to keep on going the way they are forever.'

'With you,' Ana answered. 'Once we leave here, we won't have to be a secret any more – all of this sneaking around will come to an end.'

'It's dangerous,' Frida whispered, leaning her head against Ana's knee. 'But I'll do whatever you want.'

Ana raised her lover's face and pressed a long, tender kiss to her lips. But Frida was already feeling greedy. Their escape loomed ahead, and it made her blood flow hotter. The risk was immense, but if afterwards Ana were hers and hers alone, and she were Ana's . . . At Nesebar they were at the mercy of the satyrs, prisoners of their own free will. Maybe the risk was worth it. Nor did Frida care about consequences at this moment, as she caressed Ana's full breasts.

Ana moaned softly in protest: 'Frida.'

'Mitchell can't hear,' Frida said, pulling off her own nightgown. 'Shhh.'

CHAPTER 38

Bienvenidos a Ecuador! Didi was sitting on the floor of the room she had turned over to Samuel, looking at the faded postcard she had managed to grab that night when Nadia and Kati had come to take her away. When Harju had shown her the copy of Elina's plane ticket to Ecuador, she instantly knew where her mother might be. All the pieces clicked into place.

'I'm so freaking jealous.'

Didi started. She was so lost in thought considering her potential next steps that she hadn't noticed Samuel enter.

'You got to see a real live volcano,' Samuel went on. 'All I got was a postcard like that. And when you came home, you had a piece of lava from Cotopaxi. I thought it was so incredibly cool, but you wouldn't even let me touch it.'

The memory made Didi smile the way she was in the postcard photograph. In it, she was a little girl sitting on Elina's lap in the square of a small Ecuadorian town. Now she had to somehow get past Samuel – who to top it all off was wearing a sleeveless gray T-shirt – without wanting to fall into his arms.

Samuel didn't make it easy on her. As soon as she stood up, he came over next to her.

'I've been reading about allergic reactions,' Samuel said. 'I was wondering if there could be something that made me faint out there in the woods or the first time we kissed. But I couldn't come up with a good explanation.'

'I have to go,' Didi said.

'And there's something weird about Kati and Nadia. I can't exactly put my finger on it, but whenever I'm with them, I have this feeling that they have some secret they're not letting me in on. You too . . .'

Didi practically pushed Samuel out of her way. She had already tossed her most necessary belongings into the bag she was taking with her, and she snatched it up from the sofa. She had a plan, and she wasn't going to let Samuel stand in her way under any circumstances – or Kati and Nadia either. So she had to get out of the apartment before they came home.

'Where are you going?' Samuel yelled. 'What's going on here?'

Didi felt like she owed Samuel an explanation, and she weighed her words carefully. She read pain and panic in his eyes, and she also saw that Samuel seriously believed he could help her. But that was impossible. What had happened earlier at the cafe with the detective, and then that strange dark man and ice-cold blonde, had made her cautious. She didn't want to give Samuel the tiniest clue of how afraid she was. She was no longer in control of the situation; all she wanted to do was to get away. That would be best for Samuel, too.

'Samuel, don't stay here,' Didi urged with all of her heart. 'Nothing good will come of it.'

'What are you talking about?'

'Promise me you won't stay here.'

Samuel grabbed Didi by the shoulders. Evidently he had been thinking about something and he wanted to stop Didi so he could get a proper answer.

'Are you sick or something? Is that why you want to leave me?' Samuel's touch ate away at Didi's resolve. She knew that Samuel would find the truth incomprehensible, but a story that held a seed of the truth might be enough. She was just about to answer when she realized she was looking at something familiar. A silver pendant on a leather thong hung against Samuel's bare chest. The pendant bore three oak leaves.

'Where did you get that?' Didi asked.

'My dad,' Samuel answered, bewildered.

A second ago Didi had been on the verge of confiding in Samuel, but now things were more confusing than ever.

'I have to go,' Didi said as rudely as she could, pulling the door shut behind her as fast as possible so Samuel wouldn't see her tears.

'This doesn't make any sense!' Samuel yelled, even though he wasn't sure Didi could still hear him. 'You're ice cold, and then you're totally hot. We move two steps forward and then suddenly everything's a huge mess again!'

Samuel stared in disbelief at the door that had been practically slammed in his face. He went into the living room and sat down to think things through. The way Didi set him off was infuriating. Then he was having these inexplicable fainting spells, even though he had always been strong as an ox. And if that weren't enough, he was starting to doubt his own mental health.

But now he was in the apartment alone. It was time to take advantage of the situation. There was an old dresser in the living room. He opened the topmost drawers. There had to be some clue somewhere as to the identity of these strange women who had taken Didi under their wing, some clue as to what this was all about. He looked for documents, for any information at all, and was prepared to tear the flat apart without worrying about the consequences. And then the doorbell rang.

Two men were standing at the door.

'Good evening,' said the older one, who was wearing a trench coat that had seen better days. 'We're looking for Desirée Tasson. She was supposed to pay us a visit at police headquarters at eleven today, but she never showed up.'

'Didi's not at home,' Samuel said. 'And I don't think she's coming back.'

'You don't say,' the detective replied, stretching out his neck to get a better view of the apartment. 'And who are you?'

'Samuel Koski, a friend.'

'I'll give you my card, Mr Koski. Give us a call if you hear anything about Desirée.'

Samuel closed the door. Luckily the police hadn't tried to enter. This was a new turn of events, though, and now he was even more desperate to find out something, anything. Samuel ran into Kati's room and looked around, not knowing where to begin. He had never been in there before. *You can't exactly accuse her of being a neat freak*, he thought, as he took in the unmade bed and the clothes thrown hither and thither, most of which were made of leather. There was something seriously kinky about that chick. Samuel saw a laptop on Kati's desk. Maybe he'd find something useful on it. He opened it.

'What are you doing in here?'

Samuel almost jumped out of his skin. Kati had appeared soundlessly behind him.

He turned towards Kati and answered her directly to her face, even though her expression made his skin crawl. 'I'm looking for something that would explain who you are and where you're from.'

'You're not going to find anything,' Kati said, shoving him out of the room with a firm push.

But Samuel had the courage to speak his piece now, since it felt like he had nothing left to lose: 'This isn't normal.'

'Pack up your stuff and get out of here,' Kati said, leaving him standing there.

Samuel saw Nadia in the living room. She came over to him silently and took his hand. Nadia's gaze was empathetic, but her tone was impassive. 'You should do what Kati told you to.' Samuel nodded and headed for his own room. He had no idea where he would go, but there was no way he was going to stay here any more.

'Do you know where Didi is?' Nadia asked.

'Didi split,' Samuel said before shutting himself in his room. 'She packed and split.'

Nadia looked at Samuel's closed door for a moment and then followed Kati out onto the balcony. They sat there in silence until the front door shut and they knew Samuel had gone.

Suddenly Nadia felt a hand around her throat, and the stiletto knife glittered in Kati's other hand.

'I've sworn to take care of Didi,' Kati hissed. 'You're hiding something from me.'

Nadia closed her eyes. She had no intention of answering until Kati had released her. Apparently the other nymph was able to read her thoughts, because the knife whirled back into Kati's pocket. Her other hand remained at Nadia's throat.

'Erik's here,' Nadia said, focusing her gaze on the moon that was now just a quarter full. She had been keeping secrets inside for so long, they had started boiling in her veins like poison. She had to get it all out. 'Besides, you've been keeping a few secrets from me, too. Like the fact that the love of my life, who was supposedly killed centuries ago, is alive after all.'

Kati's grip on Nadia's throat eased off, but her gaze remained impassive. Kati knew that despite her soft demeanor, Nadia was capable of being utterly ruthless. But the knowledge of Erik's presence made her re-evaluate the situation. She had to be careful about what she revealed.

'Come on, tell me,' Nadia demanded. 'Did you lie to me about Jesper?'

'We have to find Didi,' Kati said. 'Where is she?'

'Probably pretty far by now. The cash stash is empty.'

CHAPTER 39

Erik was enjoying a leisurely dinner in his hotel suite. He was not in the least perturbed by the fact that Frida was waiting impatiently in the background, or that the man in front of him was sweating bullets. Erik eyed him as he carved a slice of bloody entrecote and nodded at Frida, indicating that she should feel free to pour more wine. Jesper had casually seated himself in an armchair and didn't make the slightest sign of lifting a finger.

Erik paused for a moment to consider the piece of meat on his fork. He put the fork in his mouth and chewed carefully before turning once more to look at the young detective before him.

'Am I understanding correctly?' Erik asked. 'You did know where the girl was, but now you no longer do?'

'We're not totally sure,' Hannula explained. 'The kid, Samuel Koski, said that she might have left the country.'

'But you did know where Desirée Tasson was living,' Erik repeated, articulating every word very clearly.

'I didn't receive that information until today,' Hannula said, an edge of panic in his voice. 'And neither did my boss. I had to finish up at work, and then I came straight here.'

Erik nudged his plate aside and sipped a mouthful of red wine. The next time he lifted his head and looked at Hannula, his eyes were glowing red.

'You will find Desirée,' Erik said. 'Then you will come back here and tell me where she is.'

'I'll do my best.' Hannula nodded and turned around, hoping to leave, but suddenly Jesper was standing in front of him.

'No, you won't do your best,' Erik said. 'You will find her. Or else you can say goodbye to your wife and your child. I will allow you time to do that before your own demise; I am not unreasonable.'

Jesper stepped aside, and Hannula hightailed it out of the suite.

Jesper stretched out his arms. 'Do you need me right now? I could head down to the health club.'

Erik didn't answer, he just gave a barely perceptible nod, and Jesper went into his own room. Erik waited a moment for him to leave, and then he focused his attention on Frida.

'I'm going to have to break my word,' he said drily. The nymph's rage was palpable, although she hadn't betrayed the slightest reaction. 'You misjudged the situation when you introduced our little redhead to me. She spooked. Now Desirée has disappeared, and our deal is off.'

Before he knew it, Frida was behind him, holding a broad-bladed knife to his throat.

'I didn't break the deal,' Frida hissed.

Erik grabbed the front of Frida's blouse in his vise-like grip and hurled her to the ground. Frida's head struck the floor, and she was momentarily unable to move. Erik took his time and calmly straddled her, making any resistance totally pointless.

'I don't care about Ekaterina, and I don't care about you,' Erik said, almost politely. 'But I must have Desirée!'

Frida was seething with rage. This amused Erik and he slightly loosened his grip. He was caught completely off guard when a plate crashed violently into his temple. This time, it was Erik who fell to the plush carpet. Frida sprang to her feet, and Erik didn't have time to roll out from under the blow aimed at his diaphragm. In an instant, the nymph had the knife pressed up against Erik's throat again. Erik grinned through the pain. Good lord, this nymph was hungry for vengeance.

'I didn't betray you, so the deal is on,' Frida said. 'Kati is mine!'

As he left for the hotel gym, Jesper sensed that Erik and Frida would fight, but he thrust the thought from his mind. He grabbed his gym bag from the back of the chair, but it was all for show. He quickly took the elevator to the second floor, and when the doors opened, he glanced around.

At first he didn't see anyone, but then Nadia stepped out from behind a pillar and Jesper rushed over, eagerly hungry for her.

Nadia grabbed him by the front of his shirt and pulled him into her. They backed into a dark corner and kissed passionately. Jesper's hands had barely made it under the hem of Nadia's white cotton dress before she laughed and took off running down the corridor.

'Not here, Jesper.'

They tried the door to the staff stairway, and it was open. They wrapped themselves up in each other's bodies and whirled into the dim stairwell. Nadia's hands were unbuttoning Jesper's trousers when there was a sudden thud and Jesper fell to the hard floor. The next blow struck Jesper in the esophagus and he lost his breath. Nadia cried out in a panic, ready to fight, when she realized she was staring into Kati's ice-cold eyes.

Kati bent down next to Jesper and grabbed the satyr by his blond crop. 'What have you done with Didi?'

'Ekaterina,' Jesper rasped, but his expression was amused. 'Of course you used Nadia as bait. For you, Nadia is nothing but a useful tool . . .'

A fresh blow instantly silenced Jesper. Kati left the satyr on the floor and walked over to Nadia, waiting for her to pick a side.

'We don't have Didi,' Jesper coughed.

'Jesper has no reason to lie,' Nadia assured Kati, but the mountain nymph tossed him furiously against the wall.

'Why should I believe you? Kati asked, barely holding back her rage. 'You're responsible for what has happened to Didi.'

Jesper had crawled up to his knees, and gradually rose to his feet. He was leaning heavily against the railing, trying to breathe. Nadia wrenched free from Kati's grasp and rushed over to him.

'Nadia and I have been holding Erik off,' Jesper said.

'Feel free to give our greetings to Erik,' Kati spat. 'None of us will ever return to his covey. Just the opposite. This time I'm the hunter, and Erik is the hunted.'

Kati walked down the staircase a few steps. Nadia held Jesper's hand and watched her descend.

'Nadia, are you coming or not?' Kati asked.

Nadia's dark brown eyes were molten as she removed her hand from the satyr's grasp. Jesper lunged for it, but in vain.

'Forgive me,' Nadia said, as she followed Kati down the darkened stairs.

CHAPTER 40

It was at the airport that Didi became aware of how helpless she really was. She had never traveled alone before, and when she added to that the fear of being caught, it felt like she was bathing in a cold sweat at every security check. It wasn't until she made it onto the plane that she had time to properly consider what she had done and what she was doing now. Under other circumstances, Didi might have even laughed at the knowledge that her taking all of Kati's money must have thrown the mountain nymph into a total tizzy. But this theft was on a much more serious level than some minor annoyance. Yet emptying Kati's stash had been the only way of carrying out her plan.

Whatever that plan is, Didi thought as she snuggled under her blanket and tried to edge away from the man sitting next to her, who was eyeing her extremely appreciatively. She had no guarantees that her mother was where she imagined she would be. Still, her hunch had been so strong that she had been compelled to act. And to leave Samuel. She needed to get some distance from everything. She was dangerous to Samuel, and she herself was in danger. The nymphs and the police were on her tail, not to mention that strange dark man from the cafe who had made her skin crawl. What exactly had happened there? The questions crisscrossed Didi's mind, and there was no way she could ever have slept, even if she had dared.

Didi had been traveling for almost two days straight when the bus pulled into the square at Latacunga. The landscapes had started to look familiar before they arrived at the village, and Didi remembered the strange sensations she had experienced when Elina had brought her there as a small child. At first she had had a hard time not being put off by the unfamiliar smells and all the other differences, but gradually she had warmed up to the locals' lack of affectation and unhurried way of life. Mom seemed so much more relaxed, quicker to smile, than she ever did at home.

Now Didi realized that this tiny town in a remote corner of Ecuador was Elina's spiritual homeland, and she had perhaps been yearning for it all these years. That's why Elina had to be here now, too.

Didi looked around for a moment so she could get back into the vibe of the place. The colors and scents were the same, but the scale was different. As a child, she had thought that the plaza was enormous, but as it turned out, it was just a little village square. Food and clothes were being sold on stands, and on the church steps a little distance away someone was playing a guitar and someone else was reading a paper; close by children were playing football. As if of their own volition, Didi's feet started leading her down a narrow lane towards the edge of town, until she saw a small, red stucco house. The shutters were drawn, but a dark green linen shirt hung on the line. Didi gasped. There couldn't be a clearer sign of her mother's presence. She practically ran up the stairs of the house.

She waited a second before she knocked. There was no response, but Didi's keen hearing could make out the scrape of chair against floor from inside.

'I'm here,' Didi said in a loud voice, and took a couple of steps backwards.

The door flew open, and Elina immediately wrapped Didi in her arms. Not many months earlier, Didi would have tried to wriggle free of her mother's embrace as fast as she could, but now her body was overtaken by weariness from her long journey, and she allowed herself to rest in her mother's arms for a moment. It wasn't until she pulled back from Elina that she realized that her mother was still holding a rifle in one hand.

'Why do you have a gun?' Didi asked.

Elina didn't answer. She just stared at her daughter, utterly surprised: 'How did you know where to find me?'

'We were on vacation here over ten years ago,' Didi said. 'I remember this place.'

'That wasn't exactly a vacation.' Elina led Didi in and sat her down at a small, battered kitchen table. 'It was just too dangerous at home for a while.'

Didi looked around the small house and the way it had been decorated. Everything was familiar from before; cozy. Beyond the shutters, the sky was already growing dark, and even though Didi wished more than anything that she could forget all about it, a full moon was rising.

A question occurred to Didi. She had journeyed here simply imagining that she would meet her mother, but she hadn't given a second thought to what her mother's life had been like since they had parted ways. She had just assumed that Elina would welcome her with open arms. And she had, but something about Elina had changed.

'Why did you come here?' Didi asked.

'I left you in good hands,' Elina answered.

'You mean Kati's?' Didi snapped.

Elina smiled and shook her head. 'You haven't changed a bit.'

'I'm a totally different person,' Didi said.

Elina took Didi's hand and stroked it. This was exactly the kind of tenderness, the kind of care Didi was yearning for. She was more than ready to unburden all of her feelings on Elina, when she caught something overly familiar in the older woman's eyes. Elina was looking her over like a doctor, feeling the veins in her hands.

'You might be totally different. But Didi, I know you're not human.'

Elina's words were like a slap in the face, and Didi quickly pulled her hands back.

'You're hungry, even now,' Elina continued. 'I can see it in your veins. It might seem difficult, but you'll get used to it.'

'No one can get used to killing.'

Elina weighed Didi's words for a moment.

'So Johannes wasn't the only one?' Elina waited for Didi to nod. 'You had to stay alive.'

Didi was completely thrown by the comment. So Elina accepted her for who she was. Wasn't that wrong, though? And why hadn't Elina done anything to prepare her for the future? Didi was so frustrated she felt like raging, like screaming, but she had to control herself. Maybe if she could explain how she felt, she would be able to get help.

'I'm afraid of that feeling,' Didi said. 'I'm overcome by desire. And afterwards it's like there's an electric current running through my body. I taste and smell everything so distinctly, I can make out every single blade of grass . . .'

Didi fell silent. She waited for Elina to respond by offering words of comfort, of consolation, or maybe by offering some concrete assistance, like medicine.

'I'm not your mother, and you're not my daughter,' Elina said. 'You should get used to that as soon as possible, because there's no point fighting it.'

'What if I don't want to?' Didi asked.

'Go,' Elina urged her. 'You need nourishment. The old Jeep around back is mine.'

Didi was in a state of complete shock. The brusque rejection was too much for her, and at the same time she could feel the rays of the moon reach her in spite of the shutters covering the windows. Maybe Elina could sense it too, because she went over to the side table and got the car keys.

Didi held out her hand and accepted the keys with trembling

fingers. She had just barely found her mother – or foster mother – and now she was already driving Didi out the door to have sex with some total stranger, presumably a very unlucky one. Elina, who had always warned her about boys. Elina, who had tried to keep her sheltered as long as possible. *I wish there could have been some sort of middle ground,* Didi thought, but she could already feel the spasms in her belly. She had no desire to feel the same pain she had suffered the night of the masquerade ball, and that kicked her into gear.

I wonder if Elina knows that Laura and I used to sneak out at the cabin and drive down the dirt road, Didi thought as she climbed up behind the wheel. For a second she imagined how they used to turn the radio on full blast and shriek as they raced down the bumpy road. But tonight was no joyride. She headed out of town, remembering that as a child she had seen a few bars out along the road there where the music echoed and people drank, laughed, and danced outside. A place like that would be the perfect place to hunt tonight.

To hunt . . . Didi had to admit that she knew exactly what she was doing. She wasn't just going off to flirt with boys at the local pub; she had to seduce someone for real.

Dim, colored lights were already gleaming up ahead. Didi saw a small, modest-looking bar and pulled up in front of it. Boys were sitting around outside drinking beer, and a few old men were playing backgammon, drinking coffee and *aguardiente*.

Didi got out of the car and heard the languid rhythms and soft strains of a marimba. She let them infuse her steps as she walked slowly towards the younger men. They all looked up. She swept her red hair back from her forehead and eyed each of them in turn. She took a few dance steps. One of the young men, an Indian who looked powerfully built, stood and handed Didi a bottle of beer.

'*Por favor,*' he said, eyeing Didi as she took a small sip to quench her thirst.

Didi looked into his almost-black eyes and felt the nymph inside her take over. It was like being possessed, and this time she gave in without resisting. She stepped closer to the boy and let him lead her in a dance. *This is the first time I'm doing this alone*, she thought victoriously, pulling her hair free of her ponytail. The boy wrapped a fist around her red tresses and said something in Spanish. Didi let out a tinkling laugh.

It feels so good to dance, Didi thought as she swayed to the music, but she couldn't allow the rhythms to numb her. The moon was already high in the sky, and the nagging sensation was running through her veins. She had to get the boy somewhere out of sight, somewhere where they could be alone.

'Do you want to come to my place?' Didi asked, grabbing him by the hand. Her tone of voice told him all he needed to know, and he followed her to the car.

Didi put the key in the ignition and glanced over at the boy, who looked bewildered. For a second Didi felt like she should kick this one out and find some old backgammon-playing grandpa whose days were numbered anyway, but one glance at the taut pecs bursting out under the fabric of the boy's shirt made her refocus on her own desires. Didi placed a warm hand on his thigh, stretched her face forward, and kissed him softly. She felt the boy relax. Didi looked him in the eye, started up the Jeep and drove off, still heading out of town. She drew the boy's free hand down to the hem of her skirt, where the fabric met her thigh.

A little further down the road, Didi pulled off onto the shoulder and parked under the trees. She looked at the boy again. *If I wait too long, I'm going to start feeling bad*, she thought, *and I can't afford that.* Didi slid smoothly from her seat into the boy's waiting arms. She pressed her warm lips to his lips, and didn't stop him when his hands fondled her full breasts under their nearly nonexistent covering of thin fabric. The moon was almost at its zenith, and the hot current inside Didi began to take over. She let the top of her dress slide down. The boy gently nipped at her nipples, whispering something. Didi moaned. This is the way it was supposed to happen. She opened the car door, pulled the boy out, and a second later they were on the ground. It was a warm night, and from somewhere in the distance she sensed the humid, misty cloud forest, its mosses and tree ferns. She was an orchid wrapping itself around a powerful tree trunk, glowing white in the light of the moon, opening, giving off scent.

The next time she opened her eyes, she was looking straight into the boy's eyes and he was smiling blissfully. The next instant, his gaze was empty, extinguished. Didi waited for the horror to come, the horror that had surged through her when Johannes died. It never did. Instead, her skin started to glow; she was filled with a current of electricity. She rose from the ground, pulled on her panties, and slipped into her dress. There were plenty of bushes conveniently nearby, and she grabbed the naked boy by the feet and hid him in the brush. A few extra leaves on top and it was as if nothing had ever happened.

Didi was so deliciously exhausted that when she made it back to Elina's she could barely say a word. Elina had made up a small bed for her in the back room, and Didi collapsed onto it. She fell into a sweet, deep slumber.

From time to time, she woke up to the sound of Elina busying herself about the house, but then she would drift back off to sleep. By the time she woke to the inviting aroma of food, it was the following evening.

Didi sat up in her bed and stretched pleasurably. The cool linen sheets that had softened in countless washes caressed her skin, and she would have loved to sink back into bed, but the lure of the food was overwhelming. She rose from her bed and saw a dress set out for her on the back of a chair, as well as a pair of simple white panties. The dress had a butterfly motif that was evidently local. Didi dressed and then she went into the kitchen, enticed by the tantalizing smells.

Elina had laid the table with plantains, tomato salad, a dish of herb-laced quinoa dotted with peanuts, and fried chicken. Healthy and nutritious, as always.

'This looks so good!' Didi exhaled. This time it didn't cross her mind to whine and try to wheedle money for a burger.

'I thought you might be hungry,' Elina said, sizing Didi up.

Before she even sat down properly, Didi reached for the chicken with her bare hands and tore at the flesh that was so tender it almost fell off the bone. Elina spooned everything else onto Didi's plate and watched her feast as she drank thick coffee. Didi also registered that her mother had some *aguardiente* in her glass, which was not like her. But that didn't matter now; the only thing that mattered was the aromatic food before her.

Gradually Didi sated her hunger, and she sighed. She was completely satisfied and intended on saying so out loud when she realized that Elina had not been watching her eat out of pure joy at her healthy appetite. Elina was also observing her. And that's all it took. The dead boy's smile and the image of the life fading from his eyes flashed back to Didi's mind. She had taken another human life. She had robbed someone of a family member, of someone they loved. She had coldly dragged the body into the bushes and let the forest hide her deed. Had she even bothered to close the boy's eyes? She hadn't even asked him his name . . .

The food that a moment earlier had warmed her stomach struggled to come up and Didi lunged into the bathroom. She retched it all out in spasms, and was still holding onto the toilet with both hands when Elina walked in, wiped her face, and led her back to bed.

'What have I done?' Didi's voice was raw from the vomiting, and she could taste the blood in her mouth.

'You're alive, that's the important thing,' Elina said.

CHAPTER 41

The next day, Didi put on a sun hat and worked in Elina's tiny yard, doing whatever Elina asked her to. She staked the tomatoes, turned the soil, spread the beans out to dry. She was eager to help her mother, because sweating in the scorching yard helped her forget what she had done. She knew in the back of her mind that she couldn't put off dealing with it forever. But for once she had the patience to wait until she was able to express her feelings rationally, instead of just blurting them out.

'How can you drink that swill?' Didi asked Elina, as they moved into the shade to eat and Elina boiled herself another cup of thick coffee in a small enamel bowl.

'I couldn't live without coffee,' Elina laughed.

When she heard those words, Didi lowered her face to the table. Elina couldn't live without coffee, she couldn't live without men. But Elina wouldn't die from lack of caffeine.

'What should I do, Mom?' Didi finally asked. 'I don't want to kill anyone else. I'd rather die.'

'No,' Elina said. 'When you were entrusted to my care, I made a promise. I promised to care for you and protect you in any way possible.'

Didi took Elina by the hand and waited for her to look her in the eye.

'You made that promise. And you're a doctor. A doctor is

supposed to protect and help everyone. You can't protect a killer.'

Elina shivered as Didi uttered the final sentence. For the first time, Didi saw how at a loss Elina was when faced with the situation.

'Isn't there some medicine for this?' Didi asked. 'I want to be free of this!'

'Have you talked to Nadia about it?' Elina asked. 'In the world of the nymphs, she's considered a healer, but she has also studied traditional medicine. Over the years I've had a hunch that she's performed some tests. Unfortunately, she's never discussed them with me.'

'Nadia did take some samples from me,' Didi said thoughtfully.

'You have to go back to Nadia and Kati anyway.'

'Why?' Didi huffed. 'They don't even like me. They think I always do everything wrong.'

'They can still help you,' Elina answered. 'Kati is strong and stubborn, and Nadia longs for freedom in her own way, but they are the only ones who can completely understand you.'

Elina rose from the table and drained her glass of water. She took her dishes to the sink and was about to start washing them, but Didi took the rag from her.

'Let me do that,' Didi said.

'Wow. There's a first time for everything,' Elina said, as she wrapped a scarf around her head. 'I'm going to go out and do a little more work in the garden.'

Didi washed the dishes, which gave her time to consider what Elina had said in peace. Nadia hadn't taken all those samples and analyzed her reactions for no reason. And Nadia was a healer. Didi had always just been so hell-bent on battling the older nymphs and the way they thought that she hadn't known to ask the right questions. Still, she didn't want to go back to them just yet.

Didi wandered around Elina's little home. It was compact and tidy. All the fabrics were the naturally dyed cottons and linens that Elina was so fond of. The bookshelves were filled with a range of herbals, botanicals and plant guides, all thumbed through many times. Didi picked one that specifically covered the plants of the South American rainforest, and browsed through it for a couple of hours without realizing how much time had passed. It was already growing dark when she heard Elina sprint into the house.

Elina's face was sweaty from her yard work, but her eyes were burning with a combination of fear and rage. Didi sprang to her feet.

'Someone's coming!' Elina said, getting her rifle from the corner. 'Go into the back room and shut the door. Use the furniture to barricade yourself in.'

'Who is it?' Didi asked, frozen in place.

'Go!'

With that, Elina's dread spread to Didi, and she raced into the little room and twisted the lock. She could hear someone kick in the door to the main room with a grunt. Elina cried out. Didi started shoving the dresser and bed over in front of the door, but even as she was doing it she wondered how anything was going to stop the monster that was wreaking havoc in the kitchen.

Then she heard a gunshot and the sounds of a fistfight. Didi couldn't take it any more. She had to get out there to help Elina. She thrust the dresser out of her way and twisted open the lock with trembling fingers.

The kitchen had been demolished. A man Didi had never seen before was straddling Elina. Two thick horns were jutting out of his forehead, and his eyes were two glowing red orbs, just like in Didi's nightmare. He was choking Elina, but suddenly he coughed and fell to the side, holding his chest. A curious carved knife protruded from his breast, a stream of blood dripping down the blade. Elina held onto the handle for a moment longer, but then her grip loosened.

The first sensation Didi registered was a powerful smell of iron. She leapt over to her mother's side and raised Elina's head. It wasn't until she was holding Elina that she dared to look down. There was a huge gash in Elina's stomach. Her shirt was colored through with congealing blood. Didi quickly scanned around, desperately trying to think where she could find bandages. She didn't want to leave Elina's side even for a minute. Most of all, she was worried about Elina's dreamy expression; it was as if she didn't feel the slightest pain.

'Mom?' Didi said. 'What should I do?'

Elina had to struggle to open her eyes one last time. Didi tried to raise her mother's head higher.

'Is it dead?' Elina asked faintly.

'I guess,' Didi whispered. She didn't know if it was a man or a monster or both. 'What was it?'

'A satyr,' Elina said, fumbling at her neck and pulling off a leather thong bearing an oak pendant. 'Take this.'

'I can't take your necklace,' Didi said. She was doing everything in her power to reject what she already knew in her heart to be true.

'It was against orders, but I still loved you like my own child,' Elina said.

'Mom . . .'

'Take that *nomos* dagger and hide it,' Elina whispered. 'Promise me you'll go back to Kati and Nadia. Burn all of this.'

Didi didn't answer. Elina looked at her almost angrily.

'Promise!'

'I promise,' Didi said.

'And now I've fulfilled my own promise,' Elina said. One heartbeat later, she was dead.

It was pitch dark by the time Didi rose from her mother's side. She stroked Elina's hair one last time and folded her arms across her chest. Then she pulled out the faded bedspread and lowered it over her. She didn't know what else to do.

Didi stared at the dead satyr, its face contorted in its final roar. She didn't want to touch the beast, but she had given her word. She took a deep breath, grabbed hold of the dagger with both hands, and pulled it out of the satyr's chest. As soon as she gripped the weapon, she felt a current of powerful energy, but it was impossible to say whether it was good or bad. She wiped the dagger clean and wrapped it in a towel. After that, she doused the house in *aguardiente*. A minute later she was sitting in the Jeep, and then she turned to take a final look at the burning house – the burning house that was now her mother's funeral pyre.

CHAPTER 42

It had rapidly become evident to Kati that the situation demanded action, which suited her eminently. It was clear that the satyrs were closing in, and so were the police. She had to figure out as quickly as possible what the satyrs knew. So Kati went right to the source.

Detective Heikki Hannula was sitting at his desk in his office when Kati shut the door behind her, the only source of light the pallid glow of his desk lamp.

'What have you told the satyrs about us?' Kati asked, stepping right up in front of the young detective.

'About who?' Hannula asked.

'I'm in no mood for games,' Kati said. 'About us nymphs.'

Hannula jabbed a ballpoint pen into the desk and stared at Kati, who was dressed in skintight leather yet again. A black silk top peered out from under the zipper of her jacket, and under that, pale skin rose intensely in time to her breathing. That probably should have been proof enough.

But Hannula couldn't help himself: 'How do I know that you're one of those . . . nymphs?'

Kati leaned in closer, and Hannula caught a whiff of her alluring skin. Perhaps he even expected a caress from her. Instead, Kati pressed her palm to his heart, and Hannula felt as if he had been administered an electric shock. He stopped breathing for a second.

When he recovered, Kati was sitting on the edge of his desk, clearly waiting for an answer.

'How did they get their hooks into you?' Kati asked, her tone no more sympathetic.

'I was at a bar with my wife, or she was just my girlfriend at the time. She was pregnant.' Now Hannula felt that it might just be easiest to spill the beans. 'Some crazy guy started harassing Heidi and being a total dick. I lost it. I broke his arm. It would have been a bigger deal, but "luckily" there were a couple of young lawyers there.'

'Satyrs,' said Kati, who knew how they operated.

'They settled everything right there on the spot, threatened the douche bag with a big court case. We had a kid on the way . . . I wanted to hang on to my job, and the guys said that a little favor down the road was all the payment they needed.'

Kati considered what she had heard. Nadia might trust Jesper, but she didn't trust a single satyr. And one of the satyrs was more dangerous to them than the rest.

'Does Erik know?' Kati asked.

Hannula shook his head, looking exhausted. Kati grabbed the phone from the pocket of the jacket hanging from the back of the chair.

'You don't mind if I send a text message from your phone, do you?'

'To who?' Hannula asked, knowing full well that he wouldn't be able to decline.

'To Erik,' Kati smiled without a trace of warmth. 'I'm going to make myself a date with a satyr.'

Frida lay in the dark hotel room next to Erik as he slept, utterly relaxed. That night, Erik had danced, drunk, and screwed to his satyr heart's content, and now he was breathing satisfied and steadily. But Frida couldn't sleep. These nights she spent plotting revenge were long. If she closed her eyes, her thoughts immediately flew to the past. She was running through the dim forest, weaving between the trees and leaping over rocks. On many prior occasions like this, she had been the happy huntress, but on this particular night, she was the prey. The barking of dogs echoed in the distance, and she could hear her companions panting. Rose, Kati, Nadia and Ana-Claudia tried to maintain a steady pace, but it was getting harder and harder. Ana-Claudia in particular, who was finer-boned than the others, started to lag, and they had to stop and wait for her from time to time. Now they could see the beams of flashlights in the distance, and Frida knew they had to keep going.

'Frida, I can't do it any more.' Ana-Claudia stopped in her tracks and doubled over, holding her sides.

'We can't stop now!' Kati said.

'The dogs haven't caught our scent yet, the rest of you keep on going,' Frida said, running back to Ana, even though she knew that if she and her lover didn't keep up with the others, the ship that Kati had arranged to carry them off would sail without them.

The other nymphs looked on silently. Ana-Claudia smiled weakly at them.

'We have to keep going,' Kati said.

'Would you leave your own beloved to the mercy of the satyrs?' Frida asked Kati, and saw the answer in her eyes.

'Kati, don't let Frida sacrifice her life on my behalf,' Ana said.

'Go!' Frida shouted. 'I'm staying here.'

She was determined, but her heart still froze when the other nymphs turned and continued their flight. All except Kati. Suddenly Frida felt Kati's powerful hand around her throat, and no matter how hard she struggled, the other nymph didn't relent. She sensed Kati nod at Ana-Claudia, who started back in the direction whence they had come.

'Tomorrow you will board the boat and look into the morning sun,' Ana said to Frida. 'And at that moment I will be with you, because you are free.'

Then the darkness had swallowed Ana. Frida tried to free herself from Kati's grip, but Kati didn't release her for several minutes. Frida immediately drew her hunting knife from its sheath. If she had the time, she would have gladly slain Kati. They stared each other down like the worst arch-enemies.

'If you follow Ana, you go at your own risk,' Kati said. But Frida had no choice. There was only one thing she could do. She wanted to be with Ana, now and forever. She turned and sprang off in pursuit of her lover. The barking of the dogs grew louder and louder, and she hoped she would catch up to her soul sister before Ana ended up in the satyrs' hands. Frida didn't even want to imagine what would befall her if that happened. Nor did she have time to imagine, because Lucas stepped out from behind a tree and slammed her in the breastbone with a stout branch, knocking her to the underbrush so hard that she almost passed out. Somehow Frida managed to drag herself up.

It only took a few moments before the satyrs had circled her from all directions. They stood there silently; the hounds were leashed. Mitchell stepped into the crossbeams and hurled Ana-Claudia down at Frida's side. Ana-Claudia didn't even seem to see the satyrs any more.

'I loved you for six hundred years,' Ana said, and bewilderment and love could be heard mingling in her voice.

Frida was on the verge of answering, but Ana knew where her lover kept her knife and was quicker than thought. Ana raised the knife to her throat and slashed. Warm blood spurted onto Frida's face, and an animal cry escaped her lips. Ana-Claudia sank to her knees and then to the earth. Frida collapsed on top of her, desperate to feel her final breath.

The same nightmare every night, Frida thought in Erik's luxurious bed, *and I'm not even sleeping*. Nor would it end if she killed Kati, she knew that. But at least she'd be able to take some pleasure in the vengeance.

Frida heard Erik's cell phone buzz on the coffee table. She waited to see if the satyr would react, but the evening's reveling had taken its toll. Frida warily snuck out of the bed and crept over to the phone, naked. She opened the message. A smile rose to her lips and she reread it, just to be sure. Coming face to face with Kati at nighttime was beyond her wildest dreams. She sent a reply.

Kati loved retreating to the mountains. She felt at home in the steep rock slopes above the treetops, where it was beautiful and barren. It was hard to find such spots in cities, but Kati had always been good at improvising. Now she stepped out onto the flat roof of the mid-century hotel and waited for Erik Mann. She had arrived in plenty of time, enjoyed the sensation of the wind above the city, knowing that all the pointless hubbub lay below.

She inhaled deeply. Even though the air wasn't fresh the way it was in the Carpathians, it still soothed her. She had to stay calm yet ready for anything. She hadn't spoken with Erik since the nymphs had fled from Nesebar, but a couple of times curiosity had gotten the better of her, and she had sought out places where she could observe the satyr. She had belonged to Erik's covey, after all, and had even admired him in her own fashion. But those times had passed.

Kati sensed that it was about to rain, but it didn't bother her. She imagined what it would feel like to look at Erik's storm-lashed corpse at her feet. If she were careful enough, she would rid herself of her enemy for once and for all. They would be safe.

Suddenly Kati registered movement out of the corner of her eye. She turned and saw Frida. She should have been surprised, she supposed, because in all likelihood Frida should have died ages ago. But on the other hand, she had rarely seen a nymph as strong as Frida. And now that nymph had tricked her.

Then Kati noticed that Frida was carrying her trusted weapon, her hunting bow. Frida raised it and tensed.

'You killed Ana,' Frida said.

'Ana knew exactly what she was doing,' Kati replied, as she felt the first drops of rain on her face. She also knew that this was about something much deeper, and now was the time for straight talk. 'I didn't take Ana from you. Erik did. We wanted to be free of the satyrs. Ana wanted to be free so you two could love each other without fear.'

'You don't know anything!' Frida yelled.

'Give me a break, Frida. Your little affair was not the love story of the millennium,' Kati said, to whip Frida into a rage, because she knew she didn't stand a chance against the bow.

Kati succeeded. Frida cursed and threw the bow aside. The first blow struck Kati in the knee and the second hit her in the neck, knocking Kati off balance. Frida was immediately at her throat, but Kati grabbed hold of Frida's wrists. The two nymphs were extremely well matched.

'This is for Ana-Claudia,' Frida hissed. 'I'm going to break your neck.'

'Ana sacrificed herself so you could be free,' Kati said.

That made Frida pause for a moment, and Kati took advantage of the hesitation. She flipped herself on top of the blonde nymph. The rain was whipping the nymphs mercilessly, but they barely noticed.

'Think about what Ana would have wanted,' Kati said. 'Either you can die now, or you can help us get rid of Erik. Forever.'

CHAPTER 43

During her long return flight, Didi had hidden her eyes, which were swollen from crying, behind a sleeping mask. Other than that, she had managed to make herself comfortable in her business class seat, which almost leaned back into a bed. She had wanted to leave Ecuador behind as fast as possible, and the only tickets still available were the most expensive ones. *At least the money I stole from Kati is going to a good cause*, Didi thought, although it would be lying to say she wasn't afraid of the consequences. The plane tickets had used up almost all of remaining funds from Kati's stash, and Didi took a bus from the airport to the center of town. A minor lapse in style.

On the plane, she had shivered under her blanket from equal parts exhaustion and fear. She couldn't get the horrible monster that had mauled Elina out of her mind. Up until now, satyrs had been some sort of mythical creature from fairy tales – like nymphs used to be – but that man's strength and brutality, the overwhelming smell of blood, and Elina's fading eyes came back to haunt Didi over and over.

And Didi didn't just have the satyrs to fear; Kati's fury would doubtless reach new heights. Nadia's presumably silent disapproval would be almost as bad.

So I've got satyrs, cops and nymphs after me, Didi thought, but most of all she was afraid of herself and what she might do. The very idea that she could run into Samuel at the full moon was paralyzing.

It was evening by the time Didi fit the key into the lock of her apartment door. She moved as quietly as possible, because if there were any way she could, she wanted to postpone the inevitable confrontation until the following morning. She closed the door behind her softly and was creeping towards her room when she realized that the apartment was empty. Nadia and Kati clearly weren't at home. A wave of relief washed over her, and then disappointment. She had run away, after all. The older nymphs should have been beside themselves with worry, they should have been there nagging her about coming home on time and asking where on earth she had been. Nadia should have dashed into the kitchen to prepare her a nourishing meal and a restorative herbal infusion. Kati should have shouted and sworn that she would never help Didi again, no matter what.

But maybe it was better this way. Didi walked into her room and tossed her shoulder bag onto her bed. At the same time she caught a faint whiff of Samuel's scent, and she sank to the bed, inhaling deeply. She missed Samuel. She noticed that when she thought about him, she thought about security and all the good things a girl could hope for from life.

The unfortunate truth of the matter was that she was the one who posed a threat to Samuel. The more she dared to desire Samuel, the greater the danger he was in.

And then Didi was too exhausted to think about anything any more. She took off her clothes and let them drop to the floor. She would throw them in the trash the next morning. She took a hot shower and felt some of the tension melt away from her body. She found the nightgown with the roses and lace straps folded prettily in her dresser drawer, no doubt by Nadia, and she slipped into it. She was on the verge of slipping under the blanket when she remembered the thing that she had so effectively shut out of her mind. She opened her bag and pulled out a box. She didn't dare to open it, because she didn't have the energy to cry any more. Elina's oak-leaf necklace. She hid it in the back of the dresser drawer. Then she pulled a wrapped towel from her bag and forced herself to unroll it with trembling fingers, so she could believe that it had all been real. *Nomos*, Elina had said. She stared at the knife for a moment and heard the death rattle that rose from the satyr's chest. Then she quickly wrapped the dagger back in the towel and shoved the box under her bed. The very first time she had touched the knife she had sensed the vibrations it gave off rising up her arm and settling in the pit of her stomach. She didn't know what the knife was, but she had no intention of telling a soul that it was in her possession.

Didi sat up with a start when someone yanked the blanket off her. She was disoriented, the morning sun was shining in her eyes, and it took a moment for her to realize that Kati was standing at the foot of the bed, eyes blazing.

'Where's my money?' Kati yelled.

Didi collapsed back onto the pillows in relief. Finally, something normal.

'What difference does it make?' Didi asked. 'You can always steal more.'

'I have to pay the rent and our bills! We already sink enough money into you as it is, even though you don't seem able to get that through your head.'

'We were worried,' said Nadia, who had entered the room with a steaming cup of tea. She handed it to Didi, who sat up a little straighter. 'Where were you?'

'Ecuador.'

'What the hell?' Kati snapped.

'Elina's dead,' Didi said. 'A satyr killed my mother.'

Kati stared at Didi and Nadia in turn, weighing what she had just heard.

'OK,' she said after a moment's consideration. 'We're going to

have to talk more about all this later, but right now you and I have
to go.'

'Where?' Didi asked. 'I just got back.'

'You've been called in to police headquarters, and I'm coming
with you.'

'You have to go,' Nadia agreed. 'Kati will help you, and that way
it'll be out of the way.'

'You don't have to lie,' Kati said. 'You can talk about Johannes
totally openly, for instance. If you get into a tight spot, just answer
their question with another question.'

Didi would have loved to curl back up under her blankets, but
now was clearly not the time to argue with the older nymphs. It
would be best to focus on the most critical problem.

'What should I wear?' Didi asked.

CHAPTER 44

Didi tentatively took a seat across from Detective Harju. He was shuffling papers from one stack to another, looking absent-minded. Kati stood behind Didi in her usual black leather gear, like a seen-it-all security guard and a lawyer wrapped up in one. The younger police officer, Detective Heikki Hannula, settled for listening from a seat in the corner.

'All right,' Detective Harju said. 'Let's get started here. I'm pretty confused by a couple of things related to these incidents, and I'd be grateful if I could get a few answers from you.'

'Of course,' Didi said with a slight smile. Even though Kati had drummed into her head about how little information she should give, there was still something fatherly and gentle about this Detective Harju. Which is why she was thrown off when Harju went right for the jugular.

'You were dating Johannes Metso,' Harju stated. 'What about Janne Malasmaa?'

Didi gulped and tried to remember the instructions Kati had given her. 'Are you asking if I was dating Janne Malasmaa?'

'Were you two a couple?' Harju clarified.

'No.'

Immediately after Didi denied it, Harju suddenly popped up, walked over to her and tugged a strand of red hair from her head. She yelped.

'You don't mind if we conduct another DNA test, do you?'
Harju asked, putting the lock of hair into a bag with feigned
nonchalance. 'The previous test isn't valid, since your roommate
might have had access to it.'

Didi glanced at Kati, but for some reason the other nymph was
focused on looking around the room and didn't offer her the tiniest
bit of assistance.

Harju was already moving on to the next question: 'Were you at
the student masquerade ball last month?'

'When?' Didi asked.

Now Hannula stepped up to the table and set down a blurry,
grainy photograph of a redheaded woman in a Venetian mask and a
taller, rather broad-shouldered dark-haired woman in a mask of her
own.

'Isn't that you in this photograph?' Harju asked, looking Didi
straight in the eye. Didi's vocal cords were paralyzed.

'It doesn't matter,' Kati said. 'I heard from Heikki that there
wasn't necessarily any crime involved in the deaths of those boys at
the ball. Which means you have no reason to interrogate us, especially
if we weren't there in the first place.'

Harju turned to Hannula and gave him a questioning glance, but
the other detective's face gave nothing away.

'Which is why we're leaving now.' Kati was already pulling up
the zipper of her leather jacket. She signaled for Didi to stand up. 'I
hope you won't be bothering us about this matter again.'

Kati led Didi out of the police station at a half run. 'And now for
once you might want to do exactly what I tell you to. You have no
idea how much trouble you've caused us.'

'If you guys would actually tell me something, then maybe
everything would be a lot easier,' Didi retorted, as Kati shoved the
motorcycle helmet into her hands. 'Where are we going?'

'You're going to work,' Kati said sweetly. 'That's what you
wanted, right? A normal life, a job, and going to the university. Now

is the perfect opportunity to show the police that everything is continuing as it used to and you don't have anything on your conscience. Besides, your boss has probably been wondering where you've been these past few days.'

Didi suddenly realized that she hadn't let Valtteri know about her trip. Her departure had been spontaneous, and she hadn't even been sure if she'd ever be coming back.

She started waving at Valtteri, who was out wiping the tables on the terrace, before they even pulled up at the cafe.

'And you better come straight home from work,' Kati warned Didi in a low voice, as she dropped her off.

Didi sighed and started to prepare some story to tell Valtteri. But in the end, the truth was enough.

'I'm sorry I left without saying anything,' Didi said, and tears sprang to her eyes. 'My mother died.'

Valtteri immediately gave her a sympathetic hug.

'That's all right,' he said. 'You don't have to come to work today, either, if you don't feel like it.'

'I want to work,' Didi said, extracting herself from his embrace. 'I'll feel better if I stay busy and make sure I'm around other people.'

'Good, because there's someone inside who's been looking for you.'

Didi didn't have time to protest before Valtteri was dragging her inside and sitting her down at a table, right across from Samuel's astonished gaze. *Out of the frying pan and into the fire*, Didi thought. *I'd rather serve beer to some smelly old hung-over drunk.*

Didi and Samuel sat there looking at each other without saying a word.

'I should really go put on my uniform,' Didi finally said.

'Didi, this doesn't make any sense,' Samuel said. 'Why are the police looking for you?'

'It's a long story . . .'

'That's fine,' Samuel said. 'And it doesn't make any difference, but there's one thing that keeps bugging me.'

'What?' Didi asked.

'Sometimes you act like you want me, and the next second you're treating me like dirt.'

Didi thought feverishly. She had to come up with some explanation that would keep Samuel far enough from her. Maybe a mixture of the truth and fiction would be best.

'You know that I was dating Johannes,' Didi started tentatively. 'Johannes died while we were . . .'

Samuel had lowered his head. He had also clearly given some thought to the matter, and Didi was relieved when he took her hand in his own.

'While you were doing it?' Samuel asked, and Didi nodded.

'I've been totally locked up ever since. I feel like I can't be with anyone while that's still going through my mind. It would be forcing it somehow. And that's not right.'

'Of course not.'

Didi looked at Samuel and for a second the thought crossed her mind about how easy it was to hoodwink someone so compassionate. But it was in Samuel's own best interests. She decided to add some fuel to the fire.

'Besides, I've known you for so long. You're almost like a big brother to me . . .'

And Didi instantly regretted that she had raised the topic.

'I'm not your brother,' Samuel said, eyes burning. He got up from the table.

Didi waited for Samuel to leave, but he just stood there at her side. Didi held her breath. She could feel Samuel lean down and whisper right into her ear.

'If a brother felt this way about his sister, it would be illegal,' he said, and then he walked out.

CHAPTER 45

Kati had intentionally leaked to Detective Harju that his younger colleague had revealed information about the investigation to her. And so she wasn't the least bit surprised that not long after the interrogation, Detective Hannula sent her a curt text message indicating a time and a place for them to meet. Good. She had some things she wanted to ask him, too.

That evening Kati pulled up at a small auto body shop, where men were milling around, working on all kinds of vehicles. Many of them eyed both Kati and her gleaming black Kawasaki approvingly. She found the milieu appealing herself: men in overalls wielding tools. Unfortunately, Erik also popped into her mind; a satyr was a man, too, and like all men, he loved everything with an engine that purred. Kati turned and fixed her steely eyes on Hannula.

The detective was working on a vintage American hot rod. He lowered the hood as Kati walked up.

'Fixing up a little surprise for the wife,' Hannula explained, a little awkwardly.

People are so strange, Kati thought for the umpteenth time. The wife would probably be a lot happier to have her husband at home hanging out with her, not wasting his evenings at some body shop.

'You wanted to talk.'

'That was a dirty trick, telling Harju about our conversations,' Hannula said.

'Maybe you don't have much room to complain,' Kati retorted, stepping so aggressively towards Hannula that he instinctively stepped back. 'There were only three personal items in Harju's office. An Indian dream-catcher to keep nightmares away. A picture of a girl who was clearly his daughter. And a mug shot of this man, Mauri Laasonen.'

Kati had made a careful note of the picture. In it, a burly guy with a buzz-cut was staring into the camera, his mouth nothing more than a crease and his chin thrust defiantly forward.

'Harju's home was broken into when Hanna was the only one at home. She was one spunky little girl,' Hannula said, smiling at the memory. 'She attacked the intruders, and Laasonen flew into a rage. He beat Hanna so badly he sent her to the ICU. She eventually died.'

'Was Laasonen convicted?'

'There was some snafu with the evidence, and the case fell apart. Harju tried to get Laasonen for all kinds of things. It became an obsession. His wife eventually divorced him and moved away.'

Kati sensed that there might be some useful material here: 'Is Laasonen still alive?'

Hannula nodded slowly, his eyes glued to Kati. 'What are you going to do?'

'We'll see,' Kati smiled, before turning her back on Hannula.

'Are you going to help me get them off my back?' Hannula asked.

Kati turned around. She felt like keeping Hannula in suspense a little longer, and jiggled her motorcycle keys, supposedly thinking.

'Not for your sake,' she finally said. 'But the satyrs won't be bothering you any more, because they won't be bothering anyone.'

* * *

Kati drove to the nearest shopping center. A plan had taken shape during the ride, and now she needed certain props. She had quite a few irons in the fire, it was true, but this little diversion would help her solve some bigger problems. In under an hour, Kati had picked out the perfect outfit, a blond wig, and a few other accessories. Laasonen was about to get the surprise of his life.

CHAPTER 46

'You're not going to lock me up again, are you?' Didi asked once she realized that Nadia and Kati were leading her up to the attic where they had first kept her. Of course she had done wrong when she took Kati's money, and maybe she was a little annoying from time to time, but this was going a little overboard, wasn't it?

'No,' Nadia laughed. 'But it is time for you to meet a certain someone.'

Kati shoved open the creaking door, and Didi saw a very blond, beautiful, athletic woman. She realized right away that it was the same woman who had been at the cafe with the man who had acted so strangely. The woman returned her gaze, equally curious. When Nadia rushed over to the woman and began to tend the bruises that were visible on her face and her clearly broken rib bones, the woman – and now Didi realized that she was a nymph – gave herself over to Nadia's ministrations with complete confidence. Nadia had that sort of effect on people.

'This is Frida,' Kati said.

'We've met,' Didi said.

Both Nadia and Kati looked at her and then at Frida, perplexed.

'I went to the cafe,' Frida said. 'With Erik.'

'What the hell?!' Kati hissed, but Nadia gently touched her shoulder.

'All of us escaped the satyrs together, but Frida stayed behind,'

Nadia explained to Didi. 'We belonged to Erik's covey.'

'Who's Erik?' Didi asked.

'He's the bad guy in this story,' Kati said. 'Not me. Even though that's what you seem to think.'

'He was at the cafe, too,' Didi said, gazing around the attic that had grown so familiar to her. So much had happened in such a short time, and this is where it had all begun. What she wanted most of all was to rush out of there, if that would only erase the rest of it.

'Erik spared my life.' Frida's voice was flat.

'Only because he wants Didi,' Kati said, watching how the traces of her battle with Frida faded under Nadia's healing hands. 'Have you thought about what I said? The satyrs killed Ana, and with your help we could rid ourselves of Erik for good.'

'I wouldn't be here if I hadn't thought about it,' Frida replied. The lingering enmity between the two powerful nymphs could be sensed in the air. 'Do you have a plan?'

'Of course,' Kati said, leaning casually against a ceiling beam.

'What is it?'

'We strike first.'

Didi looked at the older nymphs in astonishment. She had seen a satyr enraged, and she had no illusions about what their fate would be if they rose up against several of the satyrs at once.

'Shouldn't we hide? We could go away somewhere,' Didi suggested, but no one listened to her.

Frida pulled Kati and Nadia a little further away and talked with them in a low voice. Apparently they reached some sort of understanding, but no one bothered to explain it to Didi. Didi started to get irritated. They were treating her like a baby again. Apparently Nadia sensed it, because she took Didi by the hand. A soothing sensation spread out from her fingers, and Didi took a breath.

'Should we go home?' Nadia suggested. 'Let's have a girls' night in, just you and me.'

'What about Frida and Kati?'

'I think they have other plans,' Nadia said.

Didi let Nadia lead her along, and when the two of them made it home, Didi realized that this was exactly what she needed. It made no difference if Nadia had implanted the thought in her through her touch, because for the first time in a long time, she felt at peace. Plus, there were things that she wanted to discuss with Nadia alone.

Didi went into her room to change her clothes, but then she glanced over at her nightstand and stormed right back out. She lifted her silver picture frame up in Nadia's face. The image was of a bouquet of flowers.

'Where's my picture of Mom?' Didi asked.

Nadia removed the frame from Didi's hands and nudged the picture of the bouquet gently to the side. Elina's grave yet smiling face was revealed below. It was exactly the way Didi remembered her.

'As far as I'm concerned you can keep the photo,' Nadia said. 'Just be careful, or Kati will destroy it. She told you you couldn't keep anything from your former life.'

Didi had already told the nymphs how she had found Elina and what the consequences had been. But she hadn't said anything about the conversation she and Elina had had, and it was constantly replaying through her mind. Didi settled down on the couch at Nadia's side, and wondered again how the other nymph always managed to look so beautiful, so naturally fresh. But now she had to focus on getting Nadia on board with her plan. She pulled a bottle of white wine from the cooler, poured Nadia a glass, and handed it to her.

'Have you ever wondered if there was any way of treating our needs with medication?'

'Being a nymph isn't a disease,' Nadia said.

Didi considered the best way of phrasing all the things she had been thinking about since her trip.

'You tend yourself with water,' Didi said. 'I need flowers. You've taken all kinds of samples from me. Couldn't our hormones be regulated with some sort of pill?'

Nadia took a couple of small sips from her glass. Didi could tell that something extremely serious was on her mind.

'I've taken samples from you,' Nadia said. 'Your copulin levels are extremely high. And I know you don't want to kill anyone . . .'

Didi's eyes widened. Nadia had already revealed some critical point.

'You've already started working on something!'

Nadia nodded. Didi tried to stay calm, but she was consumed by impatience.

'If I had a drug like that,' she enthused, 'I could lead a normal life.'

'You know, don't you, that a lot of people want to be anything but normal,' Nadia said. 'There hasn't been a century I've lived in where everyone wanted so badly to be an individual, to be unique.'

'Not me!' Didi's eyes flashed, and she was already imagining the day when she could come face to face with Samuel without fear.

'It's not that simple,' Nadia reminded her. 'And you can't say anything to Kati about this yet.'

'But Kati doesn't want me to kill anyone.'

'Of course not. But Kati does want to be a nymph, a free nymph. She would never approve of a drug that would turn her into something else.'

CHAPTER 47

'I don't keep track of how old I am any more,' Jesper said, swirling the whisky around in his glass.

Frida poured herself a healthy shot, too, but she didn't say anything. Jesper's blond hair gleamed in the dim light of the hotel room, and Frida noted the occasional red flicker in his eyes, but it only lasted for a fraction of a second. She decided she'd let the satyr talk. Maybe he would reveal something useful.

'You'd think you'd get jaded over the centuries.' Jesper tossed back his whisky and immediately poured himself another. 'And yet Ninette . . . Nadia takes my breath away every time.'

Frida didn't react, but it was difficult for her to grasp what she was hearing. The satyrs she knew didn't give a fig for nymphs or their lives. As a matter of fact, she had heard how Erik had slain the remainder of his own covey to prove to the leaders of the satyrs, to the Conclave, that he was loyal to the end.

'What did Nadia say to you?' Frida asked.

'I told her and Kati to run,' Jesper said. 'Nadia told me to choose sides.'

Nadia really was audacious, Frida thought. Under that soft exterior and the endless lacy frills was a nymph who knew what she wanted.

'Goddammit!' Jesper shouted in frustration, and his eyes flashed again. 'My brain tells me that the only way to protect you renegades is to talk to Erik and convince him that he ought to spare your lives. Otherwise you'll become martyrs, which will only feed into that legend of the knot and the nymph with the red hair.'

Jesper's voice was so low it was hoarse, and Frida knew how to handle a satyr in that state. Besides, she felt like getting crazy, too, like drinking and dancing.

'You want to have some fun?' Frida asked.

'You're on,' Jesper answered. 'Who do you think can last longer?'

Frida dropped down in front of Jesper, pulled off his boots, and then put the music on. *Luckily this luxury suite Erik booked has good soundproofing*, Frida thought a second later, as the rock music sent Jesper leaping around the room, whisky bottle in his hand.

The smoky, peaty whisky warmed Frida's throat. She had no interest in the satyr's frenetic dance. What she wanted was to whirl like a dervish, removed from time and space. But Jesper's words kept echoing through her mind. She had never thought that a satyr could love, and yet Jesper had looked both anguished and blissful when he uttered Nadia's name.

Frida's mind wandered back to the first time she had seen Ana-Claudia. She had lowered herself into the pools of soft, soothing water that had been Ana's brown eyes, curious yet tranquil. Frida had resisted for a while, but she was hopelessly lost. Nymphs were not supposed to love one other. Ana had bided her time, knowing that the harder Frida struggled, the more irreversibly she would be entangled in her web. And when Frida finally gave in to her feelings, she regretted every moment she had spent apart from Ana. Frida had experienced utter satisfaction in a satyr's arms, but it wasn't until she was with Ana that she felt her soul soar.

Yet the nymphs belonged to satyrs. Frida and Ana-Claudia had had to conceal their feelings carefully and keep their shared moments of bliss a secret; they had to pretend to warm the beds of satyrs willingly, even though every moment apart was agony. Sometimes months would pass before they could find a moment to spend together. At times Ana-Claudia was afraid Mitchell suspected something, but she and her lover were skilled actors. Frida knew how to hide her feelings well, even now. Everything except for the revenge that she had tended like a rare blossom as she languished in chains. Would she ever be able to give it up? It had kept her alive, after all.

On the other hand, Frida had felt her breast leap with genuine joy when the three well-proportioned nymphs walked in through the attic door. In an instant she was back with her covey, felt its strength and unity. Before that moment, she would have never admitted to missing the companionship of her own kind. In addition, the young redheaded nymph Erik lusted after so greatly reminded her of the very freedom that Ana-Claudia had so tenaciously pursued, and for which she had died.

Frida had learned to stay on her guard so well that she wasn't the slightest bit perturbed when Erik suddenly appeared before her. Erik watched Jesper's dancing, which at this stage looked like a combination of martial arts and jive, and for a moment he allowed himself to feel the beat, too. Then he nodded his head to the side, signaling to Frida that she should follow him into the other room. Frida had no reason not to obey. On the contrary, it was in her best interests to play the sweetest, most docile nymph imaginable.

Frida followed Erik into his suite, which was of course a couple of degrees more luxurious than the lodgings she shared with Jesper.

'I want your opinion,' Erik said, walking over to the mirror to make sure that the dark suit he was wearing was impeccable. He eyed Frida in the reflection.

Half a dozen dresses and with bags to match were hanging from a garment rack. Boxes of shoes had been laid out on the bed, as well as what must have been jewelry in gift boxes.

'Which one?' Frida said, but she couldn't help the nymph inside her; she let her hands caress the silks and other costly fabrics.

'You've seen Desirée,' Erik answered. 'Choose the most flattering ensemble.'

Frida almost laughed. She could have sworn that Erik was as nervous as a boy about to go on his first date. That said a lot about how important Didi was to Erik and his scheme, whatever that was.

'I'd take this red one,' Frida said, after lingering over the clothes for what seemed like an appropriate amount of time. 'Picture those flaming red locks combined with this even stronger red. And that pale flesh . . .'

Frida noticed how Erik was practically licking his lips. Sometimes it was far too easy to turn on a satyr.

'And then these beige patent leather heels. She has those gorgeous long legs, and these will make them even more beautiful.'

Erik finally turned around to look Frida in the eye: 'But will she like them?'

'Look at these price tags!' Frida cried, as she fingered the dresses. 'These are a wet dream for a teenage girl like her.'

Erik immediately clenched her wrist in a vise-like grip. 'Never denigrate Desirée in my presence again.'

'Of course not,' Frida said submissively, but she was getting a kick out of this. 'So what's your plan?'

'I'm going to arrange a face-to-face meeting somehow,' Erik said. 'I'm going to show her what I can offer her . . . No, what she can receive from me.'

Frida started to knot Erik's tie as if all she wanted to do was serve him. 'The nymph is in your power.'

'Still, I don't want to scare her off,' Erik said. 'She's young, and certainly inexperienced . . . Now go!'

The command reverberated with impatience, and Frida departed for her own rooms.

Erik waited until he was sure Frida's door had closed. Then he called Mitchell. He could picture it in his mind's eye, how the other satyr was lounging in his bathrobe like a dandy, a nymph on either side.

Erik went straight to the point: 'I'm going to meet the nymph soon.'

'I'll inform the Conclave,' Mitchell said.

'No, you won't. I will handle this personally,' Erik said emphatically. 'You will make up some fiction if necessary.'

After a moment of silence, Mitchell spoke again. 'This might result in some pretty dire consequences. Why would I sacrifice my future for you?'

'Listen to me carefully, Mitchell. You were there with me seventeen years ago in Spain, when we found that book, the legend, that Rose had led us to. Together we dismembered the last of the Oakhearts, who had managed to keep it their secret for so many years. The legend is true. I have touched the hand of the redheaded nymph.'

'Where?' Mitchell asked. He did not receive a response.

'The important thing is that I will rise and become the next ruler,' Erik said. He knew that his best tack was to appeal to Mitchell's thirst for power, which was almost as insatiable as his own. 'You will be my right hand. Which is why you will come up with some explanation for the Conclave.'

'Have you already killed Ekaterina and Ninette?' Mitchell asked.

'I'm working on it.'

Erik tossed the phone onto the bed in annoyance. Goddamn Mitchell and the Conclave! Korda had always taken from Erik what should have been his. But this time Erik would draw the longer straw. Everything would be better on the day he took his place at the head of the polished mahogany table in Zürich and Gabriel Korda was dethroned. After some of his nymphs had managed to flee Nesebar, Erik had felt like he was being constantly monitored by Korda, and he didn't care for it in the least. He had even gone so far in demonstrating his – supposed – allegiance to the Conclave as to slay the rest of his covey with his own two hands in the presence of those dignified satyrs in their dark suits. Not that it had even pained him, since he had done it with his greater plan in mind. When the nymph of legend was under his control, there would be no barriers to block him on his way to the top.

After that meeting, Erik had met Mitchell.

'You didn't tell the Conclave about *The Book of Knots*,' Mitchell had said. 'You mean to imprison the legend and seize Gabriel Korda's position. Korda is our Master.'

'And you want to be at my side when I do it,' Erik had replied. 'I heard rumors that the fugitives might be in Montpellier . . .'

Now Erik drew himself up to his full height. His eyes rose to the photo of Didi next to his bed. The knot symbol was winking coyly on the girl's naked belly. Erik took the red gown with the deep neckline from the rack and in his imagination melded it with the photograph of Didi. The words from the old leather-bound tome rose to his mind.

When the moon goes dark above the pale hills, a nymph will be born in the forest eaves, her hair is as red as the rose . . . Bearer of the Knot of Astarte, this nymph will be raised in the cities of man, and she will not fear to wage war on behalf of the freedom of all nymphs everywhere.

He had immediately understood that the nymphs had fled precisely because of that prophecy, and that the white hills referred to Montpellier.

Erik let the dress slip down to the bed, imagined for a moment that he had just slipped it off the young nymph. The time was ripe. Detective Hannula would have the privilege of doing him one final favor.

CHAPTER 48

Didi couldn't get Samuel off her mind. She tried studying for tests, eating, organizing her clothes, just about anything to keep his face from appearing in front of her eyes. She even considered taking up knitting. And it wasn't just Samuel's face that she kept imagining. That one morning when Samuel was helping Nadia in the kitchen, and he reached up to take down a bowl from the top shelf, with his shirt unbuttoned, his pecs flexed and his butt . . . Before Didi realized it, she had pulled up Samuel's number on her cell phone. Now all she had to do was come up with a good excuse, so it wouldn't seem like she was calling him out of pure lust.

'I need to ask you about your necklace,' Didi began.

'Are we friends again?' Samuel asked sulkily, but Didi could hear the warmth in his voice.

'My mom had one like it . . . Samuel?'

Samuel hadn't responded, and it took Didi a moment to realize that what she was saying sparked all kinds of memories for Samuel, too.

'I was maybe fourteen, we were on a trip somewhere,' Samuel said. 'My dad was in the hospital, and for once we were spending a lot of time together. Usually dad traveled a lot, but there in the hospital, with all those tubes going into him . . .'

'We don't have to talk about it if you don't want to,' Didi said.

'It's probably good for me to remember it,' Samuel said. 'The last night we were together, Dad put the necklace around my neck.'

'Why did my mom have one like it?'

'I have no idea,' Samuel said. 'I haven't taken mine off since that evening.'

Didi digested what she had heard, but the real reason for the call was still burning in her mind. 'What are you wearing?'

'Normal clothes,' Samuel responded slowly. 'Why?'

'I told you that I was still pretty locked up because of all of those things, but I might be able to give something a try over the phone . . .'

Were Didi's ears deceiving her, or was Samuel breathing heavily? Did she dare to keep going?

'Imagine you holding me,' Didi said, almost at a whisper. 'What if I slowly unbuttoned your pants . . .'

'This whole thing is getting pretty weird, Didi,' Samuel said.

'What do you mean?' Didi asked, offended.

'I mean, I just ran up the stairs and I'm outside your door.'

Now it was Didi's turn to gasp. At first she thought Samuel was kidding, but then the doorbell rang. She ran to the door, and there he was in the flesh. She blushed to the tips of her ears, but she let him in. It would be safest to change the subject right away, though.

'Where are you coming from this late?' Didi asked, to avoid the embarrassing silence.

'The med school.'

'You're telling me people study there all night?'

'Are you jealous?' Samuel's face broke out into a huge smile, and Didi was redder than ever now. 'That's all right. I like it. It just might mean that you're gradually starting to soften to my powers of seduction.'

'I'm not jealous,' Didi said tartly.

'So it was just a one-call-stand?'

Now Didi started to laugh, too, and they went into the living room and sat down on the sofa together.

'Didi, that phone call we just . . .'

'Can we forget it?' Didi asked in a panic.

'I'm trying to say that I'm fine with us just being here. There's no need for a big production.'

They sat next to each other for several minutes. It was hard for Didi to admit that she was maybe a little disappointed, but suddenly it felt totally normal to be with Samuel like this.

'You want to watch a movie?' Didi asked.

'I'm all sweaty,' Samuel said. 'What I'd really love to do is take a shower. We performed an autopsy today—'

'I don't need the details, thanks,' Didi said. 'Go take a bath. We'll watch a movie after you get out.'

'Are you serious?' Samuel cast a warm glance Didi's way, but he was already unbuttoning his shirt.

'I'm serious,' Didi promised. 'I'll go run the water for you.'

She went into the bathroom and turned on the tap. She felt the water to make sure it was the right temperature and lit a couple of candles. She was about to pour bubbles in, too, but then it occurred to her that Samuel might not be as thrilled about rose-scented products as she was. The water burbled into the tub, and Didi's mind was at ease. A normal evening, a normal girl and a normal boy. Top it off with some stupid zombie movie, and the evening would be perfect.

CHAPTER 49

Heikki Hannula turned the car onto the side street and tried to focus on anything other than the satyr sitting in his back seat. Kati had given him the address where he was supposed to drive. She planned to be lying there in ambush, and evidently she had convinced Harju to act as her henchman. Hannula had witnessed the expression on his older colleague's face when he had been informed of Laasonen's murder. The emotions had ranged from disbelief to ecstasy. Hannula hadn't been able to decide whether the method was exceptionally brutal or extremely merciful, when you considered everything that Kati was capable of.

When he got to the next block, Hannula stopped, but he didn't turn off the engine. He wanted to get out of there as quickly as possible. He glanced at Erik Mann in the rear-view mirror.

But the satyr didn't make the slightest move to get out of the vehicle. 'We're here,' Hannula said.

'This is where Desirée Tasson lives?' the satyr asked in an unhurried tone.

'Yes.'

Erik Mann slowly looked out of the car into the evening rain and then back at Hannula, who was starting to feel nervous about the way things were going.

'When you live for a thousand years, you learn to tell when people aren't telling the truth,' Mann said, and Hannula knew he had been caught. 'This is a trap. Desirée isn't here.'

Now the gaze that was fixed on Hannula from the back seat was positively hypnotic.

'No, she's not,' Hannula said. 'But I do know where she is.'

'Would it be too much trouble to ask you to take me to her?'

Hannula was incapable of doing anything but shaking his head. The car started moving again. There was no way he could inform Kati or Harju that the plan had gone awry. And badly. Maybe it wouldn't take them long to figure it out. All he had to do now was keep cool and do exactly what the satyr told him to. Then his bit would be done.

It was a short drive. This time, Hannula turned off the engine. He handed a slip of paper to the back seat. It had the code to the downstairs door scrawled on it.

'Top floor,' Hannula said. 'Have I repaid my debt to the satyrs?'

'Yes.' Erik glanced at the piece of paper and folded it into one of the pockets of his dark coat. He ran a palm across his hair, smoothing it in preparation for his upcoming encounter.

Then Detective Heikki Hannula felt a warm hand on his chest. A horrendous, paralyzing heat surged into his body. The birth of his little girl flashed across his mind, followed by his wife's face. And then his heart stopped.

Didi and Samuel were in the living room. The bath was waiting, but they had gotten sidetracked arguing about the right movie. Didi couldn't remember the last time she had experienced such a lovely, banal moment, and she wanted to cherish it. She was careful to make sure she didn't even brush up against Samuel as they stacked the dozen movies they liked best on the coffee table. And then the doorbell rang.

'Isn't the guest supposed to be the one who gets to decide?' Samuel asked, walking to the door.

Didi followed him. She didn't want to be separated from Samuel for a single second. In that sense, the bath would be a problem.

'We're not buying anything, and no one here is interested in religion, either,' Samuel said to the man in a dark suit, who he evidently took to be a Jehovah's Witness.

'Samuel, shut the door!' Didi yelled in terror. A shock wave of fear pummeled her with all its force, and for a moment she had to struggle to stay standing. She ran over to Samuel, who by this time had also realized that something was seriously wrong.

They pushed against the door with all of their might, trying to shut it. But they were too slow and too weak. Erik effortlessly thrust the door wide and stalked in. Samuel might be thinking that the dark stranger was a criminal, but Didi knew both of them were in mortal danger.

'He's going to kill us!' Didi grabbed Samuel's hand and sprinted towards the bathroom. Samuel stumbled behind.

They barely made it in, and Didi twisted the lock. She leaned back against the door with all of her strength.

'Who is that?' Samuel asked. He was panting and pushing against the door, too, but every ounce of Didi's effort was going into keeping their attacker out, and she couldn't answer.

And then the door behind Didi's back burst apart. She and Samuel retreated and Erik stepped in through the door frame. 'Let's not make this too difficult, shall we?' Erik said to Didi in a calm voice. 'Come with me, and that will put an end to all of this.'

He might not kill me but he will kill Samuel, Didi thought, trying to wedge herself between the two men. But Samuel was already lunging at Erik.

'You're not taking Didi anywhere!' Samuel yelled, punching Erik in the diaphragm as hard as he could. It had no effect whatsoever. Didi's eyes widened in horror when she saw Erik's eyes start to glow red. Erik's head shuddered, and two small stubs thrust forth from his forehead, instantly growing into a mighty pair of goat horns. Samuel stepped back and Erik advanced. Erik pushed Samuel into the water, and Samuel resisted in vain.

Didi saw Samuel trying to struggle to the surface, but Erik was invincible and enraged. There was no doubt in Didi's mind that he could have easily killed Samuel, but instead he took his time pounding the boy with his fists.

Didi found her feet. Elina's death at the satyr's hands had been the most horrifying thing she had ever seen. With her bare soles slipping on the wet floor, she ran to her room, fumbled around in one of her drawers and pulled out a bundle. She ran back into the bathroom with it, praying the whole time that Samuel was still alive. As she ran, she unwrapped the towel that held the knife. An instant later, she was in the bathroom, and she saw Erik holding Samuel under the water. Samuel was as limp as a rag doll. Didi was filled by a sudden, all-consuming rage. She thought about her dead mother and the lifeless-looking Samuel. She had no intention of losing anyone else she loved. She raised the knife over her head with both hands and buried it in Erik Mann's back with all of her might.

Erik immediately released Samuel, but the bubbles had stopped rising to the surface. Erik was choking on blood, and he tried to reach around to pull the knife out of his back. But now Didi was utterly focused on Samuel. She vaguely registered that Kati and Nadia had arrived on the scene. They shouted something and dragged the large satyr away, but she clung to Samuel and somehow managed to pull him into her arms. He wasn't breathing.

'I'm sorry,' Didi whispered. 'I should have told you. I'm a nymph.'

A tentative idea popped into Didi's head. She turned around and saw Nadia. 'Help him! You're a healer!'

Didi was dripping water as she dragged Nadia over to the tub. For all she cared, Erik, who was coughing and rattling in a pool of blood on the floor, could die. Didi was looking for even the tiniest sign of life in Samuel, so she didn't notice Nadia turn to Kati for permission. Kati nodded, and then started tapping away at her cell phone.

'You know what I have to do,' Nadia said to Didi. 'Are you sure you want me to do it?'

'Just don't let Samuel die.' Didi's voice was trembling, and she swallowed down the tears. But she knew exactly what she wanted.

With a few graceful movements, Nadia had stripped down until she was completely naked. She stepped into the already-cooling bath. She raised Samuel's face out of the water with both hands, pressed her forehead to the boy's brow and lay down on top of him, full length. She commanded her body to allow its warmth to move into Samuel, commanded her heart to call Samuel's heart to return, imbued her pheromones with the power to awaken Samuel's desire to live. Her lips met Samuel's, but not a single breath rose from his mouth.

Didi watched Nadia without turning away, and she barely registered that Kati had appeared behind her and was pulling her away. She didn't understand why Nadia rose from the water and shook her head.

Didi wrenched free of Kati's grip. She climbed into the tub, lay down on top of Samuel, and kissed his cold blue lips.

'You will not leave me,' Didi ordered him. And then she whispered all of the words that she had left unsaid into Samuel's ear.

'Didi, it's too late,' Kati said hesitantly.

'Leave me alone!' Didi yelled. She did not let go of Samuel's face. He looked so serene and at peace that it made her even more furious. She pressed a passionate kiss to his lips; she felt like biting them in order to elicit even the tiniest response. She could feel her own breath traveling into Samuel's body. Suddenly Samuel started to flail around like a drowning man. He drew air into his lungs, and his eyes widened in terror when he saw Didi on top of him. He shoved Didi off him and somehow crawled out of the tub.

'This can't be happening,' Samuel coughed out. He was kneeling on the floor, a steady stream of water spilling from him and pooling on the floor. Gasping for breath and supporting himself against the edge of the tub, he gradually rose to his feet. Then he pushed his way past the nymphs, taking a glance at the unconscious satyr as he did so. 'This can't be happening.'

'Samuel!' Didi lunged after him, but he pushed her out of the way and made a beeline for the front door. Now Kati stepped in his way, and she had no trouble overpowering the enfeebled Samuel. Didi watched as Kati led Samuel over to the living-room couch. Samuel was shaking and overcome with dread. Didi had expected that Samuel would be happy and relieved when he looked at her, not stare at her like she was some sort of freak.

Nadia had put her dress back on, and now she approached Samuel. She tentatively touched his shoulder, and Samuel appeared to calm down a little.

'What happened to me?' Samuel asked.

'You fell in the tub, and we helped you out,' Nadia said. 'You need to rest—'

'I couldn't breathe. I don't know if you can tell if you're dead or not, but I was dead!'

'But you're not any more,' Kati said.

'I have to get out of here!' Samuel cried, unable to look in Didi's direction. Something inside him was rocked to the very core. 'What exactly are you?'

'Nymphs,' Kati answered matter-of-factly. 'And you're not going anywhere.'

'Samuel would never give us away,' Didi said. 'Would you?'

'No. How could I, I don't even get what's going on here . . .'

'Didi just saved your life,' Nadia said, allowing her hand to rest on Samuel's.

'How can we be sure that you won't go blabbing about us to anyone?' Kati asked.

Now Samuel turned towards Didi and directed his words solely at her. 'I have never lied to you about anything. I swear to you I won't say a word about this to anyone. And now I want to leave.'

Didi couldn't believe her ears. Only a few minutes earlier she had brought Samuel back to life, an almost palpable exchange of energy had formed between them, she had spoken aloud all the feelings she had kept bottled up inside, and now Samuel was going to abandon her. The strength drained from her limbs, and she collapsed into the chair. She had never experienced such utter exhaustion. She wanted to get up and cling to Samuel, but her limbs were beyond following any orders. Didi heard Nadia calling out her name over and over from somewhere in the distance, but Didi's eyelids closed.

When Didi finally came to, Nadia, Frida and an athletic blond man were sitting on the sofa before her. Kati was explaining the situation to the man.

'We have to act quickly. The neighbors must be wondering what's been going on in here. We have to get Erik out of here and hide him somewhere where he can't escape.'

'The girl is awake,' the blond man said, fixing his eyes on Didi. They were as clear as a mountain stream.

Didi instantly felt the breath go out of her. 'That's a satyr!' she screamed.

'Correct, and I'm not exactly thrilled about it either,' Kati said. 'But Nadia assured me that Jesper will help us.'

'Is this the redhead?' Jesper chuckled, glancing at Nadia. 'You guys are willing to risk everything for a scrawny little thing like that?'

'You two take Erik,' Kati said to Frida and Jesper. 'We'll stay here and clean up this place.'

Kati glanced around the apartment, which looked like a tornado had blown through it. Housekeeping had never been her strong point, but now they would have to roll up their sleeves. She paused for a moment to reconsider. Then she grabbed her black leather jacket from the floor and marched towards the entryway, where Erik Mann lay unconscious and bound.

'On second thoughts, I'd better help Frida and Jesper,' Kati said. 'Call a carpenter and a locksmith!'

CHAPTER 50

A damp, musty smell hung in the dim cellar. Erik Mann heard a metal pole strike the wall, and he turned his head and gradually opened his eyelids. Jesper was standing there in front of him. The blond satyr struck the wall a second time with the pipe.

'Jesper,' Erik said, trying to greet his fellow satyr in a totally normal voice.

Erik slowly stood up and took stock of his surroundings. He pretended not to notice that he was shackled in chains that were bolted to the floor; he gave off the air of having just arrived at a party whose guests he didn't think too much of.

'Jesper, undo these,' Erik ordered.

'Kati has the key,' Jesper said. And then Kati stepped out of the darkness, Frida at her side.

'Since when has a satyr taken orders from a nymph?'

Frida walked up to Erik, and Jesper noted her white-hot, barely contained rage.

'There's water there,' Frida said, kicking one pail towards Erik, and then another. 'And there's your toilet. I'd advise you to use them sparingly. You might say I've had experience with similar situations.'

'Is that so?' Erik said, still coolly. 'So you've made up with your old enemy? It is Kati's fault that you suffered.'

'As a matter of fact, I've come to the conclusion that the only reason I've suffered is because of the satyrs,' Frida answered.

Jesper waited for Frida to lose her self-control and attack Erik. Instead, the nymph walked calmly over to Kati.

'I'm going to clear out of here now,' Frida said. 'It's good that revenge kept me alive, but now I need some space of my own. Feel free to be in touch if you need anything.'

Frida turned to look one final time at Erik. She wagged a playful finger at him and then disappeared into the darkness. A moment later, a heavy door thudded shut somewhere.

Erik now addressed his words to Jesper. 'You know what will happen to you when I get out of here. I already got rid of that useless boy. The prophecy has been given, and you cannot change the future. Didi will be mine.'

'You can always dream.' Kati stepped closer to the satyr in whose covey she had lived for years. She found these present circumstances extremely rewarding. She lowered a bottle of wine and a loaf of bread to the ground at a little distance from Erik.

'Is that my last supper?' Erik asked. 'Why haven't you killed me yet?'

'Didi wanted to keep you alive,' Kati answered matter-of-factly.

'Desirée?' Erik smiled. 'Of course. Even you cannot change what has been written, Ekaterina.'

'Or perhaps she wants to kill you herself,' Kati said. 'Let's go, Jesper.'

'Jesper!' Erik shouted as they walked away. 'You take orders from me!'

Jesper stopped. He turned slowly around.

'The only one I take orders from now is my heart.'

CHAPTER 51

So this is what being dumped feels like, Didi mused, trying to analyze her feelings. She was totally drained. She had seen girlfriends who had broken up with a guy or been dumped by one, and they had swung from one emotional extreme to the other, bawled their heads off one minute and partied their butts off the next. But she didn't have a clue as to what she should do. She would have loved to tell the whole story to Laura, if only she had any idea how to put everything that had happened into words. There were the satyrs, the dead Samuel who came back to life, and to whom she had confessed her love . . .

Didi moped around the house and got on Kati's nerves. She even tried to study her art history textbooks, but knew she was just going through the motions. She worked her shifts at the cafe, since there was no way she could leave Valtteri high and dry again.

Maybe it's better this way, Didi thought. The full moon was coming soon, and it would be best if she didn't see Samuel again. It would be best if she stayed really far from him. That's what she kept telling herself one cool morning as she hung around the back door of the university hospital, waiting for Samuel to get off the night shift. She was shivering so badly she had goosebumps, and she regretted her decision to go out in her thin summer dress. But like any other woman who had been rebuffed, she wanted Samuel to see what he had lost.

'Do you want to grab some breakfast?' Didi asked casually the moment she saw Samuel.

Samuel looked exhausted, Didi thought. But he had just been up all night, of course. There shouldn't have been anything wrong with his hearing, though. And yet Samuel trudged past her as if she were thin air. Didi ran after him.

'Samuel, wait!'

'Don't touch me!' Samuel flinched and moved further away.

'What's wrong with you?' Didi asked. This wasn't exactly the reaction she had been expecting.

'I can't sleep. I don't get any of this. That thing tried to kill me . . .'

Didi remembered the confusion of feelings that the knowledge of her nymph-hood and this whole new world had initially aroused in her. She tried to empathize with Samuel. 'Are you afraid?'

'Hell yeah, I'm afraid!' Samuel yelled so loudly that a cyclist who was racing past turned back to look and almost tipped over.

'I'm still the same girl that you've known since you were a kid,' Didi said. But she no longer tried to touch Samuel.

'No, you're not.' Samuel shook his head. 'You killed your former boyfriend. I'm starting to get the picture here. You'll kill me, too, if this goes on. Don't come here any more.'

Samuel stalked off as fast as he could. Didi stood still, frozen in place.

'Where are you going?'

'Somewhere far away from you!'

Didi dragged herself home, utterly demoralized. Maybe she'd been nursing some dream that Samuel would forget all the horrors as soon as he saw her and want to wrap his arms around her. On the other hand, that was exactly what was wholly impossible between them now. Didi tossed her bag to the floor.

'What is it?' asked Kati, who had been wondering what would be the smartest thing to do with the *nomos* dagger and now quietly slipped it into the kitchen drawer.

'Samuel looked at me like I was something out of a horror movie,' Didi said. And the worst part was that she felt like something unnatural too, like a monster. She killed, even when what she craved was love.

'You're not going to start crying, are you?' Kati asked. 'Men come and go, hundreds of years of experience has taught me that.'

'Not men like Samuel.'

'Just start doing normal stuff,' Kati advised. 'You're better off forgetting Samuel.'

Kati's tone was cool, but she hadn't completely forgotten the incident in the bathroom either. When Didi had rocked Samuel in her arms, she had seen herself holding Janos for the last time at the edge of the forest. In Kati's mind's eye, Janos was never old; he was always the same youth that had come to her aid and fought at her side against the satyrs.

'Why?' Didi asked.

'Humans have always been afraid of us.' Kati led Didi over to the table and had her sit down. 'You need to understand that. We're the ones who have been hunted and persecuted throughout the ages. We've been burned as witches, we've been bought and sold. You and I should feel just as horrified when we look at humans.'

'Samuel isn't going to do us any harm,' Didi said.

'Maybe not, but humans do themselves plenty of harm. All I'm saying is, don't trust Samuel blindly.'

One more thing had been bothering Didi, and for once Kati seemed like she was prepared to have a serious conversation.

'I'm afraid of satyrs,' Didi said.

'That's good,' Kati said.

'But aren't we the same species?' Didi asked. 'Don't we belong with them?'

'There's not a satyr on this earth I belong with.'

'What about Jesper? Do I need to be afraid of him? He helped us, and Nadia says—'

'Nadia says whatever she wants to say.' Kati rose from the table, supposedly bored by the topic. 'I'm a nymph and I want to be free of satyrs.'

Kati's attitude frustrated Didi. She was never going to get the answers she wanted from her. Didi rose from the table and trudged off to her room, dragging her bag along the ground because she knew how much it irritated Kati. She didn't make it all the way, though, because Nadia appeared at the doorway to her own room and silently waved Didi in.

'Do you remember what we talked about?' Nadia said quietly, shutting the door. 'Do you still want it?'

'The medicine?' Didi asked, her cheeks flushing with excitement. 'Did you do it?'

'I can't promise anything,' Nadia said. 'But the tests have been encouraging. Have you thought about the consequences? Or why you really want it?'

Was Nadia kidding? That was all Didi had been thinking about. She had analyzed every single one of her encounters with Samuel until there was nothing left to analyze.

'I want to know if I really love Samuel,' Didi answered frankly. 'Or if it's nothing more than hormone-induced insanity. Is it only because of—'

'The moon?'

'If it's something chemical I give off that makes me want any man I come across,' Didi said. 'If that medicine takes away my desires and I still want Samuel . . . Then won't that mean it's love?'

Throughout their entire conversation, Nadia's face had been grave, but now she started to laugh.

'Imagine!' Nadia giggled. 'Women want to be super-sexy and men want to be ready to hit it whenever. And now we're trying to develop a substance that will kill those urges.'

'Mom used to say that I always have to play devil's advocate . . .'

The sudden thought of Elina overwhelmed Didi with emotion, and she wasn't able to finish her sentence. She could feel Nadia's gentle touch, and their eyes met. 'Mom was a healer, too.'

'Yes, she was,' Nadia said. 'A skilled healer and a thoroughly good and loyal woman of the Oakheart family.'

They sat there for a moment in silence. Then Nadia pulled a small jar out of her dresser and tapped a single white capsule into her palm.

Didi stared at it. It might prove to be her salvation, or it might turn her into a monster forever. If it worked, she would be the old Didi once again, and Samuel would realize it.

'Didi, I don't know exactly what will happen. But it's going to be the full moon soon, so if you want to try this, you have to take it now.'

CHAPTER 52

Detective Harju entered the cafe, took a seat at one of the tables, ordered a bottle of beer and looked around. He saw no sign of the redheaded Desirée Tasson. That was fine, he could wait. He slowly drank his beer, flipped through the latest tabloid and people-watched the cafe's clientele, which appeared to consist mostly of students.

That morning, Harju had paid a visit to his colleague Heikki Hannula's family to offer his condolences. Heikki's wife had been reticent and red-eyed, but the kid played the way she always did, without the slightest comprehension of what was going on. *And so life continues*, Harju had reflected, even though his own life had been at a standstill of sorts for years, ever since Hanna's death. It was true the death of your own child was the worst thing that could happen to a person.

Harju still thought about his own daughter constantly, like today when he emptied his office at police headquarters. He had shoved papers and belongings into a garbage bag willy-nilly, until all that was left was the dream-catcher hanging from the wall.

The talisman had been of no use to him. At night Hanna appeared next to his bed and looked at him without saying a word, and every morning Harju woke up to the same bleak sensation that everything good had been robbed from his life.

The law hadn't helped Harju either, even though he had put his faith in it his entire life. Maybe he had been better at following the letter of the law than its spirit. He had hunted down criminals, but now he was giving his approval to a murder. He felt like justice had been served, that it was more of an execution than an assassination. And with that, he realized he couldn't continue as a police officer for another day.

The sound of Didi's voice roused Harju out of his reverie. He could see her standing at the counter, handing steaming cups across to customers and chatting with them. A moment later, he managed to make eye contact with her.

Didi approached Harju's table. He could see how guarded she was. He smiled reassuringly and indicated that she should take a seat at his side. He had already thought about what he would say, but Didi's frightened-yet-bright eyes and pale skin momentarily made him forget how to speak. Before him sat a killer who was innocent in some way. It was hard to grasp.

'Desirée Tasson,' Harju said officiously, because that was the only way he knew how to talk. 'You were my final case. I sent in my retirement papers today, and now I'm taking all the vacation time I never took.'

'Your last case?' Didi asked suspiciously, as if she thought Harju wanted her to confess.

'Don't get worked up,' Harju said. 'Kati gave me a pretty thorough explanation of how you ... what you have to do to survive.'

'I'm so sorry.'

'No need. I believed in the law, but the law didn't solve the most difficult case of my life.'

She felt a fresh wave of compassion for the old detective. She held out a hand, but flinched at the touch.

'Why are you angry?' Didi asked.

Harju had to think. It was true he was angry, but how did she know?

'I'm angry about what Heikki did,' Harju said, after considering for a moment. 'And about what Heikki had to experience, about what his family had to experience. The truth is that Heikki betrayed his family and lied to many people.'

'People do all kinds of things when they're in a tight spot, even though they don't necessarily mean any harm,' Didi said.

'True enough,' Harju said. 'Which is why I came to tell you that I won't give away your secret.'

As a look of surprise washed over Didi's face, Harju rose from the table and walked towards the door. He lifted the collar of his trench coat and stepped out. And when he saw the parking ticket on his windshield, he laughed out loud.

CHAPTER 53

Didi was relieved to see Harju go, but as the day went on, she started growing anxious. She somehow saw people more precisely, heard more keenly, and above all felt more intensely. She began to be careful about touching anyone and tried to block out people's scents. It was an incredible relief to make it outside at the end of her shift. She didn't want to linger, though, because some whisper of the full moon was nipping at her heels. She practically ran home; she was in a hurry anyway. Nadia had taken blood samples from her, and she wanted to know the results. She couldn't stand even the possibility that the medicine wouldn't help her.

Didi marched right into the kitchen, thinking she would see Nadia there, fiddling with herbs as usual. *And hopefully cooking, too*, Didi thought, because the sensory overload she had experienced at work had been so strong that she hadn't noticed her stomach growling. But instead of Nadia, she had been startled to discover Jesper in the kitchen. She hadn't had a single good encounter with a satyr, and now she was alone in the apartment with one.

'Hare with all of the trimmings,' Jesper said, as he poured a bottle of red wine into a cast-iron casserole. 'I've gotten used to a pretty woodsy diet, and this city chow you guys eat doesn't really do it for me.'

'Where'd you get that bunny, one of the parks?' Didi asked,

timidly entering the kitchen. She didn't want to show Jesper that she was afraid.

'Hare.' Jesper had bent down to sniff his handiwork. 'Hunted by yours truly and hung for a couple of days. Now I'm going to let it stew for a good, long time.'

Jesper suddenly rose and made right for Didi. Despite her instincts, she didn't retreat. She felt like prey, and knew that running and wriggling at this point would have just made things worse. But she still didn't dare to look Jesper in the eye when he firmly grabbed a fistful of her hair and raised it to his nostrils, inhaling deeply. Didi found it strange that the satyr's proximity wasn't in the least bit repulsive after all.

'Unbelievable,' Jesper said. 'It's still a day away and you smell as if the full moon were shining from a cloudless sky. You're going to drive the satyr boys crazy.'

Jesper went back to putting his hare in the oven, and Didi watched his practiced hands at work. Kati had led her to believe that all satyrs needed to be babied and served, but Jesper didn't appear to expect anything of the sort. Kati had told her that the satyrs were boring and pompous, but Jesper seemed relaxed and like he had a good sense of humor. What else hadn't Kati told her? Now was the perfect opportunity for Didi to clear up a couple of things.

'What's Erik like?'

'Some believe that Erik is our next leader, our next Master,' Jesper said and shrugged. 'I've never belonged to Erik's band, but everyone else tried to get in it.'

Didi posed her most burning question next: 'Why does Erik want me?'

'Erik has these theories,' Jesper said. 'He's quite the professor. It has something to do with the phases of the moon and that tummy tattoo of yours . . . Can I see it?'

The question was so frank that Didi assented and lifted the hem of her dress until the tattoo was visible. Jesper stared at it without blinking, until Didi lowered the thin cotton fabric.

'What's so special about my knot?' Didi asked.

'I don't have a clue. But something is, because Erik was prepared to sacrifice everything for you.'

Didi sensed that Jesper wasn't interested in divulging any more information to her, and because it looked like it would be a while before they ate, she took some blue cheese – which Kati was probably saving for the moment when she returned from spending the full moon with a couple of presumably very happy young men – some crackers, and a couple of apples and went to her room.

Didi snacked and fell asleep. She didn't wake up until late that evening. She wanted to talk to Nadia, and she didn't feel like being alone. The full moon was rising in the sky, and she didn't know if she could trust herself. What if she were overtaken by a horrendous lust, headed out to wander the city streets, and a dead boy was found again the next morning? Didi shivered with dread. She remembered Detective Harju, who knew she had killed people but had still let her go. That couldn't be right.

Didi went over to her armoire to pull out a nightgown when her eyes lit on a T-shirt bunched up in the corner. It was Samuel's. It still smelled of him, and she immediately missed him immensely, both as a friend and . . . Didi tried to push the thought from her mind. In the first place, Samuel had made it clear that he considered her some sort of monster, and in the second, she might kill Samuel if the medicine didn't work.

Didi glanced out the window and saw the bright disc peering out between the clouds. But she was no longer afraid; she just stared at it downright defiantly. This time she would win, and while she was at it, she would discover what her true feelings for Samuel were.

It was a full moon. She would go back to sleep and wake up in the morning in her own bed.

Nevertheless, some irresistible force drew Didi to the window.

She pressed her palm to the pane, as if to feel the moonbeams, but all she could feel was the cool glass. Then something caught her eye. A moth fluttered towards her hand. Its wings were silvery; they were beating right in front of her face. Then it was followed by another moth, and another ... In an instant it felt like there were thousands of them, and Didi pulled her hand back, horror-struck. The moths fluttered for a moment as if in confusion, but then they vanished just as quickly as they had appeared.

Didi went to bed. In the morning she would ask Nadia about the test results.

CHAPTER 54

'At least yesterday, there were no anomalies in your blood,' Nadia said.

'What does that mean?' Didi asked. She didn't know if the results were good or bad.

'I didn't find any elevated hormone levels or any other changes, either,' Nadia said. 'Did you have any symptoms?'

'I felt a little strange, maybe . . . But in the morning everything was fine.'

Nadia set a teacup down in front of Didi and took a seat herself. Didi looked at her closely. There was a certain radiance about the older nymph this morning.

'Were you with Jesper at the full moon?' Didi asked, even though she already knew the answer. 'What does it feel like with a satyr?'

'Natural,' Nadia answered frankly. 'It feels right. I've never experienced anything like it with a human.'

'But you've never loved a human, have you?'

Nadia didn't answer. She had had all kinds of feelings for humans. She felt a need to care for and heal them; she had coworkers that she liked. There were also nymphs that she couldn't stand no matter how hard she tried, and satyrs that she simply hated. And one satyr that she loved.

'No, I haven't,' Nadia answered, pulling back a little from Didi when Kati clomped in.

Kati headed right for the fridge, yawning as she opened the door with a yank.

'What a night!'

'I'll second that,' Nadia said, with a languid smile.

'Hmmm,' said Kati, turning towards her. 'And what about our little nymphet? Did you manage to handle things cleanly this time, or do we have to worry that a body or two are going to pop up somewhere? And who ate my cheese? I was saving it for this morning!'

Didi found herself so incredibly irritated by Kati's nonchalant attitude that she didn't care if she watched her tongue any more.

'I didn't have a man,' Didi announced. 'Nadia gave me some medicine, and it helped.'

'What are you talking about? Nadia, what the hell were you thinking?' Kati's eyes bored into each of the nymphs in turn. 'Didi could have died! Why do you guys have to take risks like that?'

'I don't want to kill any more,' Didi said.

But Kati was looking at Nadia more angrily than Didi. 'You know it's our job to protect Didi.'

'That's not enough,' Didi said. 'I need to protect myself, too. You might be in control of your own powers, but I'm not in control of mine.'

'Kati's right, though,' Nadia interjected herself between them. 'You just told me that you had some reaction—'

'It was so vague, I can't even really describe it,' Didi said. 'It's like all of my senses were in overdrive. And at night I went to the window and all these moths started to gather around me.'

'I've never heard of anything like that. It could be something other than the medicine,' Nadia said. 'You're still developing as a nymph.'

'It makes no difference,' said Kati, who was on the verge of exploding. 'Those tests end now. We can't help you if you don't follow the rules.'

'Fuck your rules,' Didi said. 'I never asked you for help. You just want to find some way to keep me chained up. You're just like the satyrs!'

And with that, Didi rushed out, leaving Kati staring accusatorily at Nadia.

Didi was curled up in bed. She had tried to snub Kati with the jab about the satyrs, but the truth of the matter was that they had aroused her interest. Jesper's proximity had been downright electric. And with Erik, Didi felt something else, too. The first time Didi saw him, she thought deep down that he was staggeringly handsome. If you liked older men, that was. Then she had touched Erik's hand and felt something remarkable. At their second encounter, she had buried a dagger in the satyr's back. Still, it had been sort of titillating to imagine how badly Erik wanted her . . . To top it all off, she felt like she was putting all of them in danger, because she was the one Erik was hunting. Wouldn't it be easiest to make an end of all this by figuring out what it was Erik wanted and give it to him? What would it feel like with a satyr? At least Nadia had glowed after spending the night in Jesper's arms.

Didi shook these thoughts from her mind. She wanted company, someone totally normal to talk to, maybe a little gossip about the newest shades of lip gloss. She called Laura, and a moment later her friend was looking at her from the screen of her laptop.

'How are things going with Samuel?' Laura asked right off the bat.

'Did you have to remind me?' Didi huffed. 'I spilled my heart out to him, and he took off.'

Laura reprimanded her. 'You should call me more often. I'm totally out of the loop.'

'It's not like life's exactly glamorous here,' Didi said, but she gave an appropriately exaggerated description of her day, her job, and all the amazing shopping. That's the kind of stuff Laura wanted to hear about, after all.

But Didi couldn't get Erik out of her mind. She decided to test out what Laura's thoughts were. 'There are a lot of really good-looking men here, all ages, all body types, all styles . . . Have you ever wondered what it would be like with a guy who's a little older?'

'Wait, do you already have someone new in the works?' Laura was clearly hungry for juicy gossip, and leaned in closer to the screen.

'Of course not. I was just thinking . . .'

Didi wanted so badly to tell someone about all of the things that had happened to her. It felt like a mistake getting in touch with Laura, because now she either had to keep secrets from her friend or lie to her face.

'I guess I could be with someone a little older,' Laura laughed. 'But he'd need to be able to compensate for his age in a lot of other ways. In the first place, he would have to be insanely hot, he couldn't have any old man flab or those gross liver spots, and then he'd have to be insanely rich, too.'

And there it is, Didi thought. Both of the criteria were fulfilled, but in her particular situation that didn't make any difference. Then she noticed Laura jump.

'What's wrong?' Didi asked. 'Did Lasse come home?'

'Let's stay in touch,' Laura said. 'I have so much to tell you!'

Didi was alone. She should have been happy about the fact that the full moon hadn't swept her up in its power, but instead what she felt was empty.

At least at work Didi felt a little better. The cafe was really busy, and when a squall drove a crowd of customers inside, the first young man in line ordered a coffee and a croissant.

'Four euros and fifty cents.' Didi handed him his order and took his money, and when their hands touched Didi instantly knew what was going through his head. She couldn't hold back. 'Just so you know, I don't find it the least bit flattering that someone I've never met before wants to screw me.'

The young man looked at Didi, startled, and disappeared with his coffee. It felt to Didi as if some stranger had spoken with her mouth, but she tried to focus on serving the next customer.

'Are there free refills?' asked the girl, who appeared to be the third wheel in a trio of young people.

Didi poured more coffee into the cup the girl was holding out, but her sense of smell caught a slight whiff. Didi turned to look at the girl's friend.

'Your friend smells like your boyfriend,' Didi said. 'And she's gotten laid today, but you haven't.'

The girl with the boyfriend narrowed her eyes at Didi as if she were speaking a foreign language.

'Your friend and your boyfriend are screwing,' Didi explained patiently. 'You might want to give a little thought to your future.'

The girl turned towards her boyfriend and started screaming at him right then and there, her cheeks blazing. The other girl slunk away as fast as her feet would carry her.

Didi's head was hammering. She felt so dizzy that she had to lean against the counter. She had been able to sense other people's experiences before, but now they were washing over her in a flood, overloading her mind. Didi would have fallen to the floor if someone hadn't suddenly supported her and led her into the back room.

'Another server will be right out!' Kati yelled over her shoulder at the confused customers before closing the door behind her.

'What are you doing here?' Didi sank down to a stool, still holding her forehead. She was gradually starting to feel better.

'I came to see how you're doing,' Kati said. 'And it's a good thing I did, too.'

'Could Nadia be right?'

'About the medicine?' Kati asked.

'About me still developing,' Didi answered. 'I sense everything so distinctly. I can't even control it any more. I say whatever pops into my head.'

'Listen to me.' Kati grabbed Didi by the shoulders and shook her. 'That medicine might be doing you more harm than good. You can't wait to see whether it's going to keep you healthy. You have to find a man!'

'That's exactly the problem,' Didi said. 'I kill every man I'm with. Nymphs are supposed to partner with satyrs. That's the way it's meant to be.'

'Don't ever say that!' Kati raged.

'We're the same species.'

'You don't know anything about it.'

'How could I?' Didi said, looking defiantly at Kati. 'I've never even had a chance to try it out.'

'This is all Nadia's fault,' Kati said. 'She's always trying to come up with ways of fixing all kinds of things that don't need to be fixed. I knew that when she started hanging out with Jesper again, you'd start getting all kinds of harebrained ideas.'

'Doesn't Nadia love Jesper? Isn't Jesper a satyr?'

'Nadia will come to her senses,' Kati said, as if the decision were in her hands.

'What about that satyr that wants me?' Didi asked, tuning her senses with every ounce of concentration she could manage. 'Erik Mann. Did you kill him?'

'You don't need to think about that. Let's go home.'

'I have to wait for Valtteri,' Didi said. 'I'll come home in a minute.'

It was a big fat lie, of course. Didi pulled out her phone and looked up Samuel's number.

CHAPTER 55

'What do you want?' Samuel evidently didn't want to look Didi in the face; he concentrated on wiping down the examination counters at the pathology department with uncharacteristic vigor.

'I just wanted to see how you're doing,' Didi said, and there was some truth in it. She waited for a vibration to surge towards her from Samuel like it had from the customers at the cafe so she could figure out what Samuel was really thinking, but her senses seemed to be blocked. 'Where are you living these days?'

'Here.'

'Here?' Didi looked around the morgue. 'You can't live here.'

'Sleep, at least. It's really quiet,' Samuel said, tossing away the rag.

Their eyes met properly for the first time, and Didi felt the familiar flicker in her breast. She felt inspired to take a hopeful step towards Samuel, but he backed up.

'Didi, I can't take this any more,' Samuel said. 'I don't want to be with you.'

'You're lying,' Didi said, sure of herself. 'You love me.'

'That makes no difference. We're not meant to be together. We don't belong together.'

The feeling of soft hope and tenderness that Didi had felt in her breast started to turn into seething irritation. How dare Samuel resist her? She was an enchantress, a nymph! But Didi managed to calm herself. After all, with Samuel, she wanted to be a totally normal girl. Besides, she had to concentrate. She had wanted to see Samuel, but she wanted something more, too.

'Actually, I need some help,' Didi said.

'As usual, you have an ulterior motive,' Samuel said bitterly. 'I knew you wouldn't come here just to talk about feelings or because you were worried about whether I had a place to stay.'

Didi didn't tell Samuel that when she had been in Kati's presence, she had focused her senses and caught a glimpse of a dark house and then a cellar. She had to get to Tammisaari.

'You have a car,' Didi said. 'I want to go back out to that manor.'

'Why? We didn't find anything last time we were there.'

'I know, but I just got this feeling that I should go back out there.' Didi was skirting the truth, and she could feel Samuel's eyes analyzing every tiny move she made.

'That creature is out there,' Samuel said slowly. 'I don't want to see it again. And I don't get why you would, either.'

'For the same reason as last time,' Didi said. 'I want to know more about myself. And if that satyr is nothing more than a creature to you, then neither am I.'

'The answer is no. Could you please leave now? Visitors aren't even supposed to come in here.'

Didi had to wheel around so Samuel wouldn't see her face contort with restrained fury. A beast inside her was raging, struggling to get free. She had to leave and fast.

Outside, Didi leaned heavily against the wall and panted. She didn't know what was happening to her, but there were terrifying moments when she didn't feel like she could control herself. Some electric force was coursing through her veins that wanted to go on a rampage, to destroy, to realize all of its desires that instant.

It took her a second to calm down. Then she noticed that she had been so excited about her plan when she headed out to meet Samuel that she had left her purse at work. She had to go back.

Didi slipped into the staff dressing room through the back door and realized she was still wearing her uniform. She opened her locker and the first thing she saw was herself in the small mirror. She looked different somehow. Her soft features were strained, and her eyes looked like they were on fire. Didi started pulling off her shirt and immediately saw them on her arms. Bruises. She frantically started searching every inch of her body. There were bruises on her stomach and her legs, too. What did it mean?

But she didn't have any more time to think about it, because the server working the evening shift came in to get a pack of cigarettes from her locker.

'Oh, Didi, you're still here. Someone was just asking for you out there.'

Didi had no idea who it could be. She slowly changed her clothes and then peeked out the door and into the cafe. It was Laura. Joy immediately bubbled up inside Didi, and she exhaled with relief. The sight of her best friend instantaneously took her back to a time when everything had been totally normal. She flew into Laura's arms. The girls giggled loudly and hugged each other.

'It's so good to see you!' Didi sighed. 'What are you doing here?'

It was only then that Didi saw that Lasse was there, too. Her exuberance instantly turned into annoyance. She had been craving the everyday companionship of her friend so badly. Not some boring old nymphs and their never-ending crises. Putting forth all of her good will, Didi just barely managed to mumble a greeting: 'Hey, Lasse.'

Laura grabbed Didi by the hand. She seemed overjoyed. 'Look!'

Didi looked at Laura's ring finger and saw the gold ring with the puny diamond. Lasse had always been cheap . . . Didi tried to keep her negative thoughts at bay. She wanted to be happy for her best friend.

'There's no way I could tell you over the phone,' Laura babbled. 'Lasse proposed out of the blue, and I've been a complete mess ever since.'

Didi glanced at Lasse, who was smiling a little crookedly. Didi knew that Laura couldn't stop talking when she was nervous or afraid. So she looked at Laura a little more closely, and noticed that her hair had been parted over to one side to cover up a Band-Aid.

'How did that happen?' Didi asked.

'Everything's fine now,' Laura rushed to explain. 'We've made up. We're so happy. Right, Lasse? Sometimes you love someone so much that you get all kinds of feelings that you can't really help. And Lasse will never do it again.'

Didi pictured herself knocking the table out of the way and throwing Lasse against the wall. But she managed to smile sweetly at the newly engaged couple. Then, concealing her disgust, she took Lasse by the hand and started leading him away. 'You don't mind if I borrow Lasse for a minute, do you?'

Laura didn't have time to protest before Didi had pulled Lasse into the back room. She leaned against the table with feigned casualness, took a chocolate chip cookie from the plate, and bit.

'Congratulations,' Didi said.

'The only reason I'm here is because Laura told me I had to come,' Lasse said.

'You don't love Laura,' Didi said, and the cookie crumbled in her fingers. 'You're sick.'

'I don't want you to see Laura any more,' Lasse said. 'You're a bad example.'

Didi's hands shook and her heart was pounding. What an idiot! She had never been able to understand what Laura saw in Lasse. Laura could have had a much better boyfriend, but for some reason she was hooked on this total chauvinist pig.

'I've never told Laura how you came on to me,' Didi said. 'I'm going to tell her now.'

Lasse took a step closer to Didi and smiled lewdly. 'Ooooh, Ms Fire-crotch's panties must be dripping wet,' he said. 'Laura's going to believe me when I tell her that you came on to me.'

Up to this point, Didi had kept her gaze fixed on the floor so she could control herself, but now she raised her eyes to Lasse's and she could feel the beast caged within blaze out through them. It felt good to give in to it. She kicked Lasse in the crotch and let him fall to the floor, wailing. In a flash she was on top of him, grabbing hold of his hair and slamming his head into the floor. Then her hands made their way to Lasse's neck, and she started to squeeze. Lasse's face went red as he flailed around.

'If I even suspect that you've done anything to Laura, I'll hunt you down,' Didi said in a hoarse voice. The beast inside her had been awakened, and now it was going berserk. 'And when I find you, it's not going to be pretty.'

She slammed Lasse's skull into the floor a final time, and the blow was so hard that he lost consciousness. She sat on him for a minute and felt calmer. Suddenly she had a brilliant idea. She searched Lasse's coat pockets and then his pants until she found his car keys. A second later, she was running out the back door and onto the street. She pressed the unlock button on Lasse's remote and saw the lights of a car blink further off. What a coincidence, Lasse had started driving his lecherous old man's gorgeous Benz. *The apple didn't fall far from the tree*, Didi thought, as she remembered how Lasse's father's eyes had narrowed with lust when she had visited the house with Laura. Sending the car rolling off a bridge sounded tempting. But Tammisaari beckoned.

CHAPTER 56

E rik was lying on the cold, clammy stone floor. His white dress shirt was soiled and crusted at the back with dried blood. The wound still ached, but it had quickly begun to heal. He didn't bother struggling against the chains; he preferred to gather his strength. The nymphs could have killed him right away, but for some reason he was still alive. Nor had he by any means given up on his plan. He had touched Desirée Volanté Tasson, and he was more certain than ever that she was what he wanted.

Erik sacrificed a momentary thought to that group of captive nymphs that the hunters he had sent out had brought before him, washed, brushed and naked. Something about each of those individual nymphs had given his satyrs – who had searched far and wide, to the furthest reaches of the globe – reason to believe that one of them would be the nymph of legend. And Erik had to admit, some of them were very sweet, downright delicious. In particular, Erik remembered Milena, whom he had felt so hopeful about. Erik had let his hands wander over buttocks, the curves of waists, beautifully formed breasts, but not a single one carried the knot tattoo on her belly, and so Erik turned them over to the other satyrs. That had been a wise decision, since he had never met a nymph like Didi. And then that delicate redhead had buried a *nomos* dagger in his back over some measly human, and without the slightest hesitation. Hadn't she felt how she and Erik belonged together?

Erik took a bottle of red wine from the basket that had been set down next to him and popped open the cork. He took a few thirsty gulps before he heard a new sound. Someone was coming down the stairs. The lights flickered on and then burned steadily.

And there she was: Desirée was standing in front of Erik in a dress with red flowers, a poplin coat hastily wrapped around her. Erik inhaled, filling his lungs with oxygen. The very sight of her made up for much suffering. But Didi kept her distance, stayed out of his reach.

'You were afraid of me back in the cafe.'

The girl's voice trembled, but there was also determination in it. Erik calculated how to best handle the situation.

'You get right to the point, don't you?' Erik answered in a low voice. 'Yes. And I'm still afraid of you.'

'What is it you want?' Didi asked.

'You.'

'You don't know me.'

'No, I don't. And you don't know me either,' Erik said. 'But I do know that we are meant to be together. Release me, and I'll tell you everything that Ekaterina hasn't revealed to you yet.'

Erik noted how Didi raised an eyebrow at this, and he could tell that he had pulled the right string. Kati tried to keep as much as possible to herself, and having secrets sometimes proved to be her downfall. But Didi was not such easy prey. The nymph took a couple of steps backwards.

'When the moon goes dark, we shall become one,' Erik intoned beguilingly. 'After that, the future is ours. As long as you bear the mark.'

He was throwing down a challenge to Didi. Someone else might have played coy, but Didi was clearly aware of her special status. Erik's heart thundered as Didi slowly began to lift the hem of her skirt until it rose above her stomach. Then he saw it, the Knot of Astarte. No one could ever claim that the legend was nothing more than a fable.

Erik smiled at Didi. He held out his hand, and the nymph came to him. He took her red tresses in his fist and let them slide between his fingers. He saw the white breasts heave beneath the thin fabric of her dress. And then the coat was slipping from the nymph's shoulders, and she drew his hand straight to her heart. Didi let it rest there for a moment, and Erik realized, nearly intoxicated, that she was already opening his trousers. He jumped back.

'I don't have the energy to fight it any more,' Didi said, a cool glow in her eyes. 'You want me and I need someone who won't die when they enter me.'

'Unfortunately, that's impossible,' Erik said, his eyes nevertheless lingering on Didi's erect nipples.

'Don't forget, I know what you feel,' Didi whispered in his ear.

'The legend forbids it!' Now Erik was shouting. He couldn't give in to his desires; he had to keep the greater goal in mind. His dark eyes started to glow like embers. 'I can't be with you before the lunar eclipse.'

'I won't kill you,' Didi said seductively.

'I'll kill you if I'm with you. The legend dies with satyrs. That's why I can't touch you.'

Didi slapped him across the face. 'You asshole! I'm offering myself to you. All men want me for this!'

Didi put her hand between her legs. She was frenzied with rage.

'You're the legend,' Erik now said in a low, commanding voice. 'You bear the knot. Go and feed. Find a man or you will die!'

The nymph hissed at him. Erik took a threatening stride towards Didi so she would really leave. He had seen many nymphs who had been at death's door, and Didi must be saved from that fate. Didi stared at him with her already-glazed eyes, but then she turned and staggered up the stairs. Erik heard the door to the cellar slam shut. He closed his eyes and prayed that Didi would find someone soon.

* * *

The girl stumbled headlong through the dim forest. Or at least her body was as willowy as a girl's, but her face wizened with every rattling intake of breath. Her lips were cracked, and her red hair was growing brittle and gray. She should have been shivering, but she didn't appear to feel any cold. A fire burned inside her that scorched her through and through. She made it a few yards further and then sank to her knees. She looked as if she didn't have the strength to continue. Nor did she have a purpose. Her eyes now glowed milk-white in the darkness, but she no longer cared what she saw, or if she saw anything at all.

She sat down and then collapsed over onto her side. She didn't move again. The night wind was already blowing dead leaves over her.

The bee had almost filled its honey stomach and was returning to her hive, but as she did, she followed the girl from the patch of heather. The bee, at least, knew what needed to be done. She needed to dance, to call her comrades from the hive. None of them would join her now that it was night, but in the morning, they would all follow.

CHAPTER 57

When Nadia had received a concerned text message from Samuel that Didi had asked for a ride to Tammisaari, Nadia hadn't hesitated for a second. Didi was stubborn, and there was no point trying to stop her. It would be best to just take off after her and try to clean up any messes after the fact. But might the mess be too big this time? Nadia looked at Kati's grim profile as they sped silently towards the manor. The gravel flew as Kati skidded into the courtyard, brakes squealing, and leapt out of the car.

Nadia rushed down to the cellar at Kati's heels. The lights were on, but Erik was still in chains.

'Erik, where's Didi?' Kati grabbed the satyr's lapels with both hands. In that moment, Kati didn't seem to feel the slightest fear. 'Where's Didi?'

Erik smiled as if he were at a boring cocktail party, not in reeking, filthy clothes in some moldy cellar. Nadia went back out. Didi had probably continued moving. Nadia sensed something: a faint droning. It was coming from a glade of trees. Nadia sprang into a run. She raced across the stones and through the underbrush and the buzzing grew louder and louder. Suddenly Nadia stopped. It looked like the earth was moving, and at first it was difficult for her to understand what she was seeing. It was like a blanket. A blanket of bees.

Nadia's mind was filled with wonder and terror. She saw a bright lock of red hair gleaming underneath the insects. She stepped closer, and the bees took off in flight. As they scattered, Didi was revealed beneath them, surrounded by hundreds if not thousands of dead honeybees.

'Didi!' Nadia yelled, even though she should have been yelling for Kati. She rushed over and dropped to her knees at Didi's side. Nadia felt Didi's skin. It was gray but warm. *The legend*. The thought flashed across Nadia's mind, but she had no time for further reflection, because her first task was to get Didi out of there.

Nadia could hear Kati's footfalls approaching; the other nymph stopped a little way off. The bees were still swarming above Didi, but suddenly they wheeled away, as if by single command.

Working together, Kati and Nadia lifted Didi up and carried her to the car at a half-run. Nadia climbed into the back seat with Didi, and Kati took the wheel.

'Did you leave Erik in the basement?' Nadia asked.

'Of course.'

'It's true,' Nadia said to Kati, who clearly had no intention of responding. 'You saw those bees. The legend is true.'

Nadia said the words out loud. The sight of Didi covered by bees had filled her with incredible hope and certainty.

'Did you doubt it before?' Kati asked.

'Of course.' Nadia was admitting this for the first time, even to herself. 'You did, too. But now I'm sure. We're protecting the legend.'

They didn't talk for the rest of the trip. When they got home, Nadia ordered Kati to change Didi's sheets. In the meantime, she retrieved distillations and dried herbs from her medicine chest and started mixing the right compounds for revitalizing Didi. And Nadia believed completely that they would help, because there was no room for despair. Didi had to be kept alive.

At first Kati and Nadia stripped and washed Didi. Dead bees showered down from her clothes and her hair. They lowered her carefully into a warm bath that Nadia had laced with ethereal oils. Then they dried Didi off, dressed her in a linen nightgown, and carried her to her bed that had been made with her favorite floral sheets. Nadia wanted to make sure every detail was perfect. She rubbed herbal ointments into Didi's skin and moistened her cracked lips.

Afterwards, Nadia and Kati took turns watching over Didi as she slept. When she showed the first real signs of life, Nadia carefully spooned broth into her mouth. After this, Didi would crack her eyes open from time to time, but then she would sink back into a deep sleep, almost a coma. This continued for a couple of days, during which time Nadia was glued to the patient's side. Until Kati pulled her into the living room.

'Shouldn't Didi be waking up by now?' Kati asked.

Nadia looked at her old friend. For the last few days, Kati had put on a show of being aloof, but Nadia could see the touch of redness in her eyes, hear the tremor in her voice.

'Maybe,' Nadia said, because she was worried herself. Didi still looked very weak as she lay in bed, nearly motionless.

'You know what might help,' Kati said emphatically. She glanced at Jesper, who was lounging casually on the leather sofa in the living room.

'I thought you were always opposed to satyrs under any circumstances,' Nadia said, even though she had also considered the alternative herself.

'I don't suppose it would hurt.' Kati resumed her tough-boiled attitude and walked over to kick the sofa with the tip of her boot. 'Time to start earning your keep.'

Jesper gave Nadia a questioning look when she came over and sat next to him.

'Didi needs life force,' Nadia said softly. 'You could help.'

'Aren't we going to wait for the lunar eclipse together after all?' Jesper asked. He raised Nadia's hand and her now-bare finger.

Not long ago he had slipped a ring onto it, the very ring he had given her so many decades ago at Garda as a sign of his oath. Jesper knew that Nadia kept the ring in her pocket primarily because of Kati.

'Of course. That time is ours, but Didi needs to find her way back to us. With your help, she might be able to.'

Nadia looked at the satyr that she had loved, lost, and regained. She felt no pangs of jealousy, because she believed wholly and completely in her own love. She kissed Jesper softly on the lips, took him by the hand, and led him to the door of Didi's room.

'I'll wait here.'

Jesper lingered outside the door for a moment before going in. Nadia lit a few candles in the living room and remembered all of the women that she had treated at the safe house in Morocco. The women had fled various horrible circumstances, violent spouses and relatives, and the safe house had helped them start new lives. This situation wasn't really any different. Except that Didi wasn't a woman, she was a living legend.

Nadia's thoughts involuntarily circled around to a nymph she had met years ago. Milena had been so beautiful and so fragile, and yet stronger than Nadia had ever been. She jumped when Jesper returned only a few minutes later, shirtless.

'What is it?' Nadia asked. She hadn't imagined that Jesper would need any instructions on how to proceed with a nymph.

'Didi said that she can't be with me,' Jesper answered.

'Why not?'

'Erik told her that she'll die if she's with a satyr. Didi said that she'll heal better without me.'

Jesper took Nadia into his arms and they reveled in each other's warmth for a long time. Then Nadia crept silently over to Didi's room and listened to how steadily she was breathing. Didi had spoken. Nadia felt that they had turned the corner.

* * *

It took a couple more days for Didi to regain enough strength to climb out of bed. After that, her vigor returned rapidly, and if possible, her skin was more lucid than ever, the red gloss of her hair more dazzling. Nadia's heart burst with joy to witness the other nymph blossom into her full glory.

Nadia was concentrating on preparing an infusion of fruit and flowers, when she heard bare feet on the wooden floor. Didi had bathed and now she was fresh, downright radiant. She was wearing a dress where the delicate rose print played second fiddle to her hair. Nadia handed her a fragrant cup of tea.

'What are you looking at?' Nadia asked.

'There's something different about you,' Didi said. 'You are so incredibly beautiful.'

'No, you are,' Nadia laughed. She started tidying up the kitchen.

Didi watched Nadia with her head slightly tilted, and then the sunlight struck on Nadia's ring.

'Is that from Jesper?' Didi asked.

'He gave it to me the first time in 1806, right before we were separated.' Nadia raised her hand and looked at the ornamental band. 'At the time, we were waiting for the lunar eclipse together.'

'What's been going on here while I've been slumbering away like Sleeping Beauty?'

'Jesper has found an apartment and I'm moving there,' Nadia answered. 'We're going to continue where we left off. The next lunar eclipse is a couple of months away, and we will seal our union then.'

'I thought you guys ran away from the satyrs,' Didi said, perplexed.

'The satyrs, not Jesper,' Nadia said. 'And Jesper and I aren't the only ones anticipating the lunar eclipse. It has to do with you, too.'

'How?'

'Kati thinks it would be better to wait for the right moment before we tell you,' Nadia said. 'But hundreds of nymphs around the world are waiting for it.'

Nadia looked at Didi as she digested this information and everything else she had heard. She wanted to talk about the knot, tell her more about her own experiences, but maybe Kati was right. It was better not to swamp Didi with too many mystical tales all at once.

'But for now, let's eat,' Nadia said.

CHAPTER 58

It's so fitting that I'm living in a morgue these days, Samuel reflected, since he truly didn't feel like he was among the living. He had learned to slip away from the other medical students at the end of the day under some pretense or other, and then slink back to the morgue, where at least it was quiet. So what if some guard came by now and again to rattle the doors? Samuel had stashed away some sheets and blankets for himself there and he made himself a bed on a gurney every night. And he was perfectly content. Life had tossed plenty of drama his way recently. He might not be getting the best night's sleep, but at least he wasn't anywhere near the nymphs and satyrs. Maybe if he continued to live this way long enough, he'd forget all about them and be a normal person again.

But Didi – he couldn't forget her that easily. Nadia had sent him a single solitary text message that said that Didi was doing fine. Since then it had been total silence. At first Samuel had been satisfied, but now the longing was starting to gnaw away at him. When he remembered Didi's smile or the way she giggled at the wrong moment in a movie, he felt a tingling. He had had girlfriends before, but no one had filled him with the same kind of desire Didi did. He didn't just want sex, he wanted all of her.

I'd better get to work before my thoughts wander off in totally the wrong direction, Samuel thought, pulling himself up. Besides, his solitude would be invaded before long anyway.

Samuel washed up and changed into a clean lab coat, but his whole appearance was rough around the edges, and he had dark bags under his eyes. *Coffee might improve the situation*, he thought. He headed for the canteen, still groggy. He let out a big yawn and walked straight into a young blonde, whose own cup of coffee ended up on her clothes.

'I'm so sorry!' Samuel exclaimed. The young woman was so thrown off she couldn't get a word out. 'I didn't see you . . .'

'I think I burned my fingers,' she finally said. 'Why don't you give me some first aid? Since you're a doctor.'

It took Samuel a second to realize that the woman was smiling at him.

'A doctor who doesn't get enough sleep, which is why he's such a klutz,' Samuel said, and the woman gave him a questioning look. 'It's a long story.'

'I have time,' the woman said. 'I'm waiting for my dad, he's getting some tests done.'

Samuel glanced around and decided that he wasn't in a hurry to get anywhere either. Besides, he suddenly realized it had been a long time since he had just talked to another person.

'First off, let me say that you appear to be in good shape,' Samuel said. 'Now that's a purely superficial diagnosis. The second thing I'm noting is that you seem to be in need of a coffee. Hi, I'm Samuel.'

'Jessica. Should we get some more?'

'You got that coffee over there?' Samuel asked. 'It's got to be at least a week old. I'll buy you a cup from the canteen.'

'Buy me a sweet roll, too, and we'll be even,' Jessica laughed.

In the canteen, Jessica waited at a window table as Samuel carried a tray over.

'Two mediocre coffees and two excellent sweet rolls,' Samuel said, sitting down. He gobbled down a bite to take the edge off his hunger.

'Did you say that you're living in the morgue?' Jessica asked.

'For almost three weeks now.'

'Problems at home?'

'You could say that again. I don't have one,' Samuel said. 'I was living on my boat but it burned down. Then I moved in . . . with a girl. It just didn't work out. Since then I've been shacking up here.'

Samuel looked into Jessica's bright blue eyes and discovered how easy it was to chat about this and that. Jessica told him a little bit about herself, too, where she worked, how she was at the hospital visiting her dad who was recovering from a back operation, all kinds of little things. When Samuel finally really had to leave to get to work, he found himself asking Jessica to go to the movies. That's how simple things were with humans.

CHAPTER 59

Nadia looked around the empty room for a second, but she didn't feel like she was missing out on anything. Throughout her entire existence as a nymph, she had grown accustomed to moving, to changing countries after every lunar eclipse, to jumping into a new role. She had even enjoyed it. Of course she might miss Didi and Kati and their life together now and again, but she was finally going to be starting a life with Jesper.

Kati was already on the balcony mixing rather strong drinks in honor of the going-away party. Didi was nibbling at the little shrimp sandwiches.

'When are you leaving?' Didi asked.

'Jesper will be by to pick me up soon, but I have time to have a drink and grab a bite,' Nadia said.

Kati had a large bowl of sliced limes, and she was just spinning the wide mouths of the glasses in flakes of sea salt, putting the finishing touches on some margaritas. 'Nadia will get a taste of what she thinks she's missing and realize that nothing ever changes. Then she'll come back to us, tail between her legs.'

'Stop being manipulative, Kati,' Nadia said. She turned to explain to Didi. 'Kati thinks that a real freedom fighter can't live with a satyr. But Jesper is looking out for our best interests the whole time.'

'He's a satyr.' Kati handed the glasses round and the three nymphs raised them.

The mixture of lime, tequila and crushed ice was wonderfully cool; it momentarily numbed their lips and made their laughter sparkle in the air. It wasn't long before Kati had to mix up a second round, but one question had remained nagging at Didi's mind.

'Fighting for what kind of freedom?'

'Nadia, wait just a second.' Kati pretended to remember something and went inside.

'Kati ran off so she wouldn't have to answer the question,' Didi said.

'When you've lived long enough, you know that there's a time and a place for everything,' Nadia said, licking the salt from her lips.

A moment later Kati reappeared, carrying a huge armful of water bottles. 'A going-away present from us.'

'You should have told me about this. That way I could have come up with a present, too,' Didi said, embarrassed.

'I was just trying to be polite.'

'You never think about anyone else.' Didi held out her empty glass towards Kati, who was playing bartender that evening.

The doorbell rang and Nadia looked at her friends. It was time to say goodbye. She hugged Kati first and then Didi, without wanting to say anything else. She just wanted to remember every detail of this dusky moment on the balcony, the yellow-green margaritas shimmering in their glasses, their friendship. She gave a little wave and then went and opened the door for Jesper, who was waiting outside.

Nadia was still panting as she rolled off Jesper. She pulled the luxurious eiderdown comforter over her and laughed hoarsely at Jesper's stunned expression. Even though he had known she was prepared to show her commitment in every way he'd been surprised. And during the lunar eclipse, everything would be even more uninhibited. Nadia was laying all of her expectations on it.

A moment later, Jesper was ready to demonstrate his own commitment, and Nadia didn't resist when he yanked the blanket off and slid down between her legs. Nadia wanted to feel good. She was lying on her back, one hand behind her neck. With the other, she intermittently stroked and pulled Jesper's blond hair as the satyr worshipped her with his mouth.

Later they lay swathed in the duvet in each other's arms, gazing out at the night-time vista opening up from Jesper's penthouse. Jesper poured champagne into plastic mugs and they toasted them with a light tap. The only things in the room were a mattress on the floor and a couple of lamps, but they would have plenty of time to get everything they needed. *And we'll be doing it together*, Nadia said to herself.

'What do you want to do tomorrow?' Jesper asked.

'I have to go to work.'

Jesper was totally flabbergasted. 'Why? You don't have to work any more.' He had clearly imagined that he would be getting Nadia's undivided attention for himself.

'I like my job and my coworkers.'

'Humans,' Jesper spat out the word. 'Besides, during the lunar eclipse, you guys were supposed to move, like you always do. That means you'll have to leave your job anyway. For a couple of reasons.'

Nadia knew that Jesper couldn't understand why she wanted to work, just like he couldn't understand her belief in the legend. It would be better to change the topic. 'Why don't we have any furniture?'

Jesper jumped out from under the duvet and went over to the gym bag that had been tossed into the corner of the living room. He took out a stack of catalogs and casually handed them to Nadia.

'I marked the ones I liked,' Jesper said.

'What if I want something different from the ones you marked?' Nadia asked. Irritation was boiling up inside her again.

'Mark your own, and then we'll see what each of us picked.'

Jesper eyed Nadia. He looked so confused that Nadia backed down. Over the centuries, she had heard from countless humans that this is exactly what life was like for young couples just starting out. You had to compromise. And she wasn't in the habit of being petty. She was prepared to try.

CHAPTER 60

'I had a great time tonight,' Samuel said, and he was totally serious. He had been on a date and there hadn't been the least bit of drama. No one had threatened his life or talked about death. Instead he had seen a totally inane comedy, gone to eat, and had a couple of beers afterwards. Then he had started walking Jessica home, and they had bought a couple of ice-cream cones after an overly analytical discussion of flavors.

'I had a good time, too,' Jessica said.

Samuel looked at her. Jessica was cute, with her blond hair in a little bun at her neck and her normal jeans and anorak, her blue flats. They were more or less the same age, and conversation seemed to bubble up without any effort. Samuel realized that Jessica had said something and was repeating herself now.

'This is where I live.'

'Sorry, I was sort of lost in thought,' Samuel said. 'I'm not trying to be rude, but can I just say that I love it that you're so totally normal.'

The perplexed look on Jessica's face made Samuel step in closer, and he felt her breath on his skin in the cool evening air. It could have been so easy, but he wasn't ready yet.

'I meant it as a compliment.'

Jessica pointed upwards. 'My window is the one on the second floor with the red curtains. You want to come up for some tea?'

Samuel would have loved to accept the invitation, but something inside him wouldn't let him yet, and Jessica could sense it.

'Is the morgue calling your name?' Jessica asked.

'Some other time,' Samuel said, laying a small peck on Jessica's pink mouth. Then he stepped back through the portico and out onto the street, and continued on his way, smiling and lost in thought. He felt like just walking and thinking about what it was he wanted. He wanted to forget about Didi, forget all their problems, forget the dangers and difficulties that their relationship entailed. He wanted to find a nice, normal girl who he could do nice, normal things with. Jessica was like that. Why on earth had he resisted?

Samuel walked until he felt like he couldn't take another step. He looked around to see where he was, and if there was a tram or a bus he could jump on. Then someone said his name and he knew where he was. He was in front of his former temporary home, the nymphs' apartment building. And he was looking straight into Didi's astonished eyes.

'Samuel?' Didi repeated. 'What are you doing here?'

'I don't know,' Samuel said, who always had a tendency to tell the truth. 'There were a lot of hours today when I didn't think about you at all.'

Didi, who had at first seemed overjoyed, turned away in irritation.

'I didn't mean to come here,' Samuel said. 'Or maybe I had to come to test out what it would feel like to see you.'

Samuel looked at Didi. She was wearing the olive green dress that made her red hair so enticing. Samuel desperately tried to call to mind Jessica's calm demeanor, how they had walked side by side and how their hands had brushed against each other at the ice-cream stand. He would have to work for it, but he was sure it would be worth it.

'Test out?' Didi repeated his words, and now a smile rippled across her lips. 'So how does it feel?'

'Not much like anything, really,' Samuel lied. 'Maybe this is starting to get easier already.'

Didi's smile faded as she grasped the meaning of Samuel's words, and her eyes began to flash. 'Go to hell,' she said between clenched teeth.

'What?' Samuel was startled by the rage he had aroused in Didi. 'If you don't want me, fine. But you don't have any right to come by here to figure out what you're feeling!'

Didi took a few steps in Samuel's direction, and he felt it would be best to grab her by the wrists. 'Didi, calm down . . .'

Didi wrenched free. A few passersby stared at them, and one looked like he was on the verge of coming over to make sure Didi was all right. *If they only knew*, Samuel thought. *I'm the one who should be happy he's still alive.*

Then Samuel saw the lost look in Didi's eyes, and he knew exactly how she felt. He felt an urge to stroke her hair, but luckily he didn't give in to it. He would have been a goner.

'You can't come here any more,' Didi said, backing up. Then she turned and disappeared in the opposite direction.

Samuel was left standing alone on the street. He was quaking. He hadn't realized how strong his passion for Didi truly was. When they'd been near each other's bodies, when he'd smelled Didi's scent, there had been an instant when he would have been ready for anything. Fear was the only thing that held him back. And not his normal fear of commitment, but fear for his own life. When the satyr had held his head under the surface in the nymphs' tub, he had struggled until his lungs filled with water. Everything had gone black, and his capacity to think and act had grown weaker with every heartbeat. *So this is what death feels like*, he managed to clinically analyze, as was fitting for a medical student. Fear of death was the greatest of fears, he thought now. Maybe that experience would prove useful. He could use it to free himself of Didi, and it would help him to understand his future patients better. It might even help him understand his father, who in his final moments had wanted Samuel at his side.

But there is one place I'd feel calm and safe, Samuel thought, and before long he was standing under Jessica's window. The light was still on behind the red curtains on the second floor. He picked up a few pebbles and tossed them at the window. He waited a minute and then he could make out Jessica's blond hair in the darkness. She didn't say anything, she just tossed the keys to him, and by the time he made it inside her apartment, the tea water was already boiling.

'I don't have any ulterior motives,' Samuel said as he took off his jacket and hung it on the back of the chair. 'I just feel so at peace when I'm with you.'

'In other words, you don't think about your ex when you're with me,' Jessica said. 'As long as you understand that I'm not some second choice. I can make up a bed for you on the couch there, if you want to spend the night.'

'I do,' Samuel said. And once more, he was telling the truth. He wanted it more than anything in the world.

CHAPTER 61

J esper had promised to pick up the groceries for their first meal in their new home, and Nadia had figured that they would cook together like any carefree young couple. So when Jesper started pulling all kinds of prepackaged food out of the bags – even though they were gorgeously packaged, premium quality and delicious-looking – Nadia was disappointed. But she masked her feelings and started to set everything out appetizingly. After all, Jesper had gotten the artichokes and paper-thin prosciutto she loved so much, and so many of the Mediterranean delicacies she couldn't get enough of. *I would have rather made the pesto myself,* Nadia thought, *but there will be time for that.* For Jesper, cooking was mostly about uncorking a good bottle of wine and choosing the right music.

'Kati asked me to come by tomorrow,' Nadia said. 'I'm going after work.'

'You're against satyrs, but Kati is your satyr,' Jesper said, plucking one black olive and one green olive from the plate. 'She makes the rules, limits your contacts with the outside world, and metes out the punishment if you break the rules.'

'Stop trying to provoke me,' Nadia said in dismay, because there was a grain of truth in what Jesper was saying. 'All nymphs are equal.'

'Kati always takes everything to the extreme,' Jesper said. 'Not all satyrs are bad, and not all nymphs want to flee. And those beliefs about that knot are total crap. There is no savior, there won't ever be a savior, and nothing is going to magically change with the wave of a wand.'

'We still have the right to be free if we want,' Nadia said. For her, the matter was that simple, especially since her belief in the legend was stronger than ever now.

'You want to have a family with me,' Jesper said. 'You and I are waiting together for the eclipse, for the rite. You always used to say you'd rather have a little satyr than a little nymph. Ninette . . .'

'My name is Nadia!' Nadia was so angry now that she threw a cherry tomato at Jesper. She could see that it irritated him, so she did it again. Some other time, this could have been lighthearted clowning around, play that would end in passionate sex and then another meal. But on this night, a totally different mood vibrated in the air.

'Idiot,' Nadia said, hurling a third tomato at Jesper.

She was totally caught off guard when Jesper suddenly took her by the arm, pulled a heaped handful of pesto from the bowl with his other hand, and smeared it on her face. Jesper had never been the least bit violent towards her, and this didn't cause her any pain, but the way Jesper had violated her person was an offense to her. Nadia's eyes were sparking.

'Don't you dare touch me.'

Jesper was stunned by his own actions and quickly retreated. He looked at his hand and Nadia's face.

'Come on, I'll lick it off.' He tried to make it all a game, but Nadia spun around on her heels.

She leaned against the edge of the bathroom sink, staring at her face, which was covered by green blotches of basil. *Jesper is a satyr first and foremost*, she thought. *I knew it all along, but I didn't want to admit it. Maybe freedom is so close now that I can finally see everything in a new way.*

Nadia turned on the shower and took off her clothes. She needed water. She craved its soothing sound and its soft sensation on her skin. She would have preferred to slip into a fresh mountain lake or a small pool in a forest glade, but she'd have to make do with the ultra-fancy, newly installed – because Jesper really did think about her needs, she couldn't deny it – overhead rain shower.

Nadia gradually calmed down, and when Jesper appeared behind the glass door, she opened it for him, and with a few natural movements, satyr and nymph were back together. When they looked in each other's eyes, they were alone, and they had left the world behind on the other side of the door. Nadia loved Jesper with all her heart.

'I'm a satyr, and I can't change how I think,' Jesper said to Nadia later, when they were drying each other off. 'I'm just trying to protect you. But you're right. I can't make your decisions for you. I can't control you.'

Jesper's words were exactly what Nadia wanted to hear, and she was about to answer them with words of her own, followed by actions, when the doorbell rang. Jesper wrapped a towel around his waist and Nadia quickly slipped on a dress. It was Didi.

'I had a fight with Samuel,' Didi said, and Nadia wrapped her in a gentle embrace.

'Let's have a little something to eat and drink,' Nadia said.

'Now you're talking my language,' Jesper said and went to get the food and wine from the kitchen. Because the large mattress was still the only piece of furniture in the apartment, they all sat down on it and ate together.

'This isn't Nadia's pesto,' Didi said as she bit into a slice of baguette heaped with cucumber rounds.

'See, I told you.' Nadia jabbed Jesper in the side, but this time it was playful.

'We know,' Jesper said. 'I just wanted to save my nymph's energy . . .'

Didi looked at the couple and only now did she realize what she had interrupted. She blushed prettily. 'Oops, I'm so sorry . . .'

'It's fine,' Nadia said. 'We have plenty of time for that now.'

They dined and Nadia began to talk about the best meals she had ever eaten.

'She's such a typical Italian,' Jesper said to Didi. 'Even at the table, all she talks about is food.'

Nadia didn't let it bother her, she just explained her family's culinary life at length and in detail. Didi felt almost as full from the story as from the meal that had been served. But she still didn't turn down the fruit with mascarpone cream that Nadia offered. After that, she was stuffed and exhausted, as were Nadia and Jesper. The three of them lay on the mattress, sated, limbs intertwined, two nymphs and one satyr.

It could be this natural, Nadia thought as she looked at Jesper and Didi through her half-closed eyes, and a warm feeling settled into her breast.

' "One night, when the moon goes dark, a nymph will be born." ' Nadia had recited the legend's words before, but she knew that Didi was hearing them for the first time now. ' "The girl will carry within her passion, destruction, love and war. The nymph will be given the name Epithymia Tha, and her symbol will be the knot. The nymph will wage war against our masters on behalf of all nymphs. She will govern our masters, and the ultimate master is the moon . . ." '

'I've heard that fairy tale, too, dozens of versions of it,' Jesper said sleepily.

'They all mention the knot and the nymph who will save the rest of us,' Nadia said.

'Maybe master doesn't mean satyrs.' Jesper was yawning widely now. 'Maybe it just means the moon.'

Nadia looked to see what sort of effect her words had had on Didi. The younger nymph was weighing them carefully. Nadia tenderly raised the hem of Didi's skirt until the knot on her belly was exposed.

'It's not a birthmark; someone tattooed it on me when I was really little,' Didi said.

'I fled my covey because of you,' Nadia said.

'I still don't believe in it,' Didi insisted.

'Thank you, Desirée,' Jesper said.

Nadia rose from the bed and walked over to the window. Night had fallen, and it was quiet outside. Off in the distance, she could see a lone figure walking a dog.

'I have proof,' Nadia said, turning back to Didi and Jesper. 'The legend says that Didi has to die before the prophecy can be fulfilled.'

'No thanks,' Didi said.

'And then bees will bring the nymph back to life ... Didi, when Kati and I found you in the forest, you were covered in bees. You are the nymph of legend.'

Nadia went back over to Didi, who stared at her, stunned.

CHAPTER 62

Erik Mann was finally free, thanks to Desirée, who had unwittingly helped him. When the nymph had approached him, he had been forced to keep his feelings in check, and that gave him the opportunity to grab a bobby pin out of her hair and slip it into his sleeve. He had waited until he heard the car leaving – based on the noises, something truly alarming had happened, but evidently Desirée was still alive – and only then had he begun to work on unlocking his shackles. It stung his self-importance that the nymphs no longer seemed to be worried about him and disappeared without saying a word.

The house was totally dark when Erik ascended the creaking cellar stairs. Evidently the enormous manor had been without inhabitants for quite some time, because the furniture was covered and the air was a little stale. He started to wander from room to room. Not a bad place. It had plenty of space, and some style too. He was accustomed to a different sort of luxury, and yet this place had its own brand of sensible charm. But now he had to start looking for some clue as to where he was. Best of all, he might find a phone somewhere.

Erik peered under the sheets and then he saw a large sideboard that might have all sorts of things concealed within its depths. He opened one door and then another, but was immediately disappointed. Then he noticed a couple of smaller drawers and searched them. A red gleam rose to his eyes. He hadn't anticipated this. An oak-leaf pendant. What did it mean? As far as he knew, the Oakhearts had been decimated, but evidently Didi's foster mother belonged to the family, and now another pendant had also appeared out of nowhere to haunt him.

Erik wasn't allowed any more time to ponder this conundrum, though. He heard the sound of a car. Had the nymphs returned? At least this time he would be prepared. Languishing in chains had by no means weakened him; it had instilled him with renewed determination and strength. His eyes grew even redder as he opened a small gap in the curtains and looked out.

A tall, slender, wavy-haired man of about fifty rose from the driver's seat. His companion was a blond girl of about ten. They started to unpack the car, and before long the key to the house was being fit into the lock.

'Should we fix dinner right away?' the man asked the girl.

'How about tea? I'm not very hungry,' the girl answered. 'You make it.'

Erik stood motionlessly in the next room. He could feel the man sense his presence, and he waited. The instant the man entered, Erik struck him in the chest with all of his might. The man fell to his knees but leapt right back up. The girl ran behind the sofa. Erik was surprised by how quickly the man recovered. He was even more surprised to receive a sharp kick to his kidneys. Erik would have continued fighting if the wound from the *nomos* dagger didn't continue to give him so much pain. He hurled a chair at the man and ran out into the dark.

'He's not coming back,' Matias van der Haas gasped to his daughter.

'Should I call the police?' Matilda asked.

'Make tea. I have to check something.'

Matias went down the stairs to the basement. The lights were on, and he immediately noticed the chains and the empty wine bottles. He walked past them, went to the darkest corner of the cellar and yanked out a dusty old chest. He opened the lid, and from under the false bottom, he pulled out a leather satchel bearing an embroidered oak tree. He sighed in relief and opened the bag. The bundle within contained the instruments that he would doubtlessly come to need: two metal bottles, a *nomos* dagger, tongs, a tranquilizer gun and darts, and a round, bluish glass in a brass frame.

He replaced everything in the chest and went back upstairs to rejoin his daughter.

CHAPTER 63

Didi wasn't necessarily a morning person, but she didn't want to hang around watching Nadia and Jesper's blossoming happiness, nor did she want to be bossed around by Kati all day. So she went in to work early. She polished the counters, set out the baked goods and filled the salt-shakers.

'Boy trouble, huh?' asked the ever-perceptive Valtteri.

'I don't have a boy,' said Didi.

'My point exactly.'

'I'm going to go outside and set out the terrace tables.'

Didi might have craved fresh air, but she regretted her decision the moment she stepped out on the terrace. Samuel was sitting there with an attractive blonde. At first Didi thought she would turn around and walk away without making a fuss, but then she got mad. Did Samuel seriously have to come to her restaurant to show off his new squeeze? Didi decided she'd show him that she could deal with things like a mature adult.

As Didi approached, Samuel and the woman were laughing at something, and the woman brushed Samuel's cheek. Didi tried to think of a way she could use a cappuccino spoon as a weapon, but as soon as the idea came to her, she buried it. Instead she gave a beautiful smile.

'Hi. What can I get you two?' Didi asked, and before Samuel had time to take over the situation, she held out a hand to the woman. 'I'm Desirée.'

'Jessica.'

'Samuel and I have had a pretty convoluted relationship. I don't know if he told you about it.'

'A little,' Jessica said, but she gave Samuel an inquiring look. 'I could take a glass of dry white wine.'

Samuel finally managed to say something: 'Jessica has offered me a place to stay. I don't have to sleep at the pathology unit any more.'

'And a café au lait for you, I presume,' Didi said. 'Like always.'

Didi was already headed off to get their drinks, but she wheeled back around to face Samuel. 'I had a crush on you when I was nine years old, when you saved me from a spider. I had a crush on you again at the beginning of the summer, when you saved me from a bee. I didn't want to fall in love, but I still did.'

'I don't believe you,' said Samuel.

'You don't believe that I love you?' Didi tossed her dish towel over her shoulder and stood there with her hands on her hips.

'One minute you run away, the next minute you call me names. Then you ask for help, then you back off. What kind of love is that, supposedly?'

'Samuel,' Jessica said in cautionary tone.

That was the last straw for Didi. She had no need for anyone's pity, especially from the woman Samuel apparently lived with now. Didi moved like a snake, grabbing Jessica by the wrist without knowing herself what she intended to do next. She could feel the other woman's pulse, and it filled her with a rage that throbbed through her temples. At first she couldn't comprehend Jessica's expression. The blonde girl was writhing in pain, even though Didi wasn't squeezing very hard. And then just as quickly as she had grabbed Jessica's wrist, Didi let it go.

'I'm sorry,' Didi whispered. 'I didn't mean to.'

'This is exactly what I was talking about,' Samuel said.

'I hate being this way, too!' Didi said. 'And I love you. What am I supposed to do?'

Samuel didn't answer, he just concentrated on making sure Jessica was OK. Didi backed inside and watched through the window as, a moment later, Samuel wrapped his arm around Jessica and they walked away.

Didi stared at her hand. Before, its touch had communicated other people's feelings to her with an astounding clarity. Now her touch could also cause pain. Of course Samuel didn't want to be with her. She was a monster.

CHAPTER 64

For some reason, lately Nadia's thoughts had been going back to Essaouira more and more frequently, to the whitewashed women's safe house. She had felt at home there. Over the course of history, she had observed the fates of many women, but everything had come to a climax there in Morocco. She witnessed all the things that could be done to women just because they were women. They were treated like property, worse than animals. Their freedom was stripped away. But Nadia didn't want to think about that; she wanted to think about the future. She wanted to heal and see women move on from the safe house towards a better life. It didn't happen all of the time, of course, but her heart still filled with hope.

And of course Nadia remembered Milena in particular. The young woman had been at death's door when she showed up at the safe house, and at first glance Nadia had recognized her as a nymph. She was beautiful, blonde, and clear-browed, but her life-light was fading. Nadia was prepared to do anything to help her, as it was the full moon, but she couldn't convince Milena to join her in her search for nourishment. Milena had wanted to live free of the satyrs, which is why she had fled her covey. She didn't want to obey anyone any more, neither her masters nor the moon. She was already in the throes of incredible pain, but she accepted her fate. Nadia had been forced to venture out by herself to feed, even though Milena had prayed for her to stay with her. By the time Nadia returned, Milena had passed away, but a smile had remained on the nymph's chapped lips.

Nadia was eager to wipe the memory from her mind, and perhaps that's why she made love to Jesper until they were panting and sweating. Getting a satyr to beg for a break was quite an achievement.

Nadia was still lying on top of her satyr, looking at his drowsy smile. The truth flashed across her mind in the blink of an eye.

'I'm jealous,' Nadia said. 'You're thinking about Didi.'

'Desirée Volanté, desire and will.' The perspiring Jesper savored the words. 'Even though I don't believe in that fairy tale of yours, there is something peculiar about that redhead. Her scent is so much stronger than with any of the rest of you. It's trapped in this blanket.'

Jesper drew the duvet up to his face and inhaled deeply. He offered it to Nadia, too, but she turned away.

'It's like a drug,' Jesper said, his voice raw. 'I'm ready for a new round. Maybe that's the power of that nymph. Satyrs will start drooling after Didi. What a legend!'

Nadia was irritated and she rolled off Jesper. Jesper didn't have to subscribe to her beliefs, but he didn't need to make fun of them, either. She didn't know all of the ways Desirée could change nymphs' lives, but the prophecy promised them freedom. The freedom to choose whom to love and when. Nadia rose from the mattress and went over to the window. There was a question she wanted to ask, but the answer scared her so much that she didn't dare to look Jesper in the eye.

'Would you have completed your task, if I hadn't been among those who were being hunted?'

'You mean would I have captured the redhead and killed the rest of the nymphs?' Jesper asked. 'Probably. I had orders.'

At least Jesper was honest, Nadia thought, but at the same time she silently cursed Kati, who had been proved right once again.

Nadia walked over to the mattress and Jesper raised his arms, ready to wrap her once more in his embrace, but she bent over and picked up her clothes from the floor.

'Ninette, stop,' Jesper said. 'I promised to live by your rules.'

'You're a satyr and you can't change. This might last a moment or even a couple of decades, but before long I'll be in the same situation I was in before the escape. I wouldn't be able to stand that.'

Jesper stood up and took a step closer to Nadia. Nadia thought about how beautiful the naked satyr was to her, how much she loved him, but she could no longer diverge from the path she had chosen. They were too close to their goal.

Nadia slowly drew the ring from her finger and held it out to Jesper. He didn't want to accept it. Nadia grabbed his hand, opened the palm, and pressed the symbol of their beautifully patinated, centuries-long union into it.

'I told you I'm on your side,' Jesper said.

'But you can't change,' Nadia said. 'I've already changed and I have to make a choice. I can't live with you.'

'Don't leave me,' Jesper said.

'I have to.' It was torture for Nadia to say the words out loud, but she couldn't think of any other way. 'If I stay, when it comes down to it, I'll be nothing more than a nymph to you. I want to be free. I want us all to be free.'

A moment later, Nadia closed the door silently behind her. And then all she wanted was to be with her sister nymphs. She ran down the stairs and almost all the way to the apartment. It didn't even bother her that once again, Kati would have the chance to tell her I told you so.

As Nadia stepped onto the balcony where Kati was leaning against the railing the way she always did and Didi was sitting in the lounge chair under a blanket, she felt like she had come home.

'I'm moving back in,' Nadia said.

'I have a new skill,' Didi said.

'I went out to the manor.' Kati filled a glass of wine and handed it to Nadia. 'Erik has escaped.'

Nadia looked at Kati, sensing that she had discovered something else at the manor, too, but this time she let Kati keep her secrets to herself without pestering her. The important thing was that they were together again. The following night, a full moon would be shining in the sky.

CHAPTER 65

Erik knew that his absence had not gone unnoticed. He was equally certain that Mitchell had used the situation to his advantage and cemented his union with Gabriel Korda. And yet he also knew Korda well enough to know that he seriously doubted Korda would fully trust a satyr who had betrayed his master. On the other hand, Korda wanted to retain his place as Master, and Mitchell lusted for a seat as a permanent member of the Conclave. If they managed to play Erik out ... So Erik just had to make sure that didn't happen. He had been so close to Desirée and to everything he wanted that he had no intention of backing down now. Up to this point, Korda had been a step ahead of him in everything he aimed for and had pushed Erik aside as soon as he was on the verge of reaching whatever he sought, whether it was status or wealth. That would not be happening again.

Erik called Mitchell as if he had been fully in control of the situation the whole time.

'I was taking care of a few things you don't need to know about for the time being,' he said. 'And now Jesper Janssen can be moved to the list of those to be eliminated. I'll stay here for a while longer.'

Erik hung up before Mitchell had a chance to ask any questions. In the first place, he had no intention of lowering himself by being interrogated, and in the second, he was waiting for a friend who was extremely punctual. So Erik poured out the cognac beforehand.

Erik rarely liked humans, but Roland Gyllen, who was almost 70, had been a pleasant acquaintance for years now. Gyllen had known that he was making a deal of sorts with the devil – or a satyr – but he had done it to secure the future of his descendants. With Erik's help, his enterprise's downward slide had been turned to profit, and the documents had been drawn up in such a way that Gyllen's wastrel children couldn't squander their own future, or his grandchildren's.

When Gyllen arrived, he and Erik made small talk while enjoying a glass of cognac. Gyllen was old and wise, and in the end, he finally brought up the subject himself.

'I presume you require a favor in return for your earlier services,' Gyllen said.

Erik looked at his friend and remembered the vigorous middle-aged businessman with whom he had drawn up the original agreement. Now Gyllen had grown stouter, his skin was pale, and he had no longer stood as tall, but he still possessed the charisma of a leader.

Erik settled into his chair, assuming a more comfortable position. Gyllen was also one of the few humans Erik trusted. Usually when humans got something, they immediately started lusting for more and, almost without exception, greed proved to be their downfall. Gyllen had always stuck to their agreements without presenting any further demands. That's why Erik had decided to speak as frankly as he could.

'I have found a spouse,' Erik said. Gyllen raised his eyebrows. 'I need an extremely quiet place where we will not be disturbed.'

Gyllen considered the matter for a moment. Erik saw that the old man's curiosity had been piqued, but he clearly kept it in check.

'I have a log cabin in the countryside. There aren't neighbors nearby. I've often retreated there myself to think from time to time, and gain some perspective. Would that do?'

Erik smiled. If Gyllen called the place a log cabin, there was no doubt it was a luxury villa decked out with all modern comforts. He raised his snifter to signify a done deal.

'Humor me for a moment longer,' Gyllen said. 'I know that this was a repayment, but I would like to ask for something myself. You've probably already divined what it is.'

'I have,' Erik said. 'I'll arrange it when you give the signal.'

'Good,' Gyllen said and rose, a little shakily. 'The keys and directions will be delivered to you tomorrow. Feel free to stay as long as you like. As you can probably guess, I don't have any use for it any more.'

CHAPTER 66

Didi was tired. It had thundered during the night, and she had slept restlessly. She could also already feel the approach of the next night's full moon. She had been in a hurry to get to her lecture that morning, but had yawned through it constantly, even though the topic had captured her imagination – the virgin of Orleans. Afterwards, she had worked a long shift at Valtteri's cafe. Luckily it was almost time to close, and the last customer was getting ready to leave. Valtteri had perched himself at the counter with a cup of tea and the newspaper.

'You've had quite a few admirers today,' he said.

Didi knew it, and it exhausted her. Men's eyes lingered on her, undressed her. It made her feel naked. She wanted to get home and away from all this. She hadn't taken any more of the medicine Nadia had prepared; she had just decided to stay within four walls during the critical period. She no longer remembered barely anything about how she had passed out in the forest, but she did remember the horrendous, gut-wrenching agony and was terrified of it.

Didi wiped the cafe counter and moved an empty cup into the sink. She remembered the blond man who had ordered the cappuccino half an hour earlier and given her a sweet smile. As she moved the cup, a slip of paper was exposed beneath it. It was an invitation for a drink, with a name and a phone number. Didi threw it in the trash without a second's hesitation.

'That boy was here, too,' Valtteri said, giving her an analytical look.

'Samuel?' Didi immediately asked. 'Did he ask for me?'

'No. He had company. What was it, Jenni or Janika . . . ?'

'Jessica.' Didi turned away from Valtteri and concentrated intently on rinsing out a rag. With her free hand, she fumbled around in the trash and retrieved the piece of paper, which she slipped into her apron pocket.

'You come have a cup of tea, too,' Valtteri said in an inviting tone.

Didi glanced at her sweet, lovely boss and recognized the symptoms. A sheep-like gaze, accelerated breathing . . . This was getting impossible. Didi wanted to keep both her job and Valtteri's friendship. There was only one thing to do.

'Valtteri, would you mind if I took a couple of days off?' Didi asked. 'I need to study for a test and I have a couple of other things . . .'

'Go ahead,' Valtteri said, even though he looked disappointed. 'As long as you don't totally disappear again.'

'I won't,' Didi promised, already taking off her apron. 'Thanks.'

Didi went into the bathroom and put on her favorite new dress. She had been walking down the street with Nadia when she had seen it in a shop window. 'That has your name written all over it!' Nadia had cried, and they had stepped inside.

The dress was sky blue; it had spaghetti straps and was dotted with pink and red flowers. It was cut snugly under the breasts, but the hem was as light as a breeze. It had been a little too expensive, but Nadia had encouraged her to buy it, and Didi hadn't regretted it for an instant.

She slipped her feet into blue ballerina flats and pulled on a blue sweater. The blue color lifted the russet glory of her hair to a totally new dimension. In her old life as a normal girl, she had never worn a color like that. Being a nymph had its own challenges, but it had also brought Didi a new confidence that she enjoyed.

She stepped out of the cafe. Just a minute ago she had been totally sure that she wanted to go home, but now something was gnawing at her. She reached into her pocket and pulled out the slip of paper that the blond man had left her and considered it for a moment. She could have a little fun, too. Samuel had found someone new right away, so why shouldn't she live a little, as well? There wasn't any harm in it. She'd meet the guy, flirt a little and then she'd go home like a good little girl. *Unlike those other two, who don't have the same concerns I do,* she thought. Already that morning Kati's eyes had been flickering like the eyes of a predator, and Nadia had announced that she wouldn't be back until morning, after she took care of some errands that involved Jesper. Didi had understood without it being made explicit that Nadia wanted to spend the night with someone who would wipe the memories of love from her mind. As if that were possible.

Didi tapped a number into her cell phone and paused in the doorway to wait for an answer. She never got it. Someone put a rag with a strange smell up to her face. She struggled against it as hard as she could, but before long she felt her legs give way. And then her eyes were going dim. She struggled to keep from losing consciousness and felt someone toss her over his shoulders and carry her out through the doorway into a van. Then she was chained to the floor of the van by one of her ankles, and the van started off.

By exerting an unbelievable effort, Didi managed to open her eyes a little and slightly raise her head, which was as heavy as lead. She couldn't give in yet. She groped around her pocket, where she had shoved her cell phone during the ambush, and pulled up a number. She pressed what she hoped was the right button. A moment later, she heard Kati's voice.

'Didi? Didi?' Kati repeated.

Didi cracked open her mouth to answer, but her vocal cords would no longer obey. And then she dropped her head and was dead to the world.

CHAPTER 67

Kati had been having an exceptionally pleasurable evening. She had seduced a man who seemed like a good catch, made long, skillful love to her, and then sank into a deep, well-deserved slumber. Kati might have considered lounging there at his side for a while, but Didi's phone call changed her mind. She had to get to the apartment and fast.

'Nadia?' she asked softly as she opened the door, but the apartment had echoed emptily. She called Nadia's number and was frustrated to hear it immediately ring in the living room. She had made Nadia swear that she would always carry her phone with her. Was it really that difficult to follow a simple instruction? The point was to ensure all of their safety.

She found Nadia's phone and checked the most recent calls and messages. Frida's name popped up, and Kati opened the message. All it contained were map coordinates. That meant Frida was in trouble. Kati immediately checked Nadia's passport stash. Her passport was gone. Goddammit, Nadia! Nadia couldn't help herself when it came to helping others. She'd bounce right up with her herbs and potions and head out the door without considering the risks or consequences.

Kati moved into Didi's room and cursed at herself. Apparently the girl had not been by the apartment, which meant something must have happened to her along the way. Kati slammed her fist into the wall and sank down onto Didi's bed to sit and think. If Didi was in

Erik's clutches, she might never see the girl again. Erik had probably had Didi kidnapped in his typical way, without getting his own hands dirty at this stage, and that meant Didi's current location would be almost impossible to figure out. Unless . . . Kati weighed the alternatives for a moment, and then she made the call. Soon a low, slightly wary male voice answered.

'Harju.'

Kati got right to the point. 'I need help.' She explained the situation to Harju. 'Is there any way you could find out what might have happened to Didi?'

'Big Brother is always watching nowadays,' Harju said. 'There are cameras everywhere. If she was abducted somewhere in the downtown area, then there's got to be a trace of it somewhere. I'll get in touch with an old friend of mine and get back to you as soon as possible.'

Up to this point, Kati had been able to act, but now she had to wait. She felt her worst fears rising to the surface, as well as memories that she had a hard time living with.

The harbor at Tarragona reeked of oil and old fish. The car that the trio was driving had overheated, and the sun was beating down. Nadia and Kati had lifted the sickly Rose from the car into the shade to rest. They were exhausted by their flight, but they all knew that this was no time for them to slow down.

'If the satyrs don't kill us, this junk will,' Kati said, sick of the chips and chocolate bars they had lived on for the last few days. They hadn't dared to stop anywhere to eat. She opened a bottle of water and took a deep, long swig.

Nadia had unfastened the buttons of her pale cotton dress, and beads of sweat were glistening on her forehead. But she wasn't concerned about herself; she was worried about Rose. 'Her fever's gone up again. We need to find a place where I can take care of your sister.'

'We have to keep going,' Kati said, examining Nadia with her eyes. 'What do you think is wrong with her?'

'I don't understand,' Nadia said. 'Maybe it's some parasite.'

'Let's get her that medicine you were talking about.'

'I don't think Rose is going to survive the journey,' Nadia said. Rose's symptoms were unusual, and until now she hadn't really been able to help her, just alleviate the symptoms.

'Maybe it's best for us to split up, and that way at least we won't all get caught,' Kati said. 'You take the car. I'll let Rose rest for a while and then I'll think of some way of getting us to Italy.'

'It will be too easy for them to find you,' Nadia protested.

'Take the car! We'll contact you, and then you can come help us.'

Nadia eyed Kati a little strangely. Kati clearly wanted to get rid of her, but she knew that there was no point asking Kati for an explanation. Besides, the most important thing was for them to survive. Nadia held out a hand and Kati pressed the car key into it.

After Nadia left, Kati went over to her sister.

'Why did you drive Ninette off?' Rose asked. Her lips were chapped and her skin was gray. Kati was terrified for her sister.

'Your pregnancy is starting to show. I'm not taking any risks at this point,' Kati said. 'It's easier for me if you're the only one I have to protect and look after.'

'Are we even going to Italy?' Rose asked. She had been listening in on her sister's conversation.

'No,' Kati said, drawing the collar of her smudged white shirt lower. 'Wait here. I'm going to arrange some transportation for us.'

So Kati had managed to finagle them passage to France via ship, and they had eventually made it to the city of Montpellier. Once they arrived, Kati was ready to settle down. She found a place that seemed safe for her and Rose, an abandoned building where she could come and go without being noticed. She acquired a mattress for Rose, found them something to eat, and asked around for information about other nymphs. For a while it seemed like Rose was doing better, but the closer she got to the birth, the worse she felt.

Then came the night when the contractions began. *It's too early*, Kati thought, but she couldn't say it out loud to Rose. She just calmed her.

'I want Ninette,' Rose panted.

'We're safe here,' Kati said. 'After the baby is born, we'll continue. As soon as you and the baby are strong enough.'

Suddenly Rose gripped Kati's arms with unbelievable strength. Kati could feel her sister's fingers digging into her flesh, and saw Rose's demanding eyes.

'Ekaterina, promise me,' Rose said, as the pain of the contractions washed over her. 'If something happens to me, promise me you will take care of the child as if it were your own.'

'Nothing is going to happen to you.'

'Promise me. Say it out loud,' Rose said, completely frenzied.

'I promise.' Kati turned away. Few people had seen tears in her eyes, and no one was going to see them now, either.

A few hours later, Kati was holding a crying newborn in her arms.

'You were right,' she said to Rose, as if her sister could still hear her. 'It's a girl.'

Rose was lying in the bloody sheets, her eyes glassy but at peace. Perhaps she had been able to hear her daughter's first cry.

Kati looked at the child. She had sacrificed everything for her, and now she didn't know if she hated or loved this tiny newcomer. But she didn't intend to stand there and ponder it much longer. She had given Rose her word, and she intended to act accordingly. It was best to stick to the plan. The legend, even if it were made up, would be the child's best protection now.

Kati wrapped the child in a towel and carried it through the lanes of old Montpellier. She slipped in through a low threshold, dug out a roll of bills, and explained what the tattoo should look like. When it was ready, she called a number that she had acquired in good time before the birth. The satyrs may have thought they had rid the world of Oakhearts years ago, but Kati had never allowed her bond to them to be severed. Now she needed the Oakhearts' help more than ever.

A woman answered, and she and Kati agreed to meet at the small inn where the woman lived. Kati made sure that the tattoo artist would never say another word to anyone, took back the money, and headed out. She was careful to check that no one was following her. The child was strangely calm; it didn't cry at all, it just gazed at her with its bright eyes. Kati thought she could already see the start of her sister's red hair on the child's head, but maybe she was just imagining things.

Some time later, Kati knocked on the door of a room at the inn. A tall woman with dark hair opened it. Kati gave her a questioning glance, and the woman drew a pendant out from under her blouse. It bore the oak leaves. Kati nodded and handed over the child without a word.

'Won't you come in?' the woman asked. She took the baby into the safety of her arms without hesitating, as if it were the most natural thing in the world.

'No. I don't want to know where you're taking the girl, as long as you take her so far away that I can't find you.'

'I'll take care of her,' the woman assured Kati.

'When Desirée comes of age as a nymph, send a message to this number,' Kati said, slipping a piece of paper to the woman. 'Give me the coordinates, and I will find you.'

The woman was on the verge of saying something else, but Kati pressed the door to. She soundlessly walked out of the inn and didn't stop until she was blocks away. *Rose*, she thought, *I promised to care for your child as best I could, and that's why it's better that she lives with someone else*. Still, Kati couldn't help but shed a few tears before heading off in search of a bottle of cognac.

* * *

Kati was roused from her reverie when Harju called and announced he was on his way to pick her up.

'We started going through the surveillance cameras in the vicinity of Didi's workplace, and we struck gold,' Harju explained in the car. 'The girl was taken from the doorway there and out to a dark-colored van. It was pretty easy to follow the movements of the van to a certain parking garage.'

A moment later, they were driving down the ramp to the parking lot, and Kati could feel her heart pounding. The van was at the far end of the garage, and there was no one around. Kati had promised to protect Didi, and this had still happened. She didn't have the faintest idea what she would find in the car. She could sense Harju's gaze, but in no way did she want to reveal her feelings. On the contrary, she presented a calmer front than ever.

Harju parked and they got out of the car. Kati walked lazily over to the van. She didn't hear any sounds coming from it.

'In this camera shot, there was another similar van in the lot here,' Harju said. 'They had been driven into a corner where it was impossible to see exactly what took place down there.'

But Kati wasn't really listening, she was looking at a stain on the rear bumper. When she looked a little closer, she knew it was blood.

'Do you mind if I open it?' Kati asked, flicking out her stiletto knife before Harju could protest. She picked the lock in a flash, and the doors to the cargo space flew back.

Kati gave a silent sigh of relief. There was a body on the floor of the van, but it wasn't Didi's. A youngish man with short hair was lying there naked and covered in bruises, his limbs spread-eagled. For some reason, he was wearing dark sunglasses. Both Kati and Harju had seen similar cases before.

'At least Erik fed Didi in time,' Kati said steadily, even though she was wondering what sort of treatment Didi might receive at the satyrs' hands. Erik always looked out for his own interests, and in the end, it was all the same to him whether he had his way with Didi through vice or virtue. The brutality of a maddened satyr knew no bounds. It might be better for Didi to die before she had a chance to experience it.

'This van was stolen a few days ago, so as far as that's concerned, we're at a dead end.' Harju looked at the dark, grim-looking nymph from a distance, unsure of what was going through her head. 'On the other hand, that other vehicle, the one that was waiting here, is registered to the Gyllen Group.'

'You already asked about it, I presume?'

'I called there and for some reason I was connected to the head honcho himself, Roland Gyllen,' Harju said. 'He explained that there was no way he could keep track of the hundreds of cars his company owns.'

'Erik knows how to pick useful partners,' Kati said. 'Where did the car go?'

'It'll probably be found in some nearby forest. I doubt the person who is behind all this is using it any more,' Harju said.

'Are you telling me that the trail stops here?' Kati asked, almost growling.

Just to be on the safe side, Harju took a couple of steps backwards before nodding.

CHAPTER 68

Samuel had sunk into Jessica's soft beige sofa to browse through her photo albums. Her family on vacation, her family at Christmas, her family at reunions. Jessica blowing out five candles, her cheeks red and round. Jessica on her new bike. Jessica and her little brother setting up a teepee.

Samuel's brain couldn't wrap itself around the photos. There had been nothing wrong with his own childhood. His mother and father had loved him and each other, genuinely so, but they didn't have any relatives. Sometimes they would host guests, but he felt like something lay hidden behind the facades. He saw it in the glances that his mother cast at his father. Or in the way Mom said goodbye to Dad as he left on one of his many business trips. Samuel's hand rose to his throat to make sure that his pendant was still there, and he started when Jessica sat down next to him. Jessica in an ironed T-shirt and jeans. How was it possible that a woman could be so fresh and sweet?

'Are you looking for secrets?' Jessica asked.

'Every picture in this album is so perfect somehow,' Samuel said. 'Family, traditions, smiles. Everything.'

'Is there something weird about that?'

'No,' Samuel said. 'Or yes. Suddenly I feel like I've missed out on something.'

Jessica grabbed Samuel by the hand and he felt the warmth of her skin. He had been staying at Jessica's place, sleeping on her sofa. That morning they had eaten cold cereal and yogurt together, laughed, watched TV. All the normal stuff had felt so good to Samuel that he had no desire to speed things up and take a single step forward. But he still wanted it, and he sensed that Jessica did, too.

Samuel looked Jessica in the eye and saw the invitation there. He bent over a little and pressed a light kiss to her lips. He and Jessica smiled at each other.

'I never would have guessed that I'd fall in love with a man who spills coffee on my shirt,' Jessica said.

Samuel laughed, but he knew Jessica was presenting a serious matter lightly. He wanted to respond, but something held him back. He remembered the roller-coaster of emotions that Didi took him for every time he saw her, and convinced himself that that wasn't really what he craved. He lifted Jessica's chin up with a finger and kissed her again, this time a little longer and deeper.

'You want some coffee?' Samuel asked.

'Sure, why not?' Jessica said, but Samuel caught a flash of disappointment in her blue eyes.

Samuel went into Jessica's compact kitchen, where everything was tidy and in its place. The first time he had walked into Jessica's apartment, Samuel had noticed that this was a woman who had built herself a nest where everything was exactly the way she wanted it. Clean and simple. Then the nymphs' kitchen flashed through his mind, with its herbs, odors, bottles of wine. Large glass canisters filled with the brazil nuts that Nadia in particular loved.

Samuel tried to concentrate on the aroma of the brewing coffee. He set the pastel green mugs out on the table and filled them.

'Have you tried to call Didi?' Jessica asked in the most casual tone she could manage.

'A couple of times,' Samuel answered. He didn't want to lie, but he also couldn't tell Jessica that he had made at least a dozen attempts.

'Why?'

'I've known Didi since I was a kid.' Samuel pulled Jessica into his arms and hugged her as he spoke. He wanted her to understand that there was nothing simplistic about his relationship with Didi. 'Even as a kid I'd get this strange feeling when Didi was in trouble. Now I have it constantly.'

Samuel might have continued, but he felt Jessica's lips on his neck. Jessica was nipping at him lightly, and she wrapped his neck hairs in her fingers.

Samuel felt himself getting aroused. Maybe everything could be this simple from here on out, without any deeper analysis. That's what he'd been missing. He pressed his mouth to Jessica's and discreetly began to push her towards the bedroom as he unbuttoned her smooth white top. It smelled faintly of detergent. He didn't resist at all as Jessica undid the zipper to his pants and felt his hardness. They fell into bed. Samuel wondered what had taken him so long, why he had kept telling himself he shouldn't rush things. By this time, he had pulled Jessica's jeans down. He closed his eyes and hoped that he'd be able to hold off for a while.

And at that moment, as he closed his eyes, he found himself in utter darkness. He could sense the fear that Didi was definitely feeling at that exact instant. His hips were right up against Jessica, but now he rolled away.

Jessica whispered in his ear: 'I'll make you forget her.' But Samuel didn't feel an ounce of desire any more.

'If it were a rational decision, I would stay here for the rest of my life,' Samuel said, lowering a hand to Jessica's collar. 'But this has nothing to do with being rational.'

CHAPTER 69

The room was almost pitch dark when Didi cautiously opened her eyes. The only light was coming in from underneath a closed door. The windows were covered with blackout shades that had been nailed to the frames. A small red light blinked at the ceiling; Didi figured that it had to be a camera. So someone was observing her. She didn't want to immediately reveal that she was awake or, especially, how afraid she was.

Fragments of earlier events started coming back to her. The man who smelled faintly of sweat who had knocked her out, the rattling van where she had been chained up . . . By the time the doors had opened, Didi had been conscious and in pain. The influence of the moon had started to take effect, and she was seared with greater anguish than ever before. Then that sweaty man had been pushed into the back of the van and she had done it, the thing that a nymph does during the full moon without asking permission or forgiveness. After that, she must have been knocked out again, because she didn't remember anything about the trip to the place where she found herself now.

Didi cautiously felt around, getting a sense of her surroundings. The bed was big and comfortable, the sheets felt smooth and satiny, and the comforter was lightweight down. She realized that she wasn't wearing a bra, she was only wearing panties. *Luckily I picked the pretty red ones*, she thought. It would have been unbearable to be kidnapped in her old cotton underwear. She avoided thinking about how someone had touched her, stripped her when she had been completely unconscious. She couldn't afford fear of any sort.

Didi's eyes circled the large room and made out a streamlined dresser and an armoire.

'If you look more carefully, you'll notice there's a nightgown on the hanger,' a low male voice said from a speaker at the ceiling.

Erik! Didi started and sat up. Erik had also been in the parking garage. The memory was now surprisingly clear. Erik was the one who had pushed that man into the van. Didi wanted to clear her head and think for a moment. She dreaded the thought that she had been with two satyrs. Which is why she had to take the reins herself now. She knew that Erik wanted her. She might be able to use that to her advantage.

'You can also turn on the light on the nightstand,' Erik's voice said. 'I'm going to assure you right away that all of the potential escape routes have been blocked, so you should save your strength for something other than attempting to break out.'

Didi didn't have any time to think about the right tactics. She would have to trust her instincts and use situations to her advantage as they arose. This was one of those opportunities. She turned on the light and immediately saw the cream-colored silk nightgown. She rose languidly from the bed and slipped into it. Her instincts were to hurry and hide her nakedness, but she decided to move as naturally as possible, as if the eye at the ceiling wasn't following her every move.

The lingerie was as light as a dream. The lacy hem came halfway down her thigh, no more, but at least she wasn't only in her panties any more.

'The door is open,' Erik's voice said through the speaker. 'Come out here.'

'You come here,' Didi said.

'No, no,' Erik chuckled. 'Patience, my little nymph. The time for that will come.'

'Wishful thinking,' Didi snorted, but she still went to the door.

Didi had assumed that she would get a better understanding of where she was, but the large windows in the living room had been covered as well. The space was illuminated by pools of mood lighting, and the furniture was stylish and simple. But it didn't offer any sort of clue as to where she was.

Erik stepped out from around a corner, and Didi jumped and took a couple of steps backwards. The satyr was dressed in an impeccable dark suit and a knotted scarf. Every blue-black hair was in place, and his beard was smooth. The only time Didi had seen men like this was in the ads for department stores. Nor did Erik fit that mold, either. In the ads, people were pretending to be something, but Erik radiated a genuine confidence and self-control . . . *and danger*, Didi thought.

'I suppose you know that Kati is looking for me and will be knocking at the door any minute now?' Didi tossed the question into the air as if she weren't afraid of anything, and poured a glass of red wine for herself from the bottle on the table. She tasted it and found the dark flavor strange and bitter. So she hadn't developed into a woman of the world yet, but she had no intention of showing that to Erik.

'Nebbiolo is my favorite grape,' Erik smiled, and Didi wasn't sure if her performance had convinced him. 'And Kati isn't coming here, because Kati doesn't know where you are.'

'What is this place?' Didi asked.

'This is our place. That's all you need to know. You look lovely, by the way. Aren't you grateful that I arranged some nourishment for you? Your eyes were like milk and your skin was dry when I served him to you. And afterwards you slept for a couple of days. Your skin was positively glowing in the dark.'

'Someone a little less sweaty next time, thanks.' Didi didn't want to devote a single minute to thinking about the incident in the van. 'Why am I here?'

A large contemporary sofa stood in the middle of the living room, with a glass coffee table in front of it. A leather-bound book had been laid out on top of the table; it was clearly very old. Erik now indicated the sofa, and made it clear that Didi had better sit down. Didi decided to give in to the satyr's request. Erik took a seat at her side.

'What is this?' Didi asked, referring to the book.

'*The Book of the Knot*. It's written in Ancient Greek, and before we do anything else, we're going to read it together . . .'

'I don't know Greek! And I don't feel like reading right now.'

'Tsk tsk,' Erik said. 'One thing at a time. The nymphs have been telling you lies, and I intend to correct them. If, after that, you still want to leave, you may do so freely.'

Didi grabbed hold of the heavy book and laid it on her lap. Her knot pattern, her tattoo, was on the cover. Even though she had made a fuss, now she wanted to know more. She opened the first page and smelled the old leather, the dust, the hands of the nymphs and satyrs that had carried it here. Her eyes traveled across the ancient letters, took in the lovely curves. She raised her eyes to Erik.

'Are you ready?' Erik asked. ' "When the moon goes dark above the pale hills, a nymph will be born in the forest eaves . . ." '

Both Erik's voice and story had been equally hypnotic, and as the plot advanced, Didi had lost her sense of time. She didn't know if she had been sitting at the satyr's side for thirty minutes or several hours. At one point, she shivered, and Erik had lit a fire in the fireplace and brought her a woolen blanket. The satyr hadn't made any moves on her, nor had he tried to force her to do anything. The only thing he had aroused was Didi's thirst for information.

' "When the Nymph of the Knot has come into her own, the full moon will cover the Earth in shadow,"' Erik continued reading. ' "The satyr whose veins flow with the blood of Silenos may pass the Eleusinian Mysteries with the Nymph of the Knot at Telesterion. And when the eclipse is at its fullest, the Nymph of the Knot will be impregnated by two potent forces: the satyr and the red moon. Afterwards, a new Silenos will be born on the Earth . . . "'

Now Didi was listening, eyes wide. She hadn't understood half of the legend, and yet it still fascinated her. But now it had taken a new turn and she needed further explanations. Besides, she had to pee.

'Are you of the kin of Silenos? What does that mean?' Didi rose from the sofa and stretched. The blanket fell from her and she felt the satyr's gaze on her skin. It didn't bother her in the least.

'Listen to the end,' Erik said, his eyes glowing.

'I need to go to the bathroom first . . .' Didi walked across the living room. She flipped a switch, thinking she had turned on the bathroom lights, but the sight before her eyes silenced her mid-sentence.

The beautiful pale light revealed an empty crib, above which hung a playful mobile of tiny birds and airplanes. There were toys and soft baby books on the shelves. Her eyes moved over to the diaper-changing table, which was stocked with all of the requisite materials.

Didi could feel Erik right behind her, and she decided to play it as cool as possible. It wasn't going to be easy. Back on the sofa, she had sensed the heat radiating from the satyr's body, and it called to her more powerfully than she cared to admit to herself. She felt that if she gave Erik even an inch, she would be lost for good. She turned to look at the satyr.

'I want to think about this a little,' Didi said.

'Be my guest,' Erik said, his tone extremely polite.

'I'm hungry and I want to bathe,' Didi said.

'Of course,' Erik said. 'Take a bath and change your clothes.

You'll find everything you need in your closet. I'll prepare us a meal in the meantime.'

Following Erik's directions, Didi entered a bathroom that was as sumptuous as the other rooms. She was alone, and she started running the tap into the large, oval tub. A bottle of oil scented with essence of rose had been left on the edge of the bath, and she poured a little in. The bubbling water and the ethereal smell immediately made her think of Nadia. She wished she had the older, more experienced nymph's advice and healing hands at her disposal, but now she had to manage on her own. Nadia had said that everything was natural with satyrs. Kati, on the other hand, hated them. What did she feel about satyrs herself? And above all, how did she feel about Erik? Conflicting thoughts filled Didi's head as she lowered herself into the warm bath.

Didi heard Erik moving around the living room and kitchen, but she didn't let it rush her. She wanted to be the one to set the pace, and to decide everything else, too . . . As long as she could figure out what she wanted first. Erik was prepared to offer her the world on a platter, there was no doubt about that. All Didi had to do was give in, and after that she would live a life of luxury. Why hadn't she agreed to it? But then all she had to do was remember Samuel's steady gaze, and she knew how impossible it was for her to even imagine wanting anyone else.

A plan started to form in her mind, but she wasn't completely sure how to carry it out. She lounged in the water for a good long while before climbing out of the tub. She dried herself with an enormous, plush waffle towel and then helped herself to another, which she wrapped around her body. She opened the door and saw the satyr waiting at the already-set table, but she didn't even glance in his direction. She just slowly walked past him to the door of her room and let the towel drop to the floor.

'Would you pick that up, please,' she said to Erik, without a hint of a request in her voice. Now she was fully naked.

In her bedroom, Didi took her time opening the doors of her

armoire, and what she saw made her gasp. If Laura had been there, they would have shrieked and jumped around the room with joy. The hangers were hung with expensive designer clothes, doubtless in the perfect size. The materials were skin-caressing wools, silks, linens. The shoe rack held countless pairs of matching heels and sandals and even a few pairs of flats. The drawer of the dresser was ajar, and Didi opened it all the way. Beautiful bras in every shade lay side by side, along with matching panties. Her only problem now was having too many choices. And men were made to wait.

Didi picked one dress after another and gazed at her reflection. After trying a few on, she had a definite favorite in mind. A cherry red dress a little longer than a miniskirt, made of soft, lightweight wool. The hem draped and flowed prettily. The cut revealed her glowing shoulders, and the color set off her hair. The fit wasn't too tight; it was classy, restrained. For footwear, Didi chose pale patent leather high-heeled sandals that she definitely wouldn't have dared to wear out in the city cobblestones. But for the present situation, they were perfect.

Didi dabbed a little pink gloss on her lips, but that would do it. She was certain that a satyr would want a nymph to be as natural as possible. And at least for the time being, she had to prove that she was eager to please.

For a while now, Didi had heard the music flowing in from the living room. Her feet easily picked up the South American rhythm, and yet she still hesitated. She wanted Samuel, but she couldn't bind a human to herself, a human to whom she could never give everything that love entailed. Was she truly certain about what she wanted? What if making love to the satyr was such a mind-blowing experience that it made her forget everything else?

Didi glanced at herself in the mirror once more. Her glossy hair was still a little damp, and she bit her lower lip a couple of times. She stroked the fabric of the dress and felt every single smooth fiber against her skin. And then she was ready.

She opened the door and stepped out into the living room. A beautiful dinner with crystal and china had been laid out on the table near the window. Erik stood next to it. His white shirt was unbuttoned enough to reveal that his chest was rising and falling a little more rapidly than normal.

'Smoked duck and salad,' Erik announced, but his own hungry gaze didn't leave Didi for an instant.

Didi walked towards Erik, her waist swaying in time to the music. The satyr held out a hand to her and led her into a dance step. No one had ever led Didi with such a sure hand. She remembered how much she had hated slow dances, with some boy who was a little too drunk pressing himself too tightly against her. This was far from that.

'For millennia, nymphs have told a tale about a savior, but things aren't so simple,' Erik said. His grip grew a little firmer, but not disturbingly so. 'Didi, I find myself in love with you already, and before long I will be your slave. I will help you realize the legend and conceive the next Silenos.'

Didi didn't have time to react before Erik had twirled her around so he was behind her. Erik's hands were resting on her hips, moving her from side to side. She could feel Erik's breathing on the back of her neck and a moment later, she felt his beard there, too. Didi shivered, but it was better to let Erik think that it was more out of lust than fear.

'You can tell me about Silenos some other time,' Didi said. 'I feel like dancing now, but not to this.'

Didi quickly whirled out of Erik's grasp and pressed a couple of buttons on the player until she found a station she liked. At first the satyr looked perturbed, as if she had broken the spell, but when the lighthearted pop beats filled the room and Didi took her first steps in time to them, his expression softened.

Didi let the music overtake her. The hem of her red dress swung, blazing like a flame, and her red hair kept the same rhythm. She danced by herself with her eyes closed, as if she had forgotten the world around her. She could feel the satyr's eyes glued to her. She lifted her hair away from her neck and then let it cascade down her back again. She rolled her bare shoulders, and the glare of the fire in the hearth lent color to her skin. Didi let her head fall back and opened her lips. She was a full-blooded nymph, and she knew exactly the sort of desire she was capable of inspiring.

Then Didi opened her eyes and took a few dance steps towards Erik. She wanted to seduce, to play. To test her power. She smiled enticingly, but Erik had had enough, and he grabbed her hips with a growl and flung her down onto the sofa. Didi was beneath the strong, heavy satyr when his burning red gaze started to drill into her. A surge of dread flooded over her. She had temporarily forgotten that the danger was real, and that's why she had toyed with it. She had imagined she was in control of the situation, but now she saw the horns thrusting forth from Erik's forehead. She remembered everything that she had momentarily forgotten: how Erik had almost killed Samuel, how she herself had buried a dagger in his back . . .

Didi shrieked in terror, but the memory of Samuel turned the emotion to fury. She writhed out of Erik's grasp and pressed her hands to his bare neck. So much adrenaline was flowing through her that she was panting. Fear and rage surged through her veins as one and transformed into a current of energy in her hands. Her touch took Erik's breath away, making him grunt in pain and stagger backwards. Didi was stunned. For a moment, she didn't understand what had happened. Erik was standing three feet away from her, and gradually his strength returned. This was the moment when she had to act. She whipped herself into a frenzy, channeled her anger so it traveled down her arms, and pressed her palms directly onto Erik's jugular. She forced the satyr to his knees. Erik was shaking all over, and a moment later his eyes rolled back into his head. And still, Didi did not relent. With his next heartbeat, Erik rolled onto his side, unconscious.

Didi didn't hang around to see what would happen. She kicked off her heels and lunged for the door. It wasn't locked, so certain had the satyr been of his control over her. In a flash Didi was outside, scanning the terrain. The sun was shining weakly, so it had to be early morning. She saw a yard and the forest beyond. It wasn't likely that she would be able to escape a satyr in the woods, and Erik would certainly come to soon. In the other direction, Didi saw a dock and the gray gleam of a mist-shrouded lake. She had to decide now.

Didi ran to the dock and dove.

CHAPTER 70

Samuel had moved from Jessica's place back to the morgue, and the couple of nights he had spent on a gurney had been rough on him. He had slept, but when he woke up it felt like he had had a dream that wasn't a dream, more like a memory that had bubbled up from the deepest recesses of his mind.

Samuel had woken up far too early, and had the sensation that he was supposed to be somewhere totally different. So he had sat down behind the wheel of his car, and when the landscapes finally started coming properly into view, he realized that he had driven to Tammisaari and was sitting at the gate to the Van der Haas manor. This time he looked at the old iron gate, the oak-motif ornamentation on it, and pulled out his dad's old necklace from under his shirt. He held it in the warmth of his fingers for a moment and then stepped out of the car. He breathed in the brisk morning air that already omened autumn, and his breath rose like steam.

Samuel walked closer to the gate. An old woman was raking up leaves a little further off, the one he had met once before with Didi, and she stopped what she was doing when she saw him. Samuel realized he was still in his white lab coat and probably quite a sight. He waved at her in greeting and passed through the gate.

The woman continued her yard work and simply glanced at Samuel as he passed. 'My son Matias is waiting for you on the porch,' she called after him.

Samuel stretched his neck to get a better look. In the distance stood a tall, middle-aged man whose face indicated that he had seen plenty of life. He was wearing a sweater and jeans and sandy hair that came down to his collar. He looked completely normal, and yet Samuel still approached him a little timidly.

'Samuel Koski,' he said, holding out a hand, but the man shook his hand quickly and matter-of-factly.

'Matias van der Haas. Let's go inside.'

Matias led Samuel into a room that once upon a time would have been called a salon. It was furnished with an old, well-worn Gustavian dining set, where they settled themselves. Matias served coffee from the pot.

'Mother called me in Greece and told me that you had been by,' Matias said. 'You and some beautiful girl.'

'Greece?' Samuel's eyebrows rose. His strange dreams had somehow been related to Greece. 'What part of Greece were you in?'

Matias hesitated before answering. He focused his analytical gaze on Samuel and was evidently choosing his words carefully.

'We were at the very southern tip, at Lakonia. There's a place there called Velanidia. My daughter Matilda has reached the age where I wanted to show her what I've been doing my whole life.'

In his dream, Samuel had heard the same thing almost word for word from his own father. His father had proposed that Samuel and Samuel's mother join him for a trip, so Samuel would find out what Dad had been doing his whole life . . . Samuel had yawned, already bored, and said that he wasn't interested in watching someone sell prescription medications. Then Mom had laughed drily and said that Dad didn't sell prescriptions.

Samuel had been on the verge of telling Matias about his memory, but all of a sudden he found himself looking down the barrel of a gun.

'There have been several break-ins here, so I thought I'd be prepared,' Matias said. 'What were you doing here that first time, you and the girl? How did you know to find us here?'

'Didi wanted information about some symbol or crest,' Samuel said.

'Who's the girl who wanted to know about the knot?'

'Didi,' Samuel repeated. He had no intention of telling Matias about the nymphs. There was no way an adult would have even believed it. 'We've known each other since we were kids.'

'Her full name!' The barrel of the gun was only a couple of inches from Samuel's face now, and Matias' grip didn't appear to be the least bit unsteady.

'Desirée Tasson.'

A second passed that felt at least like an hour, and then Matias lowered the gun to the table. Samuel's heart started to beat a little more steadily, but he was still on edge. This hadn't been your average coffee table conversation. He had managed to push Didi out his mind, but the act of uttering her name re-awakened the fear that had been gnawing at his heart. Something was wrong.

'I don't believe that. She can't be Desirée Volanté,' Matias said, interrupting Samuel's meandering thoughts.

'What does it mean?' Samuel asked.

'In Greek it's *Epithymia Tha*,' Matias answered. 'Don't you know the old story?'

'No,' Samuel said, fumbling at his throat for the necklace as he spoke. He saw Matias' surprise when he drew it out. 'Does it have anything to do with this? Or does Greece have something to do with this somehow?'

So many questions were crisscrossing through Samuel's mind that he didn't know where to start, but if Matias could answer even one of them, maybe it would help him understand something about his strange dream.

'Where did you get the necklace?' Matias asked.

'From my father, Pentti Koski, when he died,' Samuel said. 'I was a teenager when Dad was supposed to take me on a trip to Greece with him. But something went wrong, and I don't really remember anything except the hospital.'

Matias had risen from the table and walked over to the window. Samuel didn't dare to move a muscle yet. He didn't want the gun in his face again.

'I've seen dreams about it, but I can't make any sense of them,' Samuel said, turning towards Matias. 'They feel more like memories, but I can't call them back to mind.'

'There's a person here who can help you remember,' Matias said. 'If that's truly what you want.'

CHAPTER 71

'At first I thought someone had left their laundry on the dock,' the young farmer said to Didi, eyes burning brightly.

Didi imagined she was quite a sight. She had barely had the strength to swim to the opposite shore. Then she'd lain there like a red puddle, shivering and dripping water onto the dock. She'd been dimly aware that someone had helped her into a heated sauna and shyly helped her out of her clothes. Now she was finally starting to warm up, and she could talk without her teeth chattering. She gratefully drank the honey-sweetened tea, feeling its restorative power.

'I guess I got lost,' she said, which was undeniably a lame excuse. Nevertheless, the blond, red-cheeked young man just kept smiling at her like a sheep. Didi had to speed things up here, Erik was probably on her trail. 'Do you happen to have a phone?'

A moment later Didi had a cell phone in her hands and was tapping in Kati's number, ready to get an earful for disappearing again. She didn't, though. Instead, Kati's voice was incredibly concerned. 'Didi, where are you? Are you all right?'

'Yes. I'm in . . .' Didi turned to look inquisitively at the young man.

'Hauho.'

'I'm in Hauho,' Didi said, and heard Kati take a deep breath.

'Give me the address, and I'll come get you.'

Didi gave her the address and then she just waited. Sausages, cabbage salad, and rye bread were laid out before her, and words could not describe what sort of feast it felt like to her. The young man went and got her a shirt and jeans from his own closet, which she pulled tight with a belt. And it wasn't more than a couple of hours before she was waving goodbye to the forlorn-looking farmer, and on her way home with Kati.

The car was speeding down the highway when Kati started to laugh.

'What's wrong with you?' Didi wondered.

'Erik carried you off to Hauho!'

'So?'

'I didn't know where they had taken you, and knowing Erik, I would have imagined something grandiose: Monaco or something. But Erik hid you in a visible spot. He's a clever satyr, I'll give him that.'

But Didi wasn't able to find the humor in the events of the past few days yet. What she had felt for Erik right before he had lost his self-control had been something totally new, simultaneously frightening and fascinating. And what she had done to Erik was simply frightening.

'I did something to Erik,' Didi said. 'I hurt him. Badly.'

Kati didn't say anything; she just stepped on the gas. 'Good. What else happened there, by the way?'

'Erik read some moldy old book to me that says we're meant for each other. Does anyone really believe stuff like that?'

Now Kati was handling the gearstick as if she were trying to rip it out, but she didn't answer Didi.

'Nadia thinks I'm some nymph savior, too,' Didi continued.

'You may as well be happy about that,' Kati finally said. 'Nadia will take care of you, because she firmly believes in the old legends. Erik won't lay a finger on you for the same reason. Just let everyone believe in fairy tales, if it's to your advantage.'

'Why do you protect me?' Didi asked.

'Have I ever done anything that wouldn't be to my own advantage, too?'

'No,' Didi answered, a little disappointed. Kati had seemed so relieved when she'd found her in one piece that she'd started to expect some admission of affection. Didi decided to leave it there. Besides, it wasn't until she got into the car that she had allowed herself to be totally relieved or dared to give in to her exhaustion. She slept for the rest of the trip.

When Kati opened the door to the apartment, she and Didi were welcomed by the pungent scent of basil, followed by Nadia pattering up in a flowing linen dress and bare feet. It was such a welcome sight to Didi that she collapsed in Nadia's arms.

'Where were you? I was starting to get afraid.'

'Where were you?' Kati asked. 'I was trying to get hold of you.'

'I visited Frida,' Nadia said, supposedly casually, but a glance from her informed Kati that it would be best to discuss that later. 'Tell me what happened.'

'It's a long story,' Didi said. 'I'm totally beat. Do you guys mind if I take a shower and go to bed?'

'Knock yourself out,' Kati said. 'We'll talk more tomorrow.'

'I just want to say one thing now. Lately I've realized that I haven't had any idea what your life has been like. But you still need to let me make my own decisions.'

Kati looked a little bored, and her expression indicated that there was no point in Didi even imagining anything of the sort, but Nadia nodded.

'And I don't want to talk about whether I'm some legend or not any more,' Didi continued.

'There you are,' Kati said to Nadia. 'I'm not the one filling Didi's head with some crazy fairy tales.'

'No, you're just scaring me all the time,' Didi said to Kati. 'I wished you already trusted me. And now I'm going to bed, and tomorrow I'm going to work.'

'That's too dangerous . . .' Kati couldn't continue, because Didi was wagging a forefinger at her. 'OK, I'll try. But I'm not promising anything.'

The older nymphs waited for Didi to disappear into her bedroom. Then Kati went to get a bottle of white wine from the fridge, filled two glasses, and she and Nadia sat down at the table to enjoy them.

'Are you ready to talk?' Kati asked. 'Where was Frida?'

'In France. Nimes. There's an old nunnery there where nymphs had gathered.' Nadia's eyes immediately grew wet at the memory of the place.

'Tell me,' Kati said. She knew she wasn't necessarily going to care for the story, but she still had to know.

'The nunnery was cold and dark, but it was in a remote spot.' Nadia's voice was flat as she began to recall what happened. 'Frida had chosen well. And there were such young nymphs there, all of them certain that the eclipse would change everything. The rumors about Desirée had spread and inspired them to flee, under threat of death. A few had been badly injured. I tried to save one named Eliza, whose satyr had . . .'

The memory of the young nymph whose last glance was directed her way made Nadia tremble in anguish. Kati waited until she was able to continue.

'You should have seen their faces when I told them I had met the Nymph of the Knot,' Nadia said. 'I said that it was time for a true resistance. That we have to rise up against the satyrs and demand our rights. They were all ready for it. Even though Didi doesn't believe in the legend herself, she is the nymphs' guiding star. Just the rumor of the legend can change everything.'

'Did the nymphs stay there?' Kati asked, sensing that there was more to the story.

'The satyrs found out about the place,' Nadia said. 'We had to split up and run. It was horrible. I think a lot of them died that night, and I still don't know what happened to Frida. She fought, and she shot a lot of satyrs with her bow and arrow, but then I lost sight of her. I flew back from France last night.'

Kati digested what she had heard and split what was left of the bottle between her and Nadia.

'Didi probably doesn't need to hear about this,' Kati eventually said.

'Not yet, at least,' Nadia said. 'But I don't know how long we can keep it a secret from her.'

CHAPTER 72

The old library was incredibly dim. Samuel watched as Matias drew the last of the drapes across the windows. The dark-eyed woman was lighting candles. She had introduced herself as Salma, Matias' mother. Samuel already felt like calling the whole thing off. To the soon-to-be-doctor, it smacked of total bunk, like homeopathy or something. But due to recent events, he was genuinely afraid of the possibility that some power would really take over him. Besides, Salma was a rather alarming woman, and when it came to alarming women, Samuel's quota was more or less full.

'Sit down in that chair and relax,' Salma ordered him, as if that were possible. 'Take off your shirt.'

The command was unambiguous, and Samuel obeyed. He watched as Salma fetched a silver box from the drawer of the massive old desk and pulled out a hand-rolled cigarette that smelled of herbs. He was on the verge of saying something about the dangers of drugs, but Salma had already lit up and turned back to him.

'This won't hurt,' Salma said. 'Close your eyes.'

Samuel didn't dare to obey this final instruction; he looked on in horror as the glowing tip of the cigarette approached the dip in his collarbone and pressed into his skin . . . Strangely enough, it didn't cause any pain, just a warm, tingling sensation. Salma inhaled again and pressed the cigarette to another spot on his chest, and then a third. Even though he tried to resist, Samuel's eyelids started to lower.

'Sleep,' Salma said, humming softly. 'I will guide you.'

Samuel slipped out of the library. He saw himself sitting in the chair, his head leaning against his chest, and he wanted to say something to himself, but he was incapable of resisting the movement that was carrying him further away. Then he opened his eyes, and he was with his father in the cabin of the *Robur*. Outside the window, he could see a whitewashed Greek town at the crown of a hill.

His father had just lowered a leather satchel bearing the oak symbol onto the table inside the cabin. He pulled out a bundle and unrolled it with tidy movements. A tranquilizer gun with darts, a knife, an unusual flashlight, and two metal ampules. Samuel's father picked up one of the tiny darts.

'What kind of wood are these made out of?' he asked.

'Oak,' Samuel answered, without hesitating.

'Pretty close. Poison beech is a kind of oak that doesn't grow anywhere else except Velanidia.' Dad took the dart in one hand and picked up one of the ampules in the other and held them right before Samuel's eyes. 'Each dart has been made by hand. And this ampule contains the blood of a unicorn that was sacrificed at the temple of Oxiá Koiláda.'

Samuel gave his father the scornful glances of a teenager. 'A unicorn? What a bunch of bull. That's a fairy tale. Come on, Dad, I'm already thirteen.'

'You're right, and we are the fairy tale,' Dad said, laying a broad palm on Samuel's shoulder.

Samuel wanted to see more, but his father's face faded. Samuel smelled the herbal aroma of Salma's cigarette again, and his eyes opened. He had to inhale and fill his lungs with air, and a tear started to roll down his cheek.

'I want to know more,' Samuel said.

'Don't rush things,' Matias said. 'Little by little, you're starting to remember. Taking too large a step could be dangerous.'

'Did that really happen? Why did I forget all that?'

'The reason for that will come back to you as well,' Salma said, as she returned the box to the desk drawer. 'But first there's someone you need to speak to.'

As if by command, the door to the library opened. It took Samuel a moment to grasp that it was his mother standing there in the dim light.

'You can have the salon to yourselves,' Salma said.

Samuel rose a little uncertainly, but then he went over into the parlor with his mother, and they sat down side by side on the sofa. Pauliina hugged Samuel tightly and ruffled his hair the way she used to. Samuel could smell the familiar odor of the stables on his mother. It was reassuring.

'I don't know what you've had time to talk about yet,' Pauliina said. 'I could perhaps tell you about me and my role, but I've agreed with Matias that he'll tell you about your father. Then you can make your own decision as to how you feel about everything.'

'What do you all know?' Samuel asked calmly. The bizarreness of this encounter had astounded him.

'For instance, I know why Elina wanted to move in next door back when you were little,' Pauliina said. 'She wanted to make sure that Didi would stay safe.'

'You knew what Didi was?'

Pauliina nodded, and the memory seemed to still give her pain. 'You two became inseparable, and basically, Didi started to fall in love with you. We wouldn't have controlled you much longer if Didi's feelings had continued to develop. That's when we started to monitor how much time you spent together.'

Samuel weighed his mother's words. There was really only one thing he was desperate to know about, but he was a little uncertain how to put it. It was patently obvious that Pauliina had not wanted him and Didi to have a relationship.

'Is it always impossible between a human and nymph?' Samuel asked.

'Yes,' Pauliina said. 'You don't want to hear it, but it's the truth. If you had told me about Didi, I would have tried to warn you. I want you to have a normal life.'

Samuel knew that his mother had simply been concerned about what was best for him. He hugged her one more time, and she wiped the corners of her eyes. His family wasn't in the habit of expressing their feelings.

'I'm going to go now,' Pauliina said. 'Listen to Matias.'

Pauliina stood. Samuel knew how reluctant his mother was to leave her horses for long, and he walked her out.

At her car, Pauliina turned and gave Samuel a surprisingly firm embrace. She didn't say anything, she just smiled gravely.

'See you, Mom,' Samuel said. He didn't feel like bringing any more emotion to the moment. Pauliina was generally reserved, but Samuel could tell how concerned she was.

''Bye, honey,' Pauliina said, and a moment later her car disappeared from view.

Samuel remained outside to walk a while and reflect some more on his mother's words and his own question. He had understood its magnitude only after he had said the words out loud. He had fallen in love with Didi. The fear that he had previously experienced in the face of everything new and unfamiliar and dangerous had vanished. His love for Didi was enough.

Samuel went back into the parlor. Matias was there, and he was holding an object that Samuel immediately recognized. It was the old leather satchel that he had seen in the cabin of the *Robur* during his waking dream. Matias studied Samuel's face as he placed the satchel down on the table.

'Our family history is passed down from mouth to mouth, from parents to children,' Matias said. 'Children are usually taken to the place where our story began . . .'

'To Velanidia,' said Samuel.

'I knew your father by the name Paulos. He isn't here to tell you his story, so I will do it on his behalf. Our story is bound to the Knot. We bear the secret of the Knot, and the contents of this case help us in our mission to guard it. This satchel belonged to your father.'

Samuel's gaze turned reverently from the satchel to Matias. Some tiny bud in his memory began to unfurl, and he pressed his hands against the surface of the worn leather and closed his eyes again. In that same instant, he remembered being inside the rock, down in the tunnels, and his father bending down to whisper something in his ear. He had tried to listen more closely.

'Samuel, go back,' his father was ordering him.

Samuel didn't want to obey. Something was there in the tunnel with them, and he wanted to stay with his father. The sound of the predator, whatever it was, could be heard nearby, and his dad was breathing quickly. Large wooden crates lined the walls of the tunnel. Samuel's father grabbed him by the shoulders with both hands and pushed him behind the crates.

'Don't try to be a hero, son!'

Those were Samuel's father's last words to him. His father turned towards the predator. It was so dark Samuel couldn't see what happened, but it wasn't long before Samuel's father cried out and didn't get up again . . . The assailant picked up his father's flashlight and, for a moment, Samuel looked at the creature. Then it disappeared.

Now Samuel's eyes flew open. He was absolutely certain that the creature had been a satyr. He gave Matias a questioning look. The older man nodded at the bundle. Samuel started to unroll it. He saw the very same objects his father had shown to him. And the knife . . . He had seen one like it in Didi's hands, when she buried it with all the fury of a frenzied nymph into the back of the black-haired satyr.

CHAPTER 73

Erik was standing outside the cafe, looking around. Undoubtedly Gabriel Korda had already set his lapdogs Mitchell and Lucas on him to bring him before the Conclave, but he still had time to take care of things before he would be presenting his well-rehearsed speech in front of the other satyrs. If the leader of the satyrs was expecting Erik to give up or to humiliate himself, he would be waiting for a long time. Maybe Korda wouldn't be their leader for so long after all.

Erik hadn't stopped solely to confirm that he wasn't being followed. The final events at the villa had been troubling him. He had lost his self-control with the young nymph, and that had proved a critical mistake, and dangerous, too. His powers had instantly waned when Didi pressed her hands to his throat. He had been wracked with convulsions, unable to breathe. Even worse was the ferocity that radiated from the nymph's gaze, transforming the young girl into an omnipotent Fury. Erik knew that now he had to play his cards right in order to start advancing towards his goal once again.

Erik stepped into the cafe and immediately felt a spasm of jealousy as he saw Didi laughing and chatting with a table of young men. He walked up to the counter without saying anything to her, and waited for Didi to approach with her tray. He noted an initial flash of fear in her eyes, but then she assumed a serene expression.

'I went too far,' Erik said. 'But you should know by now that you don't want to taunt a satyr if you're not prepared to play.'

Didi loaded the dish rack with the dirty cups she was carrying and washed her hands. 'I don't want to see you.'

'I have a proposal to make.' Erik grabbed Didi by the wrist to get her attention, but the way the nymph's mouth immediately drew into a taut line made him remember his true aim, and he allowed his grip to relax.

'Do you remember that last full moon?' Erik asked, and this time Didi at least glanced around to make sure that no one else was in earshot. 'I arranged nourishment for you, and you enjoyed it. You didn't have to worry about shopping for the meal or cleaning up the leftovers. Or did you?'

'I didn't ask you to do any of that. I didn't ask you to abduct me, or to almost—'

'That's something we need to discuss at a more appropriate time,' Erik said. 'But right now I have a different request. I will offer you food again, and this time the dish will be served to you of its own free will.'

Didi looked at Erik, bewildered. Of course there's no way the nymph could have understood yet, but Erik had the chance to kill two birds with one stone. He would do someone a favor, and at the same time he would insinuate himself into the nymph's good graces. All he had to do was wait for Didi to arrive at her decision without pressurizing her.

'Come with me, and you can decide yourself,' Erik said to Didi. He gazed at the girl's oval face and clean features, and for a moment was reminded of Leonardo's portrait of a lady with an ermine. Maybe he, too, would create some work of art inspired by this nymph for future generations.

Didi weighed his proposal. 'Pick me up after work tonight.'

* * *

The wood-paneled dining room and crystal chandeliers of the classic restaurant made it precisely the sort of environment in which Erik felt at home. He looked approvingly at Didi, whose red hair flowed freely across her shoulders. The nymph's outfit was also appropriate for the occasion, a dove-gray dress with a pattern in an old rose tint. Of course the satyr would have preferred to see her in a more luxurious material than lightweight cotton, and in an elegant pair of high heels instead of low-heeled boots, but the time would come. He would get satisfaction out of being able to educate Didi about the pleasures of the world on so many levels. But now he had to concentrate on the moment at hand.

Erik offered his arm to Didi and allowed the waiter to lead them to the table where Roland Gyllen was already rising to greet them.

Erik handled the introductions: 'Roland, may I present Desirée Tasson.'

The captain of industry allowed his gaze to linger on the girl. 'You're right, she does look a little like Teresa did when she was young.'

Erik pulled Didi's chair out for her. 'You can speak frankly in Roland's presence. He knows about us. I knew him and Teresa when they were still a young couple.'

Gyllen waved a finger, and a bottle of champagne was brought to the table and poured for them all without anyone inquiring about Didi's age. The first course was shellfish. Erik gazed on in satisfaction, admiring how elegantly Didi managed the situation. She ate and engaged in conversation, laughed at the right moments without calling too much attention to herself. All in all, the nymph possessed precisely the right combination of characteristics. Erik and Gyllen intermittently exchanged unspoken messages, and Erik knew Gyllen was prepared to put the agreement into effect. He sensed the old man's melancholy, and he himself took a quiet moment to reflect on the fact that their long-term friendship was coming to an end. That was the inevitable consequence with humans. At least Gyllen still knew how to enjoy life, Erik grunted, when his old friend gave the order to bring roasted guinea fowl and braised root vegetables drizzled with honey.

Dessert was being served when Erik felt Didi's soft touch on his sleeve.

'Excuse me, I'd like to speak with Erik for a moment,' Didi politely said to Gyllen. She and Erik rose from the table.

Erik showed Didi the way to a small private dining room where they could talk in peace. 'Have you made your decision?'

'I came here tonight to make up for the fact that I hurt you,' Didi said in her straightforward manner. 'Why should I agree to this?'

'I read the legend to you,' Erik said. 'We belong together, but that doesn't mean you belong to me.'

Didi looked at Erik in surprise, and it was clear that she had believed this whole time that he had considered her nothing more than an object, his property. Erik was aware this was the string he needed to pull to get Didi to bend to his will. He had to convince Didi how unique she was.

'If all I wanted was a nymph, I wouldn't be here,' Erik continued. 'But I want you, because never before has anyone like you been born into this world. You should believe in the legend.'

'You mean the way Nadia believes it?'

'The nymphs' version is a bedtime story that they use to put themselves at ease, but don't make the mistake of thinking it's the entire truth.'

And at that moment, Erik was unable to control himself any longer. He leaned forward and kissed Didi softly on the lips. He could feel Didi step backwards at first, but then she gave in to the kiss, and even responded to it. Didi's eyes were filled with astonishment as they broke apart.

'If I agree to do this, will you promise to leave Kati and Nadia alone?' Didi asked.

'I promise to leave them alone if you help me keep my promise to

Roland,' Erik answered. 'But there's one thing you must understand. The satyrs are after me now, too. I've put myself in danger because I'm prepared to help you. And that's why I have to go away for a while after tonight.'

Satyr and nymph eyed each other for a moment.

'Fine,' Didi said. 'Don't come back to the table with me.'

Erik was on the verge of saying he had never taken orders from nymphs and he wasn't about to start now, yet maybe it was better this way. He had grown fond of Gyllen, but the sight of him and Didi together might have been too much for Erik's satyr nature. Besides, Erik could already sense Mitchell's and Lucas' presence. It was wisest to pretend that he was leaving with them at his own initiative.

Erik nodded. 'I'm sorry about what happened at the villa. But you have to admit you were partially responsible. The way you moved, the way you smelled . . . There's not a satyr alive who would have had the self-control to resist.'

Erik lifted his hand to Didi's cheek for a moment longer. And then he turned and left without a backward glance.

He stepped out of the restaurant and waited for a few seconds. That was all it took for Mitchell to step up behind him like a shadow. Erik turned and looked at his former lackey without bothering to conceal his scorn.

'I'd like to go to Zurich now,' Erik said.

CHAPTER 74

Didi was standing in Roland Gyllen's enormous bedroom, wondering how exactly she had ended up there. She didn't necessarily need nourishment at that moment, nor had she ever thought that she could be with a man who was so old. Even if she were old, too! Just the thought of it gave her goosebumps.

Gyllen evidently sensed what she was thinking, because he walked up to her and led her over to the edge of the bed.

'Sit down here next to me,' Gyllen said, taking Didi by the fingers. His touch was dry and warm, his skin simultaneously smooth and wrinkled, thin and delicate. 'What's going through your mind?'

Didi chased away her fears and focused. She knew how to do this. She allowed Gyllen's thoughts and feelings to slowly flow into her through her fingertips, and after a brief moment she saw . . . Didi shivered.

'How can you not be crying right now?'

'I've cried plenty in my day.' Gyllen smiled tenderly at his own memories. 'Teresa and I were married for almost forty years. We truly loved each other for better or for worse, and we'd jokingly promise to leave this world together . . . Teresa always was bad at keeping her promises. Longing is a crueler friend than death.'

'What did your wife die of?' Didi asked.

'Cancer.'

Didi lifted her hands to the old man's face and gazed into his eyes. In them, she saw a long-lived life, profound joys, deep disappointments, and everything in between. But most of all, she saw sorrow and exhaustion.

The world no longer held any interest for Gyllen; it could not offer him anything he hadn't experienced before. Except perhaps this final encounter.

'Erik said you're compassionate,' Gyllen said. 'Will you help an old man? It's time for me to join Teresa.'

Half an hour later, Didi rose from the bed and began to slowly dress. *I will never wear these clothes again*, she thought. *I don't want to forget this, but I don't want to be constantly reminded of it either.* Then she returned to Gyllen's side, drew the blanket up to his neck, and closed the old man's already-glassy eyes.

'Everyone wants something from me,' Didi said to Roland, who seemed more capable of listening to her than anyone who was alive. 'Not just you and Erik.'

After Didi spoke the words, she realized they weren't true. A thought grew clearer in her mind.

'Wait, not everyone. There was one person who only wanted the things for me that I wanted for myself. And he's the one person I can't let get close me. That's quite a conundrum. Wouldn't you agree, Roland?'

CHAPTER 75

Erik knew the grand hall well, but he never tired of it. It was ostentatious and spoke of the power that money bequeathed. The massive antique table was polished till it gleamed, and it was circled by heavy wooden chairs upholstered in leather. The first to sit was, naturally, Gabriel Korda, who took his place at the head of the table. After he had settled himself, it was the other satyrs' turn. Erik remained standing, however. He was already anticipating the day when he would claim his place, the place that had originally belonged to him. He had no intention of submitting to interrogation, and he didn't appear the least bit nervous – unlike Mitchell, who was wearing a suit that was a touch too shiny and a tie that was a tad too gaudy.

'You can begin,' Korda said to Erik. The satyr at the head of the table tended to give the impression that he had just spent the evening at the baccarat table, and he casually unbuttoned his starched, custom-made shirt. But Erik knew that the smooth bearing and behavior were just a front. Not that Korda wasn't a master at the game; just the opposite.

'I'm hunting nymphs,' Erik said curtly.

'Is that all you have to say? Have you no defense to offer us? Rumors of heresy have been whispered in connection with your name.'

Erik noted the nods around the table. He had to turn the situation vantage somehow. So he laughed out loud. 'Have I broken some law? If so, accuse me to my face and stop plotting behind my back.'

The other satyrs burst out in impassioned protests, but Gabriel Korda raised a hand, signaling silence. It was immediately granted to him.

'I beg your pardon, did I hear you correctly, or did my ears deceive me?' Korda's voice was practically a hiss. 'Us, plotting behind your back?'

'The fellowship of satyrs is splitting at the seams more violently than it has in millennia,' Erik said. 'There's no point trying to convince ourselves that the nymphs haven't noticed. They want to test their boundaries, they are fleeing their coveys. Who is to blame for this?'

'Many believe you are,' Korda retorted.

'I'm one of you. The nymphs have told and retold the legend of the redhead raised among humans, spreading it across the world.' Erik held a pregnant pause to make sure that all ears in the room were on him. 'Consider this. That nymph has come to maturity under the protection of the Oakhearts. How is that possible? You destroyed all of the Oakhearts in Velanidia in the fourteenth century, not leaving a single soul alive. Isn't that correct?'

Both Erik and Korda observed the turmoil that this sparked among the satyrs. And then Erik decided to take control of the situation for once and for all.

'And I'm hunting down that redheaded nymph. I'm looking out for the interests of all satyrs everywhere.'

'But you haven't succeeded in catching her,' Korda said disdainfully. 'It would be a different matter if you had brought us her dead body.'

'Which would have given the nymphs a martyr and only served to strengthen their resistance,' Erik said. 'Imagine what would happen if I presented the nymph as my obedient wife. What could be a faster way of making the resistance fade?'

Out of the corner of his eye, Erik noted Mitchell watching the satyrs' approving murmurs in frustration. He knew perfectly well that Mitchell was scheming for a chair bearing his own name at the Conclave. In order to frustrate Mitchell even more, Erik now drew his own chair out from the table and sat in it, to show that it was his and his alone. The other satyrs applauded, and after the review of a few general matters, the meeting was adjourned.

Erik walked off to his own chambers in the magnificent banking house that the Conclave occupied. He hadn't been there long when Mitchell materialized, with Lucas at his heels.

'Congratulations. You spoke well,' Mitchell said. 'Some of them believed you, but Gabriel Korda didn't, and he's the one who calls the shots. You're under arrest. I've been ordered to escort you to the vaults.'

'I'm glad you came,' Erik said calmly. 'There's something I wanted to discuss with you.'

Mitchell didn't have a chance to respond before Erik's hand was burning against his chest. In his other hand, Erik brandished a dagger that he used to keep Lucas at bay. Erik was a significantly more powerful satyr than Mitchell.

'You useless little peacock,' Erik growled. 'If you want my seat, you're going to have to kill me, and that's something you're never going to be able to do. I have no intention of being arrested and imprisoned here. I'm going to see this through. Maybe you two should think about why I chose a traitor nymph and the beloved of one of the fugitives to help me with my hunt. Why I allowed a miserable little nymph to overcome me in a fight. Do you think there might just be a plan behind it all?'

Erik pulled his hand away from Mitchell's chest and handed the knife to Lucas.

'I'm going to finish what I started. And then I'm going to come for you.'

Mitchell collapsed to the floor as Erik walked out, serene as could be.

Mitchell concealed his intense agitation behind a cool smile as he and his henchmen descended into the silent vaults of the enormous building. The locks were drawn back for him, and the massive, three-foot-thick door was pulled open. He was frightened, but a lust for revenge goaded him onwards. Erik Mann would never humiliate him again.

At the far end of the long vault stood a high-backed chair, and in it sat a woman in a blue gown. Her hair was dusky and her bare shoulders powerful, despite the fact that she had been imprisoned for centuries. Her head was lowered when the satyrs entered, but now she slowly lifted it and looked at Mitchell. Mitchell flinched. He had heard that the woman's gaze could turn living beings, or at least humans, to stone. Her eyes shone as bright as sapphires.

'Erik Mann,' Mitchell said.

'Enipeus.' Aurelia's voice was low and flat as she uttered the name by which she had known the satyr. Her nostrils quivered. 'You have been near him.'

'I came here to free you,' Mitchell said. His hands trembled as he pulled a photograph of the redheaded nymph from his breast pocket. 'This is Erik's chosen one. Desirée Volanté Tasson.'

Aurelia rose, and Mitchell and the armed satyrs who accompanied him involuntarily took a few steps backwards. Aurelia walked up to Mitchell with leisurely steps.

'You want me to kill Erik and press my deadly kiss to the lips of the little nymph,' Aurelia whispered in a barely audible voice. 'Why would I do you such a favor?'

'Aurelia, you have been imprisoned for millennia, moved from cell to cell,' Mitchell said, trying to sound dignified. 'I'm offering you a chance to take your vengeance. Now you are free.'

CHAPTER 76

Didi had walked home from work because she felt like she wanted to get some fresh air. She had imagined that being outdoors would make things easier, but the problem she had experienced inside didn't disappear after all. Even men on the other side of the street turned to look at her. So many eyes were glued to her that it made her skin feel sticky. She finally arrived at the door to her building and thought she was safe from all the ogling, but in the hallway she bumped into the delivery guy from the florist's who handed her a bouquet and let his touch linger on her skin a little longer than was necessary. A hunger had instantly flared up in his eyes.

Didi ran up the stairs to her apartment, slammed the door behind her, and started to unwrap the fancy bouquet as she marched into the living room.

'I'm already losing it, and it's two weeks until the lunar eclipse,' Didi said to Nadia and Kati. 'Even the guy who delivered the flowers groped me. Every single male customer at the cafe stares at me and tries to come up with some excuse for touching me.'

'You're on heat,' Kati said.

Nadia corrected Kati, shooting a judgmental look her way: 'It's called *the glowing*.'

'Why is the lunar eclipse called the glowing?' Didi asked.

'People always want to give primitive phenomena beautiful

names.' Nadia was already sniffing the peonies and lisianthus in satisfaction.

'Because it sounds better than "on heat",' said the always-pragmatic Kati.

Nadia plucked the card out from among the flowers and handed it to Didi. The sender's name was nothing more than a first initial: E.

'That's where all the touching comes from,' Nadia explained. 'Their self-control is being put to the test. Like it is for the rest of us.'

'Someone's clearly already in its grip,' Kati said, nodding at the card.

Didi had no intention of bringing up Erik again, nor did she have any desire to think about the satyr herself. It was better to push the whole thing out of her mind.

'Erik promised to leave you two alone. I should have been more specific and told him to leave me alone, too.'

Didi tossed the card on the table, but then the delicate smell of the blooms infiltrated her senses. A sharp, sudden pain sent a quiver through her body, and the older nymphs exchanged knowing glances. All of the signs portended one thing and one thing only, and it was something you had to prepare for.

'I'll let you two ladies gossip to your hearts' content about glowings and lacy bras, hell, you can even paint each other's toenails for all I care. I'm going to bed,' Kati said. 'And don't forget to study your French, Didi. I'm going to give you a pop quiz.'

'Yes, ma'am!' Didi called at Kati's retreating back, but the older nymph's door had already slammed shut.

Didi picked up her old French textbook from the coffee table. It felt so weird, but just a few months ago she had been going to school every morning, seeing her friends, giggling with Laura. All of that was in the past now. She missed it from time to time, but the things she sensed as a nymph, those potent impulses, were like a drug. She didn't know how she could settle for a normal life without them any more, or how boring a life like that would be. She had lost a lot, but she had gained a lot too, maybe more. On the other hand, the one thing she craved more desperately than anything else was off limits to her. *That's what life in paradise is like*, Didi sighed quietly, and then she tried to concentrate on her grammar.

'Why do we have to move to France?' Didi asked Nadia, who appeared to be lost in thought.

'We always change countries and cultures at the eclipse,' Nadia said. 'We don't really age, we just mature very beautifully. People would gradually start to notice, and there's no anti-aging cream or workout in the world that would explain it.'

'And that's why we're going to France?' Didi asked, who could think of plenty of places that would be more appropriate for a young nymph.

'There are other alternatives: Canada, Bermuda, Monaco . . . Kati's arranging it, and it's best if we don't know anything about it. That way we won't give anything away by accident.'

'Do you really trust Kati that much?' Didi asked. It was true that Kati had saved her from touch-and-go situations more than once, but there was a part of Kati that remained closed off, remote.

'Kati is manipulative,' Nadia answered, fingering the ring that hung from a chain around her neck. 'Maybe I've known her so long that I've grown used to it, but at least up until now Kati has always been primarily concerned with our common good. Now get your nose in that book. Legend or not, you still need to study.'

Didi delved into her irregular verbs, but the squawk of the doorbell saved her, and she bounded off to answer it before Nadia could tell her no. Kati had been quicker, though, and she was standing by the door with her stiletto knife at the ready. Didi waited for Kati to nod, indicating permission, and then she cautiously opened the door. She instantly melted. She was looking into Samuel's blue eyes, bright as a brand-new morning after a storm.

And Samuel didn't beat around the bush. 'Is it all right if I move back in here? I have good reasons.'

Kati didn't even have a chance to get out of the way; Samuel was so determined he pushed his way into the entryway and took Didi's hand. Didi glanced at the older nymphs, slightly bewildered, but before long she and Samuel were sitting next to each other on her bed.

Didi looked at Samuel, amazed. Something had changed. Samuel was emanating a confidence that she had never seen in him before.

'What's going on?' Didi asked.

'You've been looking for your roots, and I thought I knew mine,' Samuel said. 'I thought we were supposed to be kept apart, but as a matter of fact my place is at your side. I'm an Oakheart, like your mom. It's my duty to protect you.'

Didi realized how happy Samuel was about this information, but she was stunned. She didn't want Samuel to be her protector; she wanted Samuel as a lover. And now Samuel was sounding like they should live as brother and sister. It was as if this new information had made Samuel immune to her charms.

'How do you know?' Didi managed to spit out through her confusion.

But right then, Kati threw open the door to Didi's room. Didi was on the verge of driving her out. But Samuel seemed happy about her being there.

'Maybe it would be better if I explained it to all of you at the same time,' Samuel said.

They went into the kitchen, where Nadia was waiting. Samuel lowered his shoulder bag to the table. It was old and worn and bore the familiar oak pattern.

'Why are you here?' Kati asked, not showing how astonished she was by the appearance of the bag. She had seen a similar one ages ago. *Janos*, she thought.

'To tell you about my family,' Samuel said. 'I found out that this is exactly where I belong.'

'Are you an Oakheart?' Kati asked.

'I'll help you defend yourselves against the satyrs,' Samuel said.

Nadia glanced at Kati. Elina was the last Oakheart they had had dealings with, and Nadia hadn't believed she would ever meet another. But she was prepared to accept Samuel if his story sounded true, and she didn't understand how an Oakheart bag could have ended up in the wrong hands.

'Are you going to be able to keep your pants on?' Kati asked, to disapproving glances from the two other nymphs. 'It's almost the glowing, and I for one am not going to be answerable for my actions next week.'

Kati's voice contained an unambiguous threat, but Samuel just sat there on the sofa, upright and unmoving.

'Excuse me, Samuel,' Didi said. 'The three of us need to discuss this for a moment.'

Didi cast an imperious glance at the other two nymphs, especially Kati, and the three of them moved into the kitchen.

'The glowing is going to make you fall for Samuel whether you want to or not,' Kati said as soon as they walked in. 'I can see it in both of your eyes already.'

Nadia nodded in agreement, but Didi was done listening to their prohibitions. Samuel was with them now, and Didi had no intention of giving up existing privileges. She had waited far too long for this. Besides, she was completely sure that she would be able to resist the temptation the same way she could resist the world's most scrumptious bag in some store window. All it took was a hell of a lot of willpower. Either that, or a chastity belt. But she didn't say this to Kati. Above all, she trusted in her love for Samuel. She would never do Samuel any harm.

'You've been trying to get me to destroy Samuel for months,' Didi said in a low hiss. 'And now all of a sudden you're protecting him?'

'Samuel is an Oakheart,' Kati said. The gravity in her tone made Didi reconsider things from a new perspective. 'The Oakhearts have looked out for us for thousands of years. I owe it to them to not put Samuel's life at risk.'

'Kati is right,' Nadia agreed. 'Samuel will be in danger if he stays here with us.'

'Samuel is staying, and that's final,' Didi said. 'The Legend has spoken.'

Didi went back out to the living room, where Samuel was waiting with an anxious look on his face. 'You can stay.'

Samuel stood up, and he and Didi took a few steps towards each other without knowing what to do. Then they hugged each other a little awkwardly.

'Now I know why I wasn't able to let you go,' Samuel said, sitting back down.

Say it, say it, Didi chanted silently. Her heart was beating wildly. She hadn't realized how badly she wanted to hear Samuel talk about his feelings, or at least tell her that he hadn't felt anything for Jessica.

'I belong to the family that my father and Elina also belonged to,' Samuel started to explain. 'The fact that we were neighbors when we were kids wasn't a coincidence. We Oakhearts have one mission in life, and it's tattooed on your skin.'

These weren't exactly the words Didi was hoping to hear, but she needed to figure all of this out for herself anyway.

'Why is the knot on my body, if it's a bond between nymphs and humans?' Didi asked. 'Nadia thinks it means that I'm some sort of savior for the nymphs. For Erik, it means that we're supposed to conceive some future ruler at the full moon.'

'The knot explains why you were given to the Oakhearts to be raised,' Samuel said. 'That's why we met as children.'

'So weren't the feelings between us real after all?' Didi asked. The question had been going through her mind incessantly, and this was the answer that she both feared and longed for.

'You were able to resist me during the full moon. That proves that deep down inside you knew that we were bound by something much more important than pure desire.'

Pure desire! Didi thought. If Samuel were able to say those words, then he clearly hadn't experienced real desire.

'Wait a second,' Samuel said. 'What did you say about you and Erik?'

Finally I have his attention, Didi thought, smiling sweetly.

CHAPTER 77

Nadia had had plenty of time to think on her way home from work. It had been busy at the genetic medicine clinic, but she didn't mind. She liked working there, and felt like she was accomplishing more good there than any place she had ever worked before. But the eclipse was approaching, and soon it would be time for her to say her goodbyes. She thought about why she had gotten so exasperated with Jesper over keeping her job. Then again, she knew the reason perfectly well. In times past, the thought that she was Jesper's alone had brought her boundless joy, but now it made her anxious. Age brought with it wisdom, and thus pain, and that was something you couldn't avoid.

A young couple expecting their first child had come to the clinic today and brought her pain as well, even though she had been able to give them good news. There were no signs of an inherited disease; the fever and aches were probably the result of something else. The smile of relief that spread across the parents' faces and the love that existed between them were the best rewards Nadia experienced in her work. But as she studied the child's ultrasound images, Nadia had come to realize something. She had seen these same symptoms before, the symptoms that had inspired the woman to seek out the clinic's services. Maybe the notion had already silently crept into her consciousness some other way, but now she believed she was right.

When she got back to the apartment, she found Kati in the middle of an intense set of kettle-bell lifts. Kati was no doubt trying to hold off the effects of the eclipse as long as possible.

Nadia decided to get right to the point. Maybe Kati would be more disposed to respond truthfully in her sweaty state. 'How did you find out that the Nymph of the Knot would be born in Montpellier seventeen years ago?'

'It's what it said in Mitchell's book,' Kati answered. 'There was no way I could know that the satyrs would believe in it and we would be placed in mortal danger.'

Nadia shook her head. Kati was being as disingenuous and manipulative as ever. But Nadia wasn't going to swallow a single one of Kati's lies any more.

'I saw a woman suffering from a rare hereditary disease today. The risk is that the fetus and the mother might reject each other. The symptoms were exactly the same as Rose's.'

Kati's kettle bell thudded to the parquet. The dark-haired nymph stood up straight.

'Was Rose pregnant?' Nadia asked.

'Didi is Rose's daughter,' Kati responded.

Nadia had imagined she would be infuriated with Kati, but instead the tears started to stream down her cheeks. She mourned for Rose, and a wave of compassion for both Kati and Didi washed over her. She was so overcome with emotion, she started to tremble.

A few minutes later, Nadia was relaxing in the bath. She allowed the soothing effect of the flower essence to spread into her limbs and the herbs to set her mind free.

'You can't say a word about this to Didi,' Kati said, sitting down on the edge of the tub. 'Promise me that.'

'Didi has a right to know about her mother,' Nadia said.

The nymphs looked at each other. Nadia was burning with a question she was afraid to ask, but she had to know the answer. 'Who is Didi's father? It's not Erik, is it?'

Kati shook her head. 'I would never allow Didi to submit to

Erik's games if Erik were her father. You should know that.'

'To be honest, I'm not sure what you're capable of,' Nadia said.
'You've kept so many secrets from me, weaving your schemes all
this time. Are you the one who tattooed the knot on Didi's stomach?'

'Of course not,' Kati said. 'It was an old seaman. Didi shouldn't
find out anything about this. It's better if she believes in the legend.
Her belief protects her.'

'How could you lie to me, to Frida, and to Ana-Claudia about
everything . . .'

'I was protecting all of you, too,' Kati said. 'But of course, most
of all, I was protecting Rose.'

Kati had loved her sister more than anything in the world, Nadia
had known and understood that. But she still couldn't comprehend
why Kati wouldn't admit to the consequences of her actions. All of
their lives had been thrown into turmoil the instant Kati started
laying her plans.

'Are you aware that nymphs around the world believe that fairy
tale you made up? That they're risking their lives for it?'

'So? What's wrong with that?' Kati asked, clearly bewildered.
'We want to be free of the satyrs.'

CHAPTER 78

Aurelia bided her time below the deck of the ship, silent as the shadows. The millennia had trained her how to remain invisible when she so willed, and life — or at least an existence of sorts — in the cells and vaults had accustomed her to closed spaces. For Aurelia, freedom did not mean being able to come and go as she chose. It meant one thing and one thing only: revenge. Having to endure a little discomfort along the way was secondary.

She had occasionally gone up to the deck under shelter of night, and when the seascape transformed into a barren archipelago, she had guessed that the vessel was approaching its destination. Mitchell had given her the photograph of the redheaded nymph and told her about a frigid northern city called Helsinki.

Aurelia had lived in prison, but she still had not remained unaware of changes in the world. Information trickled into her ears from insignificant sources, and she knew how to stitch it together. The satyrs offered her nourishment, but only sparingly. At each of the regular intervals where the ship had docked, she had invisibly glided onto the harbor docks and procured it for herself easily. She was capable of paralyzing a man with her gaze, awakening desire with nothing more than a breath. She also knew that she needed more strength. She intended killing Enipeus, there was not the least doubt in her mind about that, and she was already relishing the thought that he would not be an easy opponent. Besides, the redheaded nymph would also be a means of causing Enipeus pain. Or Erik, as he now called himself.

Aurelia closed her eyes and flew back to the time when she rested in the many-pillared, torch-lit hall, and the pitch-black night of Eleuis could be seen out the spacious windows. She heard the cicadas and could feel Laertes at her side. Laertes, the bodyguard who had become the guardian of her heart. She didn't know if it was fortune or misfortune that had led Enipeus to assign the task to Laertes. Maybe he presumed that the most steadfast and powerful of his men would be best equipped to resist Aurelia's charms. But Enipeus' plan had turned against him, because Aurelia had proven unable to resist Laertes. She fell in love. Until that time she had not loved anyone, nor had she ever wanted anyone so badly. And she loved Laertes so deeply she would not take his life. Their love, then, was forbidden, and remained secret. It was only allowed to flourish inside enclosed walls, in discreet, lingering glances, in fleeting touches, in soundless whispers.

Then the full moon, *dikhomēnis*, had risen at the time when day and night were of equal length. Aurelia's agony was indescribable. She dripped sweat and quaked, a fire burned within her that made her double over in pain. She tried to remain silent, but the moans and whimpers escaped her lips, and Laertes could not help noticing them. And that had proven to be their fate.

Aurelia remembered Laertes' rugged, manly face as precisely as if she had brushed her fingertips along his forehead, his straight nose, his strong jaw. Laertes had knelt before her, and Aurelia had seen her suffering reflected in his eyes.

'You cannot,' Aurelia exhaled as Laertes opened his leather belt. 'Enipeus wants this moon to kill me. If you spare me, you will be declaring war on him.'

Laertes made no response, he simply thrust his hands under her white tunic. Her skin was so feverish that Laertes flinched.

'I could never forgive myself if I didn't have the courage to save you now,' Lartes said. 'I care not if my life is forfeit. You cannot stop me.'

Aurelia pressed more tightly against her beloved, but she did not offer her mouth to him yet.

'When I press my lips to yours, breathe me in,' Aurelia said in a low voice. Her lover's scent was starting to be too much for her. 'Let my spirit flow into you. Receive me. If you die, you will kill part of me at the same time.'

And so Laertes gave in to her kiss and their love.

'Beg Enipeus for mercy for me,' Aurelia whispered as they lay in each other's arms on the white marble floor. 'I am not yet prepared to give up life, or you.'

Being exposed was inevitable, of course. The fact that Aurelia was still alive was evidence enough, nor did Laertes keep what had passed between them secret. And so the man and the nymph were brought before Enipeus. Aurelia remembered how Enipeus' near-black eyes had burned red with rage, although the satyr had conducted himself with restraint.

'Is this how a servant and a nymph defy me?' Enipeus said. 'So be it. Love each other, then.'

Laertes had time to glance in Aurelia's direction, but the nymph knew that they would never be allowed to belong to each other in happiness.

Enipeus rose from his chair and scanned the crowd until his eyes fell upon those of Laertes' brother. He stepped calmly up to the man, pressed his hand to his chest, and seconds later Laertes' brother was lying on the ground, already dead. Laertes struggled to attack Enipeus, but others held him back.

'Yes, love each other,' Enipeus repeated. 'And while you do, I will speak your punishment. I will gather together a group of satyrs whose only task henceforth will be to destroy every member of your family, be they male or female. I will not rest until the satyrs' servants have disappeared from this earth.'

What followed had been a slaughter. Laertes' family had been hunted like wild beasts. They fought back, but each day their numbers diminished. A small band tried to flee under the leadership of Laertes and Aurelia. One day they split up to avoid being caught, and the next time Aurelia saw Laertes, his body had been lowered onto a funeral pyre.

Aurelia hadn't believed that her breast was capable of containing such agony and fury. 'Who did this?'

'The nymphs requested Laertes' aid,' said one of the men. 'They begged him for protection from Enipeus. Laertes believed them.'

Aurelia collapsed to the ground. Her hatred was no longer reserved for the satyrs alone, now she also despised her own kind as well. When the funeral pyre was lit, an anguished cry of the sort that had never been heard before burst forth from her lips, and for her it hadn't seemed to fade since. That cry had kept her alive.

Aurelia had retreated into a cave for several days. Laertes' people waited outside. When she finally emerged, she began to teach the humans how they could vanquish the satyrs. She led them to the root of an ancient tree and commanded them to dig until a stout thigh bone rose from the earth.

'Silenos is the father of satyrs,' Aurelia said. 'This is Silenos' grave.'

She carved two daggers for the people: one was *anthropos*, man, and the other *gynaika*, woman, and joined together they formed the law of the family, *nomos*. Aurelia raised the blades up for all to see and bared her breast, where she had tattooed a knot with a needle. She took a piece of parchment and drew a sturdy tree on it.

'Pack up the belongings that remain to you,' Aurelia said to those listening. 'Travel southwards, to Velanidia. That is where the poison beech thrives. The tree's sap weakens satyrs. This tree is now your tree. Harken to me now: with the oaks and the daggers, you will win the war against the satyrs!'

'Where are you going?' asked one of the members of Laertes' family.

'I have my own task to complete,' Aurelia said.

'I have my own task to complete,' Aurelia repeated to herself now. The vessel had arrived at the harbor. Before she did anything else, she needed to feed again. After that, it would be a simple task to acquire clothing, and her keen senses would quickly lead her to a place where a nymph or Enipeus had recently passed. From then on, the rest would be child's play.

CHAPTER 79

D idi woke up drenched in sweat, and it wasn't because of the sun that was searing through the curtains and into her room. She had slept, but she had had truly bizarre dreams that made her feel like she needed a cold shower. And the reason for them was still lying, satisfied and sound asleep, on a mattress that had been set out on the floor next to her bed. She had to continuously restrain herself from touching Samuel, from getting too close to him, from raising his hand to her breast . . . Didi wiped her forehead. Her thoughts were revolving around one thing and one thing only.

Didi had been genuinely convinced that the arrangement could work, but then a whiff of Samuel's scent would carry into her nostrils, or she would catch a glimpse of his strong, bare chest between the buttons of his shirt and she could be overcome by a desire to rip it off his body, to yank the zipper of his trousers down. No, imagining such things was a game she had better not start playing.

Didi rose quietly from the bed so as not to disturb Samuel, took her clothes with her, and dressed in the living room. She had to thrust aside all of the urges that were assaulting her and think about what was best for everyone. It was perfectly clear that Samuel's presence was a temptation for Nadia and Kati as well, even though they could more freely satisfy their urges in other ways.

Didi had been weighing the matter for a couple of days now. She didn't know how long she could keep her promises if she continued to occupy the same space as Samuel. Perhaps there was a solution. The lunar eclipse was growing ominously close.

Erik had been bombarding her continuously with thoughtful little gifts and text messages. Didi took a final look in the mirror to make sure that she looked as feminine as the satyr liked. She was wearing an off-white dress with a tiny red collar and dainty sandals. She couldn't be too forward, either – that would also prove fatal.

A pretty, dark-haired nymph opened the door to the suite as soon as Didi knocked on it. She entered and saw that Erik was in the middle of a meal. It was still morning, but the satyr's table was set with what appeared to be game and red wine. Erik looked pleasantly surprised and rose immediately to greet Didi.

He began by introducing the two nymphs who were busying themselves around the suite, tending to secretarial duties and Erik's clothes. 'Didi, this is Jamila and this is Sofia. I'm so pleased that you finally accepted my invitation.'

'I'm allowed to be curious, aren't I?' Didi said, sitting down at the table. 'What did you want to discuss?'

'I want to convince you that I'm prepared to do everything in my power for you, if you will only agree to make the legend come true with me,' Erik said.

'You're talking about the eclipse that's about to happen,' Didi said, noticing that Erik couldn't take his eyes off her lips for a single second.

'Exactly,' Erik replied, gesturing to one of the nymphs. 'Jamila, bring those papers over here.' Jamila picked up a slim leather folder from the desk and pulled out some documents for Erik's perusal.

'The first contract covers the companies, the second covers real estate, and the third is a proposal regarding other assets,' Jamila explained.

'Both Jamila and Sofia will stay with us to serve you, if you so decide,' Erik said to Didi. 'Read through these papers. If you sign them, your future is secure.'

'I need a moment alone,' Didi said.

Didi moved over to the desk and started to read the contract. It wasn't very complicated, and she understood clearly that after the contract was signed, a substantial amount of money would immediately be hers. Wouldn't that bring freedom in and of itself? She could live wherever she wanted, do whatever she wanted, even buy Valtteri's cafe if she wanted – a little sum like that would feel like pocket change. Kati wouldn't be able to boss her around any more; instead, she'd be able to boss around those two very obedient-looking nymphs. Of course there was the little hitch that she would have to make love to Erik and allow him to impregnate her.

Make love to Erik . . . No matter how she tried to wrap her brain around it, there was no way she could think of it as making love. Erik wanted something from her, and she might give it to him, but how did you bargain with something like that? Or did she fear what sex with the satyr would be like? Nadia thought it was the most natural thing in the world, but Didi was afraid that if she decided to be with Erik, she might lose some part of herself, some humanity that lived within her. She might forget who she had been, what she wanted from life.

And all she wanted was Samuel. She would have to deny herself that forever if she agreed to this.

Evidently Erik sensed her hesitation. He snapped his fingers at Jamila, who soon carried over two glasses and a cooler containing a bottle of champagne.

'I'm not a threat to you,' Erik said. 'I chose one of your own to find you for me, along with Jesper, who was and is completely enamored of Nadia. I meant you and your friends no harm. And if you so desire, I will offer you everything noted there purely as an apology for past events. I won't demand anything in terms of the eclipse.'

The bottle popped open, and Erik poured the bubbling golden

liquid into the two champagne flutes. Didi had been curious to hear Erik's proposal; she had been almost prepared to agree, but after seeing the two subservient nymphs at his beck and call as if they were nothing but objects, she backed off. Freedom was not something that belonged to simply one of them, but to all.

'I would be binding myself to you, even if I didn't agree to everything,' Didi said. 'And I don't want to do that.' She turned towards the door, terrified the whole time that Erik would not allow her to leave, but a moment later she was in the park, breathing in the fresh air and the smell of the trees.

It only took a couple of seconds before Didi could feel the gazes of the men walking past turning towards her. One even tripped on the smooth asphalt. The glowing truly was coming, and she didn't have the faintest idea what sorts of powers would be released.

When she arrived home, she found two nymphs with grave faces sitting in the kitchen, along with Samuel.

'What is it?' Didi asked with bated breath. There was an anxious mood in the air.

'Where were you?' Kati asked. 'You can't just leave without telling us where you're going. It's too dangerous!'

Didi started to get irritated. 'I have a life, too, you know.'

'Detective Harju called,' Kati said. 'In the first place, two bodies were found at the cargo harbor. You can guess what sort of marks were on them.'

And with that, Didi was suddenly afraid. Something was on the prowl, she could sense it herself. Then she realized why everyone had been measuring her up with their eyes.

'It wasn't me!' Didi said. 'How could you even think . . .'

'And that's not all,' Kati said. 'Someone has been to the cafe. Valtteri is dead.'

Nadia and Samuel had to grab hold of Didi to keep her from collapsing to the floor. They helped her sit down.

'I would never hurt Valtteri,' Didi sobbed. 'Ever . . .'

'Of course not,' Nadia said. 'Something much stronger than us is on the move now.'

'You warned me, you said that I shouldn't get too close to humans,' Didi cried.

'It's not your fault,' Kati said, after Nadia shot her a look telling her to. 'But now we have to be prepared for anything.'

It was only then that Didi noticed that Samuel had a bundle in front of him. It was unrolled, and the tranquilizer gun was waiting to be loaded.

'So you guys know how this works, right?' Samuel asked the nymphs. 'I've never fired anything like this before.'

'Open up one of the ampules,' Kati said, taking a dart. She dipped it into the bottle and then loaded it into the gun. Moving efficiently, she showed Samuel how to release the safety.

Didi watched all this from the sidelines. Sometimes the life of the nymphs and satyrs felt like a game, and then the reality would strike her full force. When she lost Elina, she had imagined that she didn't have anything else to lose, but now she realized danger was threatening everyone who was close to her. Could she have prevented it by agreeing to Erik's plan?

Just then the doorbell rang.

A profound silence immediately fell over the kitchen. No one made a move.

'We have to answer,' Nadia said quietly.

Kati gave the dagger from the bundle to Samuel and took the gun for herself.

They nodded at each other and moved into the entryway.

'Samuel, stay here,' Didi gasped.

'I'll be careful.'

Samuel and Kati assumed positions on either side of the door. Then Samuel pushed it open. Erik lunged in and quickly pulled the door shut behind him.

'I went out to run some errands and when I got back to the suite, the nymphs were dead,' Erik said, stalking straight into the living room. The others followed.

'That doesn't concern us,' Kati blurted out. 'The best thing for us would be to kill you right here and now.'

'I can be of use to you.'

'How?' Nadia asked.

'The creature who killed those nymphs was neither satyr nor human. Or even nymph,' Erik replied. 'It was Aurelia.'

Didi no longer understood a word of what was being said, but she didn't intervene. What was perfectly clear to her was that they were all in mortal danger.

'Why would we believe in those hoary old ghost stories?' Kati asked, but Didi could hear the doubt in her voice.

'Aurelia is real,' Erik said. 'I created her. I created the myth.'

'Is Aurelia the one who it took eight satyrs to overcome and chain in the cave of Medusa, so her lust for murder could be checked?' Nadia asked.

'You've heard the stories,' Erik said. 'The important thing to know about Aurelia is that once she catches your scent, she is utterly unstoppable. We have to help each other now.'

'You stay right there, we need to discuss this,' Kati said.

Erik remained alone in the living room, and the others went back into the kitchen. They didn't have much time, and it was impossible to say how trustworthy Erik was, or what sort of danger they were truly in.

'We need to escape,' Didi said.

'Where?' Nadia asked. 'We don't have anywhere else to go.'

They looked at each other, and Kati chastised herself for not having arranged a place of refuge. She had grown careless, even with so much at stake.

'I might know a place,' Samuel said. 'Wait a little while, and I'll go arrange it.'

'You have one hour,' Kati said. 'After that we're out of here.'

Samuel pulled his jacket from the back of the chair, shrugged it on, and headed out. The nymphs went back into the living room, but in the meantime Didi slipped into her bedroom, threw a few articles of clothing into a bag, wrapped her *nomos* dagger in a towel and hid it under her clothes.

'Did the boy sneak off?' Erik asked.

'Samuel would never sneak off, no matter how much I wished he would,' Didi answered. She didn't understand how she had once been so turned on by this arrogant satyr that she had responded to his kiss.

'Right,' Erik said. 'He's an Oakheart, and self-destruction runs in the blood.'

'Leave Didi alone!' Nadia said furiously, and even Kati smiled in approval.

Then they all fell silent. All they could do was wait.

CHAPTER 80

Matias van der Haas drove out to the rendezvous Samuel had indicated. He had just been coming home from running errands in Tammisaari when the younger man had reached him. Samuel had refused to tell Matias what was going on over the phone, but he had sounded alarmed.

The events of recent days had put Matias on his guard. He sensed a threat in the air that he couldn't put his finger on. And yet he had begun preparatory measures at the manor, since he knew from experience that they never went to waste. In such instances, he preferred to be wrong.

Now he was sitting in the car and waiting. He had been replaying the conversation he had had with Samuel's mother over and over again in his head. When Pauliina had visited the manor, Matias had taken advantage of the opportunity and spoken with her. Matias wanted to be aware of what others knew about past events. Which is why, after studying Pauliina, he had asked if Samuel was an Oakheart through her husband Pentti's line. Pauliina had gazed at him coolly and informed him that when she was young, she had taken a work assignment in Lebanon and the only souvenir she had brought back was Samuel. Matias had a hard time making sense of all this, but things were certainly not what they seemed on the surface.

Matias saw Samuel walk up and open the passenger door. He slipped in.

'I want to bring the nymphs to the manor,' Samuel said immediately.

'No way,' Matias said. 'It's your job to keep them as far from the manor as possible. Erik Mann is on your tail.'

'Erik is with us, he's helping us,' Samuel said.

Matias started. Circumstances had indeed developed more quickly than he had feared.

'You will not bring them to the manor,' Matias said, opening the door to indicate that it was time for Samuel to step out. Then he sped off.

Samuel's cell phone pinged; a new text message. The number was blocked. *I'm waiting for you at the pathology unit. Didi.*

Whatever it was that had happened, Samuel couldn't hang around waiting and wondering. He had to act. He flagged down a taxi and headed out to meet Didi.

Samuel had grown more than familiar with the pathology unit, and handling corpses and spending the night there hadn't really fazed him. He had always been capable of distinguishing between the living and the dead, and a few months earlier he would have firmly denied believing in anything supernatural. But this time when he opened the door to the autopsy chamber, he immediately sensed that it felt different somehow. He just didn't know why. The room was dark, and he couldn't figure out where Didi was.

Samuel's phone rang. This time the call was from Didi.

'Where are you?' Samuel asked.

'Home. Where are you?'

'Here at the pathology unit, where you told me to come . . .'

And before Didi even spoke the words, Samuel understood: 'Samuel, it's a trap!'

Samuel allowed his eyes to circle the room. He couldn't see anything, but he could definitely sense it.

'It's here,' he said, and hung up.

CHAPTER 81

Didi was already springing to her feet when Kati stopped her.
'We won't make it there in time,' Kati said emphatically,
not wanting to say everything she was thinking out loud.

'I will not leave Samuel!' Didi shouted furiously, looking to
Nadia to back her up. But Nadia also just stood there. Didi ran over
to Erik and took him by the hand. 'Help! Please help!'

Erik sounded genuinely baffled: 'Why on earth would I help a
human?'

'You promised to do anything for me. If I agreed to what you
wanted. Help Samuel and I'm yours.'

The nymphs tried to protest at this, but Didi no longer paid them
any mind.

'Do I have your promise?' Erik said.

'If you save Samuel.'

There was no need for Erik to respond. Didi went and got her
bag, and they were already rushing down the stairs when Kati came
out and shoved the gun into Erik's hand. Erik wasn't certain if it
would be of any use against Aurelia, but he took it anyway.

Erik powered his SUV through the streets, and it wasn't long
before they were at the hospital. Didi knew a side door that led to the
pathology unit. A moment later, they were inside. Didi continued
leading Erik onwards, and she quickly found the autopsy room. Didi
stepped in. She saw Samuel with his back to the wall on the far side

of the room and sighed in relief. She also vaguely registered that Erik was no longer behind her, but she couldn't let that distract her now. All she could think about was Samuel, who was walking towards her . . . And then suddenly something came from the side and stepped between them.

Didi stopped. Before her stood a woman who radiated power and fearlessness. Her eyes were like boiling liquid, sometimes blue, sometimes red. They fixed on Didi, nailing her to the spot. Then the woman reached out a hand, and her sinewy fingers wrapped around Samuel's throat, clenching hard. Samuel could not fight back.

'What are you?' the woman asked Didi in a dark, wondering voice.

Didi was incapable of answering. All she could hear was Samuel's gradually weakening breathing, and yet she was unable to move. The woman had frozen her.

'Aurelia.' Erik's voice carried into the room from the doorway. 'I'm the one you're looking for.'

To Didi's relief, the woman's loosened her grip on Samuel and released Didi from her gaze. Didi shook herself like a prisoner freeing herself from her chains. She glanced at Erik. She didn't have the slightest idea how the satyr planned on surviving the encounter, but he had promised to save Samuel, and now he had drawn the attention of the dreadful creature to himself. Didi had no intention of hanging around to see what would happen next. She grabbed Samuel by the hand and started running for the door. Aurelia could have Erik, for all she cared.

'The car's this way!' Didi yelled to Samuel, pulling him along. 'Did you find us a place to hide?'

'Yes,' Samuel lied. 'Call Nadia and Kati and tell them to start driving towards the Tammisaari manor.'

Didi did as instructed, and soon she and Samuel were on the expressway, heading west. Didi felt like she would never breathe calmly again. The moon shone from among the scattered clouds, reminding her of what still lay ahead.

Samuel didn't say anything; he just looked straight ahead and drove. The trip went smoothly, but when they were almost in Tammisaari, Samuel pulled over at the side of the road. Without thinking about it, Didi lowered a hand to his thigh. They barely dared to breathe as they looked each other in the eye.

'Samuel, there will be an eclipse tonight,' Didi said. 'I'm afraid.'

'What are you afraid of?' Samuel asked softly. He was already inching closer to her.

'I'm afraid that this will be our last night together.'

Samuel took Didi's hands in his own. Didi knew what she wanted, and what Samuel wanted, too.

'I've killed every single person I've been with,' Didi whispered.

'If this is our last night together, I want all of you,' Samuel said.

After all that had happened on that day, Didi's resistance was non-existent. She had feared the worst so many times that all she wanted now was to be in Samuel's embrace, regardless of the consequences. She wanted to wrap her arms around Samuel's neck, to kiss him, to be as close as possible to that one person who aroused all of these feelings in her. Didi's cheek pressed against Samuel's, and she took a deep breath. She didn't know what this would lead to, but right now she didn't care. This had to be their moment.

Then they heard the hollow hoo-hooing of an owl, and they jumped apart. Didi turned her head to the skies and saw the full moon coming out from behind the clouds. They couldn't give up yet. She looked at Samuel and could tell he was thinking the same thing. When you loved someone, you wanted to breathe the same air they were breathing for years to come. Samuel started up the car.

CHAPTER 82

The manor was bathed in the blue light of the moon when Didi and Samuel arrived. The mood inside the grand hall was chilly; the Oakhearts had retreated to one side of the room. Salma and Matias were sitting at a small table, and Matias was gazing out the window. The other end of the hall was occupied by Kati and Nadia, who were clearly unwelcome guests. Both Didi and Samuel noted that the only person who was dealing with the situation completely naturally was Matias' daughter Matilda, who was sitting in an armchair reading an old book, one hand dipping into a bag of candy as if she didn't have a care in the world.

The nymphs gathered around to discuss their plan of action and Samuel walked up to Matias.

'What should we do now?' Samuel asked.

'We have an ally who will be here soon,' Matias said. 'Other than that, all we can do is wait.'

Didi split off from the nymphs and moved to the wooden sofa at the rear of the hall, away from the others. Samuel followed her. Didi felt Kati's cautionary glance when Samuel sat down next to her, but she paid the other nymph no attention.

'You smell good,' Didi said, unable to help herself. She moved a little closer to Samuel, but there was still some space between them. Didi could see that something was bothering Samuel, and she stopped talking to give him time to find the right words.

'You said in the car that you had killed every man ... How many?'

'I didn't kill you.'

Samuel seemed to be deep in thought. Didi had to hold back to keep herself from shaking him. She wanted some reaction from him, any reaction at all. Then Samuel finally grabbed her by the hand.

'I can keep my feelings under control,' Samuel said. 'Not my feelings for you, but I don't feel anything for Nadia and Kati. Shouldn't the moon and the nymphs' power of attraction be affecting me, too?'

Didi was surprised. She had considered the charms of nymphs more or less automatic. When she stepped out in the street, men had instantly started looking at her. That was supposed to be the case for all nymphs.

Didi was on the verge of saying something, but now Salma was approaching, carrying a tea tray. Didi accepted a cup and spooned in generous amounts of honey in order to get the right sort of energy. She was burning to ask Samuel more about his feelings, but evidently Matias, who had already been eyeing her and Samuel for a while, had had his fill. He marched right up to Samuel, almost quivering with rage.

'I told you not to come here! We need to do all we can to avoid the nymphs during the eclipse. Then you go and bring them here. And to top it all off, you have a killer at your heels!'

'You said that someone else was going to join us and help us,' Kati said, stepping in.

Matias turned his gaze towards her and his breathing intensified. His speech began to slur.

'This is wrong. I cannot allow you to ... Samuel must take you away from here!' Matias cried, striding out of the hall.

Samuel looked at Nadia and then Kati.

Nadia answered his unspoken question: 'The eclipse is very close. It will be even worse in a minute. During the glowing, men are unable to control themselves in our presence.'

And then she studied Samuel and Didi with an analytical eye. Didi slowly removed her hand from Samuel's grip.

'Does Samuel only react to you? Not to me or Kati at all?' Nadia asked Didi. She wanted to be sure, and she stroked Samuel's arm with her long fingers.

'Could the Oakhearts be immune?' Didi asked.

'You saw Matias,' Nadia said, but then she gathered from Didi's face that the other nymph wanted to be alone with Samuel. Nadia went over to talk to Matilda.

Didi watched Nadia entertain the girl for a moment. Nadia was always so natural with everyone, even now when they were in mortal danger. Didi placed her hand over Samuel's hand once again and waited.

'Maybe it just means that my feelings for you are genuine,' Samuel said to Didi.

In that instant, Didi felt a sweet tingling in her breast and she would have responded to Samuel, but the front door burst open. Apparently the reinforcements that Matias had told them about had finally arrived. Either that, or their enemy had entered the manor. Everyone's eyes turned towards the heavy footfalls and the shrouded figure, which slowly drew the hood back from its head.

'This is the best place you could find to hide out?' Jesper asked. 'Luckily you came by different routes. Aurelia follows scents, which gives us a little more time to prepare.'

Jesper didn't seem to care in the least that satyrs weren't popular with the inhabitants of the manor. He immediately started giving out orders regarding the security measures that needed to be taken. Didi realized that Nadia's situation was completely intolerable. She couldn't even stand to look at her former lover, who had assumed the role of leader and was bossing them around. Nadia went into the next room and banged around old pieces of furniture, supposedly following Jesper's instructions, but deep inside she was seething with rage. Didi went after her, and then Kati did, too.

'Jesper's right,' Kati said. 'We need to protect ourselves. Let's move this old chest over in front of that door.'

'Seventeen years ago I ran away because of satyrs who couldn't stop telling me what to do,' Nadia said. 'Kati, you would know how to do all of this just as well as he does.'

'We need help, and Jesper can actually help us,' Didi said.

'True,' said Kati, whose feeling was that the satyr might genuinely prove to be of use now. 'You have to set aside all of your feelings for this one night. We've been in danger before, but tonight we have a special task. We have to protect Didi.'

Suddenly Didi was ashamed. She realized that the nymphs truly were prepared to sacrifice themselves on her behalf. She had whined and acted childishly, and now all of their lives were at stake. The nymphs could have fled, left her to fend for herself, but they put her and her survival first.

'Why don't you guys leave,' Didi whispered. 'Then you'll all be saved.'

'Shut up and get over here and give us a hand,' Kati said.

Kati went over to the armoire and gestured for Nadia and Didi to help her. The armoire was heavy and it took all of their strength to move it, but at least one of the entrances to the room was blocked now. Didi looked around, trying to figure out what else they could do, when she realized that something had been revealed behind the armoire. She moved the floor lamp closer. There was a tree painted on the wall, with branches and names.

'What's this?' she asked in amazement.

'Kati, look!' Nadia said. 'The Oakhearts' family tree. And here's the Montpellier branch . . . Elina.'

Didi's lips moved slightly as she read the strange names. She didn't notice how Kati's head had lowered.

'Janos Drys,' Nadia read. 'Was your Janos an Oakheart?'

'Once upon a time I helped a few Oakhearts in Velanidia,' Kati said. 'Since then the Oakhearts have helped me. Didi wouldn't be alive if it weren't for them.'

Didi and Nadia were still reading names and years. Suddenly Didi could sense a pain from Nadia, but she didn't understand its cause. She lowered a hand to Nadia's shoulder. Nadia smiled calmly at her.

'I've lived for a long time,' Nadia said. 'A nymph's life must come to an end at some point. Mine might come to an end tonight. Nothing in this world is eternal. Except love.'

Didi was stunned by Nadia's words. They had come this far, and Didi wasn't prepared to give up anything.

'No one is going to die tonight,' Didi said. She stood up and headed for the main room. 'I wouldn't be able to take it. I've already had too much robbed from me.'

'Kati, you have to tell Didi the truth before it's too late,' Nadia said to her old friend in a low voice.

Out in the hall, Didi immediately jumped right in to assist. Jesper and Samuel were hard at work, moving furniture and making sure the doors and windows were locked, and Jesper went around double-checking everything. There was no sign of Salma.

The suspense was clearly starting to grate on Samuel, as was Jesper's know-it-all attitude.

'Should we draw the curtains?' Didi asked Samuel to help her to distract him and relieve some of the tension. She grabbed the heavy velvet fabric with both hands and drew it across, covering the enormous window's dozens of panes.

'What good is this going to do?' Samuel was irritated, and he directed his words at Jesper. 'If Aurelia is the mighty creature you claim her to be, then how are a couple of dressers and some shreds of fabric covering the windows going to hold her back?'

'They won't,' Jesper said. 'But they will slow her, and believe me, that split second of extra time to defend ourselves might mean a lot. Let's take advantage of this darkness and dimness. Make sure that there are no cracks in the curtains.'

'You don't give the orders around here, this is Oakheart property!' Samuel yelled, and in two strides he was standing right in front of Jesper. 'This entire mess is the satyrs' fault. Because of you, Didi, Nadia and Kati are in danger.'

'Calm down.' Jesper's expression was utterly cool. He had plenty of experience preparing for battle, and he knew that emotions could run hot. 'We all need to work together. Aurelia will definitely find her way here by following our scent. But there's an old trick for that. Didi, let's go out to the greenhouse.'

'You're not going anywhere together,' Samuel said, not budging from his spot.

It was as if Jesper had sensed a new side of Samuel. They stared each other down, neither one intending to be the one who gave in.

Up until now, Matilda had been reading her book, but now she set it aside and started watching what was going on.

'I'll go out there with Samuel,' Didi said. 'What should we look for?'

'I can show you,' Matilda said, already handing them flashlights.

Both Samuel and Didi calmed down as soon as they made it out into the cool evening air. Nor did the darkness feel as threatening as the tense mood that had dominated the manor. Matilda led them confidently towards a light that was gleaming a little further off. They could already make out the panes of the old greenhouse in the distance.

'How can Matias let you out here?' Didi asked Matilda.

'I shouldn't have come, but I wanted to be with you,' Matilda said, and almost tripped. Samuel grabbed hold of her.

'Thanks,' Matilda said, but she didn't let go of his hand. 'Have we ever touched each other before?'

Samuel found the question odd, but so was everything else that had happened that evening. 'I guess not. How so?'

'Does Didi know that you're imprinted on her?'

Didi and Samuel didn't understand the question, nor did Didi have time to ask in any greater detail, because Matias had appeared at the door to the greenhouse.

'Matilda!' Matias' tone contained an unspoken warning. 'They can find their way here now. You need to get to the cellar! Your grandmother is waiting for you there.'

But Matilda didn't move immediately. She smiled at Samuel, then she waved and continued on her way. A moment later, she stopped.

'There's no need for you to doubt yourself. You're a totally normal boy,' Matilda said to Samuel. And then she turned to Didi. 'And don't you doubt your feelings; they're genuine.'

Then Matilda and the beam of her flashlight were swallowed up by the sheltering shadows of the dark woods.

'What did she mean by that?' Samuel asked Matias, once they were in the greenhouse.

'You don't need to pay any attention to the nonsense of pre-adolescents,' Matias answered. 'Follow me.'

CHAPTER 83

The greenhouse was a world of its own, a riot of fragrances and colors. The climate was warm and humid, like in the tropics. Didi would have loved to take her time exploring and enjoying her surroundings, but Matias immediately brought her and Samuel pouches made of cotton.

'Gather these white petals,' Matias instructed them. 'Their fragrance will mask your scent and that of the other nymphs. These little flowers may save your lives tonight. Maybe we can succeed in throwing Aurelia off your trail.'

Didi picked one of the blooms in her palm and fingered the thick, waxy petals. The scent intensified as the petals bruised in her fingers. Then she noticed a tiny granule on the desk, and she lifted it up with her fingertip. 'What is this?'

Matias came over to her and took the granule from her. He reached for a small wooden box from the desk, collected all of the little specks that lay on the desktop, and poured them into it.

'Seeds,' Matias said. 'And these are flowers that the satyrs have almost succeeded in exterminating from the face of the earth. They would destroy these too, if they ever found this place. Which is why it is our little secret, and unfortunately now Jesper's as well.'

Didi tried to catch a closer glimpse of the box. A figure had been etched into the lid, but she didn't get a proper look at it. Matias was already putting it aside, back into one of the drawers of the desk.

'I'm going to take this first batch to the manor. In the meantime, you two should keep working here,' Matias said, before disappearing into the night.

Didi and Samuel started to gather up the delicate petals and let them fall into the pouches they carried. Now that their hands were occupied, it felt to Didi as if it were easier for her to speak to Samuel about something that had been bothering her.

'Nadia says that when the eclipse proper begins, satyrs and nymphs seek out places that remind them of our ancient homeland,' Didi said. 'And when the eclipse comes, that's the moment when unions may be formed. Never at any other time. It's the time nymphs make love according to certain rituals.'

'Rituals? What rituals?' Samuel asked. He was supposedly focusing on the task at hand, but certain thoughts had been eating away at him, too.

'I don't know much about them,' Didi said. 'But tonight is a special night for nymphs around the world, a time of celebration. Unfortunately, my first eclipse is going to be anything but a party.'

Didi's voice was so incredibly forlorn that Samuel unintentionally took a step towards her. She stepped back.

'Not now,' Didi said. 'We need to stay on our guard.'

They continued working away without even daring to look at each other. But Didi couldn't get over the feeling that she had to tell Samuel all of the things that were weighing on her mind. She led him over to the old iron bench, where they sat and stared around in silence for a moment. The greenhouse was like a miniature paradise, and if only they could be there alone, just the two of them, and shut out the rest of the world . . . But that was an impossibility, and Samuel needed to know what he was dealing with.

'Out here in the countryside, you can hear the whispering of the trees,' Didi said after a moment. 'You never hear that in the city. There are always too many other sounds, too much noise . . .'

Samuel sensed that something else altogether was going on, and he simply waited until Didi was ready to talk.

'I fell for Johannes,' Didi said quietly. 'He was a little like you. Sweet, fun. I met him when he came over to help me after I fell off my bike. Still, I think that if it hadn't have been for the moon, I wouldn't have wanted Johannes that way. I just had a crush on him. I wasn't in love.'

'You can't do anything about the way the moon affects you,' Samuel said.

'There are two things tearing me in opposite directions,' Didi went on. 'I'm a killer, and I want to be with you. Or what happens if I just accept the fact that a nymph can only be with a satyr? I don't want that. I don't want to lose the humanity that I still have within me.'

Didi looked at Samuel, her eyes pleading for help. She was terrified of this night, of what it would bring. It might take Samuel away from her forever.

'A little while ago I didn't know anything about nymphs,' Samuel said. 'When I found out, at first I was afraid of you. But I've grown to understand something crucial. You're nature spirits, and no one can control nature. So I'm not afraid any more. Not one bit. At least not for me.'

Didi started to cry.

'Did I hurt your feelings?' Samuel asked, thinking he had said something stupid.

Didi shook her head. Samuel's words were an incredible consolation, and even if everything came to an end that night, she would cherish them forever. She was not a monster in Samuel's eyes after all.

Large tears rolled down Didi's soft cheeks. 'I just wanted someone to look at me as if I were the only one in the world.'

'That's the way I look at you,' Samuel said. 'That's the way I've looked at you since the very first moment I saw you.'

Their faces were leaning in closer and closer; their lips were already sensing each other. Then a light that Samuel had never seen before lit up in Didi's eyes.

'Come with me!' she cried, and rushed over to search the desk where Matias had been working. 'Now I know what I saw.'

Didi furiously yanked the drawers open, ransacking them. Her fingers searched every nook and cranny until they struck upon the tiny round wooden box. Samuel came up next to her and shone a flashlight at it so they could see it better. The knot symbol had been etched into the lid.

'The knot has something to do with these seeds.' Didi twisted open the box and looked in. Her heart was pounding faster than ever, and she glanced outside, where the moon gleamed, cool and dim.

Didi perched herself on the edge of the desk. She felt like she was truly herself with every fiber of her being. She was a nature spirit that could not be restrained. She pulled Samuel over to her and pulled down one of the straps of her dress. She was starting to melt. She wanted Samuel, and she wanted him right now. Why on earth was he resisting? He must feel exactly the same way she did.

'Didi, it's not the right time,' Samuel said.

'Do you even think the right time exists? Can we wait for it to come?'

'I don't even dare to touch you right now,' Samuel said. 'If I did, I wouldn't be able to resist you, and then I won't be able to help you and your friends.'

But the last thing Didi wanted to hear was *No*. She was smoldering.

CHAPTER 84

Gradually the manor's grand hall was getting to the point where intruders could be kept at bay. Matias had advised the defenders how to scatter the petals at all doors and windows to confuse Aurelia's sense of smell. And then he had disappeared without a word.

Kati had uncovered an old hunting rifle somewhere, and Jesper was armed with his own knives, which Kati had eyed with more than a touch of envy. She might not have understood much about purses and handbags, but she could appreciate the handiwork of Japanese metal-smiths. She looked at the poker Nadia had armed herself with and kept her thoughts regarding its usefulness against a power like Aurelia to herself.

'I'm going to take one more look . . .' Jesper was headed in the direction of the library when there was a heavy thud at the door. The room immediately fell silent, and the defenders looked around at each other.

'Open up!' yelled a muffled voice.

'It's Erik,' Nadia said. 'We can't let him in. There are only two hours left before the eclipse.'

'I'm alone,' Erik assured them through the door.

The nymphs watched the expression on Jesper's face. Who would the satyr's loyalty belong to: to them, or to his own kind? Jesper weighed the situation for a moment, and then pulled his knife from the sheath at his belt. He gave Kati the signal to open the door.

Erik fell into the room. He was holding his side, and heaving in agony. Blood was streaming out between his fingers. The three of them carried Erik over to the sofa.

Nadia examined the wound, and Erik roared in pain.

'Luckily for you it's the glowing and you made it to a healer,' Nadia said. 'Otherwise you would be as good as dead. Bring me bandages,' she shouted to the others.

'A second ago you didn't want to even open the door. We don't have to fix him up now,' Jesper said. 'Erik won't be anything but a burden if he's injured.'

But Kati brought Nadia everything she asked for. Nadia cut off Erik's shirt and started to clean and bind the wound. Thick, red satyr blood was pumping out from it.

Nadia evaluated the situation. Binding alone would not stem this blood flow. Either they let Erik die before their eyes, or she would have to use her own methods.

'I have to kiss you,' Nadia said.

'Thank you.' Erik's voice was barely a whisper, but he smiled at Nadia. 'I know you don't have to help me.'

Jesper, on the other hand, did not smile. He was seething inside as he observed how tenderly and carefully Nadia touched the other satyr. When, on top of it all, Nadia pressed her healing kiss to the wound and then to Erik's lips, he was ready to kill someone. Nevertheless, he had to admire his darling Nadia's skill and mastery, as Erik's condition improved before their eyes. Gradually the satyr was able pull himself up to a sitting position.

Erik's eyelids lowered as if he intended to rest, but instead he sprang to his feet. He drew the knife from the unsuspecting Jesper's sheath and raised it to the other satyr's neck.

'The first time, it took eight satyrs to restrain and capture Aurelia,' Erik hissed. 'You don't imagine that these paltry weapons are going to be enough, do you?'

The satyrs were almost butting heads, but Jesper didn't move a muscle. Erik lowered the knife and handed it back to Jesper, who marched into the library.

'We need everyone now,' Kati said emphatically.

Nadia was in the library organizing her supplies, and she pretended not to see Jesper, even though he planted himself directly in front of her.

'You can't run from what exists between us,' he said.

Nadia rose from the table, and her dark eyes focused fearlessly on Jesper. 'I have chosen sides. I'm fighting for the nymphs and against the satyrs. You promised you wouldn't act the way the satyrs do, but then you started to turn me into your property right away.'

Jesper smiled, and this annoyed Nadia even more. She didn't see what was so funny about the situation.

'Look at me,' Jesper said, stepping closer to Nadia so she could feel his breath on her skin. 'I turned against the satyrs, against my own kind. I came here.'

'You can turn right back around and leave, if you did it for me.'

'Of course I did it for you,' Jesper said.

'I'm not changing my mind,' Nadia said defiantly.

'So don't,' Jesper said, wrapping his arms around her.

Nadia felt her lips opening, she felt Jesper's muscular body against hers, and in the blink of an eye all of her desires were aroused. And it wasn't solely because of the moon or the eclipse. She had known hundreds of years ago that Jesper was the only one she would ever love.

But then a voice from the doorway startled them, making them jump apart. Kati's tone was concerned: 'It's been a while since anyone has seen Didi.'

CHAPTER 85

Didi and Samuel were in the dimly lit greenhouse, entwined in each other's arms, but they jumped apart when the beam of a flashlight fell directly on them.

'Here you are,' Kati said, separating her second couple of the night.

Didi felt as if she were coming out of a trance. She didn't understand how she had let things go so far. Samuel seemed embarrassed, too.

'I don't know about you two, but I can smell something in the air,' Kati said.

Didi had to concentrate to re-orient her senses away from Samuel, but a moment later she nodded as well. 'I do, too.'

'There's no doubt about it: Aurelia is nearby,' Kati said. 'She'll start at the manor. We need to find a better hiding place.'

Didi remembered something: 'Matias kept mentioning something about a cellar.'

Peering out into the dim night, Kati pulled out her cell phone.

'Matias? Is there anywhere else around here we could hide?' Kati asked. 'A stable or a storehouse where we would only have to watch one door?'

'No,' Matias answered curtly. 'You all have to stay in the manor. I don't want you going anywhere else. And if you survive the eclipse, I want you to leave first thing in the morning.'

'So where are you?' Kati asked. 'Matias?'

But the only sound to come from the phone was a thud and a faint cry.

A chill traveled through Didi's bones, down to her very core. Her worst fears were coming true, and she didn't have the slightest idea what to do. A moment ago she was still caught up in Samuel's embrace, and had forgotten everything else around her. She realized now how completely reckless and dangerous that had been.

'Aurelia is somewhere in the vicinity,' Kati said. 'Let's go to the manor and barricade ourselves in there. We don't have anywhere else to go.'

They were outside when Samuel suddenly stopped. 'I won't abandon Matias.'

'You can't go look for him now!' Didi said. 'You can't leave me. Kati, don't let Samuel go.'

Samuel directed his words at Kati: 'Matias is my kinsman.' And then he started down the path in the other direction.

Kati grabbed Didi and held on so tightly that she was unable to follow Samuel. And then Didi's love disappeared from view.

Didi reluctantly allowed herself to be led back to the manor by Kati. She hadn't been able to follow Samuel, but she had no desire to stay in the greenhouse by herself, either. With Samuel, the big house had been as magical as a castle from a fairy tale, but without him, it was eerie and bleak.

She and Kati walked up to the house and into the grand hall. But when Didi saw Erik there, she was instantly overwhelmed with terror. She tried to turn and run.

'What's he doing here?' Didi screamed.

'Everything's OK,' Nadia said, taking Didi into her arms. She nodded at the other satyrs so they would take a hint and go into the other room.

'The eclipse is only an hour away,' Nadia said to Kati. 'This is the right moment, Kati.'

Then Nadia followed the satyrs, and Didi was left alone in the grand room with Kati.

Didi was trembling all over. More than anything she was frightened for Samuel. She didn't trust Erik at all, yet on the other hand, she did trust in the strength of the nymphs. But the unknown threat was the worst thing. She didn't know how to fight against it. What could be so horrifying that it would frighten the satyrs, too?

Didi's panic was apparent, and Kati came over and sat down next to her. Didi waited for Kati to tell her to pull herself together and be strong, but the other nymph didn't say a word. She looked at Didi and retrieved a wooden box from her leather jacket. It was the same box that Didi had last seen in the greenhouse. Now Kati placed it on the table and eyed it grimly.

'Didi, I promise you that we will make it through this.' Kati tried to keep her voice as steady and reassuring as possible. 'I swore an oath to your mother that I would protect you forever.'

Didi didn't really follow what Kati was talking about. She listened, barely daring to breathe. She sensed that the older nymph was on the verge of telling her something important.

'I had a sister,' Kati said. 'A nature nymph who was born in the flax fields of Southampton. Rose was redheaded and stubborn. Sound familiar? A satyr burned our parents to death, and Erik rescued us for his covey. Time passed, and eventually, of the two of us, Erik chose Rose for himself. And for a hundred years, Rose didn't have anything against it. Then Erik gave her an assignment in London – we can keep satyrs satisfied, but we are still nothing more than objects to them – and I didn't hear from Rose for several years. When she finally contacted me, she was pregnant. My sister was with child. And the worst thing was, she was with child to a human. The satyrs would have killed her on the spot if they had known.'

Didi had been listening to Kati's story, eyes wide. Now she could hear Kati's voice start to break, and could see the effort it took the older nymph to reveal the secrets that she had kept close to her heart for so long.

'What was Rose like?' Didi asked.

'As I said, redheaded and stubborn,' Kati laughed, but thoughts of the memories made her grow serious again. 'Compassionate and strong. And like you, difficult to control.'

'Is Desirée Rose's daughter?' Erik hadn't been able to stay away. He had silently crept back into the room, and was listening intently to Kati's tale in disbelief.

'Rose died when you were born. I promised my sister I would always look after you, always protect you,' Kati finished.

Jesper and Nadia entered the hall as well and sat down. Kati retrieved the wooden box from the table and lifted it up for Didi to see.

'In a way, it's no wonder we ended up here. The Oakhearts have always protected nymphs. That's why this box is here, too.' Kati twisted open the lid of the box and picked up one of the seeds between her fingers. 'With the help of these seeds, nymphs can procreate with humans, have children.'

'Those seeds were supposed to have vanished from the face of the earth,' Erik growled.

'They have always existed and always will. Just like the Oakhearts,' Kati said, barely capable of restraining her rage. 'You will never exterminate them, no matter how hard you try.'

Erik leaned back in his chair and considered what he had heard. 'So Rose betrayed me with a human?'

Kati paid no attention to him; she just held the seed aloft at the tip of her forefinger.

'There is a miracle hidden within this tiny seed,' Kati said. 'When you swallow a seed and Samuel swallows a seed, then the two of you can be together without fear or danger.'

Kati's story had momentarily carried Didi's thoughts away from

Samuel and what might be hunting him out there in the darkness, but now her mind was once more overwhelmed by fear.

Samuel illuminated the meandering path with his flashlight, moving as fast as he could. He had finally established his first true contact with his father's family through Matias, and he had no intention of letting it go. Salma had opened up his mind to long-lost memories, and although they bubbled to the surface in nothing more than tiny droplets, he felt like he belonged somewhere now. He had had his mother, and then he had had Didi, but the family that was thousands of years old filled him with indescribable pride and joy. It felt surprisingly good to be something other than a run-of-the-mill medical student.

Samuel stopped. He had been on the verge of walking past a small knoll, but when he took a second glance at it, he spied a door. It was a cellar covered by a thick canopy of moss and low-growing blueberries. Hidden as it was under the trees, it was almost impossible to see it. Samuel pricked up his ears to make sure that no one was following him, and then he gathered his courage, opened the door, and entered.

The cellar was much bigger than he could have imagined from the outside. Candles were burning here and there, and the air was fresh and woodsy. Samuel squinted in the dimness, and then he saw Matilda.

'What is this place?'

'Come and look,' Matilda answered.

Matilda led Samuel deeper into the cellar. Salma was there, sitting on a wooden stool.

'Are you safe here? Where is Matias?' Samuel asked. 'Didi needs me.'

Matilda walked up to a low table, where Matias' leather bag lay. She pulled out a bundle, unrolled it, and held up a *nomos* dagger.

'You need this,' Matilda said. 'This is man, *anthropos*. If you have the other one too, woman, *gynaika*, you can govern the power of satyrs and nymphs.'

'Doesn't Matias need it?'

'Not any more,' Matilda answered.

It was only now that Samuel realized that Salma's cheeks were moist with tears.

'Now you must go,' Matilda said, giving Samuel's hand a quick squeeze. 'They're waiting for you. May Alekto be with you.'

A moment later, Samuel stepped back out into the woods, and he heard the bolts slide into place as the cellar was locked behind his back. *It's not likely that the Oakhearts would open up to me now, even if I knocked*, he reflected, and headed back down the path, making his way towards the manor.

CHAPTER 86

Jesper and Erik were alone on the hall. In the old days, they would have shared a couple of bottles of red wine as music played loudly in the background. They would have exchanged anecdotes about their escapades and indulged in all the good things life had to offer. But now they just stared at the old wallpaper that covered the mansion's walls.

'So how does it feel to be at the same level as a normal satyr?' Jesper asked in a chipper tone. 'The eclipse is coming, and neither one of us has a nymph. And both of us have been bested by a nymph. Maybe times truly are changing.'

'That's what I'm hoping for,' Erik said, refusing to give Jesper the satisfaction of losing his temper.

'Doesn't it seem at all strange to you that Rose warmed your bed for so long and now you're chasing her daughter? Besides, Didi isn't even a full-blooded nymph, if the story is true.'

'Not at all,' Erik answered. 'Now that I know everything, I also see the logic in everything. Legends are nothing more than self-fulfilling prophecies, after all.'

Jesper was trying to think of a suitable quip about arrogance and its dangers when he heard something. It was nothing more than a creak, but footfalls could clearly be heard coming from the stairs. Whoever was approaching wasn't even trying to walk very quietly. And a commotion could now be heard from the other direction as well. Kati dashed into the hall, Nadia and Didi at her heels.

'What's happening?' Didi asked. The expressionless look on the satyrs' faces told her that they were waiting for something.

'Aurelia is inside,' Jesper said, reaching for one of the tranquilizer guns. 'Aurelia is an ancient nymph. As far as I know the poison should affect her, too.'

Jesper made sure that his knife was also in its place in its sheath. They were all watching the door, and Didi was on the verge of asking Jesper what they should do, when he leapt into action, jerked the door open, and instantly pulled it shut behind him. Nadia cried out, and Didi gripped her hand.

'No one come out here!' Jesper shouted. 'No matter what you hear, stay in there!'

Nadia pressed her ear to the door, but the sounds of the pummeling and the blows were too much for her, and she pulled back. They heard furniture fly, and there was a tearing sound. It was impossible to make out if the shouts were those of a woman or those of a man. Then there was a final thud, after which all was perfectly still.

They waited for a moment, and then it was Kati who went to the door and peered out. She saw two figures lying on the ground. One was the broadly grinning Jesper, and the other was a tall, dark woman lying face down.

'Goddammit,' Jesper laughed, his face bloody. 'Eight satyrs, is that what you said, Erik? You needed eight satyrs to take down Aurelia?'

Nadia was already at Jesper's side. His chest was bare, and there was a long, deep gash in it. In his moment of victory, Jesper didn't seem to care about his wound in the least.

Kati happened to glance at Didi, who was deathly pale and could barely stand on her feet. The room was heavy with the smell of blood. 'Erik, take Didi somewhere else. You're not of any use here either.'

Erik nodded in assent and led Didi into the library. Kati concentrated on helping Nadia, and together they lifted Jesper onto the sofa. Nadia started to tend his wounds. Kati went into the library to retrieve the bandages for the second time that evening. She looked around. Didi and Erik were nowhere to be seen.

'Goddammit!' Kati shouted.

'What now?' Nadia asked, as Kati rushed back out.

Kati looked around more bewildered than ever, and then cocked and raised her shotgun.

'Aurelia's body was here a second ago. Where is it now?' Kati asked.

'You have to find Didi,' Nadia said. 'I'll stay here and take care of Jesper.'

A couple of choice words about satyrs were rising to Kati's lips, but Nadia's anguished expression silenced her. She ran out.

Nadia now focused all her attention on Jesper, whose skin was already turning gray. The blood on the satyr's face had dried, but his body-wound showed no signs of closing up.

'Isn't there something you can do?' Jesper asked, sounding a little surprised.

'I need to get you in water,' Nadia said. 'There's a bathroom with a large tub at the other end of the house. Can you make it that far?'

'You'll have to help me,' Jesper said.

Nadia ran off to draw the bath. Then she returned to Jesper's side, and did what she could to help him up. She knew every movement was excruciating agony for the satyr, but there was nothing she could do about that just yet. She focused all of her willpower on getting Jesper to the bathroom before he slipped out of consciousness.

Nadia stripped off Jesper's clothes and helped him into the water. Then she dropped her own dress and panties to the floor and was climbing into the tub, but Jesper raised his hand as high as he could manage.

'Let me look at you for a little while,' Jesper whispered, a red light flickering in his eyes. 'It's better than any medicine. Your skin, your beauty . . .'

Nadia waited no longer. She straddled Jesper, poured water over the satyr's shoulders and chest, and allowed him to slide into her.

'The eclipse is just beginning, Nadia. I can feel it,' Jesper said.

'Is this our union?'

Their hips moved together as the water caressed their skin. Nadia shed tears, even though Jesper was smiling.

'Kiss me,' Jesper moaned. 'Heal me.'

Jesper's eyelids lowered until they were fully shut. Nadia held him for a moment longer, not wanting to admit that the love of her life was gone.

'Freedom,' Nadia whispered, sensing the warmth of Jesper's lips as she pressed a final kiss to them.

CHAPTER 87

Didi was so shocked by the sight of the wounded Jesper that she allowed Erik to comfort her. It was even a relief to feel someone so strong and sturdy at such a stressful moment.

'What's going to happen to us? What's going to happen to Samuel?' Didi whispered, lowering her head against the satyr's chest as he took her in his arms.

So she wasn't at all prepared to have the satyr's large hand cover her mouth with a crushing force. She tried to kick and scream, but Erik paid no attention to her struggling; he just picked her up off the ground and started dragging her outside. Once he was outdoors, he tossed Didi over his shoulder and started making for the woods.

'The eclipse is about to start,' Erik said, when they made it to the edge of the forest. 'Look at the sky. This is the moment.'

'I'm not a legend,' Didi managed to sputter out, even though her head was hanging upside down.

Didi was still trying to punch and hit the satyr as he jogged lightly into the eaves of the forest. Erik glanced around, evidently looking for a spot that suited him. They made it to a small glade that was encircled by large, ancient pines with gnarled bark. Erik chose the largest tree and carried Didi over to its base. He lowered her to the ground and pressed her fiercely against the tree.

'Desirée Volenté, desire and will,' Erik muttered, eyes already burning. 'Why do you resist, when a great future awaits you? Once the legend has been fulfilled, you will lack for nothing.'

'Stop saying that. I'm not the chosen one.' The satyr's obstinance was starting to anger Didi. She had believed she would be safe from him once the truth about her origins came out. 'My mother was a nymph and my father was a normal human. The knot is nothing more than a tattoo on my belly.'

'You're wrong,' Erik said. 'Everything is as it is described in the book. So what if Kati had it tattooed on you? According to the book, the nymph bears the knot, and you were born during the eclipse, even if you are Rose's child.'

'I will never be with you!' Didi shouted.

'That is no longer yours to decide,' Erik said. 'Imagine how much more pleasant this could have been. I would have arranged a stupendous wedding. The wine would have flowed and the celebration would have lasted for days. I would have spent a fortune on it. You would have been presented to the satyrs and the nymphs as a queen, and you would have become my spouse.'

Didi tried to wriggle and kick, but Erik was too powerful an opponent, and this time the satyr knew not to let her palm get too close.

'Every part of the legend will be fulfilled. You promised yourself to me when I saved Samuel,' Erik said.

Didi could feel Erik's loins pressing hard against her. The moon was almost in eclipse, and Didi's strength was waning. She could barely resist when Erik's hands started to reach under her skirt. Didi continued to struggle.

'Do you actually think you'll get an heir if you rape me?' Didi screamed.

'It will happen tonight. And it wouldn't be rape, if you had any sense of your status as the mother of the new Silenos . . .'

At that instant, there was a loud crack, and Erik fell against Didi and then to the ground. Didi found herself looking into Kati's steely eyes. The other nymph was standing above her, still holding up the butt of the rifle, ready for another blow if the first didn't prove forceful enough.

Erik was lying in the moss, but his eyes were now burning bright red, and the horns were thrusting forth from his brow.

'Aurelia is free,' Kati said. 'She is on the loose and on the prowl. We need to find a place to hide.'

Didi saw a beam of light approaching from the forest and was starting to panic, but this time it was Samuel who ran up to them. Didi would have cried with relief if the danger were not still so imminent.

'Are you OK?' Samuel asked. 'He wasn't able to—'

'No,' Didi whispered, realizing herself what had almost happened to her.

'Erik is the least of our worries. Aurelia is here,' Kati said.

A deep voice rose from Erik's throat. 'Nomos . . .'

Samuel started to unwrap the cloth he was carrying. Finally the pieces started falling into place in Didi's mind, too, and she fumbled around in her shoulder bag. She pulled out a bundle.

'I have one just like it,' Samuel said. 'Matilda explained that we can survive if we use both of them together.'

'You need to take Didi to safety. Do you know a good place?' Kati asked.

'You can't stay here,' Didi cried. 'You are my mother's sister . . . My real aunt!'

'Everything will be fine,' Kati said firmly. 'You two have to go.'

Samuel grabbed Didi by the hand and a second later the forest path had swallowed them up.

Kati's gaze turned to Erik, who was defiantly waiting for the final blow.

'Strip,' Kati said.

The satyr looked at her as if he couldn't believe his ears.

'Strip!' Kati said in an even more commanding voice, and started to unbuckle her belt. 'I have every intention of surviving this eclipse, even if that means significant sacrifices.'

'Where are we going?' Didi panted, struggling to keep up with Samuel.

'I know a place,' Samuel said. He was thinking about the cellar and fervently hoped the Oakhearts would let them in. It felt like just about anything could be hiding in the dark forest, and it was impossible to see a thing. He was eager to keep going, but Didi stumbled.

'Are you OK?' Samuel asked.

'It's the eclipse,' Didi panted and raised her hands to her breasts. 'I feel like I'm about to split in two. There's a sharp pain in my stomach, and my breasts ache like never before.'

Samuel had been afraid that he wouldn't be able to pick out the right meandering path in the darkness, but then he saw the mound that formed the roof of the cellar. He breathed a sigh of relief.

'What is this place?' Didi asked, exhausted.

'You'll see,' Samuel said. 'We'll find safe haven here.'

Didi looked on as Samuel lowered his fist to the door, on the verge of knocking, but at that instant they heard a rustle behind them, like the beating of the wings of a large bird. From the shadows of a large spruce a woman stepped forth; she had dusky skin and jet-black hair. Her brow was straight and her eyes were flaming ice. Her hypnotic gaze paralyzed Samuel and Didi.

'Who are you?' Didi asked in a quivering voice, even though she already knew the answer.

'I was once like you,' the creature answered, almost listlessly. 'I was imprisoned, but now I have fed and am stronger than ever. I am known as Aurelia.'

Aurelia approached soundlessly, but now Didi had recovered her sense of movement. She rapidly stepped between Samuel and Aurelia. Her protective instincts seemed to amuse Aurelia, who glided right up to her. Didi could smell Aurelia's cloying breath. She didn't know any way of repelling the ancient nymph other than the one she had used to subdue Erik. She raised her hand to Aurelia's breast and tried to direct her flow of energy against her. Aurelia twitched. *I wonder if I did it*, Didi thought for a split second, but then Aurelia burst into peals of laughter. The nymph, or whatever this creature was now, had simply been toying with her. Didi was filled with dread.

And then Samuel was pulling her out of the way.

'You don't want Didi,' Samuel said. 'She is not your enemy.'

Aurelia's gaze shifted now to Samuel and then back to Didi. Didi didn't even bat an eyelid. She wanted to show Aurelia that she was done running.

Oddly enough, the hard expression melted from Aurelia's face and for a moment her nostrils quivered like a wild animal's. She took a few steps backwards, and Didi was afraid she was gathering up speed to pounce on them.

'Your feelings perfume the air here, I can smell them,' Aurelia said, very tenderly. 'You worship each other now, and you will worship each other forever.'

Didi decided to act. She pulled out her *nomos* dagger and Samuel did the same. They held each other by the hand and refused to let go.

Aurelia stretched out her neck and now her gaze was dreamy. 'I loved a man many ages ago, and our scent was just as powerful. We belonged to one another completely, but then Erik robbed him from me.'

Didi and Samuel held their daggers at the ready, but Aurelia did not fear their blades. She started to approach again, her footfalls slow and steady.

'I mean you no harm,' Aurelia said. 'If you do not trust me, then use your daggers. If anyone knows what they are capable of, it is I, because I am the one who carved them for the Oakhearts. They are capable of taking my life.'

By this point Aurelia was standing right in front of them, and she seemed to grow in height. She was still sniffing the air. Her hand slipped into Didi's shoulder bag and lifted out the wooden box decorated with a knot. She twisted off the lid and dropped two of the seeds into the palm of her hand. Her gaze turned to Didi, and all traces of cruelty had disappeared from it. She offered one of the seeds to Didi, who took it into her mouth from Aurelia's fingers, which were as smooth as sea-polished stones.

'It's not dangerous,' Didi said to Samuel, who had been watching this communion, stunned.

Aurelia offered a seed to Samuel as well, and he also swallowed.

'The eclipse will not last much longer,' Aurelia said, looking at Samuel. 'Keep your nymph alive.'

And in a single breath, Aurelia had vanished into the forest. Only a tiny rustle among the leaves spoke of her movements now.

Didi grabbed Samuel by the hand.

'What now?' Samuel asked. 'Where are you taking me?'

'To paradise,' Didi said.

An exhausted nymph and a satisfied satyr lay on a bed of moss. Eventually they sat up and started to dress. Kati had no desire to look at Erik any more. In her mind, the satyr had done nothing but perform a necessary task. Now it was time to think about what the next step should be . . .

Then Kati saw Aurelia not more than a couple of yards away. She tried to reach for her rifle, but the icy stare of the ancient nymph stopped her in her tracks and banished all thoughts from her mind. Kati could see what was happening around her, but she was unable to react.

Nor was she certain, truth be told, whether she would have helped Erik when Aurelia glided over to him and pressed her palm directly over the satyr's heart. Aurelia's powers were so potent that Erik immediately slumped to the ground, and seconds later he was as limp as a rag doll. Aurelia gave Kati one glance. Then she grabbed the half-naked Erik by the neck and dragged her prey off into the heart of the forest.

It took a few minutes before Kati could shake herself back to awareness. She never saw Aurelia or Erik again. She cast her eyes up to the heavens. The eclipse was at its fullest.

Further off, in the greenhouse, a handful of lanterns burned. In the lush greenery of the exotic flora, a redheaded girl dropped her dress from her shoulders, and a boy spread a blanket on the ground. Didi and Samuel undressed each other slowly, savoring each moment as if the rest of the world had ceased to exist. No words needed to be spoken, as their skin and their hands spoke a language of their own. Human and nymph breathed as one, and the rhythm of their bodies was shared and natural. The moon went utterly dark, the nymph began to glow as if a million minute crystals had been dusted over her. And when she felt the essence of love at its most perfect, a shiver escaped her, and moments later they were surrounded by a cloud of butterflies.

And furthest away, in the cellar, hid the greatest secret of all. A scented bath had been drawn in the old metal tub. In it sat a blonde, blue-eyed girl, her skin caressed by the petals of the blossoms floating on the water's surface. Her grandmother twisted the girl's hair into a bun on the crown of her head and stroked the nape of the girl's neck and the tiny figure of the knot there. And just as the moon went into its eclipse, Matilda accepted the crown of flowers and blueberry branches from her grandmother and placed it on her own head. The girl's skin began to glimmer and glow, almost flicker with a flame. She closed her eyes, and saw many things no one in the history of the earth had ever seen before.